...ress having worked in ...
..., ...dio, and theatre. She has published eight ...ls, all critically acclaimed. Her books are set in London, where she was born and brought up. She has shadowed police and seen, first hand, crime being committed. Her books have been described as 'strong crime'. She writes about what is happening currently and weaves her stories around that. Some have a theatrical flavour too, because this is another area she knows well. She believes books should be entertaining, truthful, and page-turning. Reviewers often mention how well her characters are drawn. Characters take the story along and, with her acting experience, she has spent her life inventing them.

Praise for Linda Regan:

'Regan exhibits enviable control over her characters in this skilful and fascinating WhoDunnit' Colin Dexter

'One of the best up-and-coming writers' Peter Gutteridge, *Sunday Observer*

'Regan continues her sure-footed walk on the noir side. Entertaining stuff, but not for the faint-hearted' *Kirkus Reviews*

'A sound debut; I look forward to Linda Regan's next book' *Tangled Web*

'For a first novel it is extremely well written' *Encore Magazine*

'This is a book you can't put down' *Eastbourne Herald*

Also by Linda Regan and available from Headline

The DCI Banham series

Staged Death
Soho Killers
Monroe Murders
The Terror Within
The Burning Question

The DI Johnson and DS Green series

Brotherhood of Blades
Street Girls

The DI Johnson series

Guts for Garters
Sisterhoods

THE
BURNING
QUESTION

LINDA REGAN

ACCENT

First published in 2022 by Headline Accent
An imprint of HEADLINE PUBLISHING GROUP

1

Cataloguing in Publication Data is available from the British Library

ISBN 978 1 4722 8957 5

Typeset in 10.5/13pt Bembo Std by Jouve (UK), Milton Keynes

Printed and bound in Great Britain by Clays Ltd, Elcograf S.p.A.

HEADLINE PUBLISHING GROUP
An Hachette UK Company
Carmelite House
50 Victoria Embankment
London
EC4Y 0DZ

www.headline.co.uk
www.hachette.co.uk

As always, without the love and support from
my wonderful Hubby, Brian Murphy,
I would never have had the confidence
to step into a life of crime.

Darling, as always, this is dedicated,
with love, to you.

Prologue

Killing is easy. It's the walking up this road and then climbing a back wall, covered from head to toe in heavy, claustrophobic bike leather, that's the hard bit.

Disorientating is not the word. The helmet that supposedly stops anyone seeing, let alone remembering, my face, makes me feel like I'm that Liquorice Allsorts man. The one on the box who wears an oversized sweet on his head. My helmet doesn't actually look like a massive sweet, of course. Now that would really draw attention. It feels like it weighs ten tons, though, and, because it's too big for me, it slides around my face, blocking my vision, making me feel like my head is loose. I'll have to watch I don't walk into a wall, or, worse still, a person.

I know I have to wear gloves, but these fur and leather things weren't a good choice. They feel like I have some fucking animal's massive paws on the end of my arms, but they're practical. One glove has enough room for the rag, and the other holds the lighter.

I am definitely not comfortable. The leather trousers and the jacket are like bloody chainmail armour. I suppose I should be grateful the boots are a reasonable fit. Running away would be pretty hard if they weren't, and I might have to do that. All seems such a palaver. But it's a must. It's all been carefully planned. It'll keep me safe in more ways than one. And this job has to be done. But it's made riding the bike that much harder. The bike's round the corner now. I nicked the big PIZZA sign from the door of the pizza shop, hung it on the back of the bike, made it look like I was delivering a pizza. Clever thinking. I just have to hope the bike's not been nicked when I get back. That would be a fine bloody song and dance.

1

Happens a lot round here, apparently. But it won't be there long. This is going to all be over in a flash.

Literally.

Job's nearly done now, cloths already dipped in petrol from my bag. Just got to make sure it gets inside the flat somehow. Door, or window, whatever's quickest.

It's all this preparation that gets the sweat going. But again, got to be cautious. Can't get caught.

Nearly there now. I'm puffing like an eighty-a-day smoker. It's nerves, I reckon. Don't know why. No one's around. So easy and quick, and then it'll all be over. The CCTV's blocked, so that's all sorted. And, worst comes to worst, I've got a gun – a revolver. Would have to change these bastard gloves to use it, though, couldn't be sure I'd aim right.

There's gear in the bag hanging round my body: a great big spliff, rolled and ready, in the side pocket. A little treat for me when all this is done. I'll still be shaking, I reckon, so I rolled the spliff earlier. Coke will have worn off by then. Forward thinking, that's the trick. Anyway, how hard is it to push a petrol-soaked rag through a letterbox, or break the back window? I've got a heavy stone in my pocket. It's the ground-floor flat so should be easy enough to chuck the bugger through.

Here it is. I'll smash the window first, then chuck the jar and the lit rag in. There's carpet on the floor, I can see it through the back window. The building will go up like a rocket on bonfire night. A quick job guaranteed.

As soon as the flames start, it'll be a fast dash back to the bike. I'll drive like a bullet from a gun, then do a speedy stop on a safe quiet path just inside the wood to change my clothes. I'll clean the gloves and the wellingtons, wash the buggers clean so there's no DNA left on them. I'm wearing my own stuff underneath, and my trainers are on the bike, in the top box. Then I'm straight out of there, on to a safe place, laughing all the way, with that big fat spliff waiting for me.

It's good that it's been raining. Stopped now, but everyone's still indoors. OK, so the nosy ones might be looking out the window, but what would they see? Just a bloke walking the street in biker gear. I've got a pizza box in my hands, they'll think I'm delivering, I've thought that one out.

2

Here we are, then. This is it. Quick double-check. Yes, good. No one in sight. Back window broken. That was easy. Lighter and cloth at the ready, and here we go. Or, rather, here she goes.

Fuck me, that went up quick. I'm out of here.

Chapter One

It was nearly midnight when the call came through to DCI Paul Banham. There had been a massive fire in a small block of flats, the Apple Tree Apartments in Apple Tree Close, not too far away from where he lived. The remains of three bodies had been found. After the first fire officers had attended, they had called in Fire Forensics, and it was already strongly suspected as arson.

Banham had immediately assigned DI Alison Grainger as Senior Investigating Officer on the case. It helped that Alison was his partner outside of work, too. They had sat up together, for the rest of the night, with maps of the surrounding streets, getting to know the location, every alleyway and slip road, and everything that was in the vicinity of Apple Tree Close.

It was now seven in the morning, and Alison had already rung round and pulled her team together. Having had less than three hours' sleep, she was feeling fuzzy-headed. Percolated coffee bubbled in her kitchen as she wrote notes before the first meeting with her team. She intended drinking at least three cups, strong and black, before she set off for the Murder Investigation Unit. Her brain needed to be razor sharp and firing on all cylinders. Before the call had come through, and before they'd gone to sleep that evening, she and Banham had been in bed, talking through their future. It was over a year since she had miscarried their baby. The loss had shaken her badly, something she felt she couldn't talk about with Banham. It had also changed her; she no longer felt any maternal pangs. Banham continually told her that he still wanted

5

them to have a child together, but would wait until she felt ready again. She felt bad and also selfish, because she didn't feel she'd ever want a baby after losing the last one. The miscarriage had made her tougher, more ambitious, but had killed her motherly feelings. She now wanted to concentrate on work and getting promoted.

Yet she didn't feel she could tell Banham she no longer had the same feelings; that would break his heart. He had been through so much, having lost his first wife and their baby daughter to a killer – a machete-wielding murderer who, even after over twelve years, had never been found and brought to justice. So, she'd lied and told him she needed time. He was understanding and had agreed, but inside Alison now knew her only calling in life was her job – hunt down killers and give closure to those who had lost their loved ones to murder.

As she poured the coffee, she studied the map of the area around Apple Tree Close. It was a small cul-de-sac leading off a street confusingly named Apple Tree Road, with a few shops and a pub. There was CCTV on that road. *Let's hope there's something on it*, she thought, knowing how grainy and useless most of the footage usually was. The pub, too, would be likely to have cameras and it was situated almost opposite Apple Tree Close itself.

The burnt-out block was made up of three flats, and had gone up very quickly. Alison had checked the electoral register already. The resident of the ground-floor flat was presumably one of the three who had lost their lives. A Danielle Low, a woman in her early thirties, had lived there alone. The other cadavers were found in the second-floor flat: an older couple, both in their seventies, the Dowds. The first-floor resident had been spoken to by the fire officers when he arrived home from work to find his home alight. He was Del Harris, single and in his mid-thirties. Alison underlined his name as she poured more coffee. He had gone to stay with his mother in Putney. The chief fire officer had passed on a forwarding address for him.

Yesterday's weather had been rainy, on and off, so not many people would have been out and about, and Sunday was always the quietest day of the week, so not many passers-by. She wrote *CCTV check* on the pad as she drank her first coffee, then, *door-to-door* and *find where neighbours have been evacuated to and take statements.* Then, *Del Harris – DS Stephanie Green to interview him. DS Colin Crowther to talk to neighbours. DC Luke Hughes – CCTV findings, and backgrounds of victims. Trainee DC Hannah Kemp to shadow . . .?*

Alison tapped her teeth with her pen as she tried to think who the best detective would be to put her new trainee with. Then she wrote, *DS Crowther.*

'I'm off,' Alison shouted to Banham as she threw the last of her coffee down her throat and snatched her car keys from the side.

'I'll be in shortly,' came the reply. 'Keep me posted.'

He may have made her Senior Investigating Officer, she thought to herself, but still she would bet, a pound to a penny, that he would follow her around like a puppy. Not because he didn't trust her, but because, as he told her constantly, he hated not knowing where she was. Irritating though it was, she understood. Alison dealt with victims who needed closure, like Banham, all the time, and fully sympathised with their plight, but she still found his constant need to be near her, or know where she was at all times, very difficult.

She hurried out the front door, mind on the job and the new team member that she had to settle in.

Chapter Two

Trainee Detective Constable Hannah Kemp moved closer to the mirror to study her face. The scarring was minimal, but it was there. Everyone told her they didn't notice, but she felt it constantly. That happy, carefree young officer, who enjoyed her weekly girls' nights in wine bars and clubs, and was about to be married, was no longer looking back at her. The face staring out from the mirror was harder, and care-worn – but still filled with ambition. Not a bad thing for a twenty-seven-year-old woman who had been promoted from a uniformed PC to a trainee detective. She dabbed more powder over the side of her nose to cover her scars, reminding herself it was about confidence. But confidence was hard to pull off on her first day in after nearly a year away from the job.

She slid her fingers underneath her fair hair, lifting it up and away from her oval-shaped face, then turned her head to look at her profile. Yes, her nose was definitely crooked, there was a little lump on the bone that had never gone down, and the scars on her forehead were still prominent. Given the time back, though, she knew she would do the same again. So, no self-pity, she told herself. She was ready to come back.

She had put in an application for the Major Incident Team. Alison Grainger had vouched for her, given her a glowing report, and had now requested for Hannah to join her team. Opportunities like this didn't come along every day. She would grab it with both hands. Her first day on the job and already the DI had rung to tell her there had been an arson attack, and she was on board. She most certainly was!

Hannah pulled her hair away from her face, and then slid the black scrunchie from her wrist, using it to secure her hair into a neat ponytail. This would tell the team she was about to meet that she wasn't afraid of having her scars on show. They all knew her story anyway.

A second later, she pulled the scrunchie from her hair and let it fall loose again. One step at a time, she told herself.

She would get a haircut at the weekend. Her thick dark-blond mane now hung below her shoulders; it looked best when it barely touched them. She would get highlights too, jazz herself up a bit. She wasn't saving for a house, or a wedding, anymore. She could spend what she liked.

She turned her body to check her rear view. A green shirt with wide-legged grey slacks – much more comfortable than the itchy PC's uniform trousers. And her own trainers were a lot preferable to the frumpy black lace-ups she'd worn as a PC, not to mention easier to chase criminals in.

It had taken a lot to get herself to today, and here she was, part of the murder team. She had earned it, DI Grainger had told her, because she had showed such bravery in a life-threatening situation. Hannah hadn't thought of it as brave. You just dealt with the situation you were faced with. That's what police did. But here she was, in MIT. She was lucky.

She and DI Grainger had become good friends when Hannah was new on the force, when they had both been planning their weddings . . . And then through all the stuff that had happened, when Hannah retreated from the world, Alison Grainger had kept in touch and stopped her giving up. She knew she had an ally in the DI. And she wasn't going to let her down.

She pulled the Rescue Remedy phial from her bag and squeezed a couple of drops under her tongue, reminding herself she was a survivor. Now it was time to move on.

★

Alison had pinned pictures to the board at the front of the murder investigation room. She was drawing arrows from some pictures to others as Hannah entered. The DI didn't see her come in, as her back was to the room, so Hannah hovered in the doorway.

The desks were all crowded with computer equipment and papers. Some also showed the remains of early morning breakfasts: coffee cups and fast-food containers, half-eaten cakes and chocolate wrappers. Most of the detectives were standing, taking in the pictures on the board. Only DC Luke Hughes sat, in his wheelchair, behind a desk at the front of the room.

Hannah was unsure whether to announce her presence or stand at the door waiting for someone to see her. She took a step into the room and DS Crowther spotted her.

'Good morning,' he said, with his hard-to-resist smile. 'And welcome to MIT.'

Crowther was five feet, four inches, and only then with the right lifts in his shoes. The man hadn't the faintest idea of either dress sense or colour coordination. Today, he was wearing a navy-blue cardigan that had possibly been knitted fifty years ago, which had dropped and lengthened with over-washing and would now fit a stilt-walker. The T-shirt underneath the cardigan was a vivid shade of mauve. His jeans were a good fit apart from the legs; the bottoms had been rolled up to avoid him tripping over. His shoes were the seventies-style boots he always ordered, with inside lifts for maximum height. His hair, which was black and curly, had been over-gelled so it stood on end. Rumour had it that he styled it this way to look taller. It had the opposite effect. DS Stephanie Green, who argued with him constantly, referred to his hair as a hedgehog that had mated with a poodle. Nevertheless, he had a cute face, and enormous, kind, brown eyes with huge eyelashes. He was a first-class detective with a reputation for missing nothing, and remembering everything. Professional respect for him was immense, and his popularity extreme. He seemed to bring out a protective instinct in women, and always had more than his fair share of female conquests.

Hannah acknowledged him with an unsure smile, and mumbled, 'Morning,' back to him. The sound of her voice made Alison immediately turn around. She greeted her new DC in a reassuring tone.

'Hannah. Héllo, come on in.' Then, addressing the room, Alison announced, 'Please welcome our new trainee detective, Hannah Kemp. I know most of you know Hannah from her previous role as a PC, but for those who don't, she has been off on compassionate leave. She was on duty in the riots ten months back, which led to her kidnap – we will all have heard the rest of that story. She was new to the force, only a year out of Hendon, and acted with such courage, she was honoured with an award for her outstanding bravery, quick thinking, and calmness in a highly dangerous situation. She requested to come back and applied to cross over into MIT. I know it's still early days in her career, but I am delighted to have her on our team. I know she will be a great asset.'

Alison gave Hannah a reassuring smile, before continuing, 'Please everyone, be patient, help her learn the ropes, and listen to her. She has the makings of a great detective.' She turned to Hannah, who was blushing and clearly feeling a little overwhelmed. 'I know you must be feeling apprehensive,' Alison said with warmth. 'But we are your colleagues, so please feel free to come to any of us at any time for advice.'

The room broke into thunderous applause. Hannah nodded her thank you, feeling too full of painful memories to speak.

'Right, back to business,' Alison said, turning back to the whiteboard. She picked up a ruler and pointed to photos of three charred and unrecognisable cadavers.

'We have heard back from Fire Forensics who are ninety-nine per cent sure the Apple Tree Close fire was arson,' she told the room. 'A full investigation is still ongoing, so more to come on that. And the bodies have been identified: Danielle Low –' Alison pointed to a drawing of the three-storey building that had housed three flats – 'she lived alone on the ground floor. And Tom and

Ann Dowd, who lived on the second floor – the top floor. The occupier of the first-floor flat, a Del Harris, was, fortunately, away at the time of the fire. Danielle Low –' Alison pointed the ruler at a photo showing the severely charred remains of a woman – 'was found in the lounge of her ground-floor flat. The arsonist might well have known that, as the curtains weren't drawn.'

Alison turned back to the room. 'This flat was where the fire was started. So, we concentrate, first, on getting to know about Danielle.' She then pointed the ruler at the next photo – the couple whose bodies had been photographed next to each other, and again, were totally unrecognisable. 'Mr and Mrs Dowd had no chance of getting out. The flames spread within minutes. Del Harris, who lived alone, came back from work to find the building burning and surrounded by fire engines. Questions?'

'Was anything left?' Colin Crowther asked. 'Anything possessions-wise, guv? And has Forensics given us anything to go by, from the area outside? Cigarette butts? Footprints? Is there CCTV? Anyone seen in the area?'

Alison shook her head. 'Nothing at all, as yet,' she said. 'You are going to oversee the door-to-door with the uniform team, Col, as you're mentioning it. The neighbours have been evacuated for now, so that means finding out where to, and following that through. Someone must have seen something. There's a pub opposite the close, that would have been open. Get a list of any customers, and interview staff that were there yesterday. The close is tiny, and it's adjacent to a row of shops. Unfortunately, it was Sunday, but we need to know: were any of them open, or was anyone in their shop doing the accounts or whatever? Flats above the shops would have a good view of the road. Was anyone there, looking out their window?'

'Ma'am.' Crowther nodded, taking the instruction.

Alison added, 'Can you take Hannah with you, Col? Show her the area.'

The tone of his voice changed. 'Yes, ma'am,' he nodded. Alison was immediately aware of the murmur that went round the room.

'But a word in my office before you go,' she added. 'Rest of you, background checks on the victims. CCTV footage checks if we can get some. Luke will oversee all of this.'

Luke Hughes nodded from his wheelchair. 'Guv.'

She then turned to Stephanie Green. 'Can you track down Del Harris and interview him, please, Steph? He'll have something to say, I'm sure.'

'Ma'am,' Stephanie answered from the back of the room. Her fingers, which she held to her mouth as she spoke, were sticky with chocolate and crumbs from the croissant that she had just consumed. There were smears of it around her cheeks, too. Baz Butler, one of the other detectives on the team, who was walking past with fellow detectives Les Mitchell and bald-headed Nigel, handed her a serviette. There was an empty bag on her desk advertising the burger she had also eaten, and beside that was a large paper cup of coffee. Stephanie was a large woman with a large appetite, for sex as well as food. She and Colin Crowther spent most of their time making jibes at each other. She tried to seduce all the men in the building, and Crowther all the women. Alison kept out of it. Both were excellent detectives, and she was always glad to have them both on her team.

Stephanie wiped one of her chocolate-stained hands down the side of her jeans and picked up a pen.

'Del Harris was out at the time of the fire,' Alison reminded her, reading from the notes on her desk. 'I have an address for his mother in Putney, where he's staying. Find out how well he knew the others in the flats, and how well they all got on. Also, any regular visitors to the ground-floor flat he had noticed. And where he was at the time of the arson, and who saw him. He could be a suspect.'

Stephanie now had the croissant bag turned upside down and was tipping the crumbs onto her open palm. She nodded to Alison, then threw the flaky crumbs into her mouth. She then squeezed the paper bag into a ball, dropped it on her desk, and grabbed her large man's parka from the back of her chair and left the room.

'That's it, see you all later,' Alison told them, then added, 'Crowther, my office.'

The latest findings from the fire had just been placed on Alison's desk. As she opened the first page, she heard a knock at her door.

'Come in, Col,' she said. 'Have a seat.'

'Problem?' he asked.

She shook her head. 'No, just advice.'

He grinned. 'That's normally the other way round, isn't it? So, I'll presume all is good, then, in the love nest with the guv'nor?'

'Yes. This is not about Banham. Listen, I'm not going to tread on eggshells here. You and I go back too far. So, I can say to you what I wouldn't say to any of the others, though, obviously not in front of them.'

'What is it you want to say, Alison? Although, I can guess.' Crowther leaned back in his chair, folded his arms and crossed his ankles, then lifted his overgrown eyebrows and grinned. 'Don't seduce Hannah Kemp?'

Alison was staring at his socks. Either, one had faded, or they were odd socks. One was brownish and the other beige. She decided not to mention it. Normally, his dress sense was a lot worse. She adored him anyway. They were very close, having worked together for many years, and had got each other out of many a scrape. He was one of the few officers she confided in.

'Col, I want you to be serious. We both know how much Hannah suffered in that hostage situation. It broke her marriage up, before it even began.'

He stayed leaning back in his chair with his arms folded. 'I knew this was going to be one of your lectures about keeping my hands to myself.'

'This is her first day back after months of compassionate leave,' Alison argued. 'I've paired her with you because I know you'll take care of her and teach her. And that is what she needs.'

His eyebrows were raised as he nodded. 'Oh, and definitely no hanky-panky. That's what you want to say, isn't it, mate.'

'In a nutshell, yes.'

'I like women, we all know that, Ali. But I ain't that insensitive. I know what she's been through. I was there when it happened – we both were.' He paused, then added, 'Listen, that woman is strong, and resilient, and brave. She was hardly out of training when the hostage situ happened. And look how she coped. With guts and great intelligence. She'll be an asset to this team. I ain't gonna compromise that.'

'And that's why I've put her with you. She wanted to come back to work. The medical team advised her to stay off longer, but she was adamant. And she wanted to be in this department. I gave her a reference despite the fact she had had little experience even as a PC before that happened. Because, I agree, she has the makings of a great detective. But we must remember, sharp as her brain is – and it is – she's inexperienced. She is going to make mistakes. And I need someone who will cover for her and help her through them – and keep a sharp eye out and report everything back to me.'

'Course.'

'And it needs to be done discreetly.'

'I'm your man.'

Alison nodded. 'I know that. Now, listen. Her ex-fiancé, PC Peter Byfield, has been sent to another station in Chelsea. Everyone thought that best. He's still phoning her regularly, apparently, and won't give her space. She broke off the engagement because she felt she needed more time to heal. So, don't fuck with her head. Just help her. Got it?'

'Is that it, Alison? A lecture on not being lecherous?'

'No lecture, just a friend asking a friend.'

'I won't,' he assured her, standing up and heading for the door. 'Anything else, or can I go and do my job?'

'Yes, there is something else. Your socks don't match.' She shook her head. 'Oh, and your hair. I prefer it without gel.'

'Christ, don't tell me *you* fancy me too!'

She burst out laughing. 'Oh, do stop. It's a tactful way of saying you need a haircut. Now, go and find the bastard arsonist,' she said, then shook her head and added. 'I really don't know what women see in you.'

'They don't *see*, Ali, they *feel*. That's the secret.' He winked at her, then turned and left the office.

Chapter Three

The short close containing the Apple Tree Apartments was set off a small main road. As Stephanie approached it, she took a detour around the block. The CCTV cameras on the road had been sprayed with black paint, leaving them useless. The Fire Forensics unit were moving around the badly damaged building. Some were on their hands and knees in the road, outside the police cordons, scraping up tiny particles of mud, or dirt, or anything that might assist in finding the person who had set the building on fire and murdered three people. A red-and-white police *DO NOT ENTER* cordon had been secured at both ends of the main road.

Stephanie parked her green Honda, flashed her warrant card to the two PCs standing guard by the tape, and signed the book to say she was officially entering a crime scene, then donned forensic overalls. The chief fire officer, Callum, was watching her as she walked towards him. She knew him well; she'd had a one-night fling with him many years ago, when she was a uniformed PC and he a serving fire officer.

She had pulled her face mask over her mouth to block the smoky fumes that still hung in the air. She lifted it up as she neared the building to enable herself to speak. 'How's it going?' she asked, addressing Callum, who was looking serious.

'Fire was started on the ground floor,' he told her.

'Yes, we have that.'

'That's as much as we're sure of. Remnants of a petrol-filled cloth were found on the carpet where it landed, in the bedroom at the back. Also particles of a glass bottle. Arson, for sure.'

'Window was broken, I see,' Stephanie added. 'Can I go in?'

'Sorry, Steph, no, not yet.'

'What kind of bottle was it? Do we know that?'

'Looks more like a jar,' the fire officer told her. 'There were some glass fragments left that weren't from the window. All gone to Forensics, so we'll let you know more when we know.'

'Thanks.'

She looked at her notebook. Del Harris had been interviewed by the local uniforms just after the fire, and was staying in Putney with his mother. Nothing else she could find here, just yet. She thanked Callum and headed back to her car to make her way to Putney.

Hannah Kemp was sitting in the passenger seat beside Crowther in his black BMW.

'How are you feeling?' he asked her.

'Raring to go.'

'It's overseeing door-knocking. That sort of thing. So nothing too complicated to start you off.'

'That's the sort of thing we did as uniformed PCs. You're a DS, why do you have to do that?'

He smiled at her naivety. 'Our job is to find the culprit. In this case, the bastard who murdered a young woman and a retired couple. Often, a neighbour or someone will have seen something. That may well lead us to finding our killer. And yes, we call on the help of a uniformed team. Depends on the crime and availability. But it's an important job. You need to ask the right questions. Someone might just remember something that way. *And*, there is always a top man on the door-to-door.' He raised his eyebrows again. 'That's me, in this case. There aren't many neighbours around here. It's a small close, so what they saw or heard could make a lot of difference. Ask them where they were, what they remember was happening around that time for them. Push their memory buttons, that's when they'll say something they didn't know was important. Right now, we know nothing, and many of the neighbours have been evacuated. The uniformed team are already here, so let's go and get stuck in. We'll stay together.'

Crowther was aware she seemed suddenly unsettled. He put his hand on hers. 'If you're worried your ex might be on the door-to-door, then don't be. You won't be bumping into him just yet. He's on duty at another station for a while, we made sure of that. Early days for you. We're looking after you.'

'I know where he is. I'm still in touch with him. We're not engaged anymore but we talk.' She paused, then added, 'And I don't need babying.'

'Oh, we know that. You more than proved that during that hostage situation. Everyone is indebted to you for that; you have everyone's respect.' He studied her. She was tense. 'You've proved how good you are and the potential you have for rising through the ranks. Now, accept the hand of friendship that's being held out to you. Rome wasn't built in a day. I'll be your friend, and I'll be a good one.'

He winked reassuringly at her, noticing for the first time the minimal scarring around her forehead, and then her large, trusting grey eyes. OK, he had been warned not to flirt, but he was allowed to look. Scars didn't matter. She was gorgeous.

'Thank you. I appreciate it.' She smiled back, and then turned and opened the passenger door. 'Let's do this.'

Del Harris was a tall man, in his early- to mid-thirties. He worked, he told Stephanie, on the railway, which meant working odd shifts, on different days, and often at night. 'Odd hours, all of that,' he told her.

She was aware he was in shock. His eyes were vague and he constantly tapped his fingers on the table next to him. He sat on the leather sofa, opposite Stephanie, who had placed herself in an upright chair facing him.

'You were at work when it happened?' she asked, looking him straight in the eyes.

19

'I was at Clapham Junction. That's my current station. Although, I move around a lot. They do that to you. It's long shifts, so it's good to be at a station with caffs and toilets. Loads of people will have seen me there, trains from everywhere go through there. I couldn't have been anywhere near the flat at the time. Just in case you suspect I did it,' he added quickly. 'I'm sure if you showed a picture of me and asked all the passengers travelling through Clapham Junction that day if they remembered seeing me, then a lot of them would. I'm a man that stands out in a crowd.' His overly toothy mouth widened into a broad smile as he spoke.

Stephanie took an instant dislike to him. 'As I said, this is just to ask you a few questions, to help with our inquiry,' she said, raising her eyebrows at his comment. 'How well did you know Danielle, and the older couple who lived above you?'

'I knew the couple above me, but not well. The Dowds. They was quiet, kept themselves to themselves. Retired. I don't think they went out much.' He paused. 'And yes, I knew Danielle.' He put his hand to his head and rubbed his scalp. Stephanie noticed how lank his greying hair was, and how in need of a wash and a cut it was. He glanced downwards and she noticed his hair was thinning, too. He then looked up, and said, quite sincerely, 'I'm a bit in shock, so my brain isn't working well.'

'That's understandable.'

'I suppose I'd have to say I knew her quite well. Truth is, I had a fling with her, actually, if you really wanna know. It didn't last long. It was a year or so back now. When I first moved in. We both moved in about the same time, and I helped her put a few pictures up, painted her radiators. That sorta thing.' He looked straight back at Stephanie as he added, 'She paid me back in kind.'

Stephanie made no comment, but nodded for him to go on.

'It only happened twice. I knocked it on the head. Truth is, I found out she was on the game, and I didn't fancy catching anything.'

'How did you find out she was on the game?'

He shrugged.

'How did you find out?' she repeated. 'Did she have different men back?'

He shook his head.

'Well, how then?'

'It was obvious. She was unemployed, but always dressed up going somewhere. You know, low blouses, high heels. Stockings and all the gear. And she had two mobile phones.'

'Did you ever see, or suspect, a regular calling round – a man that could have been her pimp?'

He shook his head again. 'Can't say I did.'

'That's a big assumption then, Mr Harris.'

He raised his voice. 'She always had loads of cash. In teapots, spilling out of her bag, and everywhere. She had bottles of champagne around the flat, and fancy clothes and jewellery. Oh, and cocaine, too. She was off her face half the time. That don't suggest to me that she was living on unemployment benefit.'

'Was she?'

'Well, she didn't have a regular job. She said she did home hairdressing, but I never saw her do any, or any evidence of hair stuff.'

'You must have spent quite a lot of time in her flat to have noticed all this.' She was watching him closely as she questioned him. He didn't seem remotely nervous.

'She was my neighbour. Like I said, I helped her out if she needed a bit of DIY, all that, so yes, I was in there quite a bit. At first.'

'Were you in love with her?'

He looked taken aback, then shook his head. 'Hardly. She was a hooker. I'm sure of that. I knocked it on the head. Wouldn't go where all them others had been.'

Stephanie blinked. She wondered what he would say if she told him she had slept with more men than she had had takeaways in the office.

'Did she ever talk to you about being afraid of anyone?'

'No. I didn't see much of her after I worked out she was on the game. I avoided her, if you must know.' He wrinkled his nose and twisted his mouth.

21

When Stephanie said nothing, but held his stare, he looked away. When he turned back after a few seconds, he said, 'She wasn't the type of woman I wanted to associate with.'

'But she never actually admitted to you, she was on the game?'

'I'm a bloke, lady. Call it male instinct.'

'And I'm a detective sergeant, so call me sergeant, not lady.' She stood up. 'Thank you for your time.'

'Is that it?'

'For now.'

Chapter Four

The duty manager of the George pub on the main street, nearly opposite Apple Tree Close, was a Mr Lyons.

'I wasn't on duty last night,' he told Crowther. 'This is a brewery-owned pub, so we have more than one manager. I only heard about the fire today. I was surprised they said we could open. I can get you the number for head office, they'll have Harry's details. He was on last night. They'll also give you the details of the bar and waiting staff who were working. Probably only two or three of them on as it was Sunday. Carol was – she's in today, as a matter of fact. I'll see if anyone knows any of the customers who were in yesterday, too. Normally families, in for their roasts, so not the regulars.'

'I'll need your CCTV, too,' Crowther told him. 'It points straight out to the road opposite the flats.'

''Fraid it's empty, mate. I'm sorry. I checked it when I came in. I thought it might come in useful, but there's no tape in there. Are you suggesting this is arson, then?'

'Can't be sure yet,' Crowther told him curtly. He handed him a card. 'Send me the name and number of your head office contact. I'll need it by lunchtime, so get on to it now, if you please. And you said one of your staff was on yesterday – who was that again?'

Carol Whitfield was a middle-aged woman. She said she had been working, waitressing, the previous evening, but hadn't seen anything happening as she was busy serving.

'First I knew of a fire was when I heard the sirens, and, next thing, the fire officers were in the pub telling us to close up and all go home. That would have been at about quarter past five,' she added. 'I checked my watch, so I'm sure of the time. I was worried my car wasn't safe – I'd parked near them Apple Tree Apartments,' she told Crowther.

'Did you notice anything different, besides the burning building, when you went to your car? Any other cars parked there that weren't there when you came in to work?'

She shook her head. 'No, I was a bit afraid and I wanted to get out of there. I wasn't looking. Like I say, I'm surprised we were allowed to open today.'

Crowther thanked her, then reminded the manager to get on to head office and get back to him with a list of all employees working the previous day. 'And any customers' details you have,' he added.

'I'll get on to head office now.'

'Good,' Crowther told him. 'I'll expect an email shortly.'

He then went in search of Hannah, who was knocking on the doors of all the shops in the parade down from the fire.

Hannah had had no luck either. She had been walking up and down the small row of shops asking questions. 'Even Pizza on the Go closes early on a Sunday,' she told Crowther.

He thought she still looked anxious. 'Fancy a pizza?' he offered. 'It is lunchtime, and we can get a list of any staff who were on yesterday while we're waiting.'

'Great!' Hannah nodded.

They made their way into the pizza parlour, stepping around the two delivery bikes that blocked the doorway. Crowther showed his identity card to the man behind the counter. 'I understand you spoke to my colleague DC Kemp just now. We're here to order lunch, this time, but anything you can tell us about the area would be great!'

The man was in his mid-thirties, fair-haired and stocky. He had a large amount of dough in his hands, which he was kneading on

24

a wooden board. He immediately stopped and held his hand out to Crowther.

'Johnny Walsh,' he introduced himself. 'Happy to help.' He seemed friendly and spoke with a scouse accent.

'For instance, did you know or ever deliver to Apple Tree Close flats?'

'Yeah, we often delivered to number two, on the first floor. A Mr Harris. He works nights and often comes in to buy, or rings for a delivery, at the end of his shift.'

'But not the other flats?'

'No. I don't know any of them.'

'It says outside you are open seven days a week, yet you told my colleague you were closed yesterday evening?' Crowther said.

'Yes, we're open on Sundays, but not all day. I work seven days a week because it's hard to make a living. Sunday is very quiet. Most people like to go to the pub down the road for their roast these days. I wouldn't bother to open at all, but I have delivery boys on standby. They need to earn. They were here yesterday, out delivering, on and off, but we were hardly busy. You can talk to them. They're in the back, both of them. I was here, too, cooking. I closed up around five. Both the boys were out. Joseph went out on a delivery to the Barrow Estate. There was a gang there hassling him. He was nervous to leave his bike.. We had a bike nicked about a month ago. Happens a lot these days.' He shrugged. 'Gangs want motorbikes to go bloody thieving on, so my boys are targets. Poor lads, just trying to make an honest living. Anyway, Joseph phoned to say he couldn't leave his bike unattended. He needed Anthony to guard the bike. Anthony went out to help. It was the only order I'd had in three hours, so I closed up and went home. I texted them and told them to go home, too, after they'd delivered the pizza.'

'What time was this again?' Crowther asked.

'Around five.'

Crowther waited.

'That's it, that's all I can say. I closed up and went home. I came in this morning to all this. It's bloody terrible. It used to be a nice

25

neighbourhood – the worst I knew was my pizza signs being stolen off the door. Lately, it's getting a lot worse. Now this terrible fire. And only four weeks ago one of my bikes was stolen. My boys often have to go out as a two, which halves their pay. They take their life in their hands just to earn a crust.' He shook his head. 'They're good, hard-working boys. They have families. If they lose my bikes we all lose out. I'd be delivering by car, and the boys would be out of work.'

Hannah was making notes.

'No one looks out for us anymore,' Johnny added as he opened an oven door to pop the pizzas in.

'We'll have ours to take away,' Crowther told him. 'While they're cooking, do you mind if we go through to the back to talk to the delivery boys?'

'Be my guest.'

The two delivery drivers were sitting around a table. Both had their heads down, and were on their mobile phones, playing video games.

Crowther held out his identity card, and then introduced Hannah. 'It's about the arson at Apple Tree Close last night. You were both working yesterday,' he half-asked and half-told them, adding, 'when the arson took place.'

They both closed their phones and gave Crowther their attention. 'Yes, we were,' the smaller of the two said.

'Can I take your names?' Hannah asked.

'Joseph Perrino,' said the taller of the two, who was mixed race with wiry black hair.

'Anthony Rossiti,' the smaller youth said. He also had dark hair, with olive skin and rich brown eyes.

'Did you see, or hear, or notice, anyone or anything? Did anyone come in here around the time of the fire?' she asked.

Crowther gave her an approving nod.

Joseph shook his head. 'We were out on a delivery.'

'What time did you leave for the delivery?' Crowther asked.

26

'I couldn't be completely sure,' Joseph said. 'Four thirty?' he offered, looking to Anthony for confirmation. Anthony nodded.

'I had to go to the Barrow Estate,' Joseph continued. 'I had hassle there. It's a real den of iniquity, like they say, so I called Tony.'

'I went to help out,' Anthony told them. 'I watched the bikes while he delivered the pizzas. We went as quick as we could. There was a gang hanging around, not one I had seen there before. As we left, I checked my phone and Mr Walsh had texted to say he had closed up and we could both go home.'

'And did you both go home?'

Joseph shook his head. 'I didn't, I was heading back to the shop, hoping to get another delivery. I hadn't got the text. I didn't check my phone until I got back. I was hoping to get another drop 'cause I need the dough. The Barrow one was a fifty-fifty split cause Tony had to come out to help. I drove into the roadblocks when I approached the shops. I could see all the smoke and flames crackling. This road was closed off. I spoke to police at the cordons, told them I needed to get back to the shop. They told me the area had been evacuated. Everyone had been evacuated for their own safety. That's when I looked at my phone and read Mr Walsh's text telling me to go home.'

'What time was this?' Hannah asked, making notes as the boy told his story.

Joseph picked his phone up and checked it. 'The text came in at seven minutes past five. I probably got it ten minutes later.'

'You hadn't checked your phone before that?'

'No. I was on my bike. And as soon as the delivery was done, we both shot out of that Barrow Estate. There was a gang lurking, like Tony said, after our bikes. The last thing I would do is get a phone out. I got away as quickly as I could. That estate is like a snake pit. Truth is, we don't want to go there. It's hassle almost every time. But work is work.'

'And you were out longer than usual on that delivery? Both of you together, because the estate is dangerous?' Hannah confirmed.

'Yes. Do you know the place?'

'Yes.'

He shrugged. 'We often go in twos, but I went ahead, I was hoping it just might be OK, and Tony could get another delivery, then we would both get full money. We don't get salaries.'

Crowther turned to Anthony. The boy's jeans were shabby and clearly old, his black trainers grubby, and his hair was in need of a wash.

'You were here, then, up to the time Joseph called you to help?' Crowther asked again. 'I'm trying to get a rough estimate of the time the arson was started.'

'Yeah. It would have been about quarter to five I went out.' The boy nodded. 'Mr Walsh will have the chit. The time's on that.'

Hannah noticed Anthony looked worn and tired. His eyes were ringed with dark circles. She had seen many boys like him. All still young, but having grown up too fast.

'I was waiting and hoping to get a drop before we shut. Joseph called me then. I didn't check my phone straight after the drop because of the shithole we were at. I shot out of the estate just after Joseph and then stopped a few streets away. Then I read Mr Walsh's text, and I headed for home.'

'What time was this?'

Anthony scrolled down his phone. 'It was five-ish,' he said, 'when Mr Walsh texted he was closing up.'

Hannah wrote everything down, then thanked them and walked back out to the counter.

As they picked up their pizzas, they took the chit that Johnny Walsh had printed for the job on the Barrow Estate.

'The job came in at four-oh-five,' he told Crowther.' Joseph left here at four twenty-seven. It would have taken him ten minutes or so to get to the estate. I closed up just after five p.m. and drove straight home. There was no fire then.'

They were eating their pizzas in Crowther's car. 'You're doing well,' Crowther told Hannah. 'How are you feeling?'

Her stomach immediately knotted. She was feeling nervous,

confused, and anxious. 'I'll get there,' she said. 'We now know for sure that the fire was started after half past four, and the fire brigade were called at two minutes past five. So, most likely, the fire started about five or ten minutes before that, as it went up so fiercely. The area was obviously quiet, it was raining and the only people about were in the pub. But none that we can talk to yet.'

Crowther nodded. 'I'd agree the fire was started about ten minutes before the alarm was raised. Well done.'

'Bugger about the CCTV, though,' Hannah said. 'Sergeant Green said all the cameras were sprayed with black paint, or taped over, so purposely blocked off.'

Crowther nodded. 'Which points to it being a calculated attack – definitely arson – and now a triple murder case.

Chapter Five

The evening meeting was full. The whole team had made it back and all carried notebooks with pages of notes.

'The traffic cameras on buses in and out of the area are being checked,' Stephanie Green told the room. 'All the street CCTV's buggered. It's been sprayed over with black paint. The near neighbours were all evacuated, so we'll need to track each one down and interview them.'

'We are waiting on any pub staff or customers to talk to us,' Colin Crowther told them. 'But don't hold your breath. The manager told us that the first any of them knew of the fire was when fire officers came in and told them to close up and evacuate. They were allowed back in this morning, as they're on the other side of the road. However, only one person who was on yesterday was in today. She saw nothing. And there is a rota of managers. The one on today wasn't on yesterday.'

Hannah was staring at the pictures on the whiteboard at the front of the room.

'We've got the name and address of the person who called 999,' Luke Hughes told Alison. 'She's a neighbour, but obviously staying somewhere else. She'll be in later to give her statement. I'm staying on for the night; I'll take the statement and give it to you in the morning.'

'Good,' Alison told him. She always had Luke Hughes on her team. His injury, which had made him wheelchair-bound, never held him back, and his stamina and dedication to work was like no other.

'I've put out a press release,' she told the team. 'I'm hoping that might jog some memories, bring someone forward. Maybe there was someone who was walking in the rain, just around the streets, towards the pub or somewhere, not even a resident.'

'We spoke to the staff at Pizza on the Go. They shut up shop about five,' Colin Crowther told her. 'The last order of the day came in at five past four in the afternoon.'

Alison nodded. 'Fire chief said he was allowing the neighbours back in tomorrow, so back on door-to-door, then, please, and interview the neighbours we couldn't do today. Fire Forensics have now confirmed arson.' She turned back to the pictures of the three charred bodies pinned to the whiteboard. Beside them was a new photo of Danielle Low in life, smiling back at the camera. Hannah Kemp was transfixed by the girl's face.

'I have spoken to the parents of Danielle Low,' Alison said. 'They're in shock, naturally, but I was able to talk to them. They said we are welcome in their house, Danielle's childhood home. We can go through Danielle's possessions in her bedroom there. They said there's an old computer there, too. Also –' Alison turned and pointed to the new photo of Danielle on the whiteboard – 'they gave me this recent photo of our ground-floor victim.'

Hannah couldn't place where she knew her from; she just knew she did. The woman had dark-blond hair that fell between her ears and shoulders, and a wide face that Hannah recognised. She didn't recognise the name, but for sure the face staring back at her was very familiar.

'I didn't, for obvious reasons, ask her parents to identify her remains,' Alison continued. 'Danielle's teeth were intact, and they were able to provide me with her dentist's details. DC Hughes contacted the dentist, who was able to confirm a positive identification. We also have confirmation, from the son, on the couple in the top flat. Thank you, Luke.'

All heads turned to the young ginger-haired DC. Luke Hughes had lost the use of his legs in a police car-chase accident a few years back, but had declined the offer of compensation and early retirement. He was a detective, he had told the board, and if they would keep him, he would work full-time in the department, chasing up leads or doing the paperwork. Everyone respected his professionalism, computer wizardry and defiance against all odds. He worked any and all hours when needed, and was a great asset to the department.

'It wasn't rocket science,' he said. 'There was nothing left to retrieve, possessions-wise, in the flat. However, I traced their son. He was able to identify the couple by their wedding rings. So, we are a hundred per cent sure who our victims are.'

'Next, we need to build a picture of these people's lives,' Alison said. 'Find out who wanted who dead. Remember, the fire was started in the ground-floor flat – the flat of Danielle Low, so we start with her. Fire Forensics have informed us that the bedroom window was broken and then a lit, petrol-soaked cloth thrown in. So, we need to find out her close friends. Her parents said she did home hairdressing, but they don't know any of her customers.'

'I interviewed Del Harris,' Stephanie Green told the room. 'He lives directly above the flat where the fire started. He claims he had a short affair with Danielle but found out she was on the game and dropped her.' She tapped her nose. 'I took a dislike to him. Although, he has a sound alibi. He was working at the time of the fire. He works on the railways, at Clapham Junction.' She shook her head. 'He seemed cold and uncaring for someone whose home has just gone up in flames, and very up himself. I'll check out that he really was working on Sunday. Find out if anyone saw him at Clapham Junction.'

'You don't see anything but trains there,' Crowther said sarcastically.

'Oh, I'm sure you'd notice if there was a mini-skirted bird on the platform,' Steph snapped back.

Alison jumped in before they held the meeting up with their constant jibes at each other. 'What didn't you like about him?'

Stephanie looked at Colin Crowther. 'Something you'll side with me on, here,' she said. 'He doesn't approve of casual sex,' she said. 'Or having fun. He seemed too moral for this day and age. Not that I think anyone would want to jump into bed with him. He could have done with a bath and a haircut, and maybe a tube of Clearasil.'

'Must be bad, if you don't fancy jumping into bed with him,' Crowther joked. 'I thought anyone would do.'

Stephanie straightened up, like a peacock about to show its feathers. 'Speak for yourself, oh ye with the loose mouth and flies,' she retorted.

'Don't start, you two!' Alison raised her voice, noticing Hannah had gone very quiet.

'Danielle owned her flat,' Luke Hughes announced.

'Good,' Alison nodded. 'So, was she in debt? Had she upset anyone? If she was on the game, did she do drugs? Col, what have you got?'

Crowther turned to Hannah. 'Do you want to go first?' He frowned as he looked at her. 'Are you OK?'

She shrugged. 'I just thought our victim looks familiar,' she said nervously. 'But I'm probably mistaken.'

'Any thoughts, Col?' Alison asked again, dismissing Hannah's vagueness.

'We'll talk to the neighbours tomorrow, see what we get from that, ma'am. And we'll interview the staff and any customers from the George pub opposite, whose details we'll have. I'm hoping someone sneaked out for a fag and noticed something.'

'It was raining, so unlikely,' Baz Butler, the tall detective who always stood in the corner, piped up.

'Smoking is addictive,' Crowther immediately snapped back. 'If you need to have a fag, rain won't stop you. Can't believe no one saw anything.' He nodded to Hannah, encouraging her to say something.

'We interviewed the two pizza takeaway boys and the manager who owns the Pizza on the Go joint,' she said. 'They closed before the fire started, or at least before it was reported, and no other shops were open as it was a Sunday.'

'Did either of the delivery boys know the victims?' Stephanie Green asked.

'Manager said they often delivered to Del Harris, but no one else in the flats.'

The penny was beginning to drop for Hannah as she stared at the photo of Danielle Low again. She was now sure she knew who Danielle was. Only not under that name . . . What a thump in the eye for her, and on her first day back!

'I'll check on Del Harris's shifts at Clapham Junction,' Luke Hughes told them. 'I can request his time sheet from the station.'

'There's a chit for the pizza order – the manager gave it to us,' Crowther said. 'The order came in at five past four, and Joseph left the shop about half past. Anthony followed about ten or fifteen minutes after that. Johnny Walsh, the manager, then texted both of them, just after five, to say he was shutting up. Anthony went home. Joseph didn't pick up the text, so he headed back to the shop. When he approached the area, the fire brigade was already there and the street closed off.'

'Do you know where the neighbour that phoned the fire in lived?' Hannah asked. 'How near to the flats?'

'The first call actually came from the Dowds' flat,' Luke told her. 'Flat number three. They called it in at a minute past five. They would have smelt the smoke. It wouldn't have been long before the fire reached and overwhelmed them. Then another 999 call from a Mrs Fuller at two minutes past five. She's the lady coming in later tonight.'

Stephanie turned to Luke Hughes. 'Let me know when you get Harris's work sheet,' she asked, then added, 'Ma'am, is it OK if I go to Clapham Junction, talk to a few colleagues and ask around about Harris? Strange, or lucky, isn't it, that he wasn't in at the time of the fire?'

'Yes, fine by me,' Alison said. 'I'll put a list on the board of who needs interviewing, or searching out. Details urgently needed of mobile phones, banks, etcetera, for Danielle.' She turned to Luke. 'That'll be you, DC Hughes. And a visit to her parents' home will hopefully turn something up. Can you also get on to ANPR and get a list of all cars that drove through the area? See if any of them saw anything. Someone must have.'

She then noticed Hannah staring blankly at the board.

'Hannah, are you OK?

Hannah jumped to attention. 'Sorry, ma'am. Yes, I'm fine.'

'Let's hope Fire Forensics can find the remains of her mobile in the flat,' Alison said.

'Don't forget the computer at her parents',' Stephanie added.

'It's apparently a very old one, but who knows,' Alison said.

Hannah took a deep intake of breath at that.

'I've checked Danielle Low on the computer, ma'am,' Luke Hughes said. 'Since Sergeant Green said her neighbour implied she was on the game. She has no previous. She used to live with her parents in Dagenham, as you know. She bought her flat a year or so back.

Stephanie nodded. 'That tallies with what Harris said.'

'She was registered as unemployed,' Hughes told them, looking up at Alison. 'So, where did she get the money to buy the flat?' He looked at Stephanie. 'Del Harris, you said, claims she had champagne and coke around the place, and expensive clothes, and was always dolled up going somewhere. So, he presumed she was involved in prostitution.'

Hannah felt her cheeks redden.

'She could have had a sugar daddy,' Crowther suggested. 'Harris gets jealous and accuses her of being a whore. Perhaps even kills her. Motive.'

'How do you get a sugar daddy?' Stephanie asked, now tapping words into her computer.

Crowther burst out laughing. 'First, you'd have to lose a good few stone, mate, if you were thinking for yourself.'

'I'm typing "sugar daddy agencies" into Google,' Stephanie snapped. 'And I can assure you, I have more than my fair share of fellas, thank you. And I certainly don't want keeping.'

'Don't think anyone could afford your food bill,' Crowther retorted.

35

'Shut up, both of you,' Alison snapped. 'And grow up! You're both as bad as each other.'

Hannah didn't hear the bickering. Her legs felt unsteady. Her first day back, and now this . . .

'I have requested the media here to set up a press conference, too,' Alison told the room, moving quickly on. 'We want to get a front-page picture of her. At least in the papers in this area. And ASAP. See if that brings anything. I should get a full report from Fire Forensics tomorrow. Fingers crossed that will turn something up.'

Hannah lowered her eyes again.

'Meanwhile, the list of people to find and things to trace will be on the board by the end of this evening. Don't go home until you have signed your name by the jobs you're taking on. Bright and early start, please.'

Alison's phone pinged. She looked down to read the text. 'Ah, from the press office. The press conference is after this meeting. I'll have to attend.' She picked up her papers from her desk and then looked up. 'Oh, and I'm going to the pub for a half-hour now before the press call. Hannah, if you would like a welcome-to-the-team drink, I would love to buy you one.'

'Can I put that on hold?' Hannah said.

'Of course,' Alison told her, then gave Crowther a concerned look.

Hannah didn't even say goodnight to DS Crowther. She hurried out of the meeting and went straight home. She could feel her heart beating too quickly in her chest as she sped along the road to her flat. The build-up for going back to work, and starting in MIT, had been nerve-wracking enough, but seeing that picture of Danielle Low had shaken her to her boots. She *had* known her, but under another name. None of the girls had used their own names, except her. She was too naive to have thought that one out, in those days. Maybe it wasn't the same girl, but deep down, Hannah knew it was, and that would mean she was now withholding evidence. A serious crime. But then, if it wasn't the same woman she thought she remembered from her student days, she would have put her job on the line and most definitely would be taken off the case. And she would have to admit that she worked in an escort agency before joining the Met.

She walked into her flat, hung up her coat, and shivered as she put the kettle on. Alison was looking out for her, she knew that. Her new partner, Sergeant Crowther, was lovely to work for. He was helpful and respectful, charming and cheeky and sexy. They were getting on well. He was clever and kind, and, she would bet, good in bed.

She turned the kettle off and pulled a half-drunk bottle of wine from the fridge. She poured a glass and swallowed half of it in one gulp. Up until seeing that picture of Danielle Low on the whiteboard, her first day had gone well. She downed the rest of the wine, and then poured herself another glass. She walked into the bathroom and turned on the taps to run a bath. She had been OK until that photo appeared on the board. Getting back to work was all she had thought about during her long healing time and absence from the job. Now she was back, she had to prove her worth.

She put on some Ed Sheeran music from the laptop beside her and stepped into the bubble-filled bath. She had got through one day, and tomorrow was another one. Danielle Low was a face from the distant past – if it was even her . . .

I've got mixed feelings about this one. Sort of hard to let go of this bitch. It'll make a big spread in the papers. But 'Vengeance is mine, says the Lord.' They were the words. And she deserves it. Thought she was always going to get what she demanded. Well, not this time, baby. This is the time you pay, because you are going to hell.

Good thing about this one is her house is behind a high fence. There's a very long driveway after you go through the gate, so it's secluded. She has the money to buy a cottage on the outskirts, as well as the pad in town. Fucking rich cow. Got that from lying on her back. Well, now she'll be on her knees, begging, when she knows she's trapped in there and on her way to hell. She'll feel the heat accelerating and curling into her burning skin, and there she'll be – face to face with Old Nick himself.

It is fucking dark on this path. You'd think the rich bitch would fork out to have lights. Suits me, though. It's 2 a.m., and I'm dressed head to foot in black; I've got the helmet over my head. I'm well camouflaged.

Ahhh. The cottage's got a light on. Might be a night light. Mind you, she's a night bird, no arguing that. I just have to hope she's in – and alone. Her red Mercedes is in the drive, but that doesn't prove a fucking thing. This one likes to come and go in taxis. Doesn't want anyone to know her number plate or much else about her. She didn't reckon on taking me on then, clearly. I know all about you, you fucking slag.

I'm going to go round the side. I've done a recce on this one and I know it's not a mansion. Not what I'd expect her to have, although there's that fancy flat as well. She likes it here, so she says. Likes the privacy. Warm and cosy. She hates the cold. Well, she'll get some warmth in a minute . . .

Shit, the fucker of a dog has started barking.

Now the light is coming from . . . Oh, hello . . . fuck. I've been spotted. Just as well I brought the hammer and wire in case of problems. Smash the window and I'm in.

'What? Jesus! How on earth did you . . . What are you doing?'

Must act quick here. Hammer's up, give her a good fucking smack in the side of the head. She's stumbled, but now she's screaming. Can't have that.

Whack. Whack. And another big whack across her face. She's down now.

Fuck me, the dog's barking, and now that's the alarm. Christ, got to get a grip on all this. Shut the dog up, first. Oh, it's quick, just missed the fucker with the hammer. Fuck, now her eyes are open and she's trying to get up, and the dog's in the way again . . .

'You bitch. I told you not to . . .'

Right, there's another whack from the hammer. I think she's finally unconscious. Fucking wailing of that alarm, it's unnerving me. And the bastard of a dog is at me now. Jesus Christ, she's moving again. And fucking moaning. Another smash to the skull should do it. Mustn't panic, can't afford to make mistakes.

Whack!

She's out again, but I don't know if she's a goner. Ah. Luck's in. There's a carafe of brandy here. Great. I'll pour that over her. Waste of good brandy, mind. But got to get this going and get the hell out of here. Fucking alarm will be my downfall. I've hit the fucking dog with the carafe. It broke, and the dog's gone quiet. Well done me.

Oh, she's at it again: head's up and she's choking on the brandy. And kicking out at me with those long legs. She's a tough 'un to kill, this bitch. She's putting me off my stroke with those strong legs. I mustn't panic, worst thing you can do, but that alarm could wake the bloody dead. And the dog's barking at me again. I'll smash him again, too.

Christ, her eyes are staring at me, in fear. Face all podgy and swollen with the whacks. It's putting me off. Getting me a bit shaky. Oh, fuck it. That fucking alarm is driving me potty. Lighter. Where's my bloody lighter? Here, stay calm – it's in my pocket where I put it. Stay calm. I'm bloody shaking. Drop the hammer and light the rag. Done. No, take the hammer, I've held the bastard without gloves, can't be leaving clues. Hammer's got a lot of metal in it; it may not burn.

OK. Cloth's alight. And dropped on her. Oh, her hair's gone straight up. She's like one of those flambé things they light in front of you in a posh restaurant. And she's trying to scream. Stupid cow – got a mouthful of the fire. Bet that bloody hurt. Right, hammer. Got it. Fuck me, everywhere's burning so quick. I'm out of here.

Christ, that fucking alarm. And the fucking dog's outside now, barking like a fucker. The police'll be here any minute. Window? Where is it? Ah, yes, French window.

Heading for my bike and off.

Chapter Six

Hannah had set her alarm for just before six. She'd slept very little. She'd decided to say nothing about the fact she thought she knew who Danielle really was.

Today was a new day. Her second day on the team. She had got through her first.

She jumped out of bed and headed for the shower.

Alison Grainger was already in before the team assembled themselves, coffees and bacon sarnies in hand. She looked drawn and worried.

Luke Hughes also wore a solemn expression.

Stephanie Green was eating a burger, which dripped with tomato sauce. A cardboard carton of chips sat on her desk, stinking the room out. Beside that a large paper cup with a protruding straw stood in the middle of her desk, advertising the burger bar.

'There's been another arson attack on a single woman, last night,' Alison told them as the team settled into place behind their desks, or perched on stools, or leaned against the wall. 'You may or may not have picked it up on the computer. It isn't in this area, but it was sent over to us as it may be connected to our current arson investigation. The cottage was owned by a woman in her late twenties, Annabelle Perry. She was the daughter of David Perry, the late MP. Annabelle was single, and worked as a model, according to the neighbour. Fire Forensics are at the location as we speak, but arson has not been confirmed yet. Fire officers have been there since two a.m. The fire is out, so it's a waiting game. If they do confirm arson, which they highly suspect, then it's either a very large coincidence, or we have a serial arsonist on our hands, maybe one who is after young women, and we need to find them double quick.'

'Why do we think there may be a connection?' Colin Crowther asked.

'Similar scenario,' Alison told him. 'Single women, both early thirties, both at home when the fire was started. Forensics think a petrol-soaked cloth started both fires. And this time, the neighbour heard a motorbike drive off. Local officers spoke to the neighbour last night. I have a copy of the statement here.' Alison picked the statement up from her desk.

'"*I heard the alarm going off about two a.m., and knowing Annabelle Perry lived alone, I came out to see if there was anyone about. Annabelle's dog was barking furiously. I was nervous someone was in the grounds. As I walked towards the fence that divides our buildings, I saw the flames. I immediately called the fire brigade. Then I attempted to go to the house. This meant going down my drive and up Annabelle's. The flames rose so quickly, I couldn't get near it, but I could see the French window was broken. I was panicking because I believed Annabelle was in there.*

'I rushed down the path and I heard what I believe was a motorbike roar off. Her dog was in the grounds, barking and howling, and clearly very distressed. Then I heard the fire engines approaching. They told me to go back into my house. They would come and tell me if I had to evacuate. I was worried about my cats, I have six, but they all hurried inside and are safe."
That's it so far,' Alison concluded. 'We've asked the neighbour, a Mrs Gillian Hillier, to come in later this morning to talk to us.'

'If Annabelle Perry was a model, then highly likely she's on Instagram, Facebook, and Twitter,' Stephanie suggested, clicking her computer open.

'Interesting,' Crowther announced. 'A motorbike belonging to the pizza place down the road from our first victim was stolen last night. I'm just reading the crime reports from the team that worked last night. One of the boys went out on a delivery. He came back and his bike was gone.'

'Have we got a time for when the bike was stolen?' Alison asked.

'No. I'll go in and take a statement from him,' Crowther told her, then added, 'This arson was a good seven miles away from the last one.'

Hannah's hand shot up. 'Desk Sergeant Stan told me the pizza-shop owner, Johnny Walsh, called in to say one of his pizza signs was returned to him last night, the sign off the first bike that was stolen.'

'Has Stan just told you that?' Alison asked.

'Yes, as I was coming in. He told me to let you know.'

'Did he say what time?'

'Would have had to be during opening hours. The place closes at eleven p.m. on a Monday,' Crowther told them.

'And this new arson was around two a.m.,' Alison reminded them. 'Get round there and pick up whatever it is Walsh received,' she said, looking at Hannah. 'Bag it, and send straight to Forensics. Crowther, take a statement from the boy who was delivering when the bike was stolen.'

'Bike thefts are on the increase,' Hannah said. 'They use them for snatching bags and phones, these gangs. So delivery bikers are prime targets.'

Crowther nodded to back her up. 'One of those pizza-shop lads called the other one out on Sunday as he was being hassled by a gang on the Barrow Estate. He thought they were after his bike.'

'Shall I check if there's CCTV anywhere on the estate?' Hannah suggested.

A couple of detectives shook their heads, mumbling, 'Are you serious?' and, 'No chance – CCTV never works on any estates. Bit like their lifts—'

'Shut up,' Alison cut them off. 'Good idea, Hannah, and worth a try.'

'Found her!' Stephanie shouted across the room, nearly knocking her burger-bar milkshake flying. She was dipping chips into a

43

side helping of tomato sauce and eating as she spoke. 'I'll print this out. She's very pretty.'

'So was Danielle,' Crowther said. 'Her neighbour said she was on the game. Is there a connection there? Is "being a model" another word for that, these days?'

Hannah immediately felt her cheeks burning.

'Her father was indeed David Perry, the Conservative MP,' Stephanie told them. 'He was killed a few years ago in a car accident.'

As Annabelle Perry's photo hummed its way out of the printer, Hannah's stomach hit her boots. She recognised the new face immediately, and in recognising Annabelle, she knew she had been right about recognising Danielle. She knew the connection. Her heart was beating like a frightened bird as she stared at Annabelle's picture.

She looked the same as Hannah remembered her. Thick, dark-brown hair that flowed and curled as it tumbled down her long slender back. Her beautifully made-up, angular face, although a little older, hadn't changed.

Danielle, however, had dyed her hair back to its natural dark blond, and wore no make-up in the photo on the board. Hannah remembered Danielle as a peroxide blonde, with short hair, bright-red lips, and heavy eyebrows – looking more like Marilyn Monroe than herself.

Now, looking at the two dead women staring back from the board, a shudder went through her. She knew what the connection was, and she now knew for sure that by keeping schtum, she was committing the crime of withholding vital evidence in a murder inquiry. How could she have been so stupid as a hard-up student, all those years ago? She silently and shakily weighed up her options.

Chapter Seven

Hannah stood in front of the mirror in the women's toilet, studying the scar between her nose and forehead. It always glowed like Rudolph's nose when she was stressed.

Annabelle Perry had lived in Herne Hill, Danielle Low a good way away from her. But Hannah knew the connection between them must mean something, must have something to do with their deaths. She'd known these women by different names, but, like herself, they had been involved in—

She leaned closer into the mirror; her scars looked like they were on fire. Question was, could the withholding of her evidence put other women's lives at risk? That thought made her feel even worse. She made a decision to do some private snooping, see if the agency even still existed. If it did, there would be a website and photos. God forbid, photos of herself as well as Danielle and Annabelle—

The knock on the door made her jump. Then the impatient voice of Crowther, saying, 'Ready when you are.'

'Coming!' she shouted back. She got her powder out of her pocket and dabbed it liberally over her face. She then speedily pulled a brush through her hair, tying it back into a ponytail. She squeezed her lip gloss over her mouth, threw her bag over her shoulder, and breathed out deeply.

'Get your skates on,' the impatient voice of Crowther came again. 'Lots to do.'

'Coming, coming,' she shouted, heading for the door.

*

As DCI Banham walked through the murder department, heading for Alison Grainger's office, all the detectives that were in the department, working on computers, checking out both the deceaseds' lives, made subtle, or unsubtle, eye contact with each other. They watched as Banham knocked, and then walked straight into Alison's office without waiting for an invitation to 'Come in'.

Alison looked up briefly as Banham entered the room. She showed no sign of looking pleased to see him. Her gaze immediately went back to her laptop.

'Is this a personal or professional visit?' she asked, still staring at her computer.

'Both. We have a double arsonist at large.'

She looked up. 'You have confirmation, do you?'

'Confirmation has just come through from Fire Forensics. Both fires were arson, and likely the same arsonist. We need to move fast on this one. What have we got?'

Alison squeezed her lips together thoughtfully. 'The neighbour at Herne Hill heard a motorcycle drive off. And a customer who was standing outside the George pub opposite Apple Tree Close has just come in and spoken to Luke Hughes. She heard the press conference we gave out last night and came in. She said she thought she saw a delivery driver, just before the fire, walking towards the flats. She had popped outside for a cigarette, and noticed the delivery man, but thought nothing of it and went back into the pub. A few minutes later, she wasn't sure how long, just not long, she said, she heard sirens and, next thing, the firemen told everyone to evacuate. There is a pizza shop near Apple Tree Close. It closed just after five p.m. Crowther and our new trainee DC Hannah Kemp are going back to interview the delivery drivers again. They had a bike nicked last night, when one of the lads was delivering. They also had another bike stolen last month.'

'You put Hannah Kemp with Crowther?'

'Yes. Problem?'

Banham lifted his eyebrows and half-grinned. 'Crowther has seduced nearly every female in the station. Was that wise?'

'Yes, I think so.' She nodded her head. 'Best person for her. He's a first-class detective, very people-perceptive. He'll build her confidence.'

Banham shook his head in disbelief.

'I've had strong words with him. He won't seduce her. He knows what she's been through. He's a sensitive guy under all that.'

'Your case, your call.'

'Yes, it is. And I'm busy on it. So, anything else, guv?'

'Will you be late tonight? I thought of cooking us a paella.'

'Gillian Hillier, the neighbour of Annabelle Perry, this morning's victim, is coming in later. I'll know what's happening time-wise after that. So, I'll let you know.'

'In that case, I'll hang about and help you interview, then we can decide together.'

She sighed inwardly. Why did he always have to be so clingy? He was her boss, but this was her case. Before she had the chance to say she'd rather use one of her team, Banham added, 'We are short-staffed all round, and I'm waiting on permission from the top to add a few more detectives to the team as it's now a double arson. Until I can get that, I'll step in, and join you and help out.'

'OK. But remember, you may be the DCI, but I am Senior Investigating Officer, so I make the decisions.'

'Yes, ma'am!'

Crowther was driving. Hannah sat beside him, deep in thought, staring out of the window. She nearly jumped when Crowther asked, 'Are you OK?'

'Yes. Why?'

'I'm not prying. I'm here to support you. You seem distracted this morning.'

She forced a smile. 'No, I'm fine.'

They had stopped at the traffic lights at the end of the road that led to the pizza cafe. He turned to look at her. 'You've had a long time off,' he said gently. 'And now this is a bigger case than we anticipated. You are allowed to be apprehensive. Just remember, I'm here, and a good ear, if you need one.'

She liked his eyes, they were kind. And, despite the fact that his eyebrows resembled over-active otters, and he dressed like he had no lights in his house, she found him very attractive. Maybe it was because he gave her confidence . . .

'Thanks, but I'm OK, really.'

'Good.' The lights were now green, and his eyes were back on the road. 'But if you have any concerns or questions, you come to me. You can trust me.'

He drew alongside a parking space outside the pizza parlour, reversed into it, killed the engine, then turned to face her. 'I would still like to know why it took you so long to come out of the ladies' this morning, and why you've hardly said a word all the way here.'

'I'm just taking everything in, that's all,' she said quickly. She'd heard he was nicknamed Col-the-know-all, but now she knew why. Nothing escaped him. 'I'm OK. If I'm not, I'll let you know. End of. OK?'

The ringing of his phone saved the moment. He was still staring at her as he listened to the caller.

Her heart was in her boots. Was this about her? She knew he was talking to Alison.

He clicked his phone off. 'Fire Forensics have OKed the residents going back into their houses,' he told Hannah, 'and a customer standing outside the pub opposite Apple Tree Close says she saw a delivery driver shortly before the fire. Annabelle Perry's neighbour is at the station now, and said she heard a motorbike just after the cottage went up. And there have been two thefts of motorbikes from the pizza shop. Interesting?'

'Very interesting,' Hannah said, immediately back to her professional self.

'You can take a statement from Walsh, and take that pizza sign that was handed in. Have you got a forensics bag?'

'Yes,' she said, then added in a voice laced with indignation, 'I am fully trained, you know.'

'Me too,' he retorted without his usual charm. This was followed by a gentle wink, as he added, 'And training makes you aware when someone has something to say, but isn't saying it. Wouldn't you agree?' He held her gaze again, then added, 'I'm your friend, Hannah, talk to me if you need to.'

She took a deep breath. 'Thank you. But I'm fine. Really.'

'Really? My training's worn off then.'

The radio was playing a Beatles song. Johnny Walsh had his back to the door, and neither saw nor heard Crowther and Hannah enter. He was singing and tossing pizza dough. Joseph was standing at the side of the counter, dressed in motorbike gear, with a pizza box in hand, ready to speed off to deliver the finished item.

'Boss,' he called to Johnny.

Johnny stopped, then switched the music off.

'Sorry to interrupt, again,' Crowther said. 'Joseph, hold on there, mate, I need a few words. Go through to the back and I'll follow.' He turned back to Johnny. 'We've come to pick up the pizza sign that was handed back in to you. Did you know the person that brought it back?'

'No idea. Sorry.' Johnny pushed the pizza, he had finished making, into the small oven, then gave his full attention to Crowther. 'A woman. I didn't ask for her name, or, obviously, her address. I was worrying about the bike we lost. The sign hangs on the bike box. They are not attached, so always falling off. We thought it was publicity for the shop. I used to leave one on the door, too, that got nicked. Did you know we lost another bike last night? It's insured, of course, but it'll shoot my insurance right up. Bloody nuisance. And I'm down to one bike now, and I've two lads trying to earn a living. I've got a car, but they don't drive cars. Besides, they both need their jobs, and I don't want to lose them. I'm building up this business.'

'Did she say where she found the sign?' Hannah asked.

'Yes. A few streets away, in Cranbourne Road. The bike that was stolen last night, that was on the Walden Estate, quite a long way away from here.' He shook his head. 'It's hard. The world is a bad place at the moment. So many bike attacks, gangs nicking phones and bags off innocent people on the street.'

'Had you done a recent delivery in Cranbourne Road?' Hannah asked him.

Johnny shook his head. 'We haven't delivered there.'

'Did she say exactly where in Cranbourne Road she found it?' Hannah asked as Crowther followed Joseph into the back room.

Johnny shook his head. 'In the road. That was all she said. I didn't ask. I thanked her and that was it. Will it help find either of my bikes?'

'That depends. Could it be from the bike that was reported stolen last month?'

Again he shrugged. 'I couldn't say, the signs are all the same. The one from the door went a little while back. I haven't replaced it.'

'Do you have the details of any other delivery drivers you have used in the past twelve months?'

He shook his head. 'These boys have been with me all that time. They're loyal. I haven't got any others. If I did, that was way back and I'd have no details for them.'

'Thank you for this,' Hannah told him. 'I'll let Traffic know, and you can pick up a crime number for your insurance.' She had a forensic glove on as she took the sign, aware Johnny had handled it with flour-laden hands. The woman who gave it in would have handled it, too. This, she knew, meant there would be little to gain from it, but still she took it carefully and was about to push it in an evidence bag when she noticed the edge of a faint boot print on it.

'You say you didn't know the woman that brought this back, but would you recognise her again?'

'Oh, yeah, for sure. She was middle-aged, maybe older . . . a little old-fashioned looking. And she spoke in an upper-class accent.'

'And can I also ask you for the details, address and phone number, of the people Joseph was delivering to when the bike was taken last night?'

'You can. It was the Walden Estate, on Bourne Street. Give me a sec to get the pizza out of the oven and I'll check – don't want it overdone. Can't lose more profits.'

She nodded. 'Course.'

He retrieved his pizza, called to Joseph that the delivery was ready, and then turned to his computer. A minute later, after scribbling on a piece of paper, he handed the address to her.

'Thank you. I'll just wait for my sergeant and then we'll be out of your way. If you do see the woman who brought your sign back, can you get her details for us? We would like to talk to her.'

'Of course. Would you like a pizza for your lunch?'

'Thank you. But no, not today.' She turned and looked out the window as Johnny went about his work. Her mind was back on the two victims. She mulled over the idea of telling Alison in confidence all she knew, and asking for advice. Then she got out her phone.

Joseph seemed edgy as Crowther faced him. The two sat with Anthony in the back room of the shop.

'Where was that drop-off on the Sunday again?' Crowther asked. 'The one you went on and got hassled for your bike?'

'The Barrow Estate. There was a gang, not the guys that normally hang around the estate. I didn't recognise them. I knew they were after my bike. So, I took it inside the flats, then called Tony to come out and keep watch. Didn't wanna risk losing the bike. Now it's gone, and we're down to one anyway.'

'This is important,' Crowther told him. 'This is about the arson on the flats up the road. Please think very carefully: when you left to deliver to the Barrow Estate, did you notice anyone around in the road, or another motorbike?'

He shook his head. 'I had my helmet on. I see only the road ahead and behind me in my mirrors. I was hurrying. It was raining, I remember that.'

51

'OK. Can you describe the gang members that were hanging round on the estate?'

Joseph looked startled at that. 'No, man, they aren't *recognisable*. They always have masks covering their faces, and their hoods up. The leader guy asking questions was a black guy, and there was a big white guy with him, and another shorter black guy. The little black guy wore a red mask across his face and a grey hoodie.'

He looked across at Anthony, who nodded his agreement. 'I think one had khaki joggers on,' he added.

'That's helpful, thank you.' Crowther knew there were notes on all the gangs in the local area, and made a mental note to check if the descriptions matched any of their information. 'You'd never seen this gang before?' he asked again. 'Not on any streets or estates you delivered on?'

Joseph shook his head. 'No. Never seen them nowhere.' He became edgy again. 'They were different. Asked me for my pizza. I said I'd call and get 'em one. I wasn't gonna do it, of course. I rode the bike into the nearest flats, asked a guy who was coming out to lock the main door, and called Tony for backup.'

'Odd that another postcode gang were down there,' Crowther said, knowing that was extremely unusual, and eyed Joseph questioningly.

Joseph scratched his neck. 'I can only say what I saw.'

Crowther's phone pinged at that second. It was a text from Hannah. *Ask what his shoe size is*, it read. *There is a partial boot mark on this pizza sign, like someone has trod on it to try and break it.*

'Sorry about that,' Crowther said. 'By the way, what size are your boots?'

Joseph hesitated. 'Size eleven.'

'And you?' he asked, turning to Anthony, who had stood up and was leaning against the wall, listening.

'Oh . . . size nine,' he said with a confused frown.

'Thank you,' Crowther said, then turned back to Joseph. 'You've been unlucky with your bikes, haven't you? You came out from a delivery last night and the bike was gone?'

'Yes. It's shit, man.'

'What time was this?'

'About eight o'clock.'

'Did you do any more deliveries after that?'

'No, I let Tony do the rest. I was really upset.'

'What time did you finish last night?' Crowther asked Anthony.

'About ten.'

'Thank you,' Crowther said, as he noticed Johnny, through the open door, tapping the pizza box on the counter. He stood up and left the room. Joseph got up and followed, picked up the pizza, and left the shop behind him.

Chapter Eight

Gillian Hillier was in her early sixties, although she looked a lot older. Something to do with the way she dressed, Alison thought as she studied her. Her A-line skirt came to below her knees. It was patterned in grey and beige and made from a tweed-wool mixture. Her brown-leather shoes were flat brogues, and her legs were concealed in thick-denier beige tights – very unflattering. Her crimplene blouse was beige and mostly covered by a grey cardigan. She wore minimal make-up – a little compacted powder. It had clogged in the corners of her nose, Alison noted. This was accompanied by a dated, dusky-pink lipstick. Her greying hair was short and practical. She worked in a local school, she told Alison and Banham, teaching history, and lived alongside the cottage that had belonged to Annabelle Perry. Mrs Hillier had told Alison, prior to the interview, that she didn't want to be away from her cats for too long as they were all traumatised from the fire.

'They were all abandoned,' she explained, 'they were street cats, and although I've domesticated them, they often spend the night on the streets.'

'Was it the house alarm, or the motorbike roaring off, that woke you?' Alison asked her, once they had settled into the chairs in the interview room and Alison had turned the tape and the video on.

'Nothing woke me. I was already awake,' she replied sharply. 'I'm a light sleeper. I hear the cries of foxes, and cats fighting, and that keeps me awake. I worry about the cats. I live alone these days, so I'm solely responsible for their welfare. I used to foster children as well as teach, but when my husband died, I gave up the fostering. It was too much with the day job—'

Banham interrupted, 'So, you were awake when you heard the alarm. And then what?'

'To be honest, alarms go off a lot these days. It could have been a fox or a wild cat that set it off. Annabelle's dog was barking, too. No, it wasn't that which took my attention. I'm ashamed to say I didn't do anything at that moment. It was a few minutes later. I smelled smoke, and when I looked out of the window, I realised Annabelle's house was on fire. I know Annabelle well. She lives on her own, too, apart from her dog. She adores that dog. Dare I ask, did the dog escape?'

'I've no idea, I'm afraid,' Alison told her.

'I hope so,' the woman said. 'Oh, Lordy, what a way for that poor creature to go,'

Alison wanted to add, *for Annabelle, too*, but instead she said, 'I'll ask the firemen and get back to you.'

'Probably best,' Gillian added, shaking her head. 'That dog was devoted to Annabelle. I don't know what it would do without her. I couldn't take it, because of the cats. If it is alive, it will pine for her for ever. I actually hope it was burned with her. May God forgive me.'

'As I said, I will find out.'

'So, the smell of smoke,' Banham pushed on, after an impatient flick of his eyes to Alison. 'And then you saw the flames, and that brought you out?'

'Yes. I ran out. No. I picked up my phone first. The flames were leaping high in the air. I immediately called 999. Then I ran out. I thought if Annabelle was there, she would have run out, and I would take her in and help her. I was also concerned about my cats, you remember.'

'And the motorbike – can you remember exactly when you heard it?'

'While I was standing in the grounds outside my house, by the fence that divides our properties. I called out to Annabelle. When

55

she didn't answer, I started to run down my drive and intended to get as near to her cottage as I safely could. I was in my nightdress. That's when I heard a motorbike roar off. I couldn't, or wouldn't, swear, but I would say it was very near.'

'How long had you known Annabelle Perry?' Alison asked her.

'Since she moved in. It was a smallish cottage, two-bedroomed I think, on quite a chunk of land, though. I live in a larger house, five-bedroomed, but on a much smaller plot beside her.'

Banham and Alison made eye contact again.

'She was always in her garden in the summer, and on any warm day. She loved the heat . . .' Mrs Hillier paused, then composed herself. 'The heat,' she repeated squeezing her lips tightly together. 'She had another property, so I wasn't a hundred per cent sure she was in the cottage.'

'You said you heard the dog barking. Surely, she didn't leave it in the house alone when she was in her other property?' Alison asked.

'No, not really.' Gillian Hillier hesitated again. 'But she often stayed out late or all night.' The woman shrugged. 'It was none of my business. She was young and very pretty. She did spend most of the colder months in her flat. The flat was near Marylebone, so she told me. Good for shopping outings.' She smiled. 'She was obsessed with shoes. I think she had over fifty pairs. I live on a teacher's salary. She was a model. They earn a lot more money.'

'Do you know who she worked for? Which agency?' Alison asked.

'No, I'm sorry. I can't help you there. It would have been a top one – how many of them are there?'

'I've no idea either,' Alison said.

'No. Well, she always had loads of money. I remember once, she had something delivered. I was in the garden with her. She opened her purse to give the delivery driver a tip, and it was overflowing with notes. Some not English. Models work abroad a lot, too.'

'Did she ever talk about her boyfriends? Did you meet any of her friends?' Banham asked.

'No, no.' She shook her head. 'We got on well, but we were just neighbours. I didn't move in the same circles as her. I just took her deliveries in, occasionally I fed her dog, and we had the odd cup of tea. She was a very pleasant and pretty girl. Well-educated. I liked her. I found her vulnerable.'

'Do you know the address, or even the street, of her other flat?'

Gillian shook her head. 'Near Marylebone, that's all I know.'

'What kind of deliveries did she have?' Banham asked.

'Oh, I don't know, parcels from home shopping companies, you know, and groceries.'

'Thank you,' Alison said. 'That is a great help. Just finally – please think hard, if you would – is there anyone that you remember visiting her, anyone that you could describe?'

'No. As I say, I only ever took deliveries in for her, and had a cup of tea with her, and put food out for her dog. I have more to do than look out my window all day.'

'Inside her house?' Banham asked. 'Did you have a cup of tea inside her house? When you fed the dog, did you go in?'

'Oh, yes, I had done that.'

'You see, almost everything inside is completely burnt out now,' Alison told her. 'Did you ever notice any photos on the side, and did she ever say who was in any of the photos? There were the remains of picture frames in her main room.'

'Her parents. She had photos of her parents on the sideboard. They are both deceased.'

'Yes, we know that.'

'Her father was a politician. She came from a very well-to-do family.'

'Yes,' Banham said, careful to let the woman think.

'She did have a brother, Jonathan, but I don't think they were in contact.'

'Did she say why?' Alison asked.

Gillian shook her head again, then seemed to have another thought. 'I know she had a crush on the MP Christopher Burton. His photo was in her purse. I saw it there when she paid me for something I picked up from the post office for her. I remember mentioning that to her. I said, isn't that Christopher Burton? And she said it was. I asked her why she had a photo of a politician, when most young women have pop stars.' Gillian smiled at that, and then gave a little laugh. 'She told me it was because he was such a dish. Much sexier than any of the lovers she'd ever had.'

'Did she give you the impression she'd had a love affair with him?' Alison immediately asked.

The woman became defensive. 'Oh, I've no idea about that. I wouldn't have asked. None of my business. It was just his photo.'

'Well, she'd have had many opportunities to meet him if her father was a politician,' Banham pushed.

The woman bristled. 'Look, she was single, and successful and very beautiful. What she did was her own business.'

Gillian couldn't give them anything else of use. As Banham and Alison walked back towards the MIT room, Alison said, 'So, let's talk to Christopher Burton, see what he can tell us. Is he married? And let's find the brother, Jonathan. Find out why they didn't get on.'

The early evening meeting was busy and buzzing.

Banham stood beside Alison, by the whiteboard at the top of the room. Hannah knew from the presence of the DCI that things had gone up a notch, and she knew they had proof that the cases were connected, as she had dreaded, which meant it had to be related to their – *her* – past at that agency. Guilt was eating into her, but still she just couldn't bring herself to speak up.

As she pondered her own brief days at the agency, she remembered that not only were the two dead women close friends back then but also there was a third, a foreign girl, maybe Slovakian, who they used to hang around with. She couldn't remember her name, but she remembered her face quite clearly now. The three of them always sat in a group together, waiting for their 'dates'. A chill went through her. She hoped the Slovakian woman was safely back in her own country.

Banham's voice brought her back to the present.

'As most of you know by now,' he announced to the room, 'this is officially a double murder investigation. Fire Forensics have confirmed both these attacks were arson, and practically the same in deed. The public will be getting anxious, so let's get this case put to bed and find this bastard.' He turned to Alison, indicating for her to take over.

'They were a way apart in distance, seven miles to be precise,' she said. 'First thing we have, apart from that the fires were started with petrol, is that witnesses heard a motorbike being driven away from the scene in both cases. So, we concentrate on motorbike drivers.' She looked over at Luke Hughes. 'Luke, check all the motorbike clubs around London. We'll interview them all if we have to. Disappointingly, no CCTV was working on Apple Tree Close where the first arson took place, and there's nothing useful from the nearby pub on Apple Tree Road. Next, we need to find out if these women knew each other.'

'Hard, when all their possessions were burned with their homes,' Crowther pointed out.

'We are tracing Annabelle Perry's central-London flat. We're also tracking down her brother, Jonathan, and the MP Christopher Burton, who she may well have known well,' Alison said. 'We also have Danielle Low's parents' home – we've scheduled a meeting for first thing tomorrow to pick up her possessions from there,' Alison told him, then turned to Stephanie Green, 'Steph, can you do that?' she asked.

'Ma'am,' came the answer with a nod.

'And we have two motorbike thefts from the pizza shop on Apple Tree Road – one on the night before the second attack, and the other a month ago. Interesting point, I'd say,' Crowther spoke up.

Alison nodded. 'Yes, agreed. Now, I'd like to find out more about these two women, and any links between them. So, let's try and get bank statements, credit-card records, and mobile phone bills.' Again she turned to Luke, who nodded.

'On it, ma'am.'

'We also know, from her neighbour, that Annabelle Perry carried a photo of Christopher Burton in her wallet, so we need to speak to him,' Banham told them. 'And that she and the brother were estranged. But where did she hang out? And with who? Same for Danielle Low. Let's try and get that from bank and mobile records. Both women were young and single, so check clubs, social media, and social life—'

'Annabelle Perry was a model,' Stephanie interrupted. She pointed to the pictures on the whiteboard. 'She was educated at a private school in Pimlico and brought up there, too. She was also the daughter of the late David Perry MP. He was a minister, he had clout. I'll bet if we went round the top London clubs, she'd have memberships.'

'Good point,' Banham said. 'Her late father was a powerful man. She absolutely would have membership to elite nightclubs, and friends there.'

'Danielle Low,' Alison continued, 'was very different. Apparently a sex worker; more than that, we have not found out yet. Her parents are working-class, from Dagenham. Danielle went to a comprehensive school there, according to her parents. The connection, if indeed there is one, has to be from their social lives.'

'I'll talk to Del Harris again,' Stephanie suggested. She had been munching on a cheese sandwich while talking and listening, totally oblivious to the fact that she had also eaten the edges of the serviette that held it together. Her fat fingers were covered in mayonnaise, which she licked clean before carrying on. 'He seemed to know quite a bit about her. He may well know where she socialised. I also need to go to Clapham Junction station and get his time sheet for Sunday. They wouldn't see me until this evening – I'm going straight after this meeting.'

'Go for it,' Alison told her.

Hannah's conscience was getting to her. She had decided she would talk to Alison, but in private. That way, if it was all just a massive coincidence, it would only be Alison who knew her secret.

No way could she speak up in this room full of male detectives, all of whom she had yet to win their confidence and respect. But she knew it was still imperative to the case, even if she lost her job over it. And other women's lives could be at risk.

She jumped to attention when Crowther shouted her name.

'Hannah brought in the pizza sign that was found. It had a faint boot mark on it. So, it's been sent to Forensics. A lot of people had handled it, but well done to her for noticing that, and immediately bagging it.'

'Well done,' Banham said, nodding at Hannah with a small smile.

'It has a smell of petrol about it, too, sir, but then if it was attached to the back of a motorbike that would be understandable,' she added.

'Right now, it's a matter of dotting all the I's and crossing all the T's,' Alison said. 'So: bank statements, social places, and friends of these two. We'll talk to Christopher Burton and Annabelle's estranged brother. They are the priorities for tomorrow. We need to find a connection between these two women.'

'I don't think modelling is far away from prostitution,' Crowther said. 'I'd start there.'

Hannah felt her cheeks burn.

'Christ, you're a chauvinist,' Stephanie said to him.

'No, I'm not,' Crowther said, holding her furious glare. 'Who wouldn't say modelling for the middle page of a "men only" magazine isn't prostitution in its own way?'

'Catwalk modelling is an art, as is photographic,' Stephanie snapped back. She then turned to Hannah. 'Wouldn't you agree, Hannah?'

'I don't know much about modelling,' Hannah said, wanting the floor to open up and swallow her.

'Can you two shut up?' Banham said firmly. 'But I take your point, Crowther.'

'We are not wasting time discussing something that trivial,' Alison snapped at Crowther.

61

Crowther wasn't giving up. 'I don't agree that it's trivial, ma'am. It may be the connection you are looking for. Prostitution and modelling go together, not in all ways, but certainly in some ways. Don't let's forget all those Hollywood producers and the casting couch . . .'

Hannah felt her cheeks burn again.

'We need to find out who Annabelle modelled for, agency-wise,' Stephanie told him. 'And go and talk to them.' She turned back to her computer. 'It says here, on her personal website, to contact her directly. So, that would seem to me that she didn't have an agent. And I find that hard to believe, for a successful model.'

'The neighbour knew little about her work, except that she was rich,' Banham said.

'She'd have to be, if she had a pad in town, too,' Crowther said.

'I've got an agency for her,' Luke Hughes piped up. 'I don't know if it's up to date. This is quite an old picture. The agency's called Fabulous. It's in Ladbroke Grove.'

'Good, well done!' Alison told him. She turned back to Hannah. 'You can go there and interview them,' she told her.

Hannah felt her throat constrict. She just managed to nod.

'Who will go and see Christopher Burton?' Stephanie asked.

'How's about if Hannah and I pay him a call?' Crowther suggested, turning to Hannah. 'He has a reputation of liking gorgeous women. Hannah is gorgeous. Let's see what he has to say to her. Are you up for that, Hannah?'

'That is sexism at its worst, Crowther,' Stephanie said, raising her voice indignantly. 'Are you suggesting Hannah should go, and not me, because I'm a few stone overweight, and prefer jeans to a miniskirt?'

'Oh for Chrissakes, shut up, both of you,' Alison immediately snapped at them. It was a well-known fact in the department that Crowther had given Stephanie the nickname of *Stepney* Green, because once inside Stepney Green tube station, the ride was there for the taking. Stephanie, in retaliation, had nicknamed him Col-the-know-all because he was so full of himself.

'Hannah, would you like to interview Christopher Burton?' Banham asked her.

'Can I sleep on it, sir?' she said, unsure whether to upset Crowther or Stephanie.

'No,' Banham came back. 'Steph, you do it.'

'I'll ring his secretary and make you an urgent appointment,' Luke Hughes told her.

'Hannah, you can pay a visit to Fabulous tomorrow,' Alison told her. 'But first, you can go to Danielle's parents' house with Stephanie.'

'I've just found Annabelle's London address,' Luke Hughes told the room, as his fingers tapped speedily into his computer.

'Well done, Hughes,' Banham told the deskbound DC, who beamed happily at the praise.

'We'll need a search warrant for that, and ASAP,' Banham added, nodding at Crowther. 'Col, get on to your mate the magistrate, see if we can get one tonight.'

'Guv.'

'As soon as that comes through, Col, we are in there,' Banham said. 'Ring us at home tonight, if you hear back.'

Crowther raised his thumb.

'Have we got an address for the brother yet?' Alison asked Luke.

'I'll get it,' Stephanie told her. 'I'll be working late. I'm going to Clapham Junction, and then I'll be working on club memberships for both women. I'll find him then.' She turned to Luke. 'I'll keep you company in here later.'

Crowther lifted an eyebrow in Luke's direction. Luke kept his head down.

'Good. Well, that's it for today,' Alison told them. 'Lots to do. And if anyone turns anything up tonight, ring me. Or else I'll see you tomorrow, bright and early, please.'

'Chrissakes,' Crowther muttered loudly as he walked past Stephanie and out the door.

'What's up with him?' Banham asked Stephanie.

'Oh, he fancies me, I expect, and knows I'll turn him down,' she teased. She had a phone pressed between her ear and her shoulder, leaving her hands free to open a packet of cheese and onion crisps.

Banham rolled his eyes and took a sharp intake of breath as he clocked Alison smiling. 'Could you imagine those two at it?' he said quietly to her as they walked into her office for their coats. 'Crowther's half Steph's size.'

'Word is, his dick isn't,' Alison replied.

Chapter Nine

Clapham Junction was at its noisiest. It was half past seven in the evening and still in the midst of rush hour. The platforms were all packed with waiting passengers. Trains came in every few minutes, doors opened and closed, inaudible announcements came over the tannoy, and whistles went off as trains hurtled out while even more passengers arrived on the platforms.

Oh, I'd get a bloody headache working here, Stephanie thought to herself as she took her change from the confectionery machine along with her Mars Bar. She unpeeled the chocolate, then bit into it, and walked over to the ticket office.

'I need to speak to the manager,' she told the small man behind the window, who had his head down with only his bald scalp facing her.

He looked up. 'We sell tickets here, or can't you read?' His tone was clipped and sharp. 'I don't know where the manager is.'

She pressed her warrant card against the window. 'Then put out an announcement. There's a microphone in front of you. Ask him to come to the ticket office. He's expecting me.'

When the man merely stared back at her, she raised her voice. 'You can tell him Detective Sergeant Stephanie Green is here on a matter of urgency.'

Within seconds, a stocky, bespectacled, middle-aged man walked up to her, an arm outstretched to shake her hand.

'Arthur Baker, Station Manager,' he announced with an insincere smile that advertised yellowing teeth.

She ignored the outstretched hand.

'What can I do for you, madam?' he asked, retracting his arm.

'Detective Sergeant Green,' she corrected. 'You have a Del Harris in your employment, am I right?'

'Yes,' he said, a touch gingerly.

'I need his time sheet for Sunday. What time he started work and what time he left, please.'

'Well, I can tell you that. I know Del rather well. He was on at nine o'clock, day shift. I had a bevvy with him at lunch, and we both finished at five p.m.'

'Are you certain of these times?'

'Yes. I can send you his clocking in and out signature if you like. But I'm very sure because I left with him. We both parked in the car park, so I walked down there with him. He left on his motorbike, and I drove my car to pick up my wife. She finished work at five thirty p.m.'

'Harris rides a motorbike?'

The fat man frowned. 'Yes. Is he in some sort of trouble? Has he been involved in a traffic accident or something?'

'No, nothing like that.' She then handed him a card. 'Please email me a copy of his clocking on and off signatures. Within the next hour will do.'

'Why, what has he done?'

'When is he back on duty?'

The man was still frowning. 'He's just asked for some leave, as it happens. There was a fire at his home. He's staying with his mother and sorting things out. Is this to do with the fire?'

'Thank you. Let me have his clocking on and off papers within the hour, please.' She looked at him, then repeated, 'You both clocked off together?'

'Yes, we walked to the—'

'I'll be in touch if I need to ask you anything more,' she interrupted. 'Within an hour, please, his time sheet.'

She then walked speedily away from the station to her car, telling herself how lucky she was to be able to drive to work and not rely on public transport. Her head was pounding with the noise of trains roaring at her every three seconds and the continuous loud and incoherent announcements. The Mars Bar had made her feel hungry; she fancied an Indian takeaway. A hot one, that would kill the headache. She had more work to do back at the office. Young Luke would be there, too. She liked him. She would get him a curry, too; the lad worked so hard, but never complained. They had more digging to do on both the victims. They would need feeding.

'Put your feet up, I'll cook,' Banham told Alison, as she walked into their lounge, threw her file on the desk, and kicked off her shoes. 'Do you fancy that paella, and a bottle of red?'

'Yes. Great,' she muttered, picking up the case file again and slumping down on the sofa. As she started to flick through it, Banham came to perch beside her. He began kneading her neck. She exhaled, and jerked her shoulders irritably.

'Christ, you are uptight,' he said gently. 'Want to talk about it?'

'Not really. I'd like to look at the notes on my case and try and put things together.'

'I'm part of the case, too,' he said.

She turned her head slightly. 'Yes, but I am SIO. You gave this case to me.' She paused and then said, 'Look, I know you're my senior officer. So, this is even more difficult, as you are also my partner, but I still have to say it. The fact is, you walk into my meetings and take over. If this is my case, then let me run it.'

He immediately took his hands away from her shoulders.

'I've come on board to help you. We most likely have a serial arsonist on our hands,' he told her. 'We need to find them, and as quickly as we can. We can't afford another attack. The public will start screaming at us because they'll say we aren't doing our job. So far, four innocent people have been burned to death. We must pull together, as a team, and find out if there is a connection, or if they are random attacks on single women.'

'Don't you think I know that?'

'So, why resent my help? *I* am responsible, overall, for what happens in my department. I've sent a memo to all the fire stations in England. If any similar fires occur, and if anyone reports hearing a motorcycle driving off, then we will be the first to hear. You are an excellent DI, Alison. No one is trying to undermine you, darling. I'm here to support you, and get to the bottom of this ASAP.'

'Fine. But when I moved in with you, we agreed I would carry on working. I'm not ready to try for another baby. I think that is what's really bothering you. You hate me working, don't you?'

'No. But yes, I would love to marry you. And I would like to have a child, or even two, but only with you. And only when you are ready.'

Alison softened. She put her hand over his and sighed. 'I want that, too. It's just too soon for me. And I understand how you feel, and it makes me feel guilty. I think –' she took a breath and then carried on – 'until you have another baby, you won't come to terms with the murder of your daughter. And possibly not even then.'

She got up and took a bottle of red wine from the sideboard, then pulled two glasses from the cupboard and stood them on the table. Banham was watching her. He didn't answer.

'I do want to have your baby, Banny,' she said quietly. 'Very, very much, and I do want to marry you, too.' She gave him a small smile. 'But not this minute. This minute, I would like that paella. How long will it be?'

He stood up. 'I'll get it going now.'

This one was always going to be more difficult. This bitch lives on the first floor with her daughter. There's this burly guy and a girl living on the ground floor. Information is that they're going out this evening. So, a text has been sent to the bitch upstairs, telling her a special delivery is arriving. She would know that it's something worth waiting in for. And it will be a special delivery all right. It will be her last one ever.

Still, things are looking a bit tricky. The cunt lives on the first floor of a three-storey building. Still, who gives a shit who else goes up like a firework, as long as she's one of them. Got to be sure she is in there, though.

I've seen the photo of her, so I won't get it wrong. Anyway, when I press the bell, I'll know if the accent is there, then I'll be sure it's her. If she comes to the door, I could shoot her. I've got a gun, the revolver, as backup. There's a silencer on it. But that's trickier. It's quite a busy road – if someone sees, or I don't kill her outright, and she's writhing around like a spider with one leg, there could be trouble. And with this fucking leather I'm wearing, and these gloves, I'm not sure I can get the gun out quickly enough and shoot straight. Imagine if I shot it the wrong way. I'd be a goner.

And I'm good at arson. I know about fire now. You get rid of all the evidence with it. You just have to be nimble on your pins, and that's me.

I know she's a mouthy cow, so if I was to get her down to the door and shoot her, she would go off screaming before I got the chance to silence her, or she'd slam the door, or something. So I'll stick to the plan and start the fire.

The bell is marked, so I just press it.

'I've got a delivery, madam, are you alone? It's quite heavy. If no one is there, I'll go and get the other driver to help.'

69

'There is no one here but me. What is the delivery?'

'Furniture, madam. For a Madara—'

'I haven't ordered anything.'

'Let me get the other driver to help carry it, and I'll press the buzzer again when we've got it to the door. If you don't want it, then don't sign for it and we'll take it back.'

She's clicked off. But it went well. Now, I know she's in, and alone.

Jesus! She's up there in the fucking window, looking from behind the curtain. Quick, I'll turn and move away. I've got my helmet back on, so she didn't see my face. Not that it matters. In only a matter of moments, she'll be toast.

Curtain has gone back now. And I know she's in that room. Got the petrol-soaked rag. Here's the lighter and . . . Oh my God, two people have just opened the gate. Can't be the ones from the ground-floor flat. I know for certain they're out for the evening. Must be the top floor. Two guys. Jesus! Hide the jar and the cloth. Christ. I've pissed myself in panic. Fuck!

Shall I shoot them? No, I'll never get to her if I do that. Think fucking quick, mate.

The warm piss is trickling down my leg. I'll stand to the side, by the corner of the house. It's dark. I'm all in black. They might not see me.

They didn't. They've gone in and I think they were quite drunk, which will be in my favour. Curtains drawn back again. They are in with her now. She must have told them someone was at the door. All three of them looking out the fucking window. I've stepped back, thank God. And it's dark, they shouldn't be able to see me.

Job not done, but I'll put it on hold. And I'll be back. Best I get out of here now.

Fuck me, I'm pissing again.

Chapter Ten

Hannah was stirring sauce into pasta. She had dug out her old university diary and, with her free hand, was flicking through for dates. There were only a few in there. She had left the agency and gone back to waitressing in the Mexican restaurant when she discovered her job with the agency was going to be more than just escorting men to business dinners. She was a naive nineteen-year-old then, who needed funds to finish her education. It had taken three dates to realise what was expected of her at The Suite Escorts. She had innocently answered an advert for 'tall, attractive girls for part-time modelling work'. The agency had said she wasn't photogenic enough for modelling, but suggested she may like casual evening work dining with clients. No one had mentioned sex with any of them, just free dinners. Deciding it was better than eating cheap burgers or soup, she had agreed and filled in the form with her full details, not bothering to hide or change any of them. She was then registered with The Suite Escorts, at the so-called Fabulous model agency. Gosh, how had she ever been that naive? She had even told them she was a student, and at which of the London universities, with a lot of work to do, and just wanted maybe one night a week's work. Escorting a lonely businessman to a paid-for, expensive dinner, sounded great.

Her first date was fine: a manager at a wine company who needed an escort for a firm's event. She remembered she even half-enjoyed herself. He was clumsy and unattractive, walked all over her feet when he danced with her, but he had treated her well. She had been at a table with four other couples, and it was a six-course meal which she had wolfed down.

The next day, when she came in for her fee, the owner of the agency, Oluwa Marconi, had asked her how far she was prepared to go with her dates. She had replied she would happily travel at weekends, but not during the week. That's just how naive she had been then. When they told her the fee for dinner was a pittance but she could earn a lot more by giving extra services to the clients – and lots of students were doing it, as they needed the money – she had told them firmly: a nice free dinner and being someone's date was as far as she would go.

The second date was with a man who was very little, but quite fierce. It was just her and him, which made her nervous. They had eaten at the hotel restaurant. He had had very little to say, just asking her what she wanted to eat, and where she was from, and where she lived, and if she lived alone. He then told her it was taken for granted that she was going upstairs with him at the hotel after dinner. When she said she wasn't, he had got stroppy, said he had paid for her, and he wanted what he had paid for. She had handled the situation by putting him on to the agency to sort things out. That had left her nervous. She told the agency she didn't think the job would work for her. The agency assured her it was just the man trying it on, and they had banned him.

By the third date, she was wishing she hadn't started any of it. She had been sent to meet a man at the reception of a top London hotel. When she gave her name at the desk she was told to go to a room number. She had been hesitant, but had gone, telling herself she wouldn't go inside the room. The man had opened the door, stark naked, and she had fled.

The agency then called her into the office, and gave her a long lecture about the money she could earn that no one would know about. They told her it was easy. She had argued it was prostitution. They told her it was just a good way of getting through university. They introduced her to three other girls who were dressed up to the nines and sitting in the office, waiting for calls for dates for that evening, and that was when she met Annabelle, and Danielle, and the Slovakian girl . . . Maddie! She never got Maddie's real name, nor the other girls' at that time. These girls, she was told, were the agency's top escorts. They knew how to please men, and through doing so, had made themselves, as well as the agency, loads of money. These top girls were often taken for weekends to the south of France, and had lavish gifts bestowed upon them. Hannah argued that she just wanted an easy, but not unlawful, job that would pay enough to keep herself at university until she got her degree.

Oluwa Marconi had merely shaken his head and rolled his eyes. His receptionist, a pretty dark-haired woman called Camilla, was gentler. She told Hannah their clients were the cream of the crop. Most girls would sleep with them for free. These clients were all rich. They included pop stars and film stars, millionaires and people in the public eye, who demanded discretion. Hannah had told her she had ambitions to work in the police force and it was a no to anything more than dinner. Camilla had introduced her to the three top agency girls: one who looked like Marilyn Monroe – Danielle Low – and another who was definitely Annabelle Perry. And then there was 'Maddie'. The three girls had tried to persuade her it was worth it. They told her that because some of their clients were very famous, it was a pension too, as in years to come they could blackmail those celebrities. Maddie had told her she had photographic evidence of kinky sex romps with some of the men. Great for getting them to pay up for your silence, when they were too old for prostitution.

Hannah had left the agency there and then, asking them to destroy her details. Now, standing here, stirring the pasta, she wondered if they really had destroyed her details with her name and address, or if, after all these years, that part of the agency was even still in business, and God forbid, her picture on their wall of escorts.

And now she had been told she had to go and interview them . . .

Two of those women were dead. Coincidence? She didn't think so. With luck, Maddie would have returned to her own country. If not, could Hannah's withholding evidence put Maddie in danger? Although, she felt sure Maddie would have gone home to Slovakia, as she remembered she'd said she was earning money to send home to her daughter.

Hannah drained the pasta. She looked at it, but her appetite wasn't there. Those two women's faces staring out from the whiteboard were playing on her mind. Eight years ago, when she last spoke to them, in Fabulous's office, they were drinking champagne and looking gorgeous. They were each full of life, not knowing it was to be a short one, and that their ends would be terrifying.

Hannah caught sight of her reflection in the mirror. She looked awful. The scarring around the inner edge of her eye and over her cheek was glowing red and throbbing. She was a murder detective now and she owed it to those two women, and to the team, to own up to what she knew, no matter the consequences for herself. Her mind was made up. She would speak to Alison, in private, first thing in the morning. Tonight, she would make herself eat at least half the pasta, then have a warm bath and an early night.

'How are you getting on?' Stephanie asked Luke Hughes as she walked back into the murder room carrying a leaking brown-paper bag full of exceptionally pungent Indian takeaway.

Luke lifted his head from his computer. He had been deeply engrossed in checking out the Perry family and Christopher Burton. The smell of curry made him realise he hadn't eaten for hours.

'I have a lot of information on our MP, Christopher Burton,' he told Steph. 'He's still married, but there's been lots of bad press about his affairs. And, interestingly, he was known to visit prostitutes.'

'That is interesting,' Stephanie said. 'Is there any mention of where?'

She had a cupboard open and was floundering around for knives and forks and bowls and plates. 'Do you fancy a bit of curry, love? There's loads here. You must be hungry. I bet you've not taken a break. Help me out with this.'

He shook his head politely. 'No, you're all right. Never let it be said I took food from the mouth of my sergeant,' he joked.

'I'll pop a small bit on a plate for you, anyway. I'm worried you'll fade away,' she told him in a motherly way. 'There's poppadoms here by the truck load. Can't go wrong with them. Like I said, I've got loads here. I ordered for two, they've given me enough for three. Be a sin to waste it.

'OK, thank you, then. I accept. You can tell you're a mother.'

She divided two enormous portions between two plates and brought them over, with cutlery, to beside his desk. She then pulled up a chair and, before plonking herself down beside him, went back and overfilled another plate with poppadoms, a variety of bhajis, and naan bread. Luke made no comment, but seemed happy to tuck in.

'Any mention of where he picked his prossies from?' she asked.

Hughes answered with a mouthful of naan bread, 'Arrested for kerb-crawling, got a caution, but then got done when caught getting a blow job in a back street near Westminster.'

'Print out all the press cuttings we can get on his suspected trolling. Phone the press agency, see if there's any articles on him with Annabelle Perry.'

'Will do.'

'And we have a statement from Harris indicating Danielle was a prostitute. Interesting,' Stephanie said, half to herself.

'I've tried googling her. Nothing on her. If she was on the game, she probably used a different name.'

Stephanie nodded and chewed and then swallowed. 'What about Burton's wife? Do we know much about her?'

'She lives in Oxford, in their other home. He's often in the London flat on his own.'

'I'll bet she knows little about his antics,' she spoke with a mouthful of food, waving her fork around as she spoke. 'That'll help us.' Some of her lamb biryani was already bedded down the front of her light-blue denim shirt, and a little had even managed to find its way into her short brown curly hair. Luke opened the drawer in his desk and handed her a serviette.

'Where do I need to dab?' she asked. 'Do it for me.'

He pretended not to hear. He was back leaning into his computer. 'Here's the cutting.' He pressed print on one of the press stories of Burton in a car with a hooker in a Westminster side street. He then moved his cursor swiftly, while shovelling forkfuls of curry into his mouth, over to the Facebook page of Annabelle's brother, Jonathan Perry.

'This is interesting, too,' he said, after clicking and scrolling for several seconds. 'He hasn't posted on his page for a few years, so this is old but, here, he swears to have nothing to do with his sister ever again. Says he hates her. And, even more interesting –' he turned to look at Stephanie – 'on his friends list, he has the local Harley-Davidson motorbike club.'

'You are joking! But why would he want to kill his sister, what's the motive?'

'I found an article earlier, says she inherited all the money from their parents' estate, and he was left without a penny.'

'Motive,' she said, nodding, then taking an enormous bite of naan bread. 'And clever to wait a few years, but then why kill Danielle Low?'

Luke shrugged. 'No idea. We'll have to ask him.'

'We seem to be collecting bikers. Del Harris rides one, too.'

'Really?'

'I'm keeping him on the list. His time sheet for work, which is apparently winging its way over to us, says he left at five p.m. Everyone fiddles their time sheets a tidge. Say he left before that, say at twenty to five. You could do Clapham to Apple Tree Close in less than twenty minutes on a motorbike. He could have done it. It's possible. He's staying on the list.'

'But why would he kill Annabelle Perry?' Luke questioned. 'Jonathan Perry belongs to the Harley-Davidson club, obviously knows about motorbikes. Has a motive to kill his sister.'

'But why Danielle Low?' they both spoke together.

'There are many more motorbike riders around London than

ten years ago,' Hughes told her. 'That's a fact. I was googling that earlier.'

'You mean, you think these arsons may be coincidental and not connected?' She shook her head. 'I don't.'

Hughes shrugged. 'I don't think we should rule it out. Copycat killer. They exist. The DI put out a press call yesterday. And we haven't had anything from that connecting the two women. The pub customer who went out for a fag only saw a delivery guy, not the bike, and Annabelle's neighbour only heard a motorbike.'

'We need to keep digging,' Stephanie told him.

Chapter Eleven

It was four a.m. when local magistrate Donald Wheaten woke Sergeant Crowther to let him know his search warrant was now ready and awaiting collection.

Crowther rang Banham with the news. Alison immediately leaped out of bed. 'You have a lie-in,' she told Banham. 'I'm on it.'

By six a.m., Alison was in the station organising a uniformed backup crew. Crowther had arrived with the warrant, and the two of them headed for Annabelle Perry's flat, which was actually in Paddington, not Marylebone.

It was a ground-floor flat, protected by a twenty-four-hour security guard sitting behind the desk in the lobby.

Crowther flashed his card at the middle-aged, rotund, and bespectacled porter, who had been reading a copy of the *Sun*.

'Worked here long, have you, mate?' he asked him.

'Yes. Been here twenty-four years, come next March.'

'So, you knew Annabelle Perry?'

'I did, sir. She lived down the hall in number six. I read the paper yesterday.' He shook his head. 'I'm gutted, I don't mind saying. She was a sweetheart. I liked her a lot. No side to that one, not like some of the residents in the block. Was it arson, or did she leave something on?'

'Why we are here,' Crowther told him. 'Was she a bit ditzy, then? Had she left anything on before?'

'I wouldn't like to say, sir. She liked a bit of the up-your-nose

78

stuff, I'm sure of that, and often came in two sheets to the wind. She was always losing her front-door keys or her car keys. Not that she used the car much. She used black taxis around London.'

'Do you know where she hung out?' Alison asked the man. 'Any clubs she frequented? Bars she liked around here, restaurants, that sort of thing?'

'She was a clubber, that's for sure. Money was no object. She often didn't come in till the next morning, looking a lot worse for wear. And I never saw her in the same outfit twice. Often it was only half on.' He chuckled. 'Pretty girl, though. Very pretty.'

'Did she ever say where she'd been?' Alison pushed.

'Gosh no, madam, and I wouldn't ask.'

'Did she come home alone on those occasions, or did she bring men back?'

'I never saw her with a man, if I'm honest.'

'Right, let's get in then,' Crowther interrupted. 'We'll try not to upset the other residents, so, if you let us in, we won't have to break the door down.'

'Let's hope we find something,' Alison said quietly to Crowther as two uniformed PCs took their places by the front door.

It was six a.m. when Hannah walked into the station. She was hyped up and ready to tell Alison everything she knew about the agency, and the possible connection between the two victims. She walked into the MIT room, and wrinkled her nose as the smell of stale curry hit her. As she headed for Alison's office, she spotted Stephanie Green half-asleep in a chair.

'Good morning, Sergeant,' she said politely.

'If you're looking for the DI, she's out, darling,' Stephanie told her. 'On an early call to Annabelle Perry's London flat. Is there anything I can help you with?'

Hannah felt her heartbeat accelerate. She should have done this yesterday. Supposing they found something about the agency in the flat? An old agency flyer, maybe one with her photo in it, for hire as an escort . . . She didn't remember having ever done flyers, but

79

certainly the agency had taken photos, with all her cleavage hanging out, too. If only she'd known then what damage it might do in the future.

'No, it's OK. I just wanted a quick word. It can wait,' she lied. She walked down the room and sat at the desk she had been allocated. 'I'll wait for Sergeant Crowther.'

'Crowther's at the flat with the guv'nor,' Stephanie told her. 'They may be a while. So, have a coffee, or pop out for breakfast. Meanwhile, I'll find you something to do.'

'No, I'm good, thanks,' Hannah replied, feeling anything but good. 'Will there still be a morning meeting?'

'Yes. There'll be one, but they'll be at the flat for a while. I'm going out, too. I'm visiting Danielle Low's parents, in the house in Dagenham where Danielle grew up. And a visit to that Fabulous model agency is on the cards. Which one do you fancy going to?'

'I'll go to Danielle's parents,' Hannah said quickly. The last place she wanted to be was at the agency. Imagine if her picture was still up on the wall of escorts! She felt reasonably sure Oluwa Marconi wouldn't recognise her all these years later, if indeed he was still there running the place, but until she unburdened herself to Alison, she wasn't taking the chance. Especially if she was there with Stephanie Green, who she hardly knew.

'Good,' Stephanie said, taking a good look at her. 'You look a bit peaky, love. Have some coffee, and there's fresh doughnuts here. I bet you haven't eaten any breakfast, have you?'

'Yes, I have had breakfast, but thank you.' The thought of eating anything made her want to heave. 'How long before we leave?'

'No rush, love. There's a Family Liaison Officer there. Do you remember Veronica Prichard? She's there, with the mother and father. She's a trained FLO now. The mother is in a bad way. So, best to have women talking to her. I think she'll open up more to us.' She picked a doughnut from the box she had just been out and bought, then bit into it, spurting jam over the side of her mouth, which she wiped away with the cuff of her sleeve, then added,

'Only, don't let Sergeant Crowther know I said that. You know what an old chauvinist he is. Is he looking after you, love?'

'Yes. He's been great. Thank you.'

'Good. Well, at least get yourself a coffee. I need to make another call to Christopher Burton's secretary, but it's a bit early, so I'll finish my breakfast, then I'll do that, then we'll be off.' She licked the jam and sugar from her fingers and picked up her mobile. 'I'll drive.' She studied Hannah again, then spoke in a motherly fashion. 'Are you sure you're OK, love?'

'I'm fine.'

'You need to take all this step by step. It's a bigger case than we originally thought. I'm always an ear if you need one.'

'Thank you. I'm good.'

'I'm going to get you a coffee. You look all in.'

Hannah nodded politely. 'Thank you. What are we asking Danielle's parents?'

'We need to find out all we can about Danielle's life, going right back. Any friends they knew of. We don't mention she was on the game, unless they do. But find out all they knew about where she hung out, any people she talked about, that sort of thing. I'll go into her bedroom and have a root around while you do that. The mother says there is an old computer of Danielle's there. I don't know how old, but I'll grab that and send it over to computer analysis.'

Hannah felt a chill go through her. What if the old computer had the agency pictures on it?

'No rush, love. Time to grab something. I'm going to the canteen; do you want anything to eat with your coffee?'

Hannah was beginning to feel like screaming. What part of *I do not want to eat anything* did this woman not understand? 'Nothing to eat, just coffee would be great.' She was dearly wishing Alison was there and she could just get it off her chest about the escort work. Maybe they wouldn't take as dim a view of her as she imagined, but she knew for sure they would take her to task if she didn't speak up. Withholding evidence was a very serious offence, and much worse for an officer of the law. As was prostitution, although she had been too naive to know at the time that she was breaking the law of *living off immoral earnings*. She may not have been selling sex, but the men that paid the agency for her had paid for that, and she had signed her name on an agency contract to be an escort. And 'escort' was another name for a prostitute. So, now she had to speak up, and before she dug herself into a very deep hole.

She toyed with the idea of confiding in Stephanie Green, but then thought Alison might get annoyed at her for not coming to her first. Alison was the one who had kept in touch with her since the horror of the case that had involved them all, and Alison had persuaded her to come back, and had requested her on her team. How long could the flat search take?

She stared at the whiteboard at the top of the room – the pictures of the two women's faces, and then the pictures of their unrecognisable cadavers beside. The last time she had seen those two women, they had been sitting in the reception of the agency. The three of them, those two and Maddie, chatting and giggling and so full of life. Hannah prayed Maddie was back in her country now, with her daughter and family. Because if she wasn't . . . was she, too, in grave danger?

It's very, very early, still dark, and no buggers about. No lights on, either, in the house. I'm creeping around the side – no lights on in the back, either. I've been told there's a child in there, so it's best to do it during the day; the child will be at school. Possibly. No knowing for sure. Still, can't worry about the kid, although I do, well, a bit. Things have turned tricky, and I need to do it before she gets mouthy.

The gun is in my hand, the silencer is on, and, if I can get her to come to the door, all will be done and dusted.

Bell pressed. Christ, I'm sweating. This outfit is so hot and heavy, and my hands are feeling slimy. Gotta get a grip, hold the trigger firm and aim for the heart. I'm pressing that bell again. Oh, Christ, will this one ever go to the place of no return? Obviously sleeping heavily. Oh no, wrong: the buzzer is buzzing an answer to me.

'Who is it? Mama's not here.'

That's floored me. It's the kid. I can't say anything. She'll remember my voice, and that could be my downfall. And I don't want to shoot the kid. To be honest, I couldn't. If she burns, I won't know, so I'll do the fire, but not until I know that the mother is in. She deserves to burn like a live pig on a barbecue. That kid is alone. I don't know how old she is, but she sounds like quite a young kid. I can't ask if she's alone. How can I say, 'Is your mother there? Only, I want to shoot her in the heart, several times. She deserves it, you don't.' No, I'm out of here. I'll be back, and I'll get her for sure tonight. I'm doing my best. I can't help it if the stupid bitch lives on the corner of a busy road, and other people keep fucking turning up when I am about to burn their fucking building. Fuckers, the lot of them.

83

Chapter Twelve

'A framed picture of Christopher Burton in the cupboard here,' Crowther shouted from the living area of the large flat in Paddington. He was opening cupboards and finding assorted bottles of alcohol next to crystal glasses of all shapes and sizes. Then he opened a tin resembling a can of Heinz Beanz, which he had spotted was a fake with a plastic lid. He flicked the top open.

'Fucking hell, guv,' he shouted, as a wad of fifty-pound notes sprang from the tin.

'Right, so if there's wads of cash, maybe there's drugs, too,' Alison said, walking back into the living room. 'She could be a dealer.'

'Or a hooker,' Crowther added.

'Bag the money,' she told him. 'Let's try and find something to tell us where the money came from. Oh, and take that picture of Christopher Burton with us. I'll do her spare bedroom,' she said as she walked into the hall and into the back bedroom. 'You do her main one.'

'Ah, bingo!' Crowther shouted back as he entered the master bedroom. 'There's a house phone in here. I'll run this number into Luke to get a breakdown of the recent calls.'

Alison put her head through the doorway. She was pulling on forensic gloves. 'Wouldn't it be a coup if we could find her mobile, though?'

As Crowther picked the phone up to read the number, he opened the drawer in the small bedside table on which the phone stood. It was jammed. He pulled again and pushed his hand into

84

the back, pulling a couple of navy-blue socks free. They were both bulging. He emptied the contents onto the cabinet. A large stash of spice, a thick bag of coke, another of heroin, a bulging bag of grass, and a small drawstring bag of what Crowther knew to be ground cement, powdered down to adulterate a stash of drugs.

'Guv!' he bellowed. 'Need to see this.'

'I fully expect she took coke and spice. No less than one would expect from a party girl,' Alison said as she stood staring at the contents. 'Much more than a party girl needs, though, so question is, who did she deal to? And we know what would happen if you added ground cement to coke. So, what was she playing at? She wasn't short of money. She had the inheritance from her parents. All Daddy's money. That must have been a fair bit. Was she messing with someone? And maybe that someone got in first.'

Crowther was running the powder through his gloved fingers. 'Ground cement for sure,' he said. 'To cut with the supply. Can do damage to the user, too.'

'And we are told Danielle Low was taking drugs. So, was Annabelle Danielle's dealer? Is that our connection? Let's look for anything else,' Alison continued. 'An old computer – pray for a hidden mobile phone. If she wasn't expecting the fire, then she wouldn't have hidden stuff away too well. She hardly looks like a tidy person.'

Crowther had started pulling clothes from the wardrobe and checking the pockets, and opening the multitude of handbags strewn across the bottom of the wardrobe.

Alison stabbed Stephanie's number into her phone.

'We've got evidence of drugs, certainly more than just a night out's worth,' she said when Steph picked up. 'I know you are the height of tact.' She looked at Crowther as she said this, and pulled a comical face: Stephanie was not exactly known for being tactful. 'You need to find out if the parents had any evidence or suspicions that Danielle took drugs. And we're looking for anything that we can link these two with. It's a shot in the dark, and I know it's the parents' house, but we've also got this ground cement powder, so

85

Annabelle could have been dealing dirty. She would have upset a few people. I wouldn't mind betting that's the connection.'

'Luke has checked. Annabelle's record was clean,' Stephanie told her. 'Danielle Low, though, *was* arrested and brought in a few times for soliciting and suspected drug use, but it was light use and she always got off with a warning, never charged.'

'See what the parents know about all that. Show them the evidence. They might open up then. And any old mobile phones would be a wondrous help.'

'There's a computer there, ma'am, and I'm taking our new TDC with me. She was looking for you earlier. Said it was a private matter.'

'Is she OK?'

'Seems to be – if a bit jumpy and nervy. I'll get back to you, on both.'

Alison clicked off and walked into the back bedroom. She stood staring at the bed and room, and then at the photo above the black-and-gold headboard. It was of Annabelle, on a modelling shoot in her heyday. She looked gorgeous. There was no doubt she could have been a Bond actress. She was tall and willowy, with dark olive skin, long thick dark hair, and cheekbones any model would kill for.

The room looked more like a brothel parlour than a bedroom. It was floor to ceiling black and gold: black pillowcases and duvet, edged with gold piping, and black sheets. Black carpet. The bedside lights were also gold. Yet, the porter had said she never brought men back.

There was a photo of three women, one of whom was definitely Annabelle, on the side, and just in the picture was an arm – a man's arm – around two of the women. The man wore a large ring on his little finger. She bagged the photo in an evidence bag and opened a cupboard door. Handcuffs and thigh-length black patent-leather stiletto-heeled boots tumbled to the floor. Now, there was no doubt.

As she opened her mouth to yell to Crowther, he yelled first.

'Guv, think you should see this . . .'

Chapter Thirteen

It was just before eight a.m. when Banham swiped his pass on the internal door leading to the investigation rooms. Before he walked through it, he stopped in his tracks. There was a dog in the front office, tied up and whimpering. He had been deep in thought, feeling a sadness that Alison and he weren't as close as they had been. He was wondering if he was losing her, thinking of what he could do to make her happier, so he hadn't noticed the animal until it whined.

'Is that a stray, Stan?' he asked the desk sergeant as he bent down to pat the dog's silky head. The animal immediately leapt at him, paws on his shoulders, and licked Banham's face, crying loudly. Then it moved its front paws to Banham's leg and pushed with its head at his arm.

'Was this dog found wandering the streets?' Banham asked as the amused station sergeant watched the antics.

'Yes, guv. And I think it likes you.'

'Steady, steady, boy!' Banham gently coaxed, as the dog's hysteria built. 'When was it brought in?'

'The finder said she took him in yesterday. It was wandering the streets a couple of miles away, bothering everyone it passed. Overwhelming everyone. Woman was afraid it might run in the road; it must have been as mad as it is now. She took it in, so she says, and offered it some food. Says it was highly distressed, wouldn't take the food. It kept crying. Still bloody is – to tell you the truth, guv, it's driving me mad. The woman brought it here 'cause it was closer

87

than Battersea. I've rung the council, they'll pick it up and take it to their kennels, but not till the end of the day. Saddest for me, there.' He bent over his counter and addressed the dog. 'Then it's Battersea for you, mate. If you carried on like that in my house, I'd turf you out, too.' Stan afforded himself a chuckle and then leaned back on his elbow, hand on chin, to carry on doing his *Daily Mail* crossword.

Banham was stroking the dog's head very gently, and it seemed to calm the terrified animal. 'Hello, fella . . . oh no, oops –' he peeked under its tummy – 'sorry, *girlie*. Fella's a lady. No collar, no tag.'

He sniffed the animal's fur. It smelled singed.

'No wonder you're lost.' He was putting two and two together. He examined the dog more closely. Stained blood smudges were visible under its chin. 'I wonder if you've been chipped,' he muttered, half to himself.

'Battersea will do that,' Stan said without looking up. 'If the owner don't come looking in five days, then they don't care enough, for Fella or Mrs or whoever it is, so that's that.'

Banham was now examining its long silky coat. The dog whimpered slightly, then became calm, moving her head to one side and looking at him through the overgrown dark-brown and rich-chestnut fringe that covered her eyes. She then lifted a furry paw and put it on Banham's bent knees, followed by her furry head with those massive dark eyes, looking pleadingly at him. They might have been the saddest eyes he had ever seen. He ruffled his fingers through the fur on her head. It was then he felt minute shreds of glass, and he knew his instincts were right. As he examined her closely, he discovered more dried blood on the animal's pink and burned tummy.

'This poor dog would well be this distraught if it had witnessed a fire, and the death of its owner,' Banham told Stan. He stroked the distressed animal's head as he noticed the dog had the same hint of reddish-gold in its hair as Alison. If it was Annabelle Perry's dog, as he had no doubt it was, then this poor animal now had no one. But how did it get so far away from home?

88

He remembered the pain in the pit of his gut, and the feeling of isolation, when his wife and baby had been murdered. He'd felt so alone in the world and frightened and desperate. He could take care of this animal.

He stood up. Christ, Alison was right, he thought to himself, he was broody. That was supposed to happen to women, not blokes. But still he felt a strong urge to help this lonely and distressed dog. *Get a grip*, he told himself. He was a DCI for Chrissakes, working a case with four murders, and this dog was possibly vital evidence.

'I'll take the dog to my office,' he told Stan. The surprise on Stan's face made him add, 'I need to get her paws covered. They're singed, and there's dried blood and shards of glass in her coat. I believe her to be the dog that ran away from the Herne Hill house fire. She could well be carrying crucial evidence. I need to keep her away from people, and I need you to find me the nearest vet.'

Mr and Mrs Low lived off a busy main road, in a century-old, tiny semi-detached cottage. The family liaison officer, PC Prichard, who had been expecting Stephanie and Hannah, opened the front door and silently ushered them in. The front door opened straight into the sitting room; two steps the other side of that room and you were in the kitchen. This led to a tiny yard for a garden. PC Prichard stood in the kitchen listening for signs of either of the parents being up. As a response to Stephanie's raised and inquisitive eyebrows, the FLO shook her head.

'Not very communicative this morning, I'm afraid,' she said in a lowered voice.

Mrs Low walked into the kitchen at that moment. She was still in her sleeping attire, a winceyette nightdress covered over with a stained and shabby blue-candlewick dressing gown. Her lank grey hair hung down her back. It clearly hadn't seen a comb in days.

Stephanie introduced Hannah. Hannah nodded a sympathetic *good morning*.

'Come through to the lounge,' Mrs Low said. 'My husband will be with us shortly. He's still getting dressed.'

'I'll make some tea,' Prichard told them as she ushered the officers into the lounge, immediately disappearing back into the kitchen, leaving Stephanie and Hannah alone with the grief-stricken mother.

Hannah was staring at the picture on the mid-century pine sideboard. It was of a young Danielle, the way she'd looked when Hannah had met her at the agency. Danielle's hairstyle was over-peroxided then, and her red and pouted lips shone brightly. Her face was turned to look over her shoulder, imitating the famous Marilyn Monroe pose. There was no doubt, if any had remained: Hannah was one hundred per cent sure the woman she had met at that agency was this woman. She picked up the photo.

'When was this taken?' she asked Mrs Low. 'She looks like a film star.'

'She did modelling then. She used to do Marilyn Monroe look-alike photos,' Mrs Low told her with a heartbreaking crack in her voice. 'She got plenty of work.'

A short man, with bitten fingernails, cheap brown trousers, and badly cut hair, now stood in the doorway. 'She did well,' he added, placing his hand on his wife's shoulder. 'Bought her own flat with what she earned.'

'Would it be OK to look around her old bedroom?' Stephanie asked. 'We are particularly interested in any photos with other people in them, and any address books she may have kept here – and her old computer, if we may. And any old mobiles. Even if they don't work anymore.'

The woman's eyes were so puffy and swollen, Hannah was surprised she could see to lead them up the narrow and steep staircase to the tiny bedroom at the top, built over the lounge.

As Stephanie and Hannah both pulled bluebell-coloured forensic gloves on, Stephanie said, 'You are welcome to stay with us, or just leave us to it. You said she had a computer from years back?'

'You're all right, I'll wait downstairs,' Mrs Low told her. 'Yes. She had an old laptop. It's in one of the drawers, I think, or maybe on the top of her wardrobe, in a big cardboard box. I wouldn't even know how to open it. We're not computer people. Not our era. No doubt you can, though. You go ahead. Call me if you need me.'

Hannah was already opening drawers. First one contained a photo album. She pushed it under a heap of old scarves in the same drawer, dreading that there might be a picture of herself in it.

Crowther was standing in the master bedroom of Annabelle's flat with a photo album in his hand, as Alison walked back in.

He nodded his head at the pictures. 'It says here, "*First day after signing with Fabulous*", under this picture, "*Me, Danny, and Madara.*"'

Alison took hold of the edge of the album and peered in, as Crowther added, 'Danny being short for Danielle.'

Alison studied the picture of the three young girls, one looking not unlike Marilyn Monroe. The second was a very pretty, barely made-up girl, with long brown hair and big hoop earrings. Annabelle was at the far side of the picture, her dark hair worn up in a twisted bun, and heavy black make-up covering her eyes. 'Looks very different there. When was this taken, does it say?'

He shook his head. 'No date. He then turned the page, and then another, and then stopped, studying the picture he saw in front of him. 'This is interesting. "*Madara, me, and Danny, on a job*", it says on here.' He turned to Alison. 'This was taken in a restaurant at dinner.'

'There's that bloke's hand around that glass – it's just at the edge of the shot, can you see?' Alison pointed out. 'There's another photo of that picture, in the other room. It's the same bloke's arm. Same ring on his finger. I'd like to know who he is. Shame only his arm is in the shot. He's obviously been with them a few times.

'You can barely see the ring there, but perhaps we can get it blown up. Might help, who knows,' Crowther added. 'Photo's taken in a restaurant, too. What would they have been modelling in a restaurant?' he added sarcastically.

'Entertaining a client,' Alison said. 'Judging by the bedroom. My money says she was a high-class hooker, maybe a dominatrix. Danielle's neighbour tells us she was on the game. So, they were on the game together, as well as modelling for Fabulous? There's our connection. But who did they both upset enough to burn them alive?'

'More to the point, who, and where, is this Madara?' Crowther said. 'I'd say we need to find her, and urgently.'

'We need to talk to the agents at Fabulous,' Alison said. 'That's next on the list. But we'll go through everything here, first. We are looking for contact lists, address book, old mobiles, anything more like that. What bothers me is the back bedroom does look like a hooker's den, and yet the porter said she never brought men back.'

'Perhaps she snuck them in, and the porter didn't notice. It isn't the same porter all the time, never is.' Crowther was fiddling with the answer machine on the phone he had discovered. There were three messages. He pressed play.

'Need to see you.' The voice was male and well-spoken. They then hung up.

The next one was the same voice. 'Did you get the picnic? Call me.'

And the third one, again, the same male. 'Will be round soon.'

'We can trace that number, hopefully,' Crowther said, then added, 'He knows where she lives, so he's been here before. That porter said no men visited. He's either lying or skiving.'

Alison nodded. 'Play them again, I'll record it, and ask the porter if he recognises the voice.'

'Suppose it was Christopher Burton she was entertaining, sexually,' Crowther suggested. 'Newspaper articles said he had a liking for whores. He would have to keep it very quiet if he was having it away with a fellow politician's daughter, even after the guy was dead. She definitely would have to have snuck *him* in.'

'See if Steph has got us an appointment with Christopher Burton. You can interview him, too. I'll pay a visit to Fabulous. It still exists, we know that. I'll take Hannah Kemp with me. Stephanie said she seemed jumpy today and distant. I need to know she's fit to work. I can't afford mistakes. I'll see how she is, but I may have to lay her off this case.'

'That's a bit harsh, guv,' Crowther argued. 'She was fine with me. Bright, and on the button.'

'Aren't all women fine with you?' Alison teased. 'Perhaps she's missing being with you, and that's why she's moody.'

'Probably.'

'You are quick to jump to her defence,' Alison said, her tone becoming harsh. 'I hope you heeded my warning. Help her, I said. Please don't tell me you've seduced her.'

'As if.'

Alison glared at him. Then she shook her head, and walked back out of the room.

Hannah was standing on a stool, on tiptoe, fishing around on the top of the wardrobe.

Stephanie sank down onto the duvet on the tiny single bed. The duvet cover was made of pillar-box red cotton and had the word 'Hollywood' printed across it in large black lettering. She pressed the green button on her phone as it chimed with a call coming in, and 'Alison' beamed across her the screen.

'Photos?' She nodded in an answer to Alison's request from the other end. 'Yes, we are looking, ma'am. Nothing yet.'

Hannah coloured up.

Stephanie then turned to Hannah. 'We are looking for anything, anywhere, with an address or connection to a girl called "Madara", the DI's requesting.'

Hannah nearly fell off the stool at those words. Madara . . . *Maddie*! She turned to tell Stephanie that she needed to talk to Alison urgently, but Stephanie had already cut the call.

'Here's the laptop,' Hannah told Stephanie as she lifted the cardboard box down from the top of the wardrobe, knowing she couldn't, and definitely shouldn't, try and pretend it wasn't there. She already felt bad about knowing she had pushed the small photo album under Danielle's other bits in her drawer.

'It's heavy, so it's obviously old,' she mumbled as she put it on the bed and then sat beside Stephanie on the edge of the cheap red

93

duvet. They were facing a large picture, on the wall, of One Direction. The other wall was covered with different photos of Marilyn Monroe, all in different poses, and some of Danielle, dressed up and looking like the Hollywood goddess.

'I wonder if there's a cable we can charge it with, anywhere. Shall I go and ask the parents if they know?'

'No. We'll take it back with us and give it to the tech department. They'll open it in no time,' Stephanie told her.

Hannah breathed a sigh of relief: that would buy her time, if there *was* any info about the agency on it, and any pictures of herself. It looked as if it could be as old as those days.

'Keep looking,' Steph told her. 'See if we can find anything else that might help find this poor child's killer,' she said tenderly. 'DI wants us to find an address for this girl called Madara who, apparently, knew them both. There seems no sign of any other photos, apart from Marilyn Monroe, in here. She clearly loved the woman.'

Hannah's conscience got to her. 'Actually, I think there is,' she said, opening the drawer and pulling out the small album she'd hidden under the collection of old scarves and underwear. She flicked through it. Pictures of Danielle as Monroe filled it. Then she spotted a picture with Annabelle.

'Stop there,' Stephanie said. 'That's Annabelle Perry. Go on,' she told Hannah.

Hannah turned to the next page: a picture in a restaurant of three women, and a man's arm around them, stared back.

'Bingo! I wonder who that other woman is,' Steph said, as Hannah felt her cheeks burn. 'And who the arm belongs to. Take that with us,' she told Hannah.

Hannah pushed it into a forensics bag. Her secret was just getting bigger, and she needed to talk to Alison before anyone found a picture of her.

'DI also wants us to ask the parents about Danielle's drug-taking,' Steph said. 'I'll do that. It's a very delicate topic, especially with the state they're in. You phone the guv and tell her about these photos.'

★

94

Banham was on the phone talking to Gillian Hillier. She sounded relieved as he described the dog. She said it sounded exactly like Annabelle's pet, Bellizza. Who was a Tibetan terrier. Banham didn't know what a Tibetan terrier was, but the description of the dog added up.

'She has no collar or disc, and has obviously been running. Her fur is burned in places.'

He listened while the woman told him Annabelle had adored her dog. Annabelle never took her to London as the dog liked a lot of exercise, and Annabelle's garden at the cottage was large, and there were plenty of nice places nearby to walk her. Gillian reiterated that she had a lot of cats and couldn't take the dog permanently. Poor Bellizza would have to go to Battersea and hope for a nice new home.

Banham cast a glance at the dog. She was now sitting on his coat on the floor by his desk. He had sent out for dog food for her, but she wasn't eating. She looked so sad and lost. There was no way, if he had anything to do with it, that Bellizza was going to Battersea. But Alison would make the decision, he knew that, and if she said no, then that would be that, he wouldn't get to give this dog the love it was missing.

'No worries,' he said. 'She'll be here with Forensics for a bit anyway. If you think of anything else that might help us, please ring me immediately.' He hung up, put his elbow on the desk, and leaned his chin on his palm. Looking down at the frightened creature, he said very gently, 'Hello, Bellizza.'

The dog wagged her tail as a way of saying her own hello.

Right, he decided, he would take Bellizza to a vet and pay for the visit himself. If she was microchipped then he would know for sure that she had belonged to Annabelle Perry. Then he would get a forensic officer over to the vets, and have samples taken of the dried blood in her coat, and her paws and teeth checked for DNA. She may well have gone for the assailant, and could have some of his DNA on her. The dried blood could contain some drops from the killer. Something made of glass was used in the initial attack on the victim, so the killer may have cut themselves. If the assailant had previous, they would be on file, and then they would have him.

The dog would have to stay with the police while this was happening. That would get Alison used to the fact that there was dog around – a dog who needed a home. Banham had always wanted a dog, but believed it wouldn't be fair to keep one with his detective's life. But this was different. This dog, it seemed, had no one, and surely a detective's life was preferential to Battersea Dogs' Home. He would be sad to see that beautiful creature, with red-tinted hair that hung over her eyes like Alison's did sometimes, sitting mournfully in a dog pound. Alison had said it wasn't the right time for her to have a baby, but she might just accept a dog . . .

'Hello, Bellizza,' he said again. The tail wagged again. She knew her name, and seemed quite pleased that he did, too. Her eyes looked like shiny black marbles, with long black eyelashes. Alison's eyes were more like a squirrel's. He had once told her that, and she had been furious. She'd said he had no tact. He hadn't meant to be rude. It was just that they did look like a squirrel's eyes. They were busy, grey eyes, always checking around, aware of her surroundings. He had meant it as a compliment, but Alison hadn't taken it that way. She had been cross. One of the female PCs had told him later that he wasn't very good at compliments. The same PC had also said she knew he had meant well, but he wasn't very good at choosing the right words. Now he wondered, if he told Alison he had fallen for Bellizza because the dog reminded him of her, would she take that as a compliment?

Alison had two unwashed glasses carefully bagged for Forensics. She was hoping there might be DNA on them that would lead them somewhere.

Crowther walked into the kitchen. 'I've recorded these messages, and listened to them again. We need to find this bloke. Sounds like she was probably his dealer.'

'Why would the porter say no men ever came back? I don't get it.'

'Let's play him the recording. See what he says to that.'

The porter was a different one when they walked back out. This man was tiny, wore pebble glasses, and seemed nervy.

Crowther flashed his warrant. 'DS Crowther. Where's the guy that was here when we arrived?'

'Oh, gone home, sir,' the tiny man replied. 'I see all the police here. Is this about Miss Perry?' he asked. 'I heard the news. I'm gutted. Nice lass.'

'Was she?' Crowther said flatly, without taking his eyes off the man. 'Did she bring many men back at night?'

'I don't do nights, sir, I do the morning shift, but only three times a week. I'm retired, see, and I've a bit of a back problem.'

Alison rolled her eyes, then asked, 'Did you ever see anyone leaving her flat in the mornings?'

He shook his head. 'I've only ever met the brother, Jonathan, when he pops round. And the Right Honourable.'

Crowther looked at Alison. They had both read the cutting which stated Jonathan and Annabelle had fallen out over the inheritance.

'Does Jonathan Perry come here often?' Crowther pushed.

The little man shrugged. 'Seen him occasionally. Couldn't say often, but, as I say, I'm only—'

'Here three mornings a week, yes, you said,' Crowther snapped back. 'Would you recognise Jonathan's voice?'

Before the porter had the chance to answer, Crowther pressed his phone recording app, which immediately played the copy of the answerphone message 'Is this him?'

The little man shook his head. 'I wouldn't like to say. He never really spoke to me, sir.'

'And the Right Honourable?' Alison asked. 'Do you mean Christopher Burton?'

The man looked at her, then squeezed his thin lips together as he looked to the ground. 'I think I've seen him here,' he said.

'When was this?' Crowther snapped.

'Oh, more than once. Not for a bit, though. Maybe a month, maybe two. I couldn't say for sure.'

Crowther lifted his heavy eyebrows and stared at the man. 'You'll have to do better than that, mate,' he told him.

'Within the last month, then,' came the nervy reply. 'Can't be more precise, sorry.'

'Thank you for your time,' Alison said quickly and indicated with her head for them to leave.

Outside, she picked up three messages. One from Banham, one from Luke, and the other from Hannah. 'Banny thinks he's got Annabelle's dog that ran away from the fire,' she told Crowther. 'He's taken it to the vet to check if it's microchipped. Luke said Christopher Burton is out of the country, on holiday. And a wellington was found and handed in. Luke said he read the report and when he noticed it was found in the woodland not far from Apple Tree Close, he bagged it, and had it sent over to Forensics.'

'Do we know how long Burton's been out of the country?' Crowther asked.

Alison shook her head. 'No. But we'll talk to his secretary when we get back. See what she can tell us. He was obviously close to Annabelle if he visited her here. I want you to go to the lab. Give them these glasses, ask for results on them ASAP, and see what you can find out with the techies on the voice recording. Keep in touch. I'm going to get Hannah and take her on a visit to Fabulous.'

'If you have any trouble, give us a ring. It's north of the river, so watch where you park. Oh, and try not to get signed up,' Crowther teased.

'Ha ha.'

Chapter Fourteen

Hannah was very tense as she opened the passenger door and climbed in, Alison noticed.

'How are you doing?' she asked brightly.

The nod from Hannah was enough to see she wasn't doing well at all.

'You said you wanted to talk to me,' Alison spoke in a confidential tone. 'Would you like to stop for a coffee and a bite to eat? It is lunchtime. I'm starving and I haven't made an appointment with the Fabulous model agency. I thought it best to surprise them.'

'Sounds good. And yes, I do need to talk to you.' Hannah paused, and then added. 'It's about this case . . .'

Alison didn't answer; she indicated and pulled out into the traffic. Hannah watched her press play on the stereo, and then the voice of Sam Smith filled the car. 'He's got a great voice,' was all Alison said, hoping the music might calm this new DC.

They drove in silence for the next mile or so. Then Alison pulled off the road and turned into the parking bay of a North London hotel.

'They do great toasted sarnies here,' was all she said.

Colin Crowther was back in the office. He was now reading the notes he had brought back from Forensics. The boot print on the pizza-shop sign that had been handed in was light and showed nothing significant to help: probably a size-nine boot or thereabouts, but too faint to be a hundred per cent. The newly handed-in wellington boot would undergo tests. It had water inside it. It had been raining the day of the first arson attack, but not since. It also contained dark-blue fibres. Crowther then turned to the notes on the missing pizza-shop motorbikes. Neither had been picked up on any cameras, so they were no further there.

Some of the sparse CCTV from around the area had been scoured. There was nothing useful from the pub CCTV. It showed no sign of a motorbike being driven in the street around the time of the fire. It had picked up the owner of the pizza shop, Johnny Walsh, locking up and getting in his car, then driving off, at the time he had said, just after five o'clock.

'So, if one of the neighbours said she heard a motorbike,' Crowther said to Luke, 'then the bike must have come in from the back of the flats. Do we have any CCTV from that side of the area?' Crowther's feet were up on his desk and he was sipping coffee from the over-sized mug that Stephanie Green had bought him for Christmas, the words 'YOUR HEAD' written across it.

'No, sarge,' Luke told him. 'No CCTV was working over that side. Any that was there had been sprayed over with black paint.'

'We've sent over to Forensics two glasses from Annabelle Perry's London flat, and a dog-end that I fished from the bin there, as well as that wellington,' Crowther told Luke. 'So, keep pestering them for results on those, will you, mate?'

Luke nodded. 'Will do. The DCI's taken the stray dog to the vet. We're pretty sure it is Annabelle's dog. It's got blood and glass shards in its coat and burned paws.' Luke scrolled down his computer. 'I'll print this out. It's the post-mortem report on Annabelle. The skull had taken a few heavy blows before the fire started.'

'Get on to Fire Forensics,' Crowther said immediately. 'Tell them we are looking for the remains of any glass that survived the fire. We may find traces of blood, even the object that cracked the skull. Needle in a haystack, but worth a try.'

'Bellizza Perry,' the vet told Banham as he read the microchip from inside the animal's shoulder. 'That's her name.'

The vet stroked Bellizza's shaking body. 'She's certainly had a fright,' he told Banham. 'Tibetans are normally hardy dogs, but this one's very scared. You say her owner was killed in a house fire?'

'That's just confirmed it, yes.'

The vet nodded. He was now examining the dog's legs and paws. 'Her paws are burned.' He rubbed the dog's head gently. 'Dried blood in this fur, too. I'm going to get some cream rubbed on the paws and then bandage all four of them. I hope that's all right with you.'

'No, it's not, unfortunately.' Banham felt terrible saying this. 'Can you put her in a crate, or somewhere where no one can touch her?' he added. 'I will have a forensics team with you very shortly. I can't, unfortunately, let you treat her until then.'

'My job – which I took an oath to do, I'd like to remind you, Inspector – is to do my best to help the animal in my care.' The vet glared coldly at Banham. 'However, you're the boss,' he added. 'What then? When your people have examined her? Off to the local council place and then to Battersea?'

'I'm going to keep her,' Banham told him. 'I have to check it with my wife, well, girlfriend, but that's my intention.'

The pretty blonde vet's nurse, who had been standing at the end of the table, moved in to help Bellizza. Banham put his hand out to stop her.

'I'd appreciate it if no one else handles her until my forensics team are here. I'll lift her,' he said. 'I have handled her anyway, and it's one less person's DNA to worry about.'

As Banham lifted his arms to reach over and lift the dog, Bellizza leaned forward and placed her hairy chin against his elbow. One of her cracked front paws followed. Her enormous dark eyes looked appealingly at him.

'Oh, and, she knows me,' he added, unable to stop himself giving her a reassuring stroke.

The vet's voice softened. 'Knows you're going to adopt her, too, I'd say.' He half-smiled at Banham. 'I'd like to X-ray her

101

ASAP, though. If she's inhaled too much smoke, her lungs could collapse.'

Alison and Hannah gave their orders at the bar in the front of the hotel, then Alison found seats in a corner at the back of the lounge bar, where there were no other customers.

She watched Hannah nervously fiddling as she hung her bag on the back of the chair.

'Lunch is on me,' Alison said, opening the conversation. 'I was going to invite you for a meal and a chat anyway, just the two of us, to see how you were managing. You said you wanted to talk to me.' She waited, watching as Hannah picked up a beer mat and turned it on its side and then over again, her gaze downward. 'I hope Sergeant Crowther is being a help to you,' Alison said, watching her closely.

'He is,' Hannah jumped to his defence. 'I couldn't ask for a better partner.'

'Good.' The coffees arrived at the same moment, and the waiter spent a good few seconds carefully placing the cutlery and napkins. Alison used those seconds to study Hannah's anxious face. As soon as the waiter had done his bit, she pushed, 'So, what's on your mind?'

Hannah took a deep breath. 'I may lose my job over this,' she said.

This wasn't what Alison had expected. She raised her eyebrows for Hannah to carry on.

'I wasn't sure when I saw the first victim, but . . .'

Alison was ten steps ahead. 'You knew the victims?'

'Yes,' she paused. 'And no.'

'Are they toms?'

'I was a student, you see, and I needed money . . .'

'Oh, you mean—' Alison said quickly. 'Tell me, Hannah, this is important.'

Hannah told her everything. As she concluded, she added, 'You see, I truly believed I was just being booked for dinner with lonely clients. I never did anything . . . more than that.'

Before Alison could speak, the waiter arrived.

'Two toasted cheese and tomato,' he said, as he placed their lunch in front of them. Hannah immediately stopped talking.

'Will I lose my job?' she asked as soon as he turned his back. 'There's a law that says you can't live off immoral earnings. I broke that, although, I only had three dates . . .'

Alison shook her head. 'You don't have a record,' she told her. 'So, no, you definitely won't lose your job. You have confirmed the link between these women. So, that's a great help. Now, the safety of this third girl, Madara, is our main concern right now. We desperately need to trace her.'

'I would be surprised if she was still in the country. I know she had a child in Slovakia. She said she wanted to earn money and take it home with her.' Hannah paused and then said, 'Do the others have to know? I've been beside myself with worry.'

Alison shook her head. 'You don't want to know the jobs I had as a student,' she told Hannah in a reassuring tone, leaning in and lowering her voice. 'Topless go-go dancer, for one.'

Hannah nearly choked on her sandwich.

'Girls' talk for a night off,' Alison said, patting Hannah's hand. 'The last thing that will happen to you is losing your job. Let me think about how we approach it with the rest of the team. But, good news is, you are going to be a massive help with this case, and it will do your career no end of good, not bad.'

'So, do the others have to know?'

Alison shook her head. 'Maybe just Crowther. He's very sound, though. He'll keep a secret. Right now, we need to discuss how we approach Fabulous. It may not be the same people running it. If it is, do you think they'll recognise you?' Alison bit into the hot melted-cheese toastie and studied Hannah.

'It's possible.'

'Right, then we are going to give this some thought. Do you remember where they kept the files on the girls they employed?'

Hannah shook her head. 'It was so long ago. I think on the computer, on the front desk. And I know there were photos on the wall. One side models, the other escorts . . .'

'Good,' Alison looked at her. 'I am delighted to have you on my team. You had a terrible incident to deal with as a newly qualified PC. You were honoured for your quick thinking and bravery over it. You have a great career ahead of you. This will help it, if we use it to our advantage, and act a little devious.'

Hannah welled up.

'You've proved your worth to me. And, as I am driving today and we are visiting Fabulous, which of course may by now be in different hands, who knows, I am going to buy you a glass of wine.'

Hannah shook her head. 'Tempting, but no thank you, ma'am. You have one. I owe you that, and I'll drive.'

Alison shook her head. 'I need to keep my wits about me. OK, then, it's on hold. Let's do a girls' night of Prosecco and gossip soon. I'll fill you in on all the gossip in the department.' She raised her coffee cup and clinked it against Hannah's. Her eyes twinkled as she lowered her voice and added, 'I'll tell you some of the jobs I did as well as topless dancing, over that Prosecco. All between us.'

'Thanks, ma'am. And just to say, I would be up for going undercover to the agency, if it would help trace Madara. If she is still in the country, that is.'

Alison looked very thoughtful.

'I know Col Crowther would look out for me,' Hannah added. 'And I really trust him.'

'I'm not sure, but I'll give it thought,' Alison told her. 'If I did consider letting you go undercover, then you couldn't come into the agency with me today. No, you'll stay put in the car outside. Watch the comings and goings, who goes in and out, all of that.'

'So, you'll consider me going undercover?' Hannah asked again, The detective in her stirred. She had liked Madara very much and believed she could help find and save her. 'Let's see how things go.'

Chapter Fifteen

DC Luke Hughes replaced his receiver and shouted across to Crowther, 'Jonathan Perry has just been brought in, sarge. He's off his face. He was picked up as he tried to enter Annabelle's flat in Paddington. The porter called the police. He said he was there to visit his sister. He hadn't been informed of the news, apparently. He fought the police and security guard when they tried to stop him entering her flat. He was arrested and is now downstairs.'

Crowther jumped up. 'Ring the guv'nor and tell her. I'll go and get him. We'll throw him in a cell till he sobers up and then interview him.'

Before they left the hotel, Hannah went to the ladies'. She brushed her hair and then rolled it into a tight chignon bun, the way she used to wear it under her PC's hat. She then took tissues from her bag and wiped all her make-up off. With her bare face staring back at her, her scars screamed and glowed. Without any make-up, and her hair in an old-fashioned style, it was highly unlikely that Oluwa Marconi – if indeed he still owned the agency – would remember her from all those years ago. She was going to be outside anyway, keeping her head down, reading a paper, watching. This pleased her, as it meant Alison was seriously considering letting her go undercover. She would have a chance to prove her worth with her colleagues in MIT. She also felt a great sense of release now she had unburdened to Alison, and she knew her ambition, to be a top murder detective, was possible once again.

The woman at reception looked very nervous as Alison walked in holding her warrant card in front of her.

Alison took her in: she was a pretty woman, maybe mid-thirties, so she could easily have been working there since Hannah's time. The woman's dark hair was cut in a tailored bob, not unlike Mary Quant in her heyday. Her eyes were dark, large, and overly made-up. She had tanned olive skin.

'How can I help? she asked, glaring with hard eyes at Alison.

Alison didn't answer at first. She turned to study the pictures on the wall. On one side were the tall and skinny girls, some on cat-walks, others displaying clothes, taken on location assignments, as Hannah had described. The other side was clearly glamour – girls leaning forward into camera, their cleavages displayed. Some leaning over chairs, legs astride the furniture, and some with tongues peeping through their lips. Others had their dresses hitched up, and a leg protruding, advertising a stocking held by a suspender. All were showing a lot of their bodies.

Alison turned back to her. 'You're not in trouble,' she told her, after taking in the pictures, scanning them quickly for any sign of Hannah and relieved to see there was none. 'I need to talk to the owner.'

At the same moment, a tall, lanky, bearded man with narrowed eyes walked out from a door to the right of reception. He stretched his hand out to Alison. 'Oluwa Marconi,' he said to her. 'How can I help you?'

Alison made no effort to take his hand, and decided pretty quickly that the man was shifty, and that there must be a camera in a back office displaying the goings-on in reception.

'I'm investigating a double murder,' she said. 'Danielle Low and Annabelle Perry. I believe they worked here?'

He shook his head. 'I read about it. Terrible,' he said. Alison picked up the insincerity in his voice. 'Annabelle Perry worked here, yeah. But not for a long while. She used to be so popular, but then her popularity faded. She got sloppy, so I dropped her. A very pretty girl, though. I'm sorry she's died. What happened?'

Alison ignored his question. 'You took her on as an escort after her modelling popularity waned, isn't that right?'

He shook his head, answering quickly. 'That was a long time ago. It didn't work out.' Alison watched his eyes shift from her, to the iPad on the counter, and then to the woman behind it. 'When the models weren't earning enough,' he said, still avoiding eye contact, 'and they got behind on rent, they worried. It's an insecure living. So we came up with the idea of offering an escort service to our clients, dinner or a night out with the girls, for a fee. We called it Suite Escorts. Nothing illegal, just dinner with businessmen alone in London.' He turned his head again to the woman at the reception. 'Camilla, here, told me it wouldn't work, didn't you?'

Camilla nodded but didn't speak.

'She said the customers would think there was sex on offer. Of course, that wasn't the case. We are a respectable agency.'

Alison raised her eyebrows and gave him a knowing look.

'It was advertised as, if you want a beautiful woman to accompany you somewhere, to impress your friends, that sort of thing,' he quickly added. 'But it didn't work. Camilla was right, there were problems. We dropped that side. We only run models now.'

Alison turned to Camilla. 'How long have you been working here?' she asked her.

'Since just after it opened,' she said quietly.

'Where are you from?' Alison asked her.

'I am from Hong Kong, originally. My father was Italian, and my mother from Hong Kong.'

'And you?' Alison asked Oluwa.

'London,' he said dismissively. 'But my father's Italian and my mother's Nigerian. You said a double murder?' He had now moved to in front of the desk and was clicking on the iPad from there.

'Danielle Low,' Alison said to him. 'Remember her?'

He didn't look up, but nodded. 'We got rid of her a long time ago. She used to do the Marilyn Monroe lookalike stuff, but clients complained when she opened her mouth.' He managed a small chuckle at this. 'She was a drug user, too.'

'Too?'

'Yes. Annabelle sadly was as well. That ruined her career.'

'They were friendly, I believe, Annabelle and Danielle?'

'Yes, I believe they were.' Oluwa nodded. 'Long time ago. So many women come and go.'

Alison was now watching Camilla. She was moving things around and placing them under her desk.

'And there was a third friend, a Madara?'

Oluwa looked at Camilla. 'Yes, she was gorgeous. Madara Kowaska?'

Camilla shrugged, then shook her head.

'You don't remember,' he said to Camilla. 'Understandable – so many girls come and go. Slovakian, if I remember correctly,' Oluwa told Alison. 'She left. I believe she went back to her home country.'

Alison turned away. She moved to study the pictures on the far wall, the ones with the girls in the overtly sexy poses. 'How long since you gave up the escort agency?' she asked.

'Oh, a few years now.'

'I'm surprised you've still got these photos up, then. They seem very out of place for a fashion modelling agency. And very sexist in today's world.'

'We do photographic, too,' Camilla snapped. 'Bikini work, and sexy girl photos. Men's magazines and the like. That's not against the law.'

Alison ignored her. She turned to Oluwa. 'I presume you keep records,' she said, and then added, with a lacing of sarcasm, 'for tax and VAT purposes.'

He narrowed his eyes. 'Of course.'

'Good. I may need to ask for them.' She held his eye contact. 'Going back a few years, too. The law says you need to keep them for at least seven previous years. Right?

He flicked his eyes to Camilla. She remained silent.

'What I would like now,' Alison told him, 'is a list of your clients. I know the agency opened twelve years ago. So, I'd like every client since it opened and all their details.'

'I wouldn't have kept them,' he said, now sounding more annoyed than nervous. 'Because of the kind of men – married and the like, you understand – that would have wanted the girls as escorts.' The bone in his cheek moved. 'Let's just say "confidentiality" was the word. I'm sure you understand.'

Alison took another second to decide whether to threaten him, arrest him for the crime of living off immoral earnings, or to play being nice. Then Camilla spoke again.

'And the girls don't give us their full or right addresses,' she said. 'We don't ask for them. They have mobile phones, which are untraceable, and—'

'Strange that, if, as you say, everything is legitimate,' Alison cut in. 'I would have thought you would have needed their National Insurance numbers, too, for employment law.'

'They are self-employed.'

Alison ignored her. 'I believe Christopher Burton was a client of yours.'

'Sorry, who?'

'We only deal with female models.' This was Camilla again.

Alison turned and leaned in and across the desk. 'Please don't insult my intelligence or try my patience,' she threatened. 'We both know you ran an under-the-counter escort service, including prostitution. At this moment, I am not interested in your seedy dealings. I am investigating four horrific murders. My investigations have led me here, to the fact that both these girls worked for you. These women have been burned alive. To say they died a painful death is an understatement.' She turned back to Oluwa. 'So, how about you work with me, and I become nice and ignore anything illegal you may or may not have done, for now.'

'I'd like to help you, Inspector,' Oluwa said in an annoyingly laid-back way. 'But I really don't have a list of clients. My models' work span is very limited, as I'm sure you understand, so anyone

109

that was here when those women were, would have moved on by now. I have no back-dated contact details. Sorry.'

'Christopher Burton,' Alison repeated. 'He is an MP. Was he a client of yours –' her tone changed to one of sarcasm – 'when you had your escort department?'

'We had no one by that name,' Camilla said, a little too quickly.

'In that case,' Alison told her, 'you may be getting a visit from the Inland Revenue. They will want your papers and records going back the full seven years, probably longer. You need to look at getting those together.' She then took a business card from her pocket and handed it to Oluwa. 'Of course, if you change your mind, before I can get hold of Inland Revenue and the VAT office, which will be –' she hesitated, holding eye contact – 'say, in the next few hours, then please give me a call, and let me have a list of all the clients that came and went through your escort department. Incidentally, do you remember anyone who wore a very large ring on their little finger?'

'Camilla loves rings, don't you?'

Camilla looked nervous. Then she begrudgingly held up her hand, which displayed large costume rings on three of the fingers.

'Any clients that you remember who wore a large gold ring on their little finger?' Alison pushed.

Both Camilla and Oluwa shook their heads.

'And you would remember, of course, being a ring-lover,' Alison said to Camilla. 'So, wrack your brains, and I will await your call.'

Alison turned and left the building, but as she opened her car door, she noticed Camilla standing at the entrance to the agency, watching her.

Hannah had had her head buried in a newspaper. She looked up as Alison opened the door.

'Head down,' Alison whispered.

Hannah immediately obeyed.

'Was that Camilla woman there when you worked here?' Alison asked her as they drove off.

'Yup. Hard as nails, and misses nothing, that one. But I'm pretty sure she didn't see me, or would even remember me. I was too far away, and I have my hair up and no make-up on.'

Jonathan Perry had sobered up by the time Alison returned to the station.

'Who do you want to interview him, guv?' Crowther asked her.

'You do it,' she told him. 'I'll watch from behind the glass. Take Hannah in with you. It'll be good for her. She's doing well, but needs to learn more.'

She turned to Luke. 'Anything back from Forensics?' she asked him.

'No DNA on the glasses Crowther took in, ma'am, and the dog-end belonged to Annabelle Perry. I believe it was found in her bin. So, no help there. Footprint on the pizza sign has shreds of nettles, and possibly a size-nine footprint. The wellington that was found nearby is also a size nine, which is interesting. Fibres of navy-blue cloth found inside, and water in it. The water was tested: not rainwater, and not from the stream near where it was found.'

Alison frowned. 'What does that mean, not stream or rainwater?'

'They don't know, ma'am, but they do know that the wood where it was found is within five minutes' walk of the first arson. I looked it up.' He passed Alison a blown-up map of the area around Apple Tree Close. 'I think that's worth checking out.'

'Get hold of DCI Banham,' she told him. 'Tell him I am requesting a full search team on the woodland. And ASAP. Where is the DCI, by the way?'

'He took that stray dog to the vet. He thinks it belonged to Annabelle Perry. Forensics have it now. I believe he's over there.'

'Ring him, and pass that on,' she said as she headed for the corridor with the two-way window to the interview room. 'Oh, and well done.'

Chapter Sixteen

Hannah sat beside Crowther in Interview Room A. Jonathan Perry, now sober, had refused a solicitor, and was demanding to know why he had been locked up.

'For your own good, mate,' Crowther told him, after reciting the legal jargon about videoing and taping the interview, and Jonathan's right to refuse a solicitor. 'Fact is, you were off your face and we were worried you might fall under a bus.'

Jonathan shook his head, then lowered it, then looked up. 'My sister has been killed, and I had to find that out from a phone call from a friend.'

Jonathan's dark eyes reminded Crowther of the ones in the pictures of Annabelle, only his looked tired and desperate.

'Who was the phone call from?'

Jonathan sniffed a few times and rubbed his nose, rather like an inquisitive cat.

'A mutual friend. No one you know,' he said.

'So, tell me.'

'My sister's next-door neighbour. Gillian Hillier. She had my number for emergencies. Annabelle had given it to her. She was right to think that it was an emergency.' He sniffed again.

Hannah started writing notes.

'We were under the impression that you and your sister weren't on speaking terms,' Crowther told him. 'Due to you being cut out of your parents' inheritance?'

Jonathan shrugged. 'Don't believe all you read in the papers.'

Crowther ignored the sarcasm. 'So, why were you cut out of your inheritance?'

Jonathan looked down at the plain steel table. He said nothing for a couple of seconds, then looked up at Crowther. His tone changed again and he spoke in a quiet voice which seemed tinged with guilt. 'I have a drug habit. My parents put me into rehab, and I came out clean, but not for long. They sent me again, threatening if I didn't stay clean that time, they would disinherit me. I didn't, so, true to their word, they cut me out of their wills and disowned me. They left everything to Annabelle. She helps me, though. She gives me money, lets me stay in the London flat, which was my parents' anyway. She didn't turn her back on me.' He put his hands to his temples, breathed hard, and then started to sob. 'I have tried to kick the habit, again and again.' He shrugged. 'I can't do it. I need the stuff.'

'So, Annabelle got your stuff for you?'

He looked nervously from Hannah to Crowther. 'No,' he said, shaking his head defiantly.

'Listen, she's dead, mate,' Crowther reminded him. 'We're hardly going to charge her for dealing. We're interested in finding who burned her alive, in her own home. She helped you, you say, so help her back, by helping us.'

'Annabelle loved to party. Let's say she had connections.'

'We need more than that.'

'I don't know.'

'You must know she kept gear at her flat. Was she a user too?'

He looked suddenly like a rabbit caught in headlights, seemingly afraid to answer. Then he shrugged. 'Occasionally. I thought everybody did at parties.'

Crowther held his gaze. Then he asked. 'You must have met her friends?'

Jonathan shook his head. 'No.'

'Danielle Low, and a woman called Madara, do they ring any bells?'

Jonathan nodded. 'My sister used to hang around with a Danielle. Years ago, she did Monroe impersonation modelling.'

'Have you bumped into her recently, at Annabelle's flat?'

'No.' He still looked frightened.

'So, this gear at your sister's flat. Was it for you?'

'I know she had some stuff for me.'

'You must have other sources, too?'

'Annabelle knew the people with the good stuff.' He looked at Crowther and added, 'I didn't mix in her circles. She just helped me, that's all.'

'Where do you live, Mr Perry?'

'Nowhere, really. I've got a room in a flat. Annabelle got it for me. She found out I was sleeping rough, and paid six months rent there for me. Then she found out the others in the flat were doing stuff. She told me not to stay there anymore, said I could stay at her London base.'

'Yet she had drugs in the London flat. And you say she got them for you.'

He shrugged, then shook his head, 'I couldn't go cold turkey. She knew that. I don't do heroin, just snow. The guys in the flat do a lot of heroin.'

Crowther changed the subject. 'You say Annabelle hung out with Danielle Low. There was another woman, Madara. Do you know her?'

'Yes. I think they were all from the same model agency.'

'We need to trace Madara. Do you know her surname, or where she lives?'

He shook his head. 'I haven't seen, or heard of her, for years. She used to live in West London somewhere. She was the one that was caught with my father's friend, Christopher Burton, giving him a blow job in a car by Westminster Bridge. It made the press.'

'There was a picture of Christopher Burton in your sister's flat in London. Why did she have a picture of him there?' Crowther asked.

'I think Annabelle had an affair with him, too. He's a bit of a charmer. She got close to him when my parents died.' Jonathan started fiddling with his hair, which was overgrown, down to his shoulders, and in serious need of a wash. He was still rubbing his nose frequently, too. Crowther knew this to be a sign of a heavy user. Basically, he could have been a good-looking lad. Late twenties, Crowther would guess, with a very lived-in face, heart-shaped like his sister's had been. And the same big Bambi eyes as his sister. Jonathan had a bad complexion, again, Crowther knew, from drug use. After watching him fiddling in discomfort for about thirty seconds, Crowther spoke again.

'I'm surprised your sister didn't try harder to help you off the gear, if she was such a good friend,' he said.

When Jonathan frowned in puzzlement, Crowther added, 'Seems to me, she encouraged it. She helped get the gear for you. All Class A stuff. Stuff that will eventually kill you.'

Jonathan didn't answer, but his dark eyes widened. Something was getting through.

Crowther then leaned forward towards the desk. 'We found ground cement powder alongside the drugs in the flat,' he told him. 'Any idea why?'

Jonathan looked terrified. Then he shook his head. 'I've honestly no idea.'

'You were reported trying to get into Annabelle's flat. Did you know the gear was there?'

'Yes. I had a key, but I lost it.' He leaned forward. 'I don't understand. Are you saying my sister was trying to kill me?'

'Couldn't answer that, mate,' Crowther said with a dismissive shrug of his shoulder. Then he leaned into the now-quivering man. 'You let Annabelle get your gear. She risked getting done for carrying, to help you, didn't she?'

Jonathan nodded his head, and Crowther nodded back, before leaning back in his chair, folding his arms, and adding, 'Because, if she got arrested for carrying that amount, she would be done for dealing. She would get a custodial, and you would have the flat for yourself. Wouldn't you have liked that flat all to yourself?'

He shook his head vehemently. 'It wasn't like that. She made me promise not to get involved with dealers. Said she would get it for me, if and when I needed, but I wanted to stop. I swear I did.' He was breaking down now. 'Is that why they burned her, because she got involved with dealers? For God's sake,' he sobbed.

'It's possible,' Crowther told him, showing no sympathy. 'But you know where she got the gear from, don't you?'

When Jonathan didn't answer, Crowther raised his voice to shouting pitch. 'Don't you?'

Jonathan started crying. 'Madara. Madara got the drugs for Annabelle. She gets them from someone else. I swear I don't know who, but Annabelle said she was good to get them. It was always good gear.'

There was a silence while Crowther and Hannah took in the relevance of the fact Madara was still in the country.

'What is her last name?' Crowther asked after a few seconds. Then he raised his voice. 'Her last name. Think. What was it?'

'I don't know.'

Crowther pushed on. 'Where in London does she live?'

'I don't know. Annabelle wouldn't tell me. She said for my own good I wasn't to go there. The gear she had was always first class. I just took it.' He sniffed hard and wiped his nose with his wrist.

Hannah felt a great urge to pass him a tissue, but her instructions were to say nothing, just take it all in.

'Think harder.' Crowther was leaning into him. 'Annabelle must have mentioned it at some time. Where in London?'

'Earl's Court! I think.' He really broke down now. 'Christ, this awful. Was my sister trying to kill me?'

As Alison stood watching the interview through the glass panel, Banham walked up and stood beside her.

She shook her head. 'He's too weak to commit murder,' she said to Banham. 'I'd be very surprised. And we've got the connection between the two women. They both worked for that model–cum–escort agency. And now, we hear the third girl is still in the country, so we have to find her. Her name is Madara, and she lives somewhere around Earl's Court. She is Slovakian. That's all we've got. A needle in a haystack.'

'This boy's an addict,' Banham said, studying Jonathan through the glass panel. 'He's unstable. Don't rule him out.'

'What's the motive? If he kills his sister, he cuts off his drug supply. An addict wouldn't do that.'

'He would if he knew where to get the supply.' Banham shrugged. 'He's desperate. I'm suggesting we don't rule him out.' He then changed his tune. 'We've found Annabelle's dog,' he said. 'She was handed in to us as a stray. She has dried blood in her coat, and shards of glass. I've had Forensics take samples. The blood may well be some of the killer's. That could help a lot.'

'Well done. I'll get Luke to press for urgency on that.'

There was a few seconds while they both watched the end of the interview, then Banham said quietly, 'I've got the dog in my office. I need to hold on to it for now.'

She frowned. 'Why?'

'In case we need more testing.'

She shrugged nonchalantly.

Banham left it another few seconds, and then said, 'The dog is gorgeous. In fact . . . it looks like you.'

Alison blinked, took an intake of breath, and then slowly turned to look at Banham. 'What?'

'That's meant as a compliment,' he said apologetically. 'Have I said it all wrong again?'

She didn't answer, just shook her head.

117

Chapter Seventeen

Stephanie Green was on the phone when Banham and Alison walked back into the investigation room ready for the evening meeting. Steph replaced the receiver and looked up. 'Christopher Burton is in Italy, on holiday, and travelled there from his holiday in Mexico – how the other half live!' she told them. 'He's not expected back for another week. The secretary was very helpful, though,' Stephanie continued. 'She said she knew he was a close friend of the Perry family, and that he would want to know about Annabelle before reading about it in the papers. I asked if he was still in regular contact with them. She said she didn't know, but seemed to clam up after that. She also suggested he might come back when he heard the news, and was quite sure he would be happy to talk to us. But she wouldn't give us his private number.'

'What day is he due back?' Crowther asked. He had just walked into the room with Hannah and stood listening. 'We should talk to him face to face.'

'Find out when exactly he is due back,' Alison told Steph. 'And tell him to ring us ASAP, to make an appointment to meet us.'

'Never trust a politician,' Banham butted in. 'But if he's been out of the country for a while, he's not a suspect. However, as Crowther said, he knows the family and could be a big help for us.'

Banham was now standing in front of the whiteboard which bore the pictures of the two women's remains. 'Let's get a round-up of where we are,' he said, addressing the half a dozen detectives who were attending the meeting. 'Not many of us here tonight, everyone else is out on neighbourhood door-knocking. Poor buggers. So, to start, as many of you know, we have found Annabelle's dog, Bellizza. She has blood in her fur and shards of broken glass. The blood and glass is being tested as we speak. Anything back from Fire Forensics? he asked Luke.

Luke shook his head. 'Nothing in the way of usable shards of glass,' Luke said. 'They are putting a report together.'

Banham turned to Alison.

'We know Annabelle and Danielle both worked at the escort agency by the name of Fabulous or Suite Escorts,' she said. 'Hannah and I visited the place this morning. The man that owns it, Oluwa Marconi, along with his receptionist, Camilla, were very cagey with us. They say they have no records of any of their old escort clients. They don't, according to them, run an escort agency. However, there are photos all over the wall of half-dressed women, all looking very provocative. Which says to me, they are lying. I have threatened him with the Inland Revenue if he doesn't find the old records of all his clients and models.' She pointed to the photo on the board of the three women with the arm around them that displayed a large ring on one finger. 'We now urgently need to trace the third woman in the photo. We know her name is Madara Kowaska. She also worked for the model agency. She is Slovakian and lives in, or around, Earl's Court.'

'According to Jonathan Perry,' Crowther butted in, 'she gave Christopher Burton a blow job in his car by Westminster Bridge.'

'She may well be in danger,' Alison said, looking over at Luke. 'Can you see if there are any Slovakian clubs or cafes in West London, and get someone to go round them with her picture?'

'Guv.' Luke nodded.

Nigel and Baz both spoke at once, both suggesting getting a search warrant and turning the modelling agency over. Alison put her hand up to quieten them.

'Not yet,' she said. 'We believe they are still running an escort agency. I think we need to find out more about that. We need to be discreet and cunning. Hannah has offered to go undercover in there for us, and apply for work.'

'No,' Banham said quickly, immediately turning round and glaring at Hannah. 'I won't allow that.'

'With respect, sir,' Hannah argued, 'I have been in a lot worse situations.'

'Which is why I am saying no, and safeguarding you from any other foreseeable danger,' Banham told her. 'You're very new in this department, and it is my responsibility to steer you gently. Thank you for offering.' He turned back to Alison. 'The answer is no.'

Alison took an intake of breath. 'Actually, it was my idea,' she lied. 'And, as I remember it, sir, *I* am Senior Investigating Officer on this case. Hannah is happy with it. I think it's good experience for her. She has been in a dangerous position before and showed her colours. We will more than protect her. And I have already agreed it.'

The room fell into silence.

'We'll discuss this after,' Banham told her.

'Yes, we will.' Alison then turned to Stephanie. 'Any luck with the old laptop found at Danielle's parents' house, Steph?'

'Technicians opened it, no problem,' Stephanie told her. 'They have been through all her files, deleted files, everything. Nothing to help our case,' she said. 'Mainly all Marilyn Monroe research.'

'We know Annabelle, Danielle and Madara were close,' Alison said, 'and they all worked for that agency, which won't give us their client lists. Which is why we need someone inside that agency. If this Oluwa Marconi does send us a list of all their past clients, to avoid my threat of a visit from the Inland Revenue, then I'll bet a penny to a pound the list will be made up, and his excuse: clients don't give real names. Someone inside the agency could find records, and there's a good chance we could find this Madara – which now has to be our top priority.'

'I am happy to do it, sir,' Hannah said again to Banham.

'I heard you, and point taken,' he said gently in reply. 'We appreciate your offer. But you will do as you are told while you are in this department, which I run.'

Alison glared at him, but he wasn't looking.

'If I think it is too dangerous, then you will respect that decision. But I will give it thought.' He turned back to Alison. 'As I said, we'll talk about this after.' Then he said to Hannah, 'And let you know later.'

The room had once again fallen into silence. Hannah wasn't sure whether to keep quiet or argue further, this time admitting her history with the agency. But Alison had told her to keep it between the two of them, and to just tell Crowther. She looked over to Alison, who lowered her eyelids and shook her head gently, as if she had read Hannah's mind. She then became aware Crowther was watching her and had clocked the eye contact between her and Alison. That man missed nothing, it seemed. She raised her eyebrows at him. He gave a small smile, and the tiniest of winks. She winked back.

Banham and Alison were in Alison's office. There was a crate in the corner, which the vet had supplied for the dog to stay in as it awaited forensic test results. The door to the crate was open, and Banham was crouched on the floor by the dog, rubbing soothing cream into her burned pads. 'Forensics have taken samples from her paws,' he told Alison. 'Poor lady, we had to refuse cream from the vet earlier to help her. Now the testing's done, but we have to wait to see if you have smoke in your lungs, too, don't we, little lady?'

The dog licked his face.

Alison watched him. She was concerned. He often talked to her about the collie dog he had as a child, and how he wished this job allowed him the freedom to have another.

'How long will it be here?' she asked him.

'She's lost, and traumatised,' Banham answered, stroking the sad dog's head. 'She's also suffering from shock, and possibly smoke inhalation.'

'Are Forensics getting back today?'

'They said they'd try. It was marked down as urgent.'

'If the results don't come through, where will it stay? We can't leave it here overnight. It seems a bit cruel.'

'*It* is a *she*,' he half-snapped. 'Her name is Bellizza. And no, I wouldn't leave her here overnight, in the dark. The vet has given us the crate. We'll take her home with us.' He looked at her. His tone changed. 'With your permission,' he said, like a schoolboy asking for an extra portion. 'We can get some cooked chicken on the way, from the fried chicken place.'

Alison now had her head down, reading up-to-date reports on the case, hardly listening. 'Well, I hope she's house-trained,' she said. She then looked up. The penny had dropped. 'Then what? When forensic results are back? It'll have to be Battersea. We couldn't be taking her on a permanent basis.'

'Why can't we?' Banham asked her, a pleading look in his eye.

'Because we have full-time jobs, and are out all the time.'

'We could get a dog walker. We'd manage.'

'Change the subject. There's more important things to discuss. Hannah, for instance. This was my decision, you made me SIO on the case, and I would like you to back me up.'

'It's not a good idea.'

'Why? She wants to do it. She is confident and brave. She's proved that.'

'She's only been back a few days. She's a trainee. She's been through too much in her time on the force already. I can't believe you think it's a good idea.

'Because of what she's been through, she's experienced and capable,' Annabelle argued. 'And she uses her head. We'll keep her very closely monitored. Another woman's life could be in immediate danger. That agency may well have information that could save her. We need to get in there. She can do that for us. She could be in and out in an evening. She knows the layout.' She noticed him turn from the dog, to listen to her, at that remark, and immediately added, 'She was with me at the agency today. We'll keep

Crowther very near her. He won't let anything happen to her. She'd be miked. I believe she'll get results for us. Time isn't on our side.'

'You're putting up a good argument.'

'It's a good idea, Banny, that's why. Listen, you may be my other half, and my senior officer, but I am SIO on this job, please don't undermine me—'

'I am not undermining you,' Banham interrupted.

'You do it all the time.'

'I'm giving you the benefit of my experience.'

'Well, I don't agree with it. I believe, if we can get Madara Kowaska's address and clients' details, going back, then this will speed us towards solving this case.'

Banham stopped stroking the dog's head. The dog whimpered as he withdrew his hand. He looked Alison in the eye. 'You're very good at your job, we all know that. But, Alison, you are impulsive.'

'And you are bossy. But we all have our faults. Please trust my judgement. One night – that's all I ask. I'll have her on a wire and Crowther will be directly outside, and a team of uniforms standing by. She'll apply to get on their books as an escort, then hopefully get the iPad which is on the reception desk and we believe contains the info about clients and models. It won't be that hard. *And* Hannah wants to do it.'

Banham had turned back to Bellizza, and started rubbing cream into her other paw. 'I don't approve, and I don't agree. I think she is too inexperienced. However, as you say, you are SIO, so I won't pull rank.'

'Thank you.'

'Just be kind to this lady when I bring her home.' He ruffled the dog's fur.

'Do I get chicken for my tea, too?'

'Yes, but you can eat yours at the table.'

He turned the dog over and started examining the dried blood on her stomach. 'I think she climbed on top of her mistress to protect her when Annabelle had something made of glass smashed on her. There are tiny cuts on her delicate pink tummy. Poor lady, she deserves some TLC.'

'Don't we all. Strange name, isn't it? Bella's quite common for dogs but I've never heard Bellizza.'

'She was obviously well loved. That was proved by the fact she tried to save her mistress and then ran out barking for help. A dog gives back threefold, did you know that?'

'No. I prefer cats.'

He turned back to her. 'I am going against my better judgement letting you put Hannah undercover,' he told her. 'So, you owe me.'

'I'll cook the chicken,' she said. 'Well, I'll heat it up.'

He shook his head. 'Not enough. I want to save this beautiful lady from Battersea Dogs' Home. Give her a home and a lot of love.'

Alison scratched her head. This was the last thing she needed right now. 'Yes, fine. But she's your responsibility.'

There was excitement in his voice as he turned back and said to the dog, 'You are coming home with us, Bellizza. We are going to be a family.'

Alison walked out of the office, although, she felt a tinge of jealousy. She had to make sure her undercover operation was going to run smoothly. It was a large risk, and deep down, one she wasn't sure she should take.

Chapter Eighteen

Crowther had been told he was to check and recheck that Hannah's wire was working after Alison had fixed it to her clothing, and then never be further than a few yards away from her. Hannah had said she felt safe with Crowther, though she'd refrained from telling Alison she also found him desperately attractive. She had been home and changed. She was now wearing a very short red skirt and a black-leather jacket with the collar turned up. She had carefully over-made-up her face, covering her scars, gluing on false lashes, and adding a thick layer of red lip gloss. She had curled and brushed her hair. It hung seductively around her shoulders. She couldn't wear a low-cut neckline because of the microphone, so had chosen a boat-neck top in clingy black nylon; the edge of her lacy black bra showed over the neckline. Black fishnet tights completed her look. She was satisfied she looked like a tart, but also felt a little apprehensive about what could go wrong.

She was in the women's room at the station putting finishing touches to her make-up when Alison walked in.

'Wow. You look perfectly tarty!' She grinned. 'I am going to wire you – I should probably wire Crowther, too, only with rope to keep his hands to himself when he sees you looking that hot.'

Hannah blushed, Alison noticed. 'I'll be at the back of the agency, in a car, and, literally, one minute away,' she told her. 'Crowther will be outside by the entrance. We will both have access to your mike and will hear everything that goes on.' She paused and looked at Hannah. 'I have told Crowther what you told me about working there. It might come out when you're talking to Oluwa, so it was best to pre-warn him. I told him you applied there for modelling work as a student. They asked you to be an escort and you walked away. I am sure you now know he is very trustworthy. He won't breathe a word to the others.'

'He's very astute, too. He'll know I went on dates,' Hannah said.

'He's not a mouth,' Alison assured her. 'Nothing we tell him would he repeat. Which is why I put you with him. He will be a mere step away. If it looks as if they suspect anything, or anyone threatens you, or it is not working in your favour in any way, you leave, and sharpish, got it? No heroics.'

Hannah nodded. 'Yes, ma'am.'

'I've put my neck on the line with the DCI for this, because I think this is a good idea, for the case, certainly, and for you as a detective. Don't let me down.'

'No, ma'am.'

'We urgently need this Madara's details. We also want a list of their past and present clients, models, and escorts, if you can. Suss where their lists are kept and photograph them. If you can't do that, then grab that iPad on the desk and walk out, but only as a last measure, and only when it's safe. Talk to any of the escort girls if you can. Who knows what any of them know? If Oluwa offers to take you on, you need to persuade him to let you sit it out in the office for the first night, and watch and learn. Tell him you want to see the clientele coming and going, anything, but stay in there. Ask any women who are working if they knew Annabelle or Danielle, and if any remember Madara. If they do, find out if they know where she lives. Should you get bought for the evening, then, as soon as you walk out of the agency, we will arrest you and the date for prostitution.'

Again, Hannah nodded.

'All this may not happen tonight. We may have to send you back tomorrow. Rome wasn't built in a day, but let's hope we *can* do it in one. First, you have to talk your way on to their books, and try and stay in reception so you can photograph the iPad details. Then we'll weigh up the pros and cons of letting it go on. If he asks for an address for you, don't give them one, say you're sleeping on friends' sofas as you lost your job. You give them this mobile number.' Alison handed her a phone. 'Which we will have as well. The wire is minute, and I'm pinning it inside your bra, but still don't undress further than your jacket. There's an earpiece, too. It's tiny and goes right inside your ear. We can talk to you through that. You can talk to us, but only talk if you are in danger, or repeat something important that we have to know.'

Hannah pushed the bud into her ear and Alison checked, then tested, it.

'You take a taxi, and we'll be there when you get there.' She looked straight into Hannah's eyes. 'You'll be very safe, but you must follow my orders. Any problem, no heroics, you leave.' She patted Hannah's shoulder. 'I have every faith in you. Good luck.'

'Thank you. Let's hope I don't need it.'

'He'll jump at the chance of signing you up. You look terrifically tarty.'

Hannah relaxed at that. 'I hope that's not a compliment!'

Alison grinned. 'I know Crowther's tongue will be hanging out.'

Hannah watched as Alison walked back out of the door. She felt lucky. Alison was a great boss, and as for Crowther, she knew she couldn't be in safer hands. He reminded her of Dennis the Menace, wild black hair standing on end and a grin like a naughty schoolboy, but so clever, and somehow madly attractive. She had asked her ex-fiancé, Peter Byfield, to give her space. She didn't want a man in her life, or any ties, after the ordeal she had been through. She'd told him she needed to find herself again, but Peter wasn't letting go. He still rang her daily. He wouldn't give up. She no longer wanted a relationship, however, a fling, she thought to herself, with Crowther, might be just what the doctor ordered for her confidence. Maybe this tarty outfit would do the trick.

★

Crowther was waiting outside as she left the cloakroom. He made no mention of the fact that Alison had told him she had worked at the agency many years ago.

'How are you feeling?' he asked, looking her up and down and drinking in the outfit.

'Fine.' She smiled. 'Confident, knowing you will be very near.'

He held her eyes and grinned. 'The slightest hint of trouble and I'll be in the door. There's a team scattered around the street as we speak. Rest assured, you are safe.' He smiled, then winked and added, 'And if I was buying, I'd definitely choose you.'

She blushed, not knowing whether it was a compliment or a dig at her past.

He noticed. 'Meant as a compliment,' he said, then, 'If I hear you in any kind of altercation in there, I'll come in, posing as a customer. I'll ask for Madara. Say I had her a few years back and was she still around? Incidentally,' he said, pulling that little-boy-lost grin, 'you do look very fanciable.'

'And you do, too,' she said, looking him in the eye.

'Is that right?' he said, giving her the gentlest of winks.

'I'm coming with you,' Banham told Alison as she pulled her jacket from the back of her chair. 'No point in sitting at home, waiting for you to come back. I'm waiting for forensic reports back on Bellizza. I'll leave her here, in the crate the vet lent me, in your office. I'll leave the light on for her. Stan says he'll let her out for a pee, and Steph said she would, too. I sent out for some chicken. She loved it. She's wolfed it all down. She wouldn't eat earlier, but she was obviously hungry. We'll pick her up later, and get some more chicken on the way home.'

Alison shrugged. 'You're the boss,' she said, then grinned and added, 'No, I'll rephrase that: Bellizza is.'

'Well, I still don't agree with your decision to put a trainee detective in danger,' he told her. 'She's been through a lot already.'

'Exactly my point,' Alison argued. 'She *has* been through a lot,

128

and has proved herself. She doesn't panic. She deals with a situation as it arises. She's going to make a great detective. And I want to help her get there.'

'You also want to move up the ladder yourself, and it will help if you crack this case,' he told her. He put his arm around her and pulled her into him, then kissed the top of her head. 'I've told you before, you often move before you think.'

She looked at him, the flare in her grey-green eyes telling him he had said too much.

'After we have done this observation, you and I will talk further about this, on professional grounds,' he told her, now holding her gaze. 'I put my head on the block here for you.'

She stared back at him. He was a clever detective and everyone respected him. But she didn't think he would speak to any other detective inspector the way he spoke to her, just because they were a couple. Pulling rank. She also knew that despite what he said, he still wanted her to take a break from the force and have his baby. Maybe this dog was a good idea. She would keep her fingers crossed it wasn't suffering from smoke inhalation and wouldn't have to be put down.

She watched him bend down and address the dog. 'You'll be all right, sweetheart,' he said gently. 'You're safe now. We are going to look after you. We're coming back later. We'll leave the light on, in case you get frightened. Stan or Stephanie will take you for a wee, and we'll have some more chicken later.'

'Do you really believe she knows what you're saying?' Alison asked him.

'Yes,' he said, ushering her out the door and closing it gently and quietly behind them. 'You can read a dog's eyes.'

Crowther and Hannah were standing outside the station waiting for the taxi. She was aware he was staring at her.

'I'll be fine,' she told him. 'I've been through a lot worse.'

'I know you have. I'm just taking in the view.' He pulled his mouth into a small smile. 'I'm allowed to look.'

She smiled back, holding eye contact. 'I look like a panda with all this heavy eye make-up, and as for the miniskirt . . .'

'Yes, as for the miniskirt –' he grinned – 'it's hard to know where to look. You look gorgeous, even with too much make-up on. It's those big grey eyes that appeal to me. The legs ain't bad either. Do you ever hear from Peter Byfield since you broke off the engagement?' he asked casually.

'Yes. We're still good friends. He knows I'm back here, working again. He rings nearly every day. Actually, I wish he wouldn't.'

'Tell him not to.'

'He won't take no for an answer. Wants to know what I'm up to, all that. I just want space.'

'Don't tell him you're working undercover,' Crowther told her quickly and sternly, his attitude changing immediately. 'You tell no one. No matter who. That's a rule. I know he's one of us, but you never say anything. Do you understand?'

'Yes. No, I haven't, and I won't.'

'Will you be talking to him again?'

'For sure. He keeps ringing. He doesn't get it that I changed after what happened.'

Crowther nodded. 'Your taxi's here,' he told her, indicating the black Mercedes that had pulled up in front of them. 'Good luck. The driver's one of ours. He knows to take his time. I'll be there when you arrive. I'll be outside, and less than a minute away.'

She put her fingers to her sticky red lips and blew him a tiny kiss.

He watched her get in the car, then hurried round to the CID parking.

'Good evening, what have you got for us?' Stephanie asked, as the Forensics lab's number lit up her mobile screen.

'Dog is called Bellizza Perry, apparently.'

'Yup, and . . .'

'The blood found on her coat is a match to Annabelle Perry's DNA. The paws are singed, and we found drops of brandy on them.'

Steph glanced across at Luke as she repeated what Forensics were saying. Luke raised his thumb.

'And there's more,' Steph said as she listened, and repeated to Luke. 'The water inside the wellington was tested again. It wasn't from a drain or a puddle. It's some kind of purified water. How come?'

Luke started writing notes.

'Definitely not London water. That's strange, very strange. Thank you.' She clicked the phone to off. 'Where do we know that's got purer water than London?' she asked. 'We know there are stinging nettles on the pizza sign, it was found near that wood, but pure water?'

'There's a team going down to the woodland tomorrow, see what that turns up,' Luke reminded her.

'They'll hardly find a fountain of pure water,' Steph argued, leaning across her desk and picking up a packet of digestive biscuits.

'Lourdes,' Luke suddenly said. 'It's claimed the Catholic water there cures the sick.'

Steph frowned and shook her head. 'I'm not sure I get that,' she muttered, pulling open the top of the packet of digestive biscuits. 'You think someone wants to be cured of arsonism?'

'I don't know, but I don't know anywhere else.' He paused. 'A pub. There's a pub near there. They would have water filters, I'll bet.'

'Bring it up at the morning meeting,' she said. 'You can buy water filters in any department store. Perhaps someone tried to wash the sign, and used a jug with filtered water.' She threw the packet of biscuits onto his desk. 'Help yourself to biscuits. I'll make us coffee.'

Chapter Nineteen

Hannah stepped out of the car, flicked the rain, as it fell, from her jacket and walked through the door to the agency. She consciously put a strut on, and walked up to the reception desk.

Nothing much had changed. Camilla, as ever, was behind the desk, wearing a large costume ring on her little finger. There were three pretty and overly made-up girls sitting on the black-leather sofa, where she remembered sitting, under pictures of half-dressed models. Hannah knew the girls had been called in to wait for men that rang for a girl. They would be sent to wherever the man on the phone had instructed. Proof indeed that the escort side of the agency was still thriving.

Camilla looked up. 'Can I help?'

Hannah blinked her false eyelashes. She felt an immediate urge to rip them off, they were irritating the hell out of her. 'You obviously don't remember me,' she told Camilla. 'I worked for you, very briefly, as an escort, but it was years ago. I'm here because I'm in debt and need to earn money quick. Can I sign up again?'

Camilla looked at her, then, after a couple of seconds, said, 'Wait there, I'll get the boss.'

The second Camilla moved into the back room, Hannah took in the iPad on the counter, then looked up and around for cameras. When she saw none, she turned to the girls. 'Hi,' she said. 'I'm hoping to join you. Are you waiting for a date?'

The three of them seemed friendly. They all said they were.

'I'm sort of out of practice,' she said. 'Have you been doing this long?'

Two said no, and the third said she had been doing it on and off for ten years. Hannah's ears pricked up. Although she didn't remember the woman from her own brief time at the agency, the woman would likely remember Annabelle and Danielle, maybe even Madara.

'I used to work with a Slovakian girl, actually, she might have been—' Hannah immediately stopped talking as Oluwa Marconi came out from the back room. He glared at her, then looked her up and down, in a manner that Hannah would have liked to have kicked him for. She remained silent.

'Come through,' he said after a second. The same second the phone on the reception desk rang, and Camilla walked back to answer it. Hannah knew it would be a call for an escort. She hoped the girl that had been working there for ten years wouldn't be sent. She was more than keen to talk to her.

'I remember you,' Oluwa said as he offered her a seat in the back office and spoke in a cold tone. 'My memory tells me you were frigid. You earned us no money, just a lot of aggravation.'

Hannah heard Crowther laugh in her earpiece. Then Alison's voice telling him to shut up. She brought her attention quickly back to Oluwa, feeling comforted by their voices.

'I'm older and wiser now,' she told him, 'and I desperately need money.'

His cold black eyes pierced into hers. 'You're hardly model packaging, but you have big breasts.'

He looked her up and down again. She felt a strong urge to kick him in the balls, but kept silent.

'You want to earn quick money, well, you know what you have to do to earn it.'

'I presume we're talking prostitution.'

'We don't use that word.'

'But that's what it is.'

'My clients, as you will remember, are all top class and famous.

133

We have to be very discreet because of that. So, it is a matter of a very nice dinner, and then agreeing to their requests.'

'Which is prostitution by any other name.'

He sneered. 'You can earn big bucks if you don't mind the kinky clients.'

'Big money interests me, but what kind of kinky?'

'We have very rich perverts on our books.'

'Can you be more specific?'

He rolled his eyes. 'I thought you said you were wiser these days. They like different things. Some get off on nearly strangling you while they wank. Others will whip you. Walk on you. Wank in your face. They'll pay well for it. You need money. That's how you earn it.'

'Je-sus,' she heard Crowther say. 'I'm right here, my friend, keep pressing him.' Then he laughed quietly. 'Not literally, though.'

She felt the urge to smile at that remark, but concentrated on her task. 'I read about those murdered women. I met them here. Were they still working for you?'

'Slow down, darling,' Crowther whispered in her earpiece. 'Gain his trust, don't lose it.'

He shook his head dismissively. 'No.'

'I'm willing to do what your clients ask. But I don't want to end up dead.'

He shrugged. 'You have to take care of yourself,' he said. 'I'm not your bodyguard. I'm here to make money, too. We have a good source of any drugs you need, recreational, whatever. Coke is good. It'll get you through a bad night, and the next day you'll be rich.'

'Which clients pay the most? Can I see photos? And do I get a list to pick from?'

'You will go with who I say, and you will do whatever they ask you to do. That is how we both make money. Is that clear?'

'Say yes.' This was Crowther whispering again.

'It's clear. Yes,' she said immediately.

His dark eyes bore into hers. 'You have scars on your face. You didn't have those before, so life hasn't been that good to you.'

Hannah blushed with anger. Crowther must have sensed it. His voice came again in her earpiece. 'Stay calm, darling. Ask him again to tell you more about his clients.'

'No,' she said. 'Exactly why I need the protection of an agency.'

'So, you have been on the game?'

'Yes.'

'On the streets?'

'Yes.'

He glared at her again, then shrugged and said, 'I told you, you look after yourself. Some clients are more warped than others, but the more they want, the more you charge. All up to you.'

'You say they're all high up in their jobs. You don't mean pilots, so who? Film stars? Actors? Politicians?'

'Yes. That sort of thing.'

'Who, for example?'

'You ask a lot of questions. I'm putting you on trial. If you upset anyone or become picky, then you're out. Got it?'

'Can I just choose for my first outing?

'No. They choose you. You've been on the game; you know the score. Some are fat. Some can't get it up. Some will enjoy hurting you. Whoever wants you, I will sell you to them. That is how it works. We have nurse's outfits, French maid's, rubber crotchless knickers.'

She tried not to show her revulsion but he obviously picked up on her reaction. 'They ask for things like that. Recently, I had to go and buy a mermaid's outfit and a can opener.' He smiled and showed a gold tooth at the side of his mouth. 'How weird is that?'

'Fuck me,' Crowther said, and laughed again in her ear.

'Shut up, Crowther,' Alison told him from her microphone to his earpiece. 'Concentrate on the job.'

'Who likes to hurt their date?' Hannah asked.

'Listen. You said you were up for it. You want this work or not?'

'You noticed my scars. I've had a few beatings. I'm being cautious.'

'We have top gear, any drugs you want. You won't know what you did. The spice is excellent. I have a very good source.'

'Do they tell you what they like, and want, before we go out?'

'Some we know, and charge accordingly. Others you charge as they ask. Then you tell us, and we take our cut. Never try to forget to tell me what they paid, because I will find out, and any girl who tries to rip me off gets a very severe punishment. Understand?'

'Yes,' Hannah said as Crowther said quietly, 'Noted.'

'You will sit it out tonight,' Oluwa told her. 'And I will see what comes in. You will earn no money tonight. Tomorrow, you will have clients. Got it?'

'Oh, OK,' she said, feeling relieved that this was going their way, but trying to sound disappointed.

'Well done, you're doing great.' This was the voice of Crowther in her earpiece. 'Sitting it out is great. I don't have to break a hotel door down and haul you out of anywhere. Not that I wouldn't.'

Her tummy took a little turn at the thought of Crowther being heroic.

Alison's voice then came in her ear. 'Opportunity gained,' she said. 'Well done. So, you talk to the other women. Try and find out about Madara. Push for names of clients. Try and photograph his list of clients, and if worst comes to worst, just steal the iPad. Then that's it, job done. We can pull you out.'

'Can I sit and chat with the other girls while they wait?' she asked Oluwa.

He shrugged. 'Be my guest,' he said dismissively. 'It's going to be a long night.'

Burning this bitch has proved harder than imagined. Three times I've tried, and either a neighbour or that wretched child gets in the way. The helmet helps, but I didn't have it on all the time, and it's getting to a point where I could be recognised. I don't suppose it matters who else goes up with her, as long as she does. But the child is a worry. So, there is going to be a change of plan. It's not safe to hang around in the dark waiting to burn the gaff anymore. She has to go, no doubt about that. So, go she will. Nothing will be solved if she doesn't. But time's running out.

She works, not far from her flat, in the local launderette, and she does the odd night shift, finishing in the middle of the night. A cover for the drug exchanges, we well know. She takes the quick route home, which means the alleyway. Tricky – anyone could enter at any time, and she'd have to be a long way in to be sure the deed isn't seen by anyone walking past. But it's a quiet time and there's a patch behind a tree in there, that'll work a treat. I'll silence her first, of course. It's chancy, but then isn't the whole of this operation? So far, though, no one has a clue.

Tonight's her late shift and it's pissing down with rain, so anyone who has to be out in the middle of the bloody night will be hurrying along to get to their destination. Umbrellas will be up and no one will really be noticing much with their hoods up. She'll be bound to take the short cut home, because of the wind and rain, so tonight's the night.

The bike's parked up, round the corner. Clever thinking: nicked an advertising board from the fried chicken shop, just in case anyone had noticed a pizza sign before.

The hammer's in my hand. Very heavy, too. Only need one hard crack

137

if I come at her from behind and smash it into the back of her skull. Can't fail. It did the Perry bitch in, so she could burn quietly. Once this one's down, I'll drag her behind the tree, then a few more heavy whacks and she's a goner. If anyone comes up the alley while I'm whacking her, I'll just make a dash over the fence. Unlikely, though, in this heavy rain. I've got the helmet on, so no one would recognise my face. I'm not stupid. By the time I've whacked her face in, it'll be bloodied pulp and it'll take longer to recognise her. Chances are high she's in the country illegally anyway, so who'll give a fuck? She won't have time to scream. Twenty seconds at most, job done, and then I leg it.

The rain is heavy, and the clock is ticking like a fornicating dog. The odd shout from a wet cat, indicating the night has set in. I'm here and ready, behind the wide tree, halfway up the alleyway, pinned against the fence. Fucking uncomfortable, but have to stay as flat as I can. If anyone is unfortunate enough to come into the alley at the same time, I'll have to either stay here, out of sight, and abort the plan yet again, or kill that fucker, too. They'd only have themselves to blame. This job has to be done and that's the end of it.

Ah! She has just entered the alleyway. I can hear my heart beating like it's thumping against a brick wall, but my luck's in. They say Lucifer looks after his own. No one has followed her in, and I am seconds away.

My hands feel slippery. They're damp. A cross between the rain dripping from my bare wrists to inside the black leather gloves, and the sweat which is leaking from my palms. But I can't think about that. She's almost here, and still no one's behind her. My mission's almost complete. And the rain will clear away any evidence. It's finally my lucky day. Fucking umbrella she's holding might get in the way, but here we go.

I am on her. A heavy swing with my arm and the hammer hit the umbrella. She's fucking screaming. Shut up, noisy bitch. Again, I smash her, and yes, now she's stumbling. Trying to turn her head. Another swing and I hit her side on. Down. She's fucking down. Her head has stayed twisted. Christ, what an ugly cow. And she's fucking bleeding. That'll do her, she'll bleed out now. I'm dragging her. We're behind the tree. Still no one around. Mission complete. I'm heading for the next fence and out of here. Just a quick glance back. Oh, Christ, her legs are moving. She's not fucking dead? Oh, Christ, no, not completely.

Down comes the hammer again. Oh. Bloody missed. Slippery as fuck, in this rain. I need to get a move on. If someone comes into the alley, I can run, but she won't be done. She'll get taken to hospital and I'll never get to shut her up. OK. Plan B, boot in and lean on her face. Bones making a strange cracking noise, all good. I'm stronger than I thought. And yuck, there's blood spurting from her like a leaking watering can. And the noise she made. Sent a shiver right down me, of disgust. But it's stopped now. Means she's a goner. Or is she? She looks so deformed now; she could earn herself a job in the circus.

Must be sure. Still no one around. Definitely my lucky day. The only noise I'm hearing is my own heart, beating like a trapped fucking bird. Expecting a cuckoo to pop out of my chest any fucking second and tell me the time. Blood has stopped spurting too. Good sign. She's definitely dead. But there's lots of blood leaking into the alley. It looks like an abattoir here. And the noises she made sounded like a dying animal. Anyway, rain'll clear all the blood, but I must get a move on now. I've had the coke and the spliff, and the other stuff, gotta keep my wits about me.

I'm looking down the alley all the time. Still no one around. My lucky night. This was a complete success. Looks like the Red Sea has erupted. Joke. That sea isn't really red, but this flood here is. I am out of here. I'm over the next fence, just in case I meet anyone coming in. Bike's just there, all waiting. I'm feeling very, very proud of myself. Job's done, and well done at that. When this coke wears off, I will treat myself to a lot more. I've earned it. Whoops, nearly tripped as I landed from the fence in my hurry to get out of there. Keep it together, can't get sloppy now.

Chapter Twenty

'I've blown the picture up. It's the size of the screen now,' Luke told Steph as they sipped their coffees and Steph opened yet another packet of digestive biscuits. He clicked on the screen. Immediately the photo of the three women and the man's arm around them – with the gold signet ring in full view – glared back.

'Nothing too unusual about the ring. Plain gold with a large tiger's eye protruding from the centre. There's millions like that,' Luke said.

'Look closer at the hand,' Stephanie told him.

'Normal size. But definitely a man, I'd say.'

'Print copies of the photo for ma'am, and the others,' Steph told him. 'Uniforms are going to search the wood near Apple Tree Close tomorrow, see where that leads us. More urgently, we need to trace that Slovakian woman. I'm going to get on to Slovakia, see if Interpol can trace her.'

'If, indeed, Madara is her name,' Luke said.

'If indeed. We'll send Baz and a team of uniforms out visiting all the Slovakian restaurants, cafes, and clubs in West London with that photo, so we'll need a good few copies of it.'

'It's a few years old,' Luke reminded her. 'The woman may well have changed a lot.'

'It's better than nothing.'

'I've printed out that other list, too.' Luke handed it to her. 'Every single motorbike club, and all their members in London and the surrounds.'

'Well done you! So here's our next task. We'll go through them, as most of the team are out on the obbo with our trainee detective tonight and it's going to be a long night. Tomorrow we'll phone each and every one of them, ask what make their bike is, and ask where they were on the evenings of the two arsons. Have you got Del Harris on that list?'

'Yup. He's registered with a Putney club.'

'I don't like that man one little bit. I've got a bad feeling about him. See what you can dig up on him. I've got to take the guv'nor's dog out for a pee. Shall I get us a Chinese takeaway while you start all that?'

Crowther had been listening to Hannah talking to the other women. The one who had been there on and off for ten years had gone out with a client and Hannah hadn't seen her since, but others had arrived. Crowther was impressed with Hannah's work. She had asked the women about any weird clients and famous ones. He knew she was pushing to see if Christopher Burton's name came up, without actually mentioning it, but it hadn't. She was going to make a great detective. She had ridden a very bad hurdle at a very early stage of policing.

Peter Byfield then came into Crowther's mind. Hannah had broken off their engagement but Byfield was still phoning her daily. That bothered him. He was responsible for Hannah and he liked her. They worked well together. She had strength of character, she listened and learned, and she was ambitious and brave. She could do very well. Byfield should know to give her the space she had asked for. When she had come back to work after a very traumatic experience which had left her face scarred, DCI Banham had taken the precaution of sending Byfield on attachment to Chelsea, to give her the space she needed, but Byfield hadn't taken the hint. Crowther flicked through the numbers in the index on his phone. He had Byfield's mobile number in there, he had taken it at the time of the incident. He found it. He took his earpiece out and turned it to *off*, then pressed green on his phone.

Byfield picked up after a couple of rings.

'Crowther here, Sergeant Colin, remember me, mate?'

'Of course,' Byfield answered. 'Hannah is working in MIT with you. Nothing wrong, I hope.'

'Not from our end, mate,' Crowther's tone was curt. 'Hannah's doing well.'

'So, to what do I owe the pleasure of your call?'

'As I say, mate, nothing wrong with Hannah. Except she needs space.' Before Byfield could answer, Crowther spoke again. 'None of my business, in one way, and all my business in another.'

As Byfield started to speak, Crowther raised his voice and spoke over him. 'So, a bit of advice coming your way. Back off, mate, she needs to get her head together. She's told you enough times.'

The answer was only a beat later coming back, and flatly spoken when it did. 'Thanks for the call.'

'Not meant harshly. Just a nose tap. But you should heed it. How are you doing down there anyway?'

'It's got interesting. I'm on cordon duty as we speak. We've had a murder in an alleyway here, near Earl's Court.'

'Oh, murder figures are on the up around there. Is it gang related?'

'Could be. A night worker found her, and then her young daughter came looking for her. That was the difficult part. Imagine finding your mother broken up and murdered. The victim is a known dealer in the area, apparently. The face was a bit of a mess, but she had ID on her. A Slovakian woman.'

Crowther leaped to alertness. 'A Slovakian woman. Have you got a name?'

'No, sir, I don't. It'll probably be on officers' briefing in the morning, as the victim was in possession of drugs. Her daughter only called her Mama. Heartbreaking, it was. The child's only nine. She was taken to the station and the social are having to look after her.'

'Is the girl at your station still, do you know?'

'Don't know, sir. They lived quite near. She told us her mother

142

had told her not to tell people she was left alone. She knew her mother worked nights in a launderette. The murder team here are at the launderette. Something interests you here, sir?'

'Yes. I'll get on to the station. Thanks for that. And remember what I said about Hannah.'

Crowther cut the call, and immediately called Alison's personal number. As she picked up, he relayed the news.

'That sounds very interesting. Thanks, Col,' Alison told him. 'I'll get on to them now. Incidentally, why aren't you on the earpiece and what made you phone Byfield?'

'Social call. To let him know Hannah was doing fine.'

'Don't believe you're that nice, but good that you did, whatever the reason. Hannah's doing well in there. Some of the women she's talking to aren't English, but she's hammering away.'

'First sign of trouble, ma'am, and I'll be straight in,' he told Alison.

'I don't doubt it. Oh, and news from Stephanie: there's a uniformed team confirmed for tomorrow to go to the woods near Apple Tree Close. We're looking for a place with water, but not stream or pond water. The water was pure, apparently it contains no mud. Work that one out.'

'Come again?'

'The pizza sign, the one that was handed in after the first attack, had a faint boot footprint on it. The wellington boot found nearby has fibres, from navy-blue pure-wool socks, apparently, and traces of water, but no mud in the water. Water was pure.'

'Poured from a bottle then, sounds like. And wasn't the coke in Annabelle's flat in a navy-blue sock?'

'Yes. They are on that. The puzzle is the water. It hasn't come from around here.'

'So, we're looking for a lake, or a river, that hasn't been near any London earth? Doesn't sound as if that exists, if you ask me, guv. I'd say bottled water. Pick up all the empty plastic water bottles. Always loads tossed around there.'

'Good thinking,' Alison told him. 'So, Nigel and Les are in unit cars up the road, just in case anything goes tits up here. Banny and I are going to drive over to Chelsea nick, he's just said. It could be our missing Slovakian woman. I'm not waiting till it filters through on the daily PowerPoint in the morning, so I'm leaving you in charge here. And there's a uniformed team on standby, round the corner, just in case.'

'All right with you, Col?' Banham interrupted.

'Yes, sir. For sure. I'll be staying here. Even if it's an all-nighter.'

'Whatever you do, stay awake,' Alison told him. 'If she gets caught in there attempting to photograph a client list, anything could happen. Call me if there's any problem.'

'In hand, ma'am.'

Banham was speedily stabbing numbers into his phone. Chelsea's Murder Department picked up immediately.

Alison listened as Banham spoke. 'We think this may be part of our case,' he was saying. 'We are coming over to talk to the child. How old is she?' There was a long silence. All Alison could hear was the person on the other end talking in a loud and aggressive tone. Banham held the phone a few inches from his ear.

'We're on our way over,' Banham told them, then hung up.

'What did they say?' Alison asked as he blew out air and clicked his phone off. 'Who were you talking to?'

'Would you believe, Mr Pomp himself, DI David Drew.'

'Oh, God! Is he SIO on the murder?'

''Fraid so. He was as unhelpful as ever. Wouldn't give us a name. Said the child couldn't be interviewed tonight, she was traumatised, and it was too late. Said she was at the station and they were waiting for the social to come and get her.'

'Tough tits. This could well be part of our case.'

'It's only our case if we can prove it is Madara Kowaska,' Banham reminded her. 'We don't know that, as yet. It was just coincidence that Crowther was talking to Byfield. But let's go. I'll pull rank for you.'

'Of course you will.' Alison smiled, firing the ignition and reversing out of the cul-de-sac she was parked in. 'Because then we will go and get your Bellizza, and take her home.'

'That poor creature has burned paws, shards of glass in her coat, and blood on her fur and stomach. That, too, is part of *our* case,' he reminded her. 'And that evidence must be protected.'

'I know, you said.' Alison smiled.

'It wouldn't be fair to keep her in a crate in a forensic lab for the whole time she is evidence. It could be weeks. She has lost her owner. We're not that heartless.'

'Never let it be said,' Alison replied, pulling a knowing smile. 'We had better stop off on the way back, too, and get that chicken for her. You can pay.'

Chapter Twenty-one

The morning meeting was busy and buzzing. A lot had happened overnight. The team were tired, but all felt things had taken a mighty step forward.

'As you know, last night we visited Chelsea station,' Alison told them. She pointed to the picture on the whiteboard. The victim we coincidentally stumbled across, thanks to Crowther, is confirmed as Madara Kowaska. She had been lifted from the scene, and taken to the morgue; she was practically unrecognisable. She still had drugs and money about her person, so theft wasn't the motive. We were able to check her identification and confirm that she is our third woman. We met the daughter when the social worker came to take her. She spoke little English. She doesn't go to school. She told us Mama brought men back and they made money like that. She gave us her address and her front-door key. The child is in care at the moment, and we are free to search the flat this morning. Everyone's un-favourite DI, David Drew, is heading the case there, but he has agreed, finally, that it is our case and is sending all the details over, this morning. Until then, there is a brief outline of the murder, and pictures of it, on the daily murder briefing on the PowerPoint from their station.'

Alison quickly ran through it. As it finished, she said, 'Photos.' She pinned a photo of Madara with her daughter onto the board. 'The daughter had this picture in her coat pocket. We've established she was born and raised here, though Madara apparently told people her daughter was in Slovakia. The daughter told us she wasn't allowed to tell people things about Mama.'

'Which could mean anything,' Crowther pointed out.

'They found a large amount of cocaine and heroin in a washing bag tied around the victim's waist.'

'The murderer could have been scared off,' Crowther suggested. 'In which case, someone out there must have seen something.'

'We'll be having a press call and notifying every paper,' Banham told him.

Alison looked over at Stephanie, who nodded. 'I'm on to the Slovakian police, ma'am. Seeing what I can find out re family. And Les and Baz are going round Slovakian cafes and clubs with the other pictures, to see if anyone knows, or knew, her.'

'Jonathan Perry told us Annabelle got his drugs from Madara,' Alison reminded the room. 'We found cement powder with the cocaine found in Annabelle's flat. So, was Madara responsible for that? Had she made enemies because of messing with the drugs? We know she was friends with Annabelle Perry and Danielle Low from the photos we found in Danielle and Annabelle's possession. We know they all worked together at this Fabulous escort agency. Hannah, as we know, spent most of last evening undercover there.' She nodded at Hannah to take over.

Hannah stood up from behind the desk she had been given. 'They told you, ma'am, when you visited, that they had stopped operating as an escort agency, but I witnessed the opposite. The place is running a prostitution racket, and from talking to the other women, as well as the owner, drugs are freely available there—'

'So, we know we can hand all that to the drugs squad and get them closed down,' Alison interrupted. 'But first, we need to get more info on anyone in that agency who knew those three victims or was involved with them through the agency. There clearly is a link. I suspect our murderer knew them all through that place. We need their clientele and a list of their models and escorts going back several years. Hannah knows where everything is now. Last night was too difficult as the receptionist never took her eyes off her. She could make conversation with the other women but nothing more, so she's going undercover again tonight and confident she can get what we need.'

'We could get a search warrant,' Banham suggested. 'Save putting our trainee in danger again.'

'We *could*, sir,' Alison answered, sarcasm laced in her reply. 'However, I think we'll get more from Hannah being in the building. She will have strong backup, and we now know there is a list of perverted clients. We must have that. We also need to know the source the drugs come from. I wonder, did Madara tread on someone's territory there?'

'And if we sent a search party in,' Crowther added, backing Alison up, 'Marconi would, for sure, drop his mobile down the loo. He's always in the back with his mobile near him. Hannah reckons there's a lot of stuff on that. Dealers' numbers, for instance. Best Hannah nicks it, and gets out of there. Any trouble, we are right outside.'

'I wasn't able to photograph the contact list last night,' Hannah told them. 'Marconi left at about midnight and didn't come back all night. But now I know more about the place, I am confident I can deliver tonight.'

'Last chance, then,' Banham told her. 'Take the iPad on reception, and his mobile, and then walk out.'

'It's attached to something behind the desk, sir,' she said. 'I'll have to photograph it.'

'Take a cutter in your bag,' Crowther told her. 'If Marconi sees it, tell him it's for your own protection. He believes you've worked the streets. Cut the wire and walk out with the iPad.'

'We now have five victims,' Alison said. 'And we know there is a connection between the three hookers.'

'But not through arson, though, ma'am,' Baz piped up.

'We have got to use everything we can to track this killer,' Alison continued. 'Who knows who is next?'

'Only two hookers were arson victims,' Baz reminded them.

'The Slovakian woman was attacked. Could we be looking for separate killers, or a gang?'

Alison shrugged. 'It's possible. Top priority is talking to everyone and anyone who knew those women during the time the three worked together in that place. I want to talk to Jonathan Perry again, too.'

'Interesting thing was,' Hannah said, 'I saw the name "Mr Harris" written on a piece of paper that one of the escorts had. She was obviously booked to meet him later that night. I know it's a common name, but then it could also be Del Harris.'

'He belongs to a motorbike club, too,' Luke said. 'I ran a check and his name came up, he's part of the club in Putney. I checked his work records this morning. He finished work at Clapham Junction at seven o'clock last night. His mother lives in Putney. Earl's Court isn't too far. Murder happened, they reckon, at around what, two a.m.? He could have been meeting a prostitute after.'

'What time was it when you saw she had the name Mr Harris written on a piece of paper?' Crowther asked Hannah.

'It was late, maybe after three a.m., and I saw a "P" written beside it. I presumed that stood for pervert. Marconi told me there was a list of men who like perverted things and pay well for them. He wouldn't show me the list. He said if I go with any of them, because they're perverts, I'd need drugs to get through it. He told me the agency supply them. I believe they're kept behind the reception area. I will find out for sure, tonight.'

There were a few rude murmurs from around the room about the mention of perverts. Hannah coloured up.

'Shut up!' Stephanie shouted at them. 'You're getting on my nerves. Show some respect.'

'For once, I agree with you,' Crowther said to Stephanie. 'Show some respect!' he echoed to the room.

Alison underlined the name 'Del Harris' on the board. 'Madara was dealing,' she said. 'We know that from Jonathan Perry, who was a user. Annabelle was buying for him, from Madara. Danielle, too, was using, and the agency supply their girls. Did Madara cross the agency by powdering the cocaine down and selling to them? Or was Madara getting her supply from Marconi, and *he's* powdering it down to make more money? And why did *Annabelle* have the cement powder in her flat?'

'I'd like to find out more about that Camilla, and if she dishes out the drugs,' Hannah suggested.

'Talk to her tonight,' Alison said.

'Marconi left the agency last night, we know that,' Crowther said. 'I saw him leave at ten past midnight.'

'Where was he when the other two were burned?' Banham asked.

Alison shook her head. 'That we don't know.'

'I doubt he'd do his own dirty work anyway,' Crowther said.

'Can I talk to Del Harris again?' Stephanie said. 'I really took a dislike to him.'

Alison nodded. 'Talk to Jonathan Perry, too,' she told her. 'And, Hannah, if the woman that went out with this Mr Harris last night is in tonight, find out everything you can about him, and what he looked like. You also need to photograph any drugs you see in there.'

'You also need to keep your eyes peeled for anyone that comes in with a large signet ring on his finger,' Banham said as Hannah scribbled furiously in her notebook. 'Luke will show you a photo of the ring again. This is your last shot at getting inside info. Do you think you can do all that?'

'I'll give it my best, sir.'

'But your safety comes first,' Banham told her.

Luke Hughes had been clicking on his computer, and the printer beside his desk was whizzing. 'I've got more forensic results in,' he interrupted, 'plus the list of all the staff that were working at the George, the pub opposite the first arson.'

'I'll take that,' Crowther said. 'I want to talk to each of them. Get on to the pub and get them all to go there this morning. Make sure you get mobile numbers for all of them. Any of them that can't attend, get their addresses.'

'Will do.'

'Then I'll visit the pizza place again. Get full info on the stolen bikes.'

Luke picked up more papers from his printer and read aloud, 'Shards of glass in dog's fur are a match to the remnants of the glass from the French window which was broken as our murderer entered the building.'

'The dog ran away through there, barking for help when the fire accelerated,' Stephanie said. 'If only it could talk.'

'I think the DCI thinks it can,' Alison said.

'The fact that its stomach was smeared with blood proves it risked the broken shards to run for help for its mistress,' Banham said. 'Brave dog.'

'And aren't we lucky, we are adopting the brave dog!' Alison said, pulling a smile and lifting her eyebrows as she turned to Banham. 'What else?'

'We have a team of uniforms combing the woods near Apple Tree Close, looking for stinging-nettle patches and empty plastic water bottles,' Stephanie told the room. 'Forensics has discovered what they deem as "pure water", on the inside of the wellington boot found. Anyone any idea where you'd find pure water in a wooded area with nettles?'

'Puddles?' Baz shouted.

'Puddles are generally very muddy,' Luke said, shaking his head. 'We're looking for somewhere where there's clean water that you could walk in, at least up to your shin. It was on the inside of the boot. Very little mud was on the outside of the boot.'

'A drain?' someone else suggested.

'Drains aren't clean,' Crowther scoffed. 'Sounds like he washed the boot, and the water dripped inside as he poured, so from a bottle of water – that's purified, isn't it? Bottled water from a shelf, I'd say. Question is, why did he wash the wellington? Answer: because it contained his DNA. Not there now, obviously, but the fact that he did, tells me the wellington was worn by our killer. So, we need to find the other wellington, because he wouldn't just dispose of one. Tell them to bring in all the discarded plastic water bottles that they find,' he told Stephanie.

'Maybe holy water from a church?' Baz suggested. 'Perhaps our killer is religious.'

'Why would you put holy water in your wellies?' Les Mitchell piped up.

'Stay with that thought,' Alison said, shaking her head.

'Perhaps our murderer went to confession first, and took some holy water from the church,' Les suggested.

'It's possible,' Banham said. 'What else?'

'People heard motorbikes driving off at the time of the two arsons,' Alison reminded them. 'Sadly, no one has come forward and mentioned a motorbike roaring off in the case of yesterday's murder. In fact, we have very few witnesses at all, which, even in the middle of the night, seems strange in that area of London.'

'We've yet to get the full notes from Chelsea, though,' Banham told them. 'And Alison and I will be visiting the victim's flat straight after this meeting.'

'The murder of Madara Kowaska wasn't arson. She was beaten with a weapon, as Baz reminded us,' Alison said. 'Baz is right, we shouldn't lose sight of the fact.'

'Although, this latest forensic report states we do have a faint boot print on the woman's face,' Banham added. 'And a faint boot print on the pizza sign, plus that wellington boot. Forensics may be able, if there is enough of an imprint on the face of Madara Kowaska, to tie them all together, with luck on our side. But the fact it was raining will go against us, of course.'

'We have more than one picture of these three women together,' Alison told the room. 'And two of their next of kin have confirmed they were close friends, going back many years. We now know there is a connection to the agency. Coincidence? I don't think so.'

'They are checking CCTV as we speak, and Chelsea have a uniformed team door-knocking around the immediate area,' Crowther told her.

'I've been going through the motorbike clubs around London,' Luke said. 'And I just noticed, Christopher Burton has a membership of one.'

'He's out of the country, and has been for the past few weeks,' Crowther reminded him.

'He has been done for kerb-crawling, though,' Stephanie added.

'It wasn't just kerb-crawling, it was a blow job he was being given in his car in a side road by Westminster,' Luke reminded her.

'By Madara Kowaska, apparently,' Stephanie argued. 'So, clearly he has, or had, a taste for toms.'

'When is he back?' Banham asked.

'I'm in touch with his secretary,' Stephanie told Banham. 'She assures me, as soon as he is back, he will be in touch. Apparently, he's mortified about Annabelle.'

'Interesting,' Banham said.

'Jonathan Perry had a membership with a motorbike club, too, but doesn't own a bike, or belong to a club anymore,' Luke read from his paper.

'But he can still ride one,' Alison pointed out. 'And probably could steal one, too. He fell out with his sister. And he's an addict.'

'Why would he want to murder the other two?' Crowther asked.

'Let's ask him,' Alison said. 'Get his alibis. What about the pizza-delivery drivers, Col?' she asked. 'There have been two motorbike thefts from there this month.'

'They've both been alibied,' Crowther told her. 'Times of deliveries match. We have the chit for the order coming in, and the exact time the first boy, Joseph, left the shop. Second delivery lad, Anthony, went out to help when Joseph was hassled. We've picked them up on CCTV around that area, at the time they said they went, and the time they came back: they match. Both had texts on their phones from the boss, telling them to go home. This was all before the fire started. And the George pub opposite Danielle Low's street gave us their CCTV footage. It shows the owner of the pizza gaff, Johnny Walsh, locking up the shop at around the time he said, and driving off in his car in the direction of his home. They're in the clear for Danielle Low.'

'That pizza-shop sign was handed in,' Stephanie reminded Crowther.

'Anyone could nick that off the door. Neither of the stolen motorbikes have turned up,' Crowther told her. 'I'm going round there to get full descriptions and put it out to Traffic. If we can find even one of them, it'll tell us a lot. I'm also keen for us to find the woman that brought back that pizza sign, and ask where she found it.'

Banham nodded. 'Good. We'll mention that in the TV appeal later this morning. And can someone get a map drawn up of the area surrounding all the murders? Let's see if there are any churches in the vicinity, especially Catholic ones. If there are, get samples of the holy water from them. See if we can match that water. Baz could be right; our murderer may be a regular there.'

'Did anything turn up on Danielle's computer, do we know yet?' Alison asked Luke.

Hannah took an intake of breath, and blushed.

Luke shook his head. 'Nothing, guv.'

'Alison and I will talk to Madara's daughter again this morning,' Banham said.

'OK, let's get on,' Alison said. 'We all know what we're doing. Let's find this killer, or killers.'

'What shall I do?' Hannah asked.

'Stay here and help DS Green. You may be working all night again,' Alison told her.

'And, as you're staying here, you can keep an eye on the dog,' Banham told her.

Alison rolled her eyes at that.

'Her name is Bellizza,' Banham said. 'She is very sad, and missing her owner.'

'She's tied up in my office,' Alison told her. 'Take her out for a wee, but only a short one. We want to keep any evidence on her intact.'

'Yes, ma'am, I am happy to, but with respect, I would rather work. I'm OK. I'm not tired.'

'She can come with me,' Crowther spoke quickly. 'If you get tired, you can have a kip in the back of my car.'

'Oh, that's straight to the point,' Baz scoffed. 'Wear the gear for tonight, will you?' he teased Hannah.

Stephanie threw an angry glance at Baz. 'You've got a mind like a sewer,' she told him. 'I expect respect and professionalism from you. I'm fed up with you and Crowther's sexist remarks.'

'I haven't said a word!' Crowther argued.

'Hannah can curl up in the back of your car?' Stephanie said accusingly. 'She's not a pet cat. Treat her with respect.'

'Enough!' Alison shouted. 'Get on with it, all of you. I want details and accounts of everything by the evening meeting. We've all got lots to do. We need to bring this in. Another woman may be in danger, for all we know. Anyone thought of that?'

Hannah blinked. That thought hadn't occurred to her. She was around, working as an escort, at the time the three murdered women were. Maybe someone was killing off all the escorts from those days? If so, why? Was it possible she was in danger, too?

Chapter Twenty-two

There was chemistry between Crowther and herself, Hannah was sure. Hadn't he taken it upon himself to phone Peter last night and tell him to back off? Didn't that prove there was more than a professional concern towards her? And, for sure, it was mutual.

As she was assigned to the investigation room for the morning, she sat behind her desk and checked every name on the list of motorbike-club members that Luke had given her. She wanted to write a list of potential suspects who could ride motorbikes. Jonathan Perry had ceased his membership seven years previously. He no longer owned a bike. But, if he'd had a licence, then for sure he could use a motorbike. She put a tick against his name and another one next to Christopher Burton. The MP was out of the country, but he, too, could ride a motorbike. The two delivery drivers, Joseph and Anthony, weren't registered with any clubs, but rode bikes, so she added their names to the list. Del Harris, too. He had supposedly been working when the arsons happened, but had finished work in enough time to not have a clear alibi – apart from his mother, so she added his name.

She pondered over the list. Two bikes had been stolen from the pizza shop, and witnesses had heard motorbikes drive away from two of the murders. Coincidence? She didn't think so. Del Harris had his own bike, and a 'Mr Harris' was on the list of men wanting escorts for last night. Harris was a common name, though, and she knew clients rarely used their real name.

It was getting on for lunchtime when the call came from

Christopher Burton's secretary to say that, having heard the news of Annabelle Perry's death, Burton had got a flight back and was heading straight for the police station, to come in and help with their inquiry.

'He's keen,' Luke said. 'Obviously very close to Annabelle.'

'And we know he likes toms,' Stephanie added, turning to Hannah. 'Would you like to sit in on the interview? It'll be good experience. You say very little, but take it all in.'

'Thank you.'

Burton was a good-looking man, average height, fair hair thinning a little at the crown. Probably early fifties, Hannah hazarded a guess. She had seen him before, on parliamentary programmes and on the news, but never in person. He was impeccably dressed in jeans, a designer and tailored jacket, over a white shirt. He was handsomely tanned, wore an expensive watch, and sported a fresh haircut. Hannah immediately noticed his well-manicured hands. He wore a signet ring, but not a wedding ring. His signet ring was discreet, nothing like the one they had seen in the blown-up photos. Hannah thought his eyes looked a bit shifty; too many years as a politician, she told herself.

Stephanie led the conversation. 'Thank you for coming in, Mr Burton, we appreciate how busy you are, and obviously you must be tired after your journey.'

'It was only a short flight,' he told her. 'From my Italian villa.'

'And you were in Mexico too, before that?'

'Yes, I was, but flew on to Italy after. I've got a villa in Ischia. It has a maid in every week, but I wanted to check it for myself.' He smiled a little guiltily as he added, 'And I wanted to grab another three days of sunshine.' Then his tone changed. 'I couldn't believe it when I heard,' he said. 'You know, I know, or knew, the whole Perry family, very well as it happens.' He paused, looked down briefly, then added, 'I was particularly fond of Annabelle. I'm sure you know her father was a fellow MP.'

'Yes, and I'm hoping you can shed some light on Annabelle's

private life,' Stephanie told him. 'We are trying to build up a picture of places she went, people she knew, that sort of thing. What can you tell me about her?'

He hesitated as he held Stephanie's gaze, as if thinking. Then he shrugged. 'I knew her father best, obviously. As you know, we were close colleagues.' Again he hesitated, picking his words carefully. 'And through him I got to know the whole family.'

'We need to know more about Annabelle, and Jonathan, too,' Stephanie pushed. 'We know you knew them well.'

Burton gave a sympathetic smile. 'Annabelle was a wild child, very beautiful, but extremely wild. You'll know she was a model?'

Stephanie nodded. 'I believe her career was on its way out.'

'It's the sands of time, I'm afraid. Modelling careers are short, but she was still very beautiful. That long, wild, gypsy hair and those eyes. She was a stunner. But always hard to handle, according to her parents. A difficult child, and very opinionated.' Again the sympathetic smile. 'I liked her very much.'

'Do you know anything about her use of drugs?'

'No.' He shook his head. 'Annabelle wasn't a user. That was the brother, Jonathan. She may have tried the odd party drug, but that would have been when she was younger.' He shook his head again.

'You seem very sure. You must have known her very well.'

He maintained eye contact with Stephanie. 'I knew the whole family,' he said after a second. 'Annabelle wasn't a user. She didn't like drugs. Jonathan has been in and out of rehab for years. Their father tried endlessly with him. Spent a fortune trying to help him, but it did no good.' He shook his head and lowered his eyes. 'Each time, he came out of rehab clean. All looked well, but he was always back on it within a month. I'm afraid that boy is a junkie.'

'How did they get on, Annabelle and Jonathan?'

'Well.' He paused and looked taken aback. 'You're not suggesting . . .'

'As I say, we're trying to build up a picture of the woman, her friends, the places she visited, who was close to her, all of that.'

'Well, Sergeant, I didn't know her *that* well. Certainly not lately.

158

I knew her more in her youth. David and his wife died tragically, a few years back in a car accident. You may have read about it.'

'And you didn't see much of Annabelle or Jonathan after that?'

'No. Not really.'

'What does *not really* mean?'

'Well, if there was a political party do, they were invited. Sometimes one or the other would come, normally Annabelle. I saw her then. That's it really.' The sympathetic smile appeared again. 'Occasionally, she rang me, if she needed advice. I think she looked on me as a sort of uncle figure, as I was her father's closest friend. And she no longer had her father. But she had a life of her own.'

'What kind of advice did she want your opinion on?'

'Jonathan, mainly.'

'Why you? Do you know a lot about drugs?'

He gave her a cold stare. 'No. As I said, because she looked on me as an uncle figure. I had known them since they were kids. And because I knew the right people, if needed, and because she cared about Jonathan.'

'Yet she inherited her parents' estate, and happily kept the inheritance. She didn't care enough to share it with him.'

'I don't think that's true, but it's between them.'

'Not any more it isn't, she has been murdered.'

'I know she cared for her brother's welfare.'

'Did you have a love affair with her, Mr Burton?'

He looked shocked. 'No. God, no.' Stephanie watched him stumble slightly with his words. 'Whatever made you think that?'

'She had a photo of you in her London flat.'

'I know.' The words seemed to come out before he'd thought them through.

'Do you. How?'

'I visited her there.' He quickly added, 'When she wanted advice about getting Jonathan back into rehab. Whether it was worthwhile . . .' Again he paused. 'To be honest, and you may already know this. I don't doubt you don't.' He rubbed the damp from his top lip with his forefinger, pausing before he spoke. 'The reason

David left everything to Annabelle in his will was not favouritism, but because they knew Jonathan would blow it all on drugs. Annabelle wanted advice on whether to share the money with him, or use what would have been his half to keep paying for rehab. She wanted advice on whether she should let him live at the flat. I advised her to let him stay at the flat whenever he needed it, as it should have been half his, but not to give him any lump sums of money. I agreed that he would blow it.'

'She heeded your advice. She must have trusted you.'

He nodded. 'I like to think she did.'

'How did Jonathan take that?'

'Not well. He fought a lot, wrote all over Facebook that he hated her, and threatened to take her to court. She told him if he agreed to go back into rehab, and then stay clean for at least a year, she would share everything with him. She intended giving him so much every month, but only if he stayed clean.'

'But he didn't?'

'No.'

'Do you think he is desperate enough to commit murder?'

'I would say no to that, but who can say? They had a good relationship until he went off the rails. But there is no telling what a drug addict may do. I certainly hope not.'

'Did Jonathan ever ring and talk to you?'

'No, never. He knew what I would say. I was always on Annabelle's side, and she did all she could, and more, for him, in my opinion.'

'Do you know if Annabelle was seeing anyone special?'

'No, I don't. She didn't mention that to me. Anyway, she always said she was married to her dog. She took it everywhere.'

'If she looked upon you as a sort of second father, she would have told you if she had someone in her life, wouldn't she?'

'Well –' he half laughed – 'I can't really answer that. Probably only if she needed advice.'

'Did you know or meet any of the friends she hung about with?'

He shook his head. 'I was not a social friend, just someone who

160

she could trust and go to if she needed advice. Advice that her father would have given if he was alive. And that is all I can say.'

'She also had photos of a couple of her friends in her London flat.' Stephanie paused, watching him carefully, as she passed the picture of the three women with the man's arm around them across the table. 'It was next to the photo of you. Do you recognise any of these women?'

He shook his head. 'No, sorry. As I said, I didn't socialise with Annabelle, I was just there when she needed advice.'

'You don't recognise that ring, do you?' Stephanie asked.

He looked closely at the photo, then shook his head. 'I wish I could help. Sorry, I don't.'

'I am grateful for your assistance, Mr Burton.'

'Anytime. I am happy to give you all the help I can. I was very fond of Annabelle. I want to see whoever did this to her behind bars. I only wish our laws were stricter.'

Stephanie quelled the urge to remind him he was part of the political party that made the laws. 'Just one more question, Mr Burton,' she said instead, looking him straight in the eye. 'I have to ask you, did you know Annabelle had been a prostitute?'

He looked down at the table, and then up to meet Stephanie's gaze. 'Sergeant, I know you will know this about me, as it made all the national press; I won't try and hide it, and I am certainly not proud. Are you asking me that because I was done for having a whore in my car? You think I was into that scene? I made a very stupid mistake. My marriage was going through a very difficult time. It was something I regret deeply, and the repercussions that it caused for my family and colleagues were horrendous.'

'I'm asking you this to help us find Annabelle's killer.'

He sighed. 'Yes, I did know about Annabelle's escort work. Her modelling career was dwindling, so she started to do escorting. She confided in me about it because she knew about my little indiscretion. I had a quiet word with her father, who I knew wouldn't let it continue. He gave her an allowance and that was the end of that. She stopped.'

161

'How long ago was this?'

'About a year before David was killed.' He squeezed an eye closed thoughtfully. 'She was cross with me at first, but then she realised what I did was right for her in the long run, so I was forgiven and we became friends again.' He looked at Stephanie. 'I hope that mistake won't surface again with her death. Let her secret stay that way.'

'I'm afraid I can't guarantee anything. Our job is to find out who wanted to kill her, and why. Whatever that takes,' Stephanie told him. 'Thank you, Mr Burton. I appreciate you coming straight from your holiday. I'll be in touch if I need to ask you anything further.'

'Do, please. I'm more than happy to help you find her killer. I would just ask you to keep Annabelle's mistake, and mine, from being resurrected in the papers.'

'Oh, and –' Stephanie pretended to glance down at her papers – 'are you a motorbike fan?'

'Gosh!' He laughed. 'A bit past all that. I did have a motorbike once, but that was years ago.'

She held his gaze. 'You still belong to a motorbike club?'

'I pay a membership for my son. I don't ride a motorbike anymore. Nor does he, come to that. Why do you ask?'

'There was a motorbike heard driving off after two arsons, including Annabelle's,' she said dismissively. 'I wondered if you had any connections with the club you pay?'

He shook his head. 'Sorry. Can't help. I don't know why I still pay the membership. My son drives a sports car and lives in France these days. I must remember to tell my wife to stop the payments.'

'Oh and lastly, Mr Burton, are you sure you don't recognise either of the two other women in this picture? Please take a closer look.'

'No, I don't. Should I?'

'Well, quite possibly. This woman –' Stephanie's fat finger stabbed down on Madara's face – 'was the prostitute you were caught with in your car that time you regret.'

Burton looked shocked. 'I'm so sorry, Sergeant,' he said. 'As I said, that was a night I care not to remember. It was a massive, stupid mistake, and as you will also know, it was dark when I very stupidly picked up a prostitute. And I truly didn't look at her face.'

Stephanie stared at his embarrassed expression, clearly trying to embarrass him more, wondering if she should mention his earlier kerb-crawling. 'Thank you,' she said after a few long seconds. 'For coming in. I'm sure we will be in touch. I'll have someone show you out. Do you need a lift?'

'No, thank you. My driver is waiting around the corner. Discretion, you understand.'

'Rightly so,' she said sarcastically.

Chapter Twenty-three

Hannah headed straight into Alison's office, remembering she had been told to take the dog out for a wee. She clipped the new tan-leather lead that Banham had bought to its collar and headed for the front entrance. It didn't seem happy to go. She practically had to drag the dog towards the exit.

'Come on, Bellizza, you must want a pee,' she coaxed. Bellizza reluctantly went with her. As soon as she got outside, she walked along the road, making encouraging noises as Bellizza fought to go back. The poor animal's tail was hanging between its legs; she clearly didn't want to be there. Then, as they turned the corner into a side street, the dog's tail stood erect. Excited barking followed. Then it lunged forward. It had spotted, and recognised, Christopher Burton. Hannah's arm was nearly wrenched from its socket as the dog leaped towards Burton, its tail now in overdrive, wagging like it was a windscreen wiper on double time.

Burton had the car door open and was about to jump in, but had no choice but to stop. He leaned down to pat the excited animal. Bellizza licked his face as if it were an ice-cream cone. Yelps of joy were accompanying the ritual as the dog attempted to follow Burton into his car.

Hannah was taking all this in.

'This was Annabelle's dog,' Burton told her, patting the animal again. 'She recognises me.'

'She's certainly pleased to see you,' Hannah said.

'She's a friendly beast,' Burton said. 'She likes people,' he added as he withdrew his hand and then stepped into the waiting car.

'Well, she certainly knows you well,' Hannah said, half to herself, as she stood watching the car drive off.

Crowther headed into the George pub and found a crowd of the staff sitting, waiting to be interviewed. He spoke, in depth, to each of them. All but one said the pub was noisy on the Sunday, with children and families having lunch. None had noticed, or heard, anything out of the ordinary, until they were alerted by sirens screaming their way up the road. Only one person, Vera Heath, who was a waitress at the pub, said she had popped out for a cigarette break shortly before the sirens sounded and had seen a person walking up the road from a motorbike, dressed in leather and carrying a pizza box.

'I didn't take much notice – there's a pizza shop down the road, so it didn't seem unusual, like.'

The person was wearing a bike helmet, so Vera couldn't describe them. Couldn't even say if they walked like a man or a woman. When Crowther asked her to hazard a guess about their height, she said, 'Average.' Somehow, though, she remembered the registration number of the bike, or at least part of it. Crowther thanked her, told her he might talk to her again, and made his way to the pizza shop.

There were no customers about. The small shop was deserted. Johnny Walsh was cleaning around the cookers. He offered Crowther a pizza, on the house, or a coffee. Crowther refused the pizza but accepted the coffee. He asked Johnny to write down as many details, apart from the registrations, as he already had them, of the two bikes Johnny had recently reported stolen. 'And full details of both the drivers, please, Mr Walsh. National Insurance numbers, how long they've been driving, that sort of thing.'

Joseph was standing in the doorway to the back room, listening.

'It's a small business,' Johnny explained. 'I have my two delivery boys, Joseph and Anthony, and I don't keep records. I pay cash in hand on each drop they do. If there are no orders, they make no money. They still come to work, they're loyal to me. No orders at the moment. It's tough.'

Crowther nodded. 'Write down anything you can about the stolen bikes,' he said. Then he went through to the back. Joseph followed him.

Anthony was there, playing with his phone.

Crowther sat down beside him. 'Tell me everything you remember about the bike thefts,' he asked them both. 'Anyone you saw around before they were nicked. Descriptions, anything that might help me.'

'The one last month went from out the front here. No one saw nothing,' Joseph said. 'It just went. We were all in here at the time, all three of us. None of us heard nothing.'

Crowther looked at Anthony, who nodded his agreement.

'And the second one?'

'From the Walden Estate,' Joseph said. 'It was me. I was delivering. I came out and it was gone. Poof! I was sick as a pig. But it happened.'

'Describe the bike.'

'Standard delivery. Nothing more I can tell you. 'Sides, I ain't done nothing and you're beginning to hassle us.'

Crowther fixed his eyes on Joseph. The lad was a cocky bastard. Crowther decided to cut him down to size. He looked at his trainers, which were thick with mud. 'Blimey, your trainers are muddy,' he said to him. 'Where have you been with them?'

'I walked to work today, OK? No crime in that. We're a bike short, remember? Took the shortcut through the woods up the road. It's muddy in there.'

'Notice anything while you were there, anything unusual?' Crowther asked, knowing there was a uniformed team combing the woods for a wellington.

Joseph shook his head. 'Only that it was very cold,' he said.

Johnny came through with a cup of espresso and placed it in front of Crowther on the table, then handed him a piece of paper.

'Wrote down a description of the bikes that were stolen. I have no details for the boys. Don't be hard on them. They just need to earn.'

Crowther took the piece of paper. 'OK, so would you put a notice in the window now, please? It will read: "Can the woman who returned my sign please call in again". When she does, I want you to take all her details, and tell her we need to speak to her, urgently. Got it?'

'Yeah, no worries. Sorry not to have thought of it myself.'

'Anything else you can tell me about the two bikes?'

'No. You have the registration numbers. My insurance company have been informed. Soon, they won't insure me, or they'll stick it so high I'll go broke with the premium. Bad things have been happening to my business.'

Crowther looked at him. 'Worse things have been happening to those women, a lot worse things, mate,' he snapped, draining his espresso cup. 'Thanks for the coffee. I'll be back.' Then, turning to Joseph, he changed his tone. 'Don't be going anywhere, will you?' he said, aware that Joseph had mentioned walking to work through the woodland, but he made no mention of the fact there was a police team combing it. The waitress in the pub had said she had seen a delivery driver with a pizza box near the flats. Joseph might have been out at that time, and had proof, but Crowther wasn't going to let him get away with that attitude.

Alison buckled her seat belt, and dragged her fingers across her forehead. Banham was in the driver's seat, watching her.

'It doesn't get any easier interviewing the child of a murder victim, does it?' he said. 'Worse when she needs an interpreter and you have to listen to them asking the child about finding her dead mother. You did well in there. It was productive.'

'Imagine losing the only person you have in the world,' Alison said, then, realising the tactlessness of the remark, she quickly changed the subject. 'She said she doesn't have a father, although lots of men come to visit Mama. So, we know Madara was still on the game and selling drugs.'

'OK, so, after lunch, we go to the flat,' Banham said. 'We might find evidence of relatives in Slovakia there.'

'If not, she'll go into care, poor love,' Alison said. 'So sad to be nine years old, and in a country where you speak barely any of the language, and have no relatives.'

'Families are so important,' Banham said.

'You are very taken with that dog, aren't you?' Alison said, hoping he wasn't going to talk about trying for another baby.

'Bellizza? Yes.' He laughed. 'She reminds me of you.'

Alison blinked. She shook her head, lost for words.

'She has your colour hair, or similar. She has gorgeous eyes, and she's very loveable,' he said quickly.

'I'm glad, then, that we are keeping her,' Alison said, moving her body towards him. 'I want you to be happy. Are you?'

'Right now, I'm hungry, so we are going for lunch, and I'm paying.'

'This had better be a nice lunch.'

Stephanie Green walked back into the murder room carrying three large filled baguettes from the canteen. At Stephanie's instruction, Hannah was following, carrying three cappuccinos. She, Luke, and Stephanie were settling down to an office lunch.

Hannah opened a packet of serviettes, pulled three out and then handed one to Stephanie. She had noticed the DS had already eaten half of her baguette and was wiping mayonnaise from around her mouth with the cuff of her denim shirt.

'Is Crowther looking after you well?' Steph asked her, accepting the serviette, and speaking with her mouth full, as she used her other hand to pull the plastic lid from her coffee. She sipped from the cup, leaving a ring of froth around her mouth.

'Yes, thank you. He's teaching me a lot,' Hannah told her, fighting the urge not to laugh.

'Watch him, though, darling. He's a bit of a one for the women.'

'I had heard, thank you,' Hannah answered politely, keeping her own thoughts of seducing Crowther to herself. 'Changing the subject, I took Annabelle's dog for a wee. We bumped into Christopher Burton as he was getting in his car. The dog went insane, racing up to him, full of life, tail wagging, tongue out licking him. It was like a lost soul finding a friend.'

'Knows him well, then.' Stephanie nodded. 'Obviously been around Annabelle's house a lot more than he admits. We're going to chat further to Jonathan Perry, see what he says about Burton.'

'How about we invite Gillian Hillier back in?' Luke interrupted. 'She lived next door; she knows the dog. She might just know Burton's car. Do we know what he normally drives? He had a driver with him so that might have been his work vehicle.'

'Easy enough to find out,' Stephanie pointed out. 'Hannah, you check that one out. I'll check with ma'am, run it all past her.

'Something else I was thinking,' Hannah said, slightly hesitantly.

'Spit it out,' Stephanie coaxed.

'It sounds a bit silly now, but . . .'

'But?'

'That dog is called Bellizza. Sounds a bit Italian, and Burton said he visits Italy often. Just wondered if there was a connection.'

'Probably is. But where would that lead us?' Luke asked her.

'Why would she call her dog after something Italian?' Hannah said. 'There'll be a reason. My mother's got a cat called Chelsea. She says she called it that as she loved her wild teenage days in the King's Road. It crossed my mind that Annabelle may love Italy, and possibly have been there, perhaps with him.'

'Needle in a haystack,' Stephanie told her. 'But your thinking is good. You'll make a good detective. I'll run it past Alison, and ask if we can go talk to Gillian Hillier again. If she says she's seen the car parked there, then we'll get Burton in again.'

Chapter Twenty-four

The one-bedroomed flat that Madara Kowaska had lived in with her daughter was tiny and felt claustrophobic. A double bed took up most of the bedroom, and a small, shabby set of unpainted wooden drawers stood beside it. No pictures on the walls, which were covered with grubby, and dated, flocked wallpaper. The room smelled of mould and was in desperate need of a deep clean. Alison pulled back the dusty green velveteen curtains and opened a window. Then she pulled the drawers out from the chest. All were overflowing. The first contained Durex in all flavours and colours, sex toys, crotchless underwear, fluffy pink handcuffs and another set in metal; another drawer overflowed with black imitation-leather corsets and fishnet stockings. There was a nurse's outfit, a French maid's, and a mortar board.

'Hooker's stuff in here, nothing else,' she shouted to Banham as she shoved the stuff back into the chest and left the room to join him in the tiny adjoining living room.

This room housed a shabby beige Formica table. Two folding chairs were leaned against the wall. Beside them was a tiny child's bed. There were two glass ashtrays on the Formica table, both spilling over with joint stubs, making the room reek of stale cannabis. A bottle of vodka lay on its side, on the top of the only shelf in the room.

'If the daughter stood on a chair, she could reach this,' Banham said, shaking his head. 'Some people don't deserve children.' He bagged the dog-ends in a forensic bag.

Alison walked to the window. The flat was in a Victorian building just off the main Earl's Court Road. The location, which was within minutes of the alleyway where Madara had been murdered, seemed buzzing with people. There were also shops nearby. Alison knew that in this area of West London the shops would be open late, meaning people milled around well into the early hours of the morning.

'Someone must have seen something,' she said as she turned back to the room. 'Her daughter said she worked at the launderette. She was a hooker and a drug-pusher, so the launderette must have been a cover.'

'How could you let your child sleep in this mess?' Banham said, lifting the mattress that covered the tiny bed and feeling underneath it.

Alison knew his murdered baby would have been a teenager by now, and the fact that he had been robbed of the chance to be a father would be playing on his mind. She only hoped he wasn't thinking of adopting the motherless child here. The dog was more than enough.

Banham pulled his hand out from under the child's mattress and shook his head. 'Nothing there, but you're right, someone must have seen something. We'll put it out to a press conference. Someone will come forward.'

'We'll appeal to the fact there is an orphaned child here, alone in London, and in need of closure on this,' she added. She was noticing an edge of the carpet that looked loose. She kneeled down, checked her forensic gloves were clinging to her wrists and fully secure, then tugged at the edge of the carpet until she could force her hand under the carpet edge. She felt a polythene bag, which she retrieved, then another, and a third. 'One large block of hash, and this one's spice,' she told Banham as he moved in to see her pull out the third. 'And look at the cocaine in this.'

'No cement powder,' Banham noted, examining it closely.

Alison pushed her hand back under the carpet to check there was nothing else. She shook her head. 'No, but she was definitely dealing.'

'And we know Danielle was a user.'

'And we know Annabelle bought drugs for her brother, and a little recreational for herself. So, where did her powdered cement come from?'

'Annabelle was rich,' Banham said. 'And Danielle had recently bought her flat.'

'They were all still on the game,' Alison said. 'Danielle's neighbour said she was, as well as a user. Annabelle's flat looked like a hooker's boudoir. This is a tip, but full of gear. Madara was clearly making money, so my guess is, she was sending it back to Slovakia. Hopefully, we'll find relatives there, for the child.'

Banham rubbed his hand across his face in his habitual thinking manner. 'What we need to know is, who was Madara's dealer? Because that powdered cement was meant for someone, and let's say that someone found out. Are we still waiting on results from Danielle's laptop?'

Alison shook her head. 'No. It's a very old model, there's nothing current on it.' She shook her head again. 'Hannah is back in the agency tonight. Let's hope she can get a list of contacts.'

'I'm not happy about this, you know that,' Banham told Alison. 'I think you should get a search warrant and turn the place over. I have bent the rules because it's you.'

'You've bent the rules because you want the dog,' Alison argued. 'You assigned me as Senior Investigating Officer on this case because you trust my judgement. I believe it's the best way to get the client lists from there.'

'I only hope you're right.'

'Oluwa Marconi is insistent he has no back records or list of clients. Hannah knows there is a list, on Camilla's laptop, and probably on his personal mobile. If we get a search warrant it won't help. He'll dump his phone and we'll have got nowhere. Hannah is shrewd and knows the layout. I trust her. She's proved herself in the past. And I've made sure she is safe. Crowther is right outside.'

'I'm still not sure she's experienced enough.'

'I have faith in her. So, have faith in me.'

Banham shrugged. 'Your call. I trust your judgement.'

'Madara's daughter, Paola, wasn't that her name? She said she has no daddy but lots of different men came to the flat. She said there was one who beat her mama, and frightened her. She couldn't remember much about him. So, let's keep looking here. We might find clients' details. Madara didn't have anything on her like a contact list; she had her handbag with money and drugs in it, but no phone.'

Banham had walked through and was now in the tiny kitchen. He reached up to open a cupboard, but as he did, he stepped on something that felt hard underfoot. He bent down and pulled back the corner of the stained and foul-smelling green lino. 'Alison,' he called out as he pushed his hand under the lino, and pulled out an old video-cassette. Written across the back was: *I have another copy of this.* 'This looks interesting,' he shouted again to Alison.

'One minute.' Alison had been turning the bedding over. She found nothing, but then, as she flicked through the uneven rail of clothes that leaned against the wall in the corner of the room, she noticed a supermarket plastic bag hanging inside a raincoat, with an umbrella poking from it. She pulled the bag free from the hanger and then turned it upside down. A handful of old photos fell to the floor, and a dated photo album. She opened the album, and turned its pages, glancing at many different Polaroid pictures.

All the pictures were of Madara in restaurants or bars. All on different days, as her wardrobe differed in every shot and in each one she was with a different man. Alison then pulled at the bunch of photos which had been secured by a half-perished elastic band. Most were yellowed with age, faded, and stuck to each other. 'Taking these back with us,' she shouted as Banham walked into the bedroom holding the VHS cover.

'This could be telling?' he said, showing her the cover. With the words – *I have another copy of this.*

'Does it play?' she asked. 'VHS went out years ago.'

'No tape in it, just the cover with these words,' he said. 'The fact she says she's got another copy says to me there was something worth seeing on it.' Banham then leaned over Alison's shoulder as she rummaged through the loose pictures.

'Stop there,' he said, after a few photos had been looked at. He put his finger on an old Polaroid photo of Madara with a young Annabelle. The corner had been torn off, but there was still the shoulder and arm of a man next to them, and again the ring was the same as the one in the photo found in Annabelle's flat. 'Interesting,' he said. 'This man's arm features a lot. I'd like to know who he is, and if he still wears this ring.'

Alison photographed the picture with her camera, and sent it through to Luke. She followed with a message asking him to get it blown up and on the whiteboard by the evening meeting. Then she sent the photo to Hannah with the message: *Here's another picture of the arm with the same ring. Keep your eyes sharp this evening.*

'Good. Let's turn the place over and hope to find the tape that goes with this cover,' Banham said.

Stephanie had made her way back to Clapham Junction. She stood in the underpass that led to the many platforms, taking it all in. Del Harris could so easily have slipped away early on that Sunday and not have been missed. Too much to-ing and fro-ing for anyone to really notice. She had taken a dislike to the man, and to Christopher Burton, too; she felt they were both hiding something. As she stood there, the station manager approached.

'I saw you on the CCTV,' he said. 'You looked a little lost. Are you travelling today?'

'No. I wanted a word with Del Harris. Do you know where he is?'

'Straight ahead. On platform fourteen,' the little man told her with an obsequious smile. 'Anything I can help with?'

'Can you confirm what time he left here last night?'

'Nine p.m. His shift ended then, and he left then, give or take five minutes.'

She nodded and approached platform fourteen. Del Harris saw her immediately and walked over to her.

'I heard you've been asking about me,' he said. 'Do you think I burned my own home down or something?'

She ignored his question. 'Did you come to work on your bike today?' she asked.

'Yeah. It's in the bike park by the station. Problem?'

'You still drive it a lot?'

'Quickest way for me to get to work. I'm living at my mum's since the fire, and Putney to Clapham is a pig of a journey in rush hour. Easier on a bike.'

'Even with free rail travel?'

He stared coldly at her, then smiled. 'I have it on good advice that the British rail system is not the most reliable.'

'Another woman was murdered last night, in Earl's Court,' she told him, then handed him the picture of Madara with Annabelle and Danielle. She pointed to Madara. 'Did you ever see this woman with Danielle? Did she ever visit the flat, that you know of?'

He shook his head, a little too quickly, she thought. 'Take a good look, Mr Harris. And do you ever remember seeing anyone with that ring on their finger come to the flat to see Danielle?'

'No, I told you, I kept away from her after I found out she was doing drugs and on the game – not my scene.'

'You found out? You told me before you *suspected*.'

'It was pretty obvious. Don't have to be a detective to work it out. She had Rizla papers everywhere, razor blades in the loo, and sexy gear lying around, and she rubbed her nose constantly, like a pedigree cat.'

'Where did you go after you left here last night?'

'Home to my mother's.' He put his hand out to pause her as a train approached. He then dealt with a train coming in, then, as the doors closed behind the boarding passengers, he blew his whistle and flagged the train out, then turned back to her. 'Oh, am *I* a

175

suspect for Madara being murdered? Well, my mother will alibi that I was there from what, nine twenty, and all night.'

'Of course she will. How did you know her name?'

'What?'

'You said Madara. I told you another woman was murdered. I showed you a photo, but I didn't say her name.'

'Oh,' he said, again very quickly. 'Danielle had that picture on her sideboard thing. It had the women's names under it. Danielle with Madara and Annabelle.'

She held his gaze, and noted he looked away.

'You've got a good memory,' she told him. 'Seeing as you said you hadn't been in her flat for a good while.'

'It's not hard to remember three names, lady.'

'Sergeant.'

'What?'

'You don't refer to me as "lady", my title is Sergeant.'

He shook his head. 'What is this?'

'A murder inquiry.'

At that moment, another train came thundering in, with the usual loud and muffled tannoy message telling people where it was going. Harris again turned his back on Stephanie, dealt with the train, and then turned back to her.

'What is the registration of your bike?' she asked him.

'Oh, I am a suspect, then. Why would I want to murder three women?'

'Just answer the question.'

'L, M . . .'

He reeled off the rest, but Stephanie had stopped listening. She believed the registration of the bike the pub witness saw started with LW. It wasn't that far off, and the witness could have been mistaken, or short-sighted.

One thing Stephanie knew was, she didn't like this man one little bit, and normally she liked, and tried to sleep with, anything in trousers.

★

Alison and Banham were walking Bellizza. The animal was going slowly. She was still in some obvious pain and she showed little interest in sniffing at her surroundings.

'She's very depressed,' Banham said. 'She must have loved her owner very much. It's obvious she misses her.'

'Hannah said her tail whirled like a funfair ride when she saw Christopher Burton outside the station. She became very animated,' Alison reminded him. 'I'd say that's very interesting.'

'He admits he knew Annabelle. He said he'd visited the flat. He didn't mention visiting her in her cottage, though, and the neighbour said Annabelle rarely took the dog to London. So, he must have visited the cottage on a regular basis for the dog to know him and become that excited when she saw him. Sounds to me like he had a close relationship with Annabelle.'

'And he's married, and has had a sex scandal in the papers, so he doesn't want to advertise the fact. He wasn't in the country when any of the murders happened, though, so he's not a suspect. He has papers to prove it, air tickets, his secretary's word, airport CCTV, and even a tan, according to Hannah.'

'I'm not saying he's a suspect. I'm saying he knows more than he's telling us. He's protecting his position. He already has a record of picking up prostitutes, and if it got out he was having an affair with an ex-tom, who also happened to be a minister's daughter, well, how would that look?'

'Like he likes hookers, which is interesting.'

'We could talk to him again, pretend we understand his need for discretion, but ask him to tell us why the dog knows him so well. Tell him we know he is holding back on us.'

'I think we should. Hannah mentioned "Bellizza" sounded Italian. She also mentioned Burton has a villa in Italy. She cleverly said there might be a link. Let's ask him if he bought the dog for Annabelle.'

'Good idea, but he's not getting her back,' Banham said very quickly and with an air of panic at the thought.

'Never let it be said,' Alison told him, indicating to him to get a poo bag out now that Bellizza was finally doing her business.

'Let's also ask at the press call tonight for anyone who knew anything about Annabelle Perry's personal life to come forward, besides showing the photo of the ring again, and asking for witnesses for anyone who saw or heard anything around the time of Madara Kowaska's murder,' Banham said, as he tied the bag and disposed of it in the *dog litter only* bin by the side of the road.

Chapter Twenty-five

The day had passed quickly for Hannah. She was to miss the evening meeting as Oluwa Marconi had told her to be there at five p.m. If there were clients calling at that time, he'd said, they were often the dinner-and-a-quick-hand-job type. An easy start for her. Crowther told her to find any reason to stall on leaving the agency. They were all hoping the woman she had started to chat to last night would be there and she could push her for details of eight years back.

Hannah was now in the ladies' bathroom at the station, piling on thick make-up for the evening ahead. She leaned into the mirror as she attempted to glue on a second false eyelash. She held the eyelash between her thumb and finger as she stared at the scar by the side of her nose, and the one above her brow. *These scars have made me stronger,* she told herself. *Five people have been murdered. I could be dead, but I am alive, and I will get out there and help find their killer. This is my opportunity to prove my worth and I will use it.*

She leaned back in, fixed the eyelash, then sprayed a thin line of pink dye down one side of her fair hair, which hung loosely around her shoulders. Next, she pressed an artificial tattoo onto the side of her neck – a bird in flight, pretty apt for this moment, she thought as she turned, and checked her all-round view in the full-length mirror. She was wearing a brown synthetic-leather skirt, which came to her knees but the sides bore deep splits, displaying, as she walked, the top of her black hold-up fishnet stockings. For her upper body, she had chosen a pink-gingham blouse. It was feminine, with short, puffed sleeves, but buttoned up to her neck. It needed to conceal the microphone she would pin under it. She groaned as she slipped her feet into high black stiletto shoes, knowing there was little chance of her running in them; she would just about be able to walk. She was used to her trainers or comfortable flats; her job needed her to be prepared to step out and run at a second's notice. Tonight, though, she needed to look seductive, and trainers didn't go with black fishnets.

As she leaned in to pull her perfume from her handbag, Crowther walked in, knocking after he'd opened the door, then stood, his eyes taking in her outfit.

'Bet you prefer that to the itchy PC togs with the flatties,' he teased.

'I bet you do, too.'

His head moved an inch back and his eyebrows lifted as he took that in.

'Good at flirting, aren't you?'

'That's my brief for tonight.'

He moved towards her. 'My brief is to keep it professional and protect you,' he told her. 'However, seeing as you ask –' he grinned and raised his eyebrows again as his eyes moved up and down her – 'I think you look just right for –' he paused, then his grin widened – 'this assignment.' His tone then changed back to professional. 'Here's the mike and earpiece. I'll let you put that in yourself. Wouldn't want to be accused of touching you up.'

She shook her head. 'I promise I won't, and I'd rather you did it, then I know it's safe and working.'

He raised just the one eyebrow this time. 'No problem.'

As he was testing that the tiny microphone was now firmly adhered to the inside of her bra, just above her breastbone, she breathed in, raising her breast, and then said, 'Should I call you sir, or guv, when we speak on the recording?'

'Col is fine,' he told her. His eyes held hers, then he turned to walk out.

She spoke quickly, 'I wasn't meaning to flirt just then, I . . .'

'Shame,' he said, turning back as he reached the door. 'Flirting never harmed no one.'

'It's just Peter, my ex, rang me this morning. He told me you spoke to him, and told him to back off from bothering me, and I wondered . . .'

'If it was professional or personal?'

She didn't answer, but she held his gaze.

'I told you,' he said gently, 'my brief is to look after you. You are very new in the department. You've got a lot to learn. You're very brave, and very quick, and you've got a good future. We were aware he was constantly on your case. I understand he's your ex-fiancé, but you have told him you need space and he wasn't listening, so I used my position to help you out. I've heard you asking him not to keep ringing you.' He paused, then and walked back to her. He gently stroked her cheek. 'We are working together, and I've got to know you. So, on a personal level, I thought I'd lend a hand, not a heavy hand, but one letting him know. And, if he doesn't give you the space you want, you can ask me again, and I'll bring down a heavier one.'

'Thank you.'

'We all need mates, Hannah. Incidentally, you do look very . . . gorgeous. How do you feel?'

'Good. I'll be trying to find out who the man with the ring is, I'll get the lists we need, chat to anyone I can, then I'm out of there, and back in my comfy shoes.' She smiled.

'And then I'll buy you a beer. Until then, I'll have your back. And I've got a team on standby. Rest assured you are completely safe.'

Chapter Twenty-six

Alison stood by the whiteboard at the head of the murder investigation room. Banham stood beside her. The picture of the battered and murdered Madara had just been added. Beside that picture were pictures from the inside of Madara's flat, having now been blown up to maximum size. Also, pictures of the three women together in various restaurants – a large percentage of them with the same arm, and ring, in shot.

'We urgently need to find the wearer of this ring,' Banham said. 'He – presumably, it is a "he" – appears in many of the photos we've found. Old photos, I grant you, and, of course, he may not still wear this ring, but he is crucial to our inquiries.'

'So, how can we trace him?' Alison now spoke. 'What jumps out at us about this part of the arm or hand or fingers?'

'Thinnish fingers,' Stephanie said. 'Not too big, so probably not too tall.'

'Which could also mean his feet are not that large,' Banham added. 'Wellington we found is a size nine.'

'Not pale hands, although he's white.' Stephanie nodded. 'More than one photo there. All look as if his skin is regularly exposed to the elements. Are they taken near each other in time, do we know?'

'We don't know,' Alison told her. 'There are no dates or information on them. The photos have now been blown up. That's the best we can do on this. Hannah has a photo of it, too. She is looking out for the wearer.'

'I can try and enlarge that even more,' Luke told her. 'Give me a few hours.'

'Del Harris has thinnish fingers, but they were quite long, I thought,' Stephanie told them. 'And he's a tallish man.'

'Who rides a motorbike,' Alison stated. 'Nothing from the photo proves this man isn't tall, even if he has smallish hands. OK. Let's move on to suspects so far.'

'Jonathan Perry had motive to murder his sister. He could have known about the powdered cement and presumed it was intended for him, which it may have been,' said Banham.

'But why would he kill the others?' Luke piped up.

'All three of these women have links to the escort agency,' Banham said. 'I think we hold onto that and the fact that they all have a drugs connection. Madara supplied Annabelle, for instance.'

'Hannah's at the agency again tonight, as we know, with Crowther close by,' Alison reminded them. 'Her brief is to photograph the list of clients past and present, if she can safely get to the list, and talk to the women who do escort work there, and look out for anyone wearing that ring.'

'I can't see why we don't get that warrant and just make him give us his client list?' Baz Butler said. 'Hannah's very new. I am concerned for her safety.'

Banham glanced at Alison, but said nothing.

'We visited the agency,' Alison told him sharply. 'Oluwa Marconi denied having a list. He also lied, saying he no longer worked with escorts, and that the clients who used the agency gave false names. A warrant could prove fruitless, though.'

'I hope you've made the right decision, ma'am,' Baz argued, as Alison immediately prickled.

'She is the perfect undercover officer in my opinion.' Alison spoke firmly and with an air of authority, hiding her fury at being challenged at an open meeting. 'Crowther is outside the agency on an earpiece, and there is a backup uniformed team on standby.'

'We've run checks on Oluwa Marconi and Camilla Agnelli, the pair that run it,' Stephanie told them. 'He is from London, but she came to the country twelve years ago, when she got married. She is now divorced and living alone.'

'Interesting,' Alison said. 'We know they have a supply of Class A drugs in that agency, so we can arrest them any time we want.'

'We spoke to Christopher Burton this morning,' Stephanie continued. 'He arrived back from holiday this morning and came straight over to talk to us. His secretary confirmed she booked all his flights, and we checked he boarded them. I got the feeling he was fond of Annabelle and Jonathan. He also admits to having been caught with a prostitute, but said he didn't know it was Madara.'

'The dog is called Bellizza,' Luke said, 'and it knew Burton. Hannah pointed out "Bella" is Italian in itself, and that people name their dogs after things they love. Could "izza" could be short for Ischia, where Burton has his villa?'

'Yes, that is interesting,' Alison said. 'Did he buy her the dog then, I wonder?'

'He also has a membership with a motorcycle club,' Luke told them. 'He said he paid for it for his son, who now lives abroad, and just forgot to stop it.'

'Del Harris rides a motorbike, too,' Stephanie reminded them. 'He lived above Danielle Low, and escaped the fire. He thinks prostitutes are scum. His words.' She looked at Alison and raised her eyebrows. 'Also, he had time to get to Earl's Court last night, after work. Same as he did on the night of Danielle's Low's death, and Annabelle Perry's. He got home just after. Only alibi there is his mother.'

Banham nodded. 'Could be a jealous lover. He admits an affair with Danielle. But why would he want to kill the other two? And do we have anything apart from the fact he rides a motorbike?'

'Perhaps he blamed the other two for getting her into drugs and prostitution,' Baz Butler offered from his usual position against the wall. 'He finds out she was on the game, loses it, and kills her, then goes after the other two.'

'We have his boss's statement, confirming he was working at

Clapham Junction at the time of the first fire,' Stephanie came in again. 'He probably didn't notice the exact time Harris clocked off.'

'Yeah, especially at Clapham Junction.' Baz nodded. 'There are more platforms there than you've had young men, Steph,' he said with a teasing chuckle. 'Trains whizz in and out every few seconds. You could never see anyone for more than ten seconds. I'd not cross him off.'

'I agree,' Steph said. 'I've just been back to Clapham Junction. It was mayhem.'

'Keep him on the list.' Banham nodded. 'But let's keep our minds open. There were two bikes stolen from the pizza place, one just before the last murder. If our killer owns a bike, they wouldn't need to steal one. Or this could just be a coincidence. Bike thefts are up a hundred per cent over the past few months.'

'We have a press call after this meeting, then on to back Crowther up,' Alison reminded them. 'Luke, are you going to be manning the phones tonight?'

'For sure.'

'Good. Call me if anything urgent comes in. Everyone else, keep your phones open. Hannah may need us.'

'What do we know about the delivery boys at the pizza place?' Baz asked. 'Apart from the fact one of them is a size-nine footprint?'

'They have been alibied,' Alison told him. 'They were out delivering during the first murder. One went to the Barrow Estate. Joseph Perrino,' she said, reading from the notes on the desk in front of her. 'He was hassled there – a gang shadowing him. He called his colleague, Anthony Rossiti, to come and help.' She checked her notes again. 'They have both given identical statements. Neither admits to knowing any of our victims, so, at the moment, the only connection is the stolen pizza sign and the bike thefts. The owner of the pizza shop, Johnny Walsh, reported a motorbike stolen a few weeks before. He also says the pizza-shop signs are always being nicked off the door. Another bike was stolen the night before last, when Joseph was at the Walden Estate. Not that unusual, as DCI Banham says, given the rise in motorbike muggings.' She looked over to Luke for an update.

'No sighting of either, as yet,' he told her. 'But what is baffling everyone is the water stains on the inside of the wellington. From pure water, as Forensics have told us. Their testing confirms the water inside the wellington wasn't London water. It was too clear for anything found in London. Work that one out.'

'It was raining last Sunday,' Alison reminded him.

Luke shook his head. 'I mentioned that; they said no, rainwater was unlikely to be this clear.'

'Unlikely, but not impossible,' Banham corrected.

'OK. Keep going through the list of registered motorbike clubs,' Alison told him. 'Crowther suggested bottled water, did you mention that to Forensics?'

Luke nodded his head. 'They're testing different brands of bottled water.'

'Alison and I will be over at the Fabulous agency, in a side road very near the reception door, after the press call,' Banham told the room. 'We'll stay close to Hannah. Luke will be here, if anything comes up. Everyone keep your phones on.'

'I think I'll talk to Christopher Burton's wife. Let's see how happy the marriage is and what she thinks about his kerb-crawling days,' Alison added. 'Luke, can you get me their country house address?'

'On it, ma'am.'

Chapter Twenty-seven

The press call was fast and furious.

'Five victims, and you believe the murders are connected. Why?' This was a new and overly keen journalist, shouting before Banham and Alison had even had a chance to take their seats.

'I can't reveal any findings as yet,' Banham answered. 'I'm sorry.' He then nodded to the civilian police volunteer sitting at the back of the room, who was holding the controls of a screen that took up nearly half the wall. The grey-haired volunteer obliged with a click of the mouse, and a picture of Madara Kowaska immediately filled the screen.

'We are appealing for anyone who knew this woman, or saw her approach the alleyway adjacent to the row of shops by Earl's Court tube station, around two a.m. this morning,' Banham told the journalists. 'It's a busy area; even at that hour there would have been people around. Please take time to think. Were you in the area around that time? If so, we need you to come forward, even if you saw nothing. This woman worked in the local launderette and would have just finished work and been hurrying towards her home. Her name was Madara Kowaska; perhaps people in the area know her. We would like to talk to anyone who has met her. She was dressed in a khaki anorak and brown jeans. A brown handbag hung from her shoulder.'

The police volunteer clicked on the mouse again, and a picture of the bag came on to the screen. 'The bag was still on her when she was found,' Banham told the room. 'A few essentials lay strewn around it, but no phone.'

'What about CCTV?' someone shouted.

'Any, and every, bit will help,' Banham answered, avoiding telling the journalist what they already did or didn't have. 'Did anyone who was in that area at that time see anyone lurking near that alleyway? We believe our victim came out of the launderette where she worked around, or before, two a.m. She would have walked along the road and into the alleyway by the shops. Perhaps someone was already in there? Or did they follow her in?'

He nodded again to the police volunteer, who clicked on the picture of the three deceased women in the restaurant, sitting with the person whose arm was at the end of the shot, and whose hand displayed the large signet ring. 'And does anyone know the wearer of this ring, or recognise their arm and hand?' Again camera bulbs flashed wildly at the screenshot. 'If so, please call us. Our team are on hand and waiting for your call. The number is behind me, on this board. You may not remember anything, but if you were in the area, please give us a ring There is a nine-year-old girl left without her mother, and we need to find her mother's killer. We also believe the killer may kill again. So, we must find them urgently. Thank you, that's all.'

He stood up, taking Alison's elbow as he stood, much to her annoyance, and steering her out of the room and into the police building.

'Please don't steer me about like I'm a boat,' she told him sharply as they walked back along the corridor. 'I am the senior investigating officer on this case, and you made me look like a child.'

'I'll meet you in the car park,' he told her, ignoring her remark. 'Let's get up to Ladbroke Grove and give Crowther some support.'

'Crowther has requested a firearm out,' Alison told him. 'I've authorised it. I'm taking no chances with Hannah. Do I have your authority?'

'Yes. Sign one out for yourself, too, you're very good with a gun. But don't use it on me.'

Camilla was behind the reception desk when Hannah walked in. She had her head down, typing on the iPad. There were three women sitting on the black-leather sofa by the window. Hannah was relieved to note that one was the woman she had been talking to yesterday, the one who had been with the agency for ten years. Hannah needed information from that woman, and here was her chance. Camilla still hadn't looked up.

'I'm here,' Hannah said.

Camilla glanced up briefly. 'Take a seat,' she told her, immediately dropping her gaze back to her iPad.

Hannah decided to try for a sneak peek at what was on the tablet. She leaned over the desk and nearer to Camilla, where she could see what the woman was typing, if only from an upside-down view. 'I'm a bit nervous,' she told her. 'I hope I get an easy date.'

Camilla ignored her.

Hannah persisted, noticing the top of a mobile phone peeking out from the pink clutch bag that lay on the shelf below the counter, next to Camilla. *Something else worth stealing*, Hannah thought as she tried to read what was on the iPad from her upside-down position.

'Can I take my time to pick an escort?' she asked, concentrating on the screen. It was a list. *Bingo*, she thought. 'If picking's the right word,' she prattled on, her eyes still glued to the upside-down writing. There were names and contact numbers. Exactly what they needed.

'Sit down. You'll be in a queue. We've got three women here already. They all want to earn tonight.'

'Has anyone booked?'

'Yes. We've had a couple of calls. Please sit down, I'm busy.'

'What are they like?' Hannah leaned in further. There was a column beside the contacts that said *'comments'*. *Very helpful and interesting*, Hannah thought.

'One is a regular, but not for you. He likes rough sex after a lot of beer. Imogen will go with him, he likes her.'

'Gosh. Do a lot of them hurt the girls?'

Camilla shrugged. 'I don't ask. I just take the money. Please sit down.'

'Have you got some good regulars?'

She shrugged. 'Yes. Please, will you sit down.'

'Any pictures?'

Oluwa came out from the back at that moment.

'You ask a lot of questions,' he said. 'Sit down. We'll let you know if you are working tonight.'

So, he had heard, or had seen, her attempted conversation with Camilla. That meant there were definitely cameras in his office, and out the back. Good – they may be able to tell the exact time he left the building last night. However, the cameras also meant she was being closely watched, so she would have to be cautious and very quick.

'I'm nervous, that's all,' she said. 'I want to know what kind of men I will have to go with. Surely, that's fair.'

His voice was sharp when he answered. 'You're lucky I am giving you a second chance. If you mess me about again, you will pay dearly. So sit the fuck down and shut the fuck up. There are three others before you. Unless someone comes in and chooses you.'

Camilla was still clicking on her iPad. Hannah looked at the receptionist's hands. She wasn't wearing the same ring as she had been last night, but she was sporting another one on the same little finger of her right hand. Her arms were long and muscular.

'You like rings,' Hannah said to her.

'Yes,' Camilla said flatly, without looking up.

'I've got a thing about rings, too,' Hannah lied, then, aware that Camilla had looked up and at her hands, she added, 'but I haven't worn any tonight. Have you got any clients with nice hands?'

'I told you to sit down and shut up,' Oluwa barked at her.

His tone made her realise she had pushed as far as she could, for now.

She sat and started to make small talk with the woman she had been chatting to yesterday. The woman had obviously seen and heard Oluwa barking at her, and gave her one-syllable answers. *Bugger*, she thought to herself.

Fifteen minutes went by, and then Camilla stood up and walked to the ladies' room, taking her pink clutch bag and her mobile with her. Hannah gave it ten seconds, then followed.

Camilla had gone into a cubicle but had left her clutch bag by the sink. Hannah quickly opened it. She pulled out the phone, then noticed there was a small handgun in the base of the bag. She heard the chain flush – there was no time to look further – so she shoved the phone back in the bag and clicked the clasp closed. As Camilla walked to the basin, Hannah had her lipstick out and was reapplying it. Camilla flicked a look at her, picked up the clutch bag, and left without washing her hands.

'Crowther, are you there?' Hannah whispered.

'Of course. Can you talk?'

'Camilla Agnelli has a handgun in her clutch bag. I just saw it.'

Chapter Twenty-eight

There was a silence. Then the voice of Banham. 'OK, Hannah, stay calm. Crowther has a firearm on him and so does Alison, and I am now putting a gun unit on standby. Try and photograph the gun and any drugs, but your safety comes first. Any problems, you get out.'

The bathroom door opened at that second, and Oluwa stood there. He gave her a hard glare before speaking. 'You were a long time,' he said. 'I wondered if you'd fallen down the toilet.'

She carried on washing her hands, and forced a smile. 'Just making sure I look my best,' she said.

She walked back into reception and settled down beside the three women.

'Have you been doing this long?' she asked the two women she hadn't met before. 'I'm Hannah, by the way. I'm new, so I'm looking for tips.'

'You'll get used to it,' the one Camilla had called Imogen said dismissively.

'Just think of the money,' the black-haired girl said to her.

'Are there any weirdoes I should avoid? I don't want to get a wrong 'un, and I'm a little nervous.'

She became aware Camilla was watching her. She lowered her voice. 'Anyone to avoid?'

'Any questions, come to me, please, Hannah,' Camilla said sharply.

'Sorry, Yes. I was just wondering—'

'We have no problem clients,' Camilla said dismissively.

'Not true,' the woman she'd spoken to last night whispered under her breath.

'I need the loo again,' Hannah said. 'It's nerves.' She got up and headed for the toilet, hoping the woman would get the message and follow her.

As she opened the door to the ladies, she heard the woman stand up to follow her, but a very sharp voice boomed out from Camilla. 'Sit down, unless you want trouble.'

'All OK?' Hannah said to Crowther, as she leaned over the basin and towards the mirror to check her eyelashes and scars.

'Yes, darling. Have you located the list?'

'It's definitely on the iPad on the counter, I've seen it. But it's not easy. I've clocked a safe, too, behind the counter. I reckon that's where the drugs are, and there is a large computer, too. Camilla is like a Rottweiler.'

'I've put in for a search warrant – as soon as it comes through, we may well come in, especially now we know there are firearms in there.' This was Banham.

'Oh, well, I'm OK. I'll get the iPad, there is inner CCTV and I have to—'

Camilla opened the door. She stood glaring at Hannah.

Hannah's heart jumped into her mouth. 'Is everything OK?' she asked.

'With me, yes. But I am doubting you. Have you got a weak bladder?'

Hannah hesitated.

'Tell her it's nerves,' Crowther's voice came in her ear.

'I won't let you down,' Hannah replied, staying very calm. 'This is my first job for a while and I am a little nervous. But I'm in debt up to my ears, so I'll get used to it.'

'You said you've been on the streets before,' Camilla said, holding her cold, bird-of-prey gaze on Hannah. 'This will be a piece of cake compared to that.'

'I'll be OK, once I get out there and get my first one over with.'

'We have some very nice men we could put you with, but they are tighter than a virgin's arsehole. No tips. Then we have others who will tip dearly, but they want the special things they like, sexually.'

'Ask what special things they want,' Crowther whispered.

'What kind of special things?' Hannah asked.

'They like to hurt you, stuff like that. It doesn't last long. Only a few bruises. I can see you have scars, so you wouldn't notice a few bruises. They pay very well.'

'Ask who they are, and how long they have been using the agency,' Crowther's voice came again in her earpiece. 'Get her to show you that list on her iPad.'

'Can I see pictures? How long have they been using your girls?'

The woman's eyes stayed pinned on Hannah. 'I have pictures, yes. Does that mean you're interested?

'Possibly.'

'Get her to show you the list, and read it out loud,' Crowther spoke quietly into her ear.

'Can I see them?'

'No. Confidentiality is our thing. But I have some good drugs you can take. You will pay for them, of course, but then you'll earn it back. And plenty more.'

'Get the source for the drugs,' Crowther half-whispered.

'Yes. Drugs will help. These men, what do they do? Is there more than one pervert on your books? Are they English?'

'English, yes, and more,' she said, raising her eyebrows. 'Generous, too. I'll get the other girls a date first. If I do, and when you are next, I will call the person I have in mind for you. I'll ask him if he would like to come and meet you.'

'This is good,' Crowther told her. 'Get him to book you and we'll arrest you both as you step outside the agency.'

'The gun unit have arrived,' Alison whispered in her ear. They are surrounding the building. You are safer than you could ever know. Go along with her.'

Hannah nodded to Camilla. 'Great. That's a yes, then. Can I get some drugs now? Do you have a stock here in the agency?'

Crowther spoke again. 'You're doing good, babe.'

'Yes, you are,' Alison agreed. 'Crowther, can you pack the "babe" in, please. She isn't a Barbie doll.'

Hannah felt herself blush and forced herself not to smile.

Banham turned to Alison. 'I think "babe" is a nice name,' he said. 'I don't like Bellizza for our dog, it's too much of a mouthful. Shall we rename her Babe?'

Alison looked at Banham. 'Babe? A dog called Babe!' She shook her head. 'No, that's an awful name for a dog.'

Luke and Stephanie were still in the office, waiting to take any calls that came through from the earlier press appeal. Apart from a few lunatics and timewasters, the incoming phone had remained silent.

'I can't believe no one has come forward with anything worth knowing,' Luke said to Stephanie.

'Oh, I can, love. People are afraid to open their mouths to us lot these days, for fear of reprisals. Also, the penny can take a while to drop, and then they'll go, "ooh, what was that number? I've just remembered."'

'Here's hoping.' He nodded, as he tapped away at his computer.

'I'll make us a cuppa,' Stephanie told him, noting his despondency. 'Think it's going to be a long night for all of us. At least we're warm in here, and there's coffee, and I've got biscuits. Guv'nor and Crowther are in their cold cars, and Hannah's in a hookers' den, hoping not to get caught.'

'We all have our burdens,' Luke mumbled.

Stephanie stared at Luke, glued to his computer screen and sitting in his wheelchair. She felt sorrier for him than herself sometimes. He was lonely. Yes, she was lonely, too, but only sometimes. Her children had grown up and gone off to university, and she, too, more often as not, went home to an empty flat, but at least she could have her affairs, casual or not, her choice. She didn't want anything permanent. Luke probably would like a relationship, but since the accident, it wasn't to be. This poor twenty-six-year-old lad had come into the Met with big ambitions, and within two years he had broken his body in a police chase and now had little or no chance of children. His detective work had become his life.

'Coffee,' she repeated as she left the room, two mugs in hand, heading for the coffee machine.

She had only walked a few steps, when Luke yelled out, 'Sarge, I think you need to see this.

Chapter Twenty-nine

A very rotund man with a face full of acne, probably in his mid to late thirties, had come in and was handing money to Camilla. He then turned and stared at the waiting women. He studied each one, giving them leering looks. Hannah could smell car oil even from where the man stood. She looked away, praying he wouldn't pick her. After a minute, he turned back and leaned across the desk to whisper to Camilla. Camilla then called the tall blonde woman over. The woman that Hannah had been chatting to last night, who had been there ten years. Hannah sighed to herself. Her chance of chatting to her was now non-existent. The man handed cash to Camilla and then walked out, followed by the tall blonde.

Everything then remained quiet. Hannah was aware that, again, Oluwa had left the building.

'Has Oluwa gone home?' she asked Camilla.

'Yes. We're open all night, so we do shifts. I do a few hours, then he comes and takes over. What's it to you?'

The evening started to drag out. The two remaining women still sat waiting to get a date, and Hannah felt that if it didn't happen soon, she wouldn't get to meet this pervert, and the team wouldn't be able to arrest Camilla for firearms, Class A drugs, and prostitution offences. She had drugs in her bag, which she had bought from Camilla, and now knew they were indeed kept in the safe behind the desk. And at least Oluwa wasn't watching her every move.

Another hour passed, then Crowther's voice whispered to her, 'Two ugly men approaching the agency.'

Hannah looked up as the men walked in and straight to the reception desk. They then turned and looked at Hannah and the other two girls. Camilla then told the escorts to stand up, Hannah included.

'The blonde is booked tonight,' Camilla told the men. Hannah knew that meant her, as the other two women were both brunettes. Money was then handed to Camilla. The two women were summoned to be introduced to the men, and Camilla quickly opened the safe and handed them a tiny bag of what Hannah knew was cocaine, and then they all left together.

'Presume you are the last one left now, babe?' Crowther said to her.

Hannah was watching Camilla, who was, again, typing on her tablet.

Another ten minutes passed, then Camilla looked up and spoke to Hannah. 'I'm going to phone this client I told you about,' she told her. 'See if he's up for it. You'll be well in the money in the morning. Bruised, and in a bit of pain, but nothing paracetamol won't cure.' With that, she lifted her iPad and left the room.

'Shit,' Hannah whispered. 'She's taken the iPad with her.' She hurried to the counter and leaned over. 'But, hey, the safe is still open. She took drugs out a few minutes ago.'

Hannah grabbed her phone and quickly moved behind the counter. She noted the large mirror on the wall behind reception. She would say she was touching up her make-up if Camilla came back in. She quickly pulled the safe door further open. There were two navy socks full of what looked like cocaine in there. Her hands were slippery with nervous perspiration as she snapped pictures of the drug-filled socks. She then moved the socks, and her eyes fell on another gun. 'There's another firearm here,' she whispered to Crowther.

She was about to photograph it, when she heard the inner door shut, and knew the door to the reception would open in two seconds. She jumped up and started to fix her make-up in front of the mirror as Camilla came through the door.

Camilla's eyes narrowed. 'What are you doing?'

'Just touching up my lippy,' Hannah said, holding a tube of lip gloss in her hand and showing it to Camilla.

'I've spoken to that client,' Camilla told her, walking over to the desk and checking around suspiciously. She obviously hadn't noticed the safe door was open much wider than when she'd left. She then turned to Hannah. 'He wants to hire you. He is on his way down to buy you dinner. You get a slap-up supper at the Savoy, and then a room is booked there for afterwards. We've told you how it works. He will pay us to hire you for supper. We will pay you the minimum fee, and anything you can negotiate with him after is another twenty per cent to us. We always find out if you double-cross us, and Oluwa will make you pay dearly if you try, so it's twenty per cent of what he gives you. Charge him dearly for each bruise.'

'Ask how he likes to hurt?' Crowther whispered in her earpiece.

'CS019 have moved in and are either side of the door. We will arrest you both as you leave with him,' Banham whispered.

'What exactly does he want me to do for it?'

'Oh, whatever, he likes causing pain,' Camilla told her casually. 'You have scars, so you're obviously a woman of the world.' Her dark eyes narrowed. 'A few more won't hurt. Think of the money.'

Hannah hid her anger. 'Who is he?' she asked.

'You'll meet him soon,' Camilla said. 'Carry on brushing your hair. He is fussy about his women. But as I say, do as he requests and you will make a killing tonight. He truly pays very well.' She paused. 'I have been with him. He bought me a diamond ring and gave me two grand.'

Hannah's ears pricked up. 'Why a diamond ring? Does he like rings or something?'

'No. But I told him that I do,' she said.

Hannah nodded. 'I'll go sniff that coke you gave me in the loo. Is it pure?'

'Comes from the best supplier in London,' Camilla told her, turning to close the safe. Hannah leaned over it.

'Why have you got a gun in the safe?' she asked, letting Crowther know where they were.

'I was on the game once, and I like to feel secure.'

Hannah hurried to the loo. 'The drugs are wrapped in the same navy socks as found in Annabelle's and Madara's flats,' she whispered to Crowther. 'So, same dealer. And, as you heard, there's another gun in the base of the safe, with bullets. I've got a photo of the socks, but not the contents or the firearms.'

'Right,' Alison said. 'This client could be our killer. Get him out in the street, ask him what he's expecting, and as soon as he mentions sex and money, we'll arrest him, then the firearms team will go in and arrest her.'

'You've got some of the drugs on you now, haven't you?' Crowther asked.

'Yes.'

'Good. First, we'll arrest you for that. Keep you out of it, and safe that way. You're doing great, by the way.'

Steph still had the empty mugs in her hand. She hurried back when Luke called her.

'What will I want to see that's more important than coffee?' she asked Luke.

'Forensic findings,' he told her. 'On the wellington boot found at the edge of that wood. They just sent this through.'

She nodded for him to read on.

'Dark blue fibres found on the inside of the boot are a match to a unique Italian brand of socks. I can't pronounce it.'

She put the empty coffee mugs on the desk and looked at him.

'I know they sell Italian socks in all good menswear outlets, but Christopher Burton has a villa on Ischia,' he said. 'And the water inside the wellington isn't a match to any bottled water sold in shops here.'

'Lots of men wear dark-blue socks,' she said. 'I've seen enough taken off, but I have to admit I haven't looked to see the make.'

'I always wear black socks,' Luke said, rubbing his head. 'It's the pure water here that gets me. Where, if not from a bottle, as Crowther suggested, do you get pure water to pour on a wellington?

'I've no idea,' Stephanie said, shaking her head. 'I'll phone this through to the guv'nor, give her something to think about while she sits outside that agency watching all those men going in and out for sex.'

Chapter Thirty

Alison had decided to move her car nearer the agency. There was a space on the other side of the road, opposite Crowther's car, where they could see clearly all the comings and goings.

As she was reversing into the parking spot, her phone started to vibrate. Banham picked it up, to Stephanie.

'It's certainly a puzzle,' he said to her, then relayed her message to Alison and in the earpiece to Crowther.

'Navy Italian socks,' Crowther repeated. 'The drugs here are in navy socks, too. Suppose whoever brings the drugs, gets them in Italy and brings them back in his socks. That spells Christopher Burton to me.'

'He wouldn't do his own dirty work,' Banham said.

'So, he has someone do it for him. Someone who he can push around. And looks like the wellington-wearer also wore navy socks. That would mean the wellington is connected to the drug courier, and, as we believed, the arsonist.'

'Christopher Burton was out of the country, but he owns an Italian villa,' Alison said. 'Coincidence? Who knows?'

'Who else has connections to Italy?' Banham said.

Crowther's voice then took all their attention. 'Fuck me,' he said loudly, making Hannah sit up in her seat back in reception. 'Fuck and fuck again.'

'What? What mate?' Banham asked urgently.

'Can you see down the street from where you are?'

'Just about, but only just about. You are the other side to us. What's going on?'

'Talk of the fucking devil. Walking down the road coming from the north – look over that way – and heading towards the gaff is none other than our seedy MP, Christopher Burton.'

'All units, stand by,' Alison spoke into her mike. 'Hannah, I know you can't answer me. I just hope you heard, and know what to expect. Christopher Burton is walking down the mews now. He looks to be heading for the agency. He will be entering there within a minute. If he is the client you are expecting, play the game. Get him outside and negotiate a payment. We'll nick him then. We'll arrest you and get you safely out of it.'

Hannah's blood rippled with a cold chill. She couldn't answer, as she was back in the reception, sitting near Camilla. Had Alison forgotten that she had sat in on the interview with Burton and Stephanie Green only yesterday? He couldn't fail to recognise her.

Alison's phone vibrated again.

Steph's voice was urgent as she spoke, as well as full of food. 'Got some more interesting info back from Forensics,' she told Alison.

'Steph, we'll call you back,' Alison told her, watching Burton, who was now only a few feet from the entrance of the agency. 'Christopher Burton is here and heading towards the agency as we speak. Hannah is going to honey-trap him for us.'

'Christ, guv,' Steph jumped three feet in the air. 'He'll recognise her. I took her with me into the interview room with him yesterday. Get her out. He knows she's a cop, guv.'

The second that came across, and into Crowther's earpiece, he leapt from his car and was now behind Burton. Banham shouted, 'No, Crowther. Stand back. Let him go in.'

'CS019, stand by,' Alison said urgently to the firearms team.

Burton's newly whitened teeth beamed against his suntanned skin as he walked into the agency. Camilla acknowledged him and then turned to Hannah. 'This is Hannah,' she told him. 'She's new and keen to please.'

The smile immediately left his face as he turned to face Hannah.

'She's a cop!' he spat at Camilla.

Camilla turned to Hannah, surprise and anger now written all over her face.

Hannah held her nerve. She knew her team were outside the door.

'She interviewed me yesterday, she's a cop,' Burton shouted as he turned to hurry out of the agency.

'Evening, sir,' Crowther said, blocking his path as he took a step outside the door.

Camilla quickly grabbed her pink clutch bag and, as she clicked it open, Hannah shouted. 'She's got a gun. Look out, Col, she's got a gun.'

Camilla now had the gun pointed at Hannah.

'Put the gun down.' Hannah's voice was calm as she spoke. 'Yes, I am a police officer. The building is surrounded—'

She hadn't got through the rest of her sentence when the door flew open. 'Drop the gun,' came the command from Jim Westgate, the sergeant in command of the CS019 Armed Response Unit. 'The building is surrounded.'

Camilla froze, gun in hand, unsure what to do. The gun was still pointed at Hannah. Then her hand moved slightly, as if she might aim and fire.

Jim Westgate was quicker. He fired a bullet into the wall behind Camilla. Camilla immediately dropped the gun.

'On the floor. Kneel. Hands on your head. Do it,' Jim Westgate's command wasn't to be messed with. 'Now.' He raised his voice. 'Now!'

Camilla dropped to her knees, then placed her hands on her head.

Hannah speedily moved to her and bent to pick up the gun.

Seeing her coming, Camilla pulled her hand from her head and punched Hannah hard in the eye.

Hannah went flying.

Crowther had been standing by the door, behind the CS019 team. He immediately rushed in to help Hannah.

Christopher Burton, seeing his chance, made for the street, but came face to face with Alison and Banham. He pushed into them, and past them, knocking Alison into the wall, but Banham grabbed him, and the uniformed backup team behind quickly pulled his hands behind his back. One officer pulled handcuffs from their waistband as Banham recited the arrest.

'I haven't done anything,' Burton shouted, trying hard to wriggle free from the cuffs and the strong uniformed police who were fighting to cuff him. 'You can't arrest me. How dare you! What's the charge?'

'You assaulted me,' Alison told him, pretending to rub her arm where he had pushed her.

'I haven't done anything,' Burton persisted. 'I'll have you for false arrest. I came in to ask for directions.'

'You've just attacked a police officer,' Banham told him. 'Don't make this worse for yourself.'

Camilla's hands were also being handcuffed. 'Lying bitch,' she shouted at Hannah, as she wriggled and tried to stop the cuffs being clipped on her. As the uniformed team took her elbow to lead her away, she aimed a mouthful of saliva at Hannah, that landed on Hannah's cheek.

Crowther quickly pulled his hand back and smacked it hard into the woman's face. Every officer in the room turned away, pretending not to see.

Burton and Camilla were taken in the back of separate meat wagons to the station. Crowther and Hannah followed in Crowther's car, and Crowther booked the prisoners in.

'You look all in,' he said to Hannah, gently touching her forehead. 'And that's a nasty bruise you're gonna have on your eye.'

'I'm fine.' Hannah shrugged and nodded. 'I've been through much worse.'

'Fancy a nice Chinese while they cool off in a cell?'

'If the guv'nor says it's OK,' Hannah said, tactfully looking over to Alison, who was standing within hearing distance.

'Yes, it's fine by me.' Alison nodded her agreement, then flashed a warning glance at Crowther. 'I need a while to go through the woman's iPad first, and then I'll send it over to the technical department. Burton has called his solicitor. He will be here in about an hour or so. So, we'll start interviewing then. That's enough time to get a meal,' she told Crowther, with another look at him that said, *a meal and nothing else*. Then she added, 'And no alcohol, please. You are still working.'

Hannah nodded. 'Thank you, ma'am.'

'No. Thank you. You've done well. I am very proud of you.'

They had barely ordered, when Hannah said, 'I was young and broke as a student and I thought escort work literally meant a nice dinner and that was all. I joined that agency and only went on a couple of dates. I quit when I realised what was going on. I kept it quiet because I was afraid it would affect my police career. Little did I know, it could help a murder case years later.'

Crowther smiled. 'I was born on a council estate, no father. I was streetwise at seven. We're all different. No one in the department has to know your history if you don't want to tell them. You did nothing wrong. And as for our DI, she worked in a pub when she was a student, as a topless dancer. Now, that's a well-kept secret, too. She told me she told you, so I'm not speaking out of turn.'

Hannah nodded and half-laughed. 'She did tell me. Can you imagine? So out of character.' The waiter started placing hot-plates on their table and then put water glasses in front of them. 'Shame we can't have a proper drink,' she said. 'I could certainly do with one.'

'I bet. Me too, as it happens. But it'll have to wait until we've interviewed Burton.' The waiter was now pouring water into their glasses. 'I want you in on the interviews. You did the hard work; you should get to charge them. Camilla Agnelli will get a custodial for threatening an officer of the law with a firearm, inciting women into prostitution, and possession of Class A drugs. They'll pick up Oluwa Marconi and he'll be done for housing firearms and drugs and inciting women into prostitution. Now, we have to push Burton. He's saying he went in for directions! At the moment, all we have is a weak charge of assaulting an officer of the law.'

'I'll need a large drink after, that's for sure.'

'I'll be right next to you in the interview room, and I'll buy your drink afterwards. You've definitely earned it.' He lifted his hand and, very gently, placed it against the side of her eye. 'We'll get pictures of this when the bruise comes out. Bastard woman. I'll make sure she goes down for that alone.'

'Thank you for being so nice to me,' she said, locking her large, seductive eyes on his.

The waiter was now placing various dishes of steaming goodies onto the hotplates. He then laid the chopsticks by their plates. She waited till he had finished.

'It'll be the middle of the night,' she reminded Crowther. 'Nowhere will be open for alcohol, will they? Then a small smile lit up her face. 'Oh, I forgot, you are Col-the-know-all, because you always know somewhere, or someone, who can get something. In this case, a drink in the middle of the night.'

He lifted his heavy eyebrows and grinned. 'True, I do. And, if you trust me, I've got a stocked-up drinks cabinet at my flat. I promise to be a perfect gentleman,' he added quickly, as he passed her the plate of duck. 'You must agree, I know a good Chinese when I taste one. The food here is delicious.'

She grinned and popped a piece of duck in her mouth. 'Mmm, it's great. And you know what? I think you are the perfect gentleman.'

'So, that's a yes, then?'

'That's a yes, then.'

Chapter Thirty-one

'So, what's the latest forensics that's come through?' Alison asked Luke and Stephanie, who were both still sitting behind their desks.

'DNA on the spliffs found in Madara's flat matches that of Annabelle Perry, Jonathan Perry, and – listen to this – Del Harris's DNA is also on one of the spliffs,' Steph told Alison.

'So, Harris had been in that flat, and recently, too, as the ends in the ashtray weren't that old,' Alison said, looking at Stephanie as if to say, you were right not to trust him.

'Can I bring him in, ma'am?' Stephanie asked. 'Bastard has been lying to us.'

'My pleasure.' Alison nodded.

'You were right,' Banham said to Alison as they sat in her office, going through the devices they had taken from the agency. 'Hannah did very well undercover in there. She kept her cool, and we've got the iPad and the laptop, and Burton and the owners of the agency.'

'Let's hope the iPad tells us a lot,' Alison said, tapping into its documents.

'Interesting, too, that Del Harris was lying. Is Steph going to knock him up in the middle of the night?'

'Yes. She's taken a dislike to him. She said it'll give her great pleasure.'

'What do you think, so far?' he asked, leaning over her shoulder as she ran through all the documents on the iPad.

'I think Burton is involved. We know he didn't kill those women. We have him on video at Gatwick boarding a plane. He was at his Italian villa. But where do the Italian socks, the man with the ring, and the pure water come into this?'

'We'll threaten to give the press the story: *Local MP found in sleazy escort agency.* We'll say, help us, and we'll do our best to stop it going to the press.'

She nodded. 'Yes, for sure.' She was engrossed in the documents she was opening. 'They're all fake names on this list. One man has called himself Elvis. He wants his escort to dress as a rocker.' She shook her head. 'Going to be hard to trace these.'

Banham bent down and stroked the dog, who had been sitting patiently in Alison's office. 'It's going to be a long night, Babe,' he told her. 'But you'll get used to our odd hours. We're all detectives here. You can join in, too. What do you think? Could you sniff out your mistress's killer?'

'By the way,' Alison said, 'when Burton's solicitor comes, you can take Babe, if that's definitely going to be her name, out for a walk. I'm taking Hannah into the interview room with Burton.'

Banham shook his head. 'She's not experienced enough. Let her watch from the screen in the office. He needs very careful handling. She could mess up. Let her interview, and charge, Camilla Agnelli. She earned that.'

Alison shook her head. 'No. She'll make Burton uncomfortable. I'll interrogate him. My decision, my risk. You've made your decision to call the dog Babe, for good or bad.'

As Hannah and Crowther walked back into the station, the banging and rattling from an angry prisoner, locked in a cell, could be heard from two passages away.

'That's Oluwa Marconi shouting,' Alison told them. 'He was arrested at his home. He's being charged with possessing firearms and Class A drugs, and inciting prostitution. No one gets bail, and no one goes home tonight, Burton included,' she told them as she stared at Hannah's eye. 'You're going to have a bruiser there. Do you want the medical officer to check that?'

'No, I'm fine, ma'am.'

'We'll definitely photograph that now, and again tomorrow, when the bruise comes out,' she told her. 'Agnelli will be done for assaulting a police officer, on top of the other charges. She'll be before a judge tomorrow, and won't get bail. She's going down.'

'Good to hear,' Crowther said.

Alison stared at him and then at Hannah. 'And Stephanie has gone to bring in Del Harris. He's been lying to us. His DNA was found on one of the spliffs we found at Madara's flat,' she told them. 'So, we'll have a full house here tonight.'

'Her hunch was right, then,' Crowther said.

Alison nodded. 'Hannah, you are with me,' she told her. 'We are interviewing Camilla first. Col, you and Banny are doing Oluwa Marconi. Good luck with that. And then, Hannah, you'll join me in the interview with Burton.'

Crowther opened his mouth to protest and then changed his mind. 'Good luck,' he said to her.

'Can I wash my face first?' Hannah asked Alison. 'I can't bear this slap on me any longer.'

Camilla sat with her hands laid flat on the desk in front of her, and her hard, dark eyes piercing into Hannah's. She had refused a solicitor, but asked that Oluwa sat with her. Alison told her that wasn't possible, that he, too, was under arrest, and they were both facing the same serious charges. Camilla then cast her eyes downwards and started turning her hands around, nervously examining her long mauve and obviously false nails.

She looked up after Alison clicked the video and tape to *on*, introduced herself, and informed the tape who was present and who they were interviewing.

Camilla spoke first. 'I work there, that's all,' she said. She glared at Hannah. 'I tried to help you. You said you were broke.'

Hannah didn't answer.

'Where did you get the guns?' Alison asked her.

'They belong to Oluwa. Nothing to do with me. He gave me the small one for protection. I only work there. The other gun has been in the safe as long as I've been there. I didn't think they were real.'

'Oh, come on, Camilla, you weren't born yesterday,' Alison pushed. 'You work with sex workers and perverts. You supply drugs. You must have known the gun in your handbag worked.'

'I didn't, and the drugs are nothing to do with me. I just pass them over when requested. I'm not responsible for the welfare of the women. I just work there.'

'I didn't request them,' Hannah said. 'You offered me class A drugs.'

'Don't add lying to a police officer to your already long list of charges,' Alison told Camilla. 'At the moment, you are under arrest for possession of firearms, assaulting a police officer, possession of Class A drugs, and inciting women into prostitution.'

Camilla shook her head. 'I only work there. I don't own the place. Not my fault if there is illegal stuff there. I manage a model agency; if they want to prostitute themselves, it's not down to me.'

Alison then leaned forward and spoke in a threatening tone. 'This is a murder inquiry. Five people have been killed. Three of those had worked as escorts for you. So, stop lying, and start answering our questions, or things are going to get a whole lot worse for you.'

Alison watched Camilla breathe deeply and bite her top lip. She knew she was getting to the woman. 'How long have you known Christopher Burton?' she asked.

'He has been a client for around ten years.'

'How regular?'

'On and off. He pays well, because he's a pervert.'

'What does he like to do to the women?'

Camilla shrugged and lifted her hands, gesturing she had no idea.

'You've been on a date with him. You told me you had,' Hannah pushed. 'So, what did he do to you?'

211

'He hurt me.'

'How? What did he actually do to you?' Alison pushed.

'He burned me with a cigarette stub. Not badly, but I'm still scarred.' She pulled her jumper down from her shoulder, revealing a large round scar at the side of her breast.

Alison and Hannah took that in.

'Why did you go with him if you knew he was a pervert?' Hannah asked her.

'He asked me. He likes Italian women. Oluwa said to keep him sweet. He does a lot for the agency and he would give me a lot of money. But he hurt and sickened me.'

'What does he do for the agency?' Alison asked her.

'He supplies us with protection, if there's a problem. And he gets the stuff for the girls, too.'

'He supplies your drugs?' Hannah pushed.

'Yes. I just hand them out. I have to. I need a job, I have no other, or I would leave. There's always a supply of drugs kept in the office safe.'

'Does he bring them in to you?'

She shook her head. 'I believe one of the girls brings them in for him. I don't know all the details. There's always a supply there. The models all take drugs to stay thin, and the escorts need them to sleep with the punters who come in and buy them. If a girl's new to the agency, she's usually given drugs free – at first.'

Alison made eye contact with Hannah.

'Does he always bring them in to you, in the same navy socks we found them in?'

'That lot came in socks, but no, not always.'

Hannah was watching Camilla closely. She now felt this woman, in a way, was a victim – she was under the power of Marconi, who used her, knowing she had no visa after her divorce, so couldn't get another job.

'Were Danielle and Madara still working for the agency when they were murdered?' Hannah asked.

Camilla shook her head. 'No, Danielle was sacked ages ago for using too heavily, and Madara left a little while back.'

'And Annabelle had left a long time before, is that right?' Hannah asked.

'Yes.'

'For the tape, I am showing Camilla a photo.' Alison pushed the photo of Madara with Danielle and Annabelle at a dinner with a man's arm in shot. The arm in the picture was wearing a large ring. 'Do you recognise this man's arm, or the ring he's wearing?' she asked.

Camilla nodded. 'Christopher Burton, for sure.'

'Why for sure?' Alison asked her.

'Because he used to wear that ring. I noticed it because I love rings. He hasn't worn it recently, but I remember it well.'

'Are you sure it is definitely Christopher Burton?' Alison asked again.

Camilla nodded. 'He punched me with that ring on. Marked my face quite badly.'

Banham and Crowther had been watching and listening to the interview on the video screen in Alison's office. They made eye contact, and then headed into Interview Room B, where Oluwa Marconi was sitting, impatiently, waiting to be questioned.

Marconi raised his voice as Crowther and Banham settled into their seats. 'I haven't done anything. I run a legal model agency. You have no right to raid my office and then come to my home and arrest me.'

'You refused a solicitor,' Banham told him. 'And we had every right. You are under arrest for possession of firearms, and possession of Class A drugs.'

Before Marconi could argue more, Crowther jumped in. 'Carries at least a five-year custodial sentence. Not to mention inciting women into prostitution. So, to put it mildly, you are in deep shit. However, better news for you is, we are conducting a murder inquiry. So, a chance to help yourself here. If you cooperate, answer our questions, and don't fuck about, we may be willing to tell the judge you helped in a murder inquiry.'

'I know nothing about drugs or firearms,' Marconi replied with an indignant shrug of his shoulders. 'I run a modelling agency. I've told you before: I let my clients take the models to dinner, for cash payments. That is all I do, and that is not illegal. If they take it further, it is nothing to do with me. If there are drugs on the premises, nothing to do with me either. It will be the models. See my assistant about that. I may own the agency, but I am not often there.'

'Who holds the key to your inner safe?'

'Camilla Agnelli, my assistant. There is a spare somewhere. I don't know where. I know nothing about drugs or firearms. If you found drugs and firearms, then talk to her.'

'Talk to us about Christopher Burton,' Banham said abruptly.

'What do you want to know? He likes women, and has dated some of our models.'

'Paying to do so?'

Marconi shrugged. 'What the women do in their time is not my concern.'

'We know he supplies your drugs,' Crowther said. 'Where does he get them from?'

Marconi rolled his eyes. 'I told you, I didn't even know there were drugs in the building, or firearms, until you woke me up and arrested me. I can only think they belong to one of the models and Camilla put them in the safe for them. Models are notorious for drug-taking, to keep thin. I run a model agency, that is it.'

'We checked your mobile,' Crowther told him. 'Burton's phone number is on your phone.'

He shrugged. 'That isn't a crime. He books the models.'

Crowther laid the photos of the three victims on the table in front of Marconi. 'Did Burton book these women?'

Marconi glanced briefly at the photos and shook his head. 'I hardly remember. Many girls come and go through our doors, as do clients. I don't remember much about any of them.'

'I'll remind you, then,' Crowther told him, leaning in and speaking in a tone that let Marconi know he was becoming bored with his lies. 'They worked for you as prostitutes.' He then sat back in his chair. 'But I think you know that. So, I'll ask you again. Did Christopher Burton book them?'

'I really don't remember.'

Crowther raised his voice and pierced Marconi with his gaze. 'Why are you trying to protect Burton?'

Marconi stayed calm. 'I'm not trying to protect Mr Burton. I know nothing about the questions you ask. I run a legitimate model agency. My books are intact. If the girls want to date any of the men that book them for modelling assignments, the men pay the model's fee, and what the models do on the side is their business. I told your other detective, I no longer run an escort agency, it became too troublesome.' He turned away and then turned and looked back at Crowther. 'I have done nothing wrong. I am tired and I would like to go home.'

'You are going nowhere, Mr Marconi. Well, to court tomorrow, and then jail, I suspect,' Crowther told him.

'Have a sleep in the cell,' Banham said sarcastically, turning to the uniformed officer on the door. 'Would you please take Mr Marconi back to his cell.' He then turned back to Marconi. 'We'll talk again when you're less tired – your memory may be better, then. Incidentally, would you like to tell me which keys, out of the many in your personal effects in reception, are the keys to your other safe? The one in the back office?'

Marconi narrowed his eyes. 'I don't have them. As I said, Camilla was there last night. She'll have them.'

'Apparently not.' Banham gave a forced smile. 'No worries, we'll break into it. Have a nice rest.'

Chapter Thirty-two

Burton's solicitor had arrived, Thomas Eden, a large, fat, middle-aged man with an extremely ruddy complexion and large bags under his eyes. Eden wore an expensive dark-grey suit over a mauve striped shirt. The jacket was left open, obviously, Alison noticed, because it was too tight to button up. His complexion, she knew, would have been reddened from rich food and too much alcohol. She wondered how many times a week bent politicians wined and dined him, and whether he was, perhaps, as sexually perverted as Burton?

She clicked the tape and video to *on*, then sat forward and looked Burton in the face. He was a good-looking man, no question of that, if you liked that sort of thing. Expensively dressed, immaculately cut, sun-bleached blond hair, slim, tanned, with grey eyes. The man was rich and powerful. Surely he didn't need to stoop to the level he did for a bit of the other, she thought with disgust.

'Where do you live, Mr Burton?'

'Thirty-eight, Under—'

'Just the town will do.'

'I live in Oxford, but spend the week in my London flat, due to my job.'

'London?'

'Yes.'

'You must know the city well, then?'

He rolled his eyes and turned to his solicitor.

'Is my client under arrest?' Thomas Eden snapped at her.

'No, not at the moment –' she pulled a false smile – 'just helping us with our inquiries.'

'Can you answer the question, Mr Burton?' Hannah then said.

'Yes, I know the city well. If you are getting at the fact that I went into that building, I merely wanted to ask them where the nearest off-licence was.'

'Have you ever been in that building before?'

'Does this have any—' The solicitor didn't get to finish the sentence.

'Yes,' Alison barked back. 'And if you don't want to be here all night, can you let Mr Burton answer the question. I will repeat, Mr Burton is helping us with our inquiries.'

'So, I am free to leave?' Burton asked.

'No. You are not. I could charge you with attacking an officer of the law, and I am considering doing just that. So, answer the question. Have you been in the building before?'

Hannah watched him put his hand to his head.

'Truth is,' he paused, bent his head down, and then looked up. 'Yes. OK, I have been in there before and tonight I wasn't looking for an off-licence. I have been in there before, to book Annabelle Perry, not because I would have slept with her, but because I wanted to get her out and help her.'

'Very noble,' Alison said with more than a lacing of sarcasm. 'You have a reputation in there as a pervert who pays for beating up women. How did that happen, if you haven't booked any of the women before?'

'Who said that? That's not remotely true. I was going in there tonight to ask if they knew anything about Annabelle's murder. I wanted to get to the bottom of it. That is not a crime in my book.'

'Noble of you, again,' Alison said curtly. She pressed the iPad she had taken from Camilla, and turned it round to show him. 'For the tape, I am showing Mr Burton a diary of his bookings at the Fabulous escort agency. According to this, you also booked Madara Kowaska, and Danielle Low, on various different nights in the past

217

few years. Also, according to this, on another night, you booked them both together. They were then both booked out from working for a few nights after that. Do I presume that was to heal their bruising?'

When he didn't answer, she carried on. 'And, according to these agency notes, also –' she paused and then said – 'for the sake of the tape, I am showing Mr Burton the notes written about him in the booking diary of Fabulous escort agency. It is written here, "*Christopher Burton. A high-profile pervert who pays very well.*" Can you tell me about that?'

'Don't answer that,' his solicitor interrupted.

'It's not true,' Burton argued, ignoring his solicitor and speaking with a raised voice to Alison. 'It must be someone with the same name as me. Or someone trying to frame me for something.'

'We know you have been done for prostitution offences. That is on record. And these notes are clear. Your name is written here, in this agency's notes, as a pervert.'

'There is no picture to prove it is me.'

She raised her hand for him to stop talking. 'Mr Burton, your sexual preferences are of no interest to me. But your connections to the murdered women are. I am running a murder case. Five people have been murdered. Three of whom had connections with this agency, and those same three women also had a connection with you. So, what I want to know is, what is the connection between these women and you? And do not lie to me. This proves you booked all three of them. So, start talking to me.'

'OK. So I have a past. But that is what it is. Stupid mistakes of the young. How can I have anything to do with their deaths? I have been out of the country.' His voice was full of panic. He then paused and looked down. When he looked up, his forehead was furrowed and he appeared on the point of breaking. 'I truly loved Annabelle, why on earth would I want her dead?'

'So, you admit you slept with her?'

He leaned on the table, and he spoke quietly. 'No, I do not. Yes, I admit I booked her out. I tried to help her – as an uncle figure.

Her father and I were close friends.' He sighed. 'And yes, I fell in love with her. She was beautiful, but that was after I helped her get away from working for the escort side of the agency.'

'Go on,' Alison said coldly.

'This was a long time ago,' he said. 'She started doing escort work there because modelling was drying up and she needed money. I found out.'

'How?'

He became irritated. 'Because she confided in me.' His voice then calmed again. 'So, I spoke to her father about it. He agreed to give her an allowance to stop her prostituting herself.' He looked at his solicitor. 'It was after that my love affair with her started. Of course I didn't kill her. I loved her.'

'Did your wife know about your affair with her, and the other escort women?' Hannah asked, speaking in a condescending manner.

'No. No, and I don't want her to find out.'

Alison breathed a bored sigh. 'Because you love her. And want your marriage to work?'

'My wife doesn't like sex. End of.'

'Hardly surprising,' Hannah snapped. 'If your idea of fun is burning and punching your partner.'

'That's enough,' Thomas Eden jumped in. 'My client's married life has nothing to do with this.'

'Oh, but I beg to differ,' Alison told him. 'It has everything to do with it. Three women, who your client has had sex with – perverted sex, too, according to these records from Fabulous – are now dead.'

'Jesus.' Burton shook his head and spoke quietly. 'I didn't kill them.'

'What size shoe are you, Mr Burton?' This was Hannah.

'Size eleven, normally.'

'And you are just back from where?'

'Mexico, and then Ischia. It's an Italian island. I went there briefly to check on the villa. My wife and I have a villa there.'

219

Hannah sat up; the penny seemed to drop. She turned to Alison. 'Isn't that where all the spas are, Ischia?'

'Yes, that's right,' he said. 'Healing spas.'

'Where the spa water is completely pure and untouched by any chemical?' Hannah pushed.

'You've done your homework,' he said flatly.

Alison made eye contact with Hannah. She had got the message.

'Do you bring bottles of it back with you? Is that allowed?' she asked him.

'Yes, it is allowed. My wife always brings some back.' He then hesitated briefly before saying, 'Why do you ask?'

'Nice for your wife. Pure water. Don't get much of it here,' Alison said, watching the puzzlement that was registering on his face.

'Isn't Mexico rife with illegal drugs?' Hannah added.

He scowled. 'How would I know?'

'What has this got to do with my client, or your inquiry?' Thomas Eden again spoke in a bullying tone.

Alison stared straight into his over-ruddy face. 'We've found a drug connection with the murdered women, and now the agency, too. The drugs we found in Madara Kowaska's and Annabelle Perry's flats, we believe, came from the same source. We also found heroin, cocaine, spice, and crystal meth at the Fabulous agency, also from that very same source.' She turned her attention back to Burton. 'What can you tell us about that?'

He shook his head nonchalantly. 'Nothing. Why would I?'

'You have already told us you wanted to help Annabelle help her brother. He's an addict. So, where did she get the drugs for her brother? As you were so in love with her, I believe you helped her. Found her a good supplier. Who was her supplier, Mr Burton?'

'I don't . . .' He stopped mid-sentence and sighed. Then he bowed his head and then lifted it. 'Madara Kowaska.'

'Who did Madara get them from?'

'I don't know.'

'She wasn't the top dog. Come on, Mr Burton, you have connections. You must know.'

'I don't. And I didn't want to get involved. It is more than my job's worth, but, yes, I wanted to help Annabelle and Jonathan.'

'What colour are your socks, Mr Burton?' Hannah asked him.

He frowned, sighed loudly, then looked down at his foot before raising his trouser leg to check, and throwing his eyes northward.

'Navy blue,' he said flatly.

'Do you always wear that colour?'

'Mostly, yes.'

'I notice you have had a membership to a motorcycle club,' Alison said. 'You had a vintage motorbike registered. Do you ride still?'

He looked suddenly uncomfortable. 'My son had a bike. I paid for the membership of a club for him. I have just forgotten to stop the direct debit. My wife probably should have done it. And, no, I don't ride a motorbike. We've been through this.'

'Such a family man, aren't you?' Alison said sarcastically. 'I'm going to ask you to remove a sock, please. I will be sending it to Forensics.'

She ignored the alarmed look on his face, and, as Thomas Eden started to speak, she put out her hand, palm up, to hush him, then leaned into the tape and spoke. 'The time is now one forty-five a.m. I am terminating this interview, but it is to be continued.'

'What's going on?' Both Eden and Burton spoke at the same time.

'I am not prepared to release you. I am detaining you for further questioning after further forensic investigation,' she told Burton, ignoring Eden's arguments that she couldn't. She waited for the sock to be handed over, then stood up, turned her back to him, and opened the door from Interview Room A. As she walked out, she said to the uniformed officer standing guard outside the door, 'Escort Mr Burton back to his cell, please.'

Hannah then followed.

'Look, OK. I've dabbled in prostitutes,' Burton shouted after them. 'I am a man, for Christ's sake.' He realised his pleas were falling on deaf ears, as Hannah and Alison were now the other end of the corridor and the uniformed PC was standing by him, looking bored and ready to take him back to his cell. He lowered his voice and, in a weak tone, turned to Thomas Eden, 'My wife doesn't do sex. What am I supposed to do?' His tone became desperate. 'This is going to ruin me. I didn't kill them. I am being framed. OK, I had sex with them, but I didn't kill them. Why would I?'

Eden patted his hand. 'We'll sort it all out,' he told him in a comforting tone. 'I'll have a word in the right ear.'

Chapter Thirty-three

Banham had been watching the interview on the screen in Alison's office. He walked back into the investigation room.

'You did well in there,' he said to Hannah.

'Forensics tests on fibres from inside the wellington tell us they come from the same fabric as the socks the drugs were found in at Annabelle's flat,' Alison reminded the detectives that were in the room. She handed Burton's sock to Nigel, the bald detective. 'Get this sock over to Forensics. Ask them to compare fibres. Tell them it's urgent. I *so* don't want to release that lying, perverted, bastard.'

'Don't hold your breath,' Banham told her. 'Even if Forensics prove it's the same material, that's still not enough to charge him with murder. You can charge him with aggravated assault, but he'll get bail, especially with that solicitor.'

'He admitted he visited the three prostitutes,' Hannah said.

'The three *murdered* prostitutes,' Alison corrected.

'Visiting prostitutes isn't against the law,' Banham reminded them. 'And he wasn't in the country when they were murdered. He can prove that.'

'He also has a membership to a motorcycle club,' Hannah pushed.

Banham rubbed his hand across his mouth, the habit he had when he was thinking. Then he said, 'I agree, everything points in his direction. But his alibi is sound. If you could prove he wasn't out of the country, then we have a case. But right now, there is not enough for the CPS to even consider it.'

'The water found in the wellington boot wasn't London water,' Hannah reminded him. 'He has a villa in Ischia. That island is famous for spas. Supposedly, it has the purest water in the world. He admits he brought some of it back. There's a connection, surely, sir?'

Banham nodded. 'I agree, lots of coincidences. But we have the CCTV from Gatwick which shows he boarded that plane, and then arrived back when he said he did.'

Crowther joined in. 'He wouldn't do his own dirty work anyway. He would employ someone to do it for him.'

Alison shook her head. 'Why would he have had Annabelle killed? I believe he loved her.'

'No idea,' Crowther said. 'Supposing we go along the lines of he employed someone to kill them, and he then left the country to give himself an alibi. Then we work out what they had against him.'

'I'd like to know where the video is for the cover we found in Madara's flat,' Banham said.

'Anything of interest on his phone?' Alison asked Luke Hughes, who was still sitting behind his desk, busying himself on his computer.

He shook his head. 'It's all business numbers. My thoughts are, he has another mobile for private use.'

'You should go home,' Banham said to Luke. 'Morning meeting is at seven. It's quarter to three now. You were up all last night.'

'I'm OK.'

'Luke sleeps very little,' Stephanie told them, 'and then, it's normally in a cell here.'

'And you know, how?' Crowther asked, the implication in his voice clear.

'Oh, don't start, you two,' Alison said. 'It's too late for jovialities.'

'So,' Banham said, looking at Alison. 'What next? You're the boss.'

'Search warrants for Burton's London pad and his Oxford home, and for Fabulous,' she told him. 'All the arrests stay here overnight.

We are going home now. Your dog – sorry, *Babe* – looks tired and hungry.'

'I'll get on to my mate the magistrate,' Crowther said, tapping digits into his phone. 'Get him out of bed. As soon as we get a warrant, I'll bell you.'

'I'm off to wake up Del Harris, and arrest him for lying to us,' Stephanie said. 'He can spend the night in a cell, too.'

Alison nodded. 'Take a few uniforms with you.'

'My money's still on him,' Stephanie told her. 'I never took to him. He rides a motorbike, could have clocked out of Clapham earlier than he said, and made it to all the murders. And now, we find out he lied to us and knows Madara. Let's see if we can find a connection for him with Christopher Burton?'

She then looked at Luke. 'That'll be all our cells full tonight – where will you nap?' she asked him.

'I'm fine,' he said sharply.

'We are all going home for the night,' Banham told the dog, whose ears were pricked up, listening to him.

Alison shook her head and threw her eyes to heaven.

'I'll give you a lift,' Crowther said to Hannah.

Alison immediately gave him a warning glance.

'I'll bell you soon as I hear on the warrant,' Crowther told her, ignoring her warning glance, as he put his hand on Hannah's shoulder to see her out of the room. He then turned to look back as he got to the door. 'If I don't call before, I'll see you first thing in the morning.'

'My feet are still killing me from the stilettos,' Hannah said as she kicked off her trainers onto the carpet in Crowther's flat.

'Feel free to take everything off,' he told her. 'I'm a gentleman. Borrow a dressing gown. There's a couple in my bedroom, and, if you want, have a warm bath. I'll chill some wine while you soak, unless you just want to snuggle up and go straight to bed. I'm sleeping on the sofa by the way. So, once you're in the bedroom, it's your space.'

'To be honest, I'm past the wine. I'm too tired. I would love a hot bath, though, and then to slide into a bed'

'Want a hot drink in the bath?'

'Have you got chocolate?'

'Coming up. I'll knock and leave it at the door. Make yourself at home; we've only got three hours before we're back.'

The hot bath made her feel sleepy. She had a quick dip and then climbed out, wrapping herself in the very fluffy black towelling robe that hung on the back of the door. As she tied the belt around her, there was a knock on the door.

'Hot chocolate outside the door,' Crowther said.

'It's OK, I'm out. I'm covered up. Come in, if you want.'

The door opened, and Crowther stood, in a dressing gown, holding a Dennis the Menace mug of hot chocolate in each hand.

He placed one mug on the cabinet just by the door, without looking at Hannah. 'I won't stay,' he said. 'I'm just outside.'

'Don't rush away. Stay and talk,' she said encouragingly.

He paused, looked down to the ground and then said, 'To be honest, I just can't be in here and not touch you.' He looked up and into her eyes. 'You are so beautiful.'

It took less than a second for her to walk to him, take the other mug out of his hand, and place it on the cabinet. Then, as he watched her, she pulled her dressing-gown cord loose, pulled it down over her shoulders, then freed her arms, and it dropped to the floor. She was completely naked as she cupped his head and pushed her mouth against his.

Chapter Thirty-four

Just before the morning meeting was due to start, Alison walked into the women's locker room and found Hannah changing from the clothes she had been wearing the night before into a clean pair of khaki trousers and a beige jumper that were hanging in her locker.

It didn't take a detective to know Hannah had not been home last night.

She spoke briskly to her. 'Starting in five,' she told her. She then walked into the incident room and glared furiously at Crowther. He didn't acknowledge it.

'OK. Busy day ahead,' she said, addressing the team. She then turned as Hannah hurried into the room. 'Nice of you to join us,' she said curtly.

'Sorry, ma'am,' Hannah said quietly.

Alison then stood silently, watching, and allowing the rest of the room to watch, too, as Hannah hurried in and settled behind a desk. She then turned her attention back to the meeting. 'Right. Long and productive night. I know we're all knackered. We are getting closer. All our cells are full, and we will have to make decisions on that this morning.'

'I've got Del Harris waiting,' Stephanie interrupted. 'He's in Interview Room C. He's waiting for the duty solicitor and is not a happy bunny.'

Luke then lifted his hand and spoke up. 'Search warrants have just arrived. The ones Sergeant Crowther organised last night.'

'Thank you,' Alison said, then turned to Crowther. 'You had a busy night – no wonder you look done in,' she said sarcastically, aware Hannah was blushing.

Luke took her attention again. 'And interesting info here. A neighbour of Danielle Low's, who lives in the road directly behind Apple Tree Close, came in about half an hour ago,' he told her. 'On her way to work. She heard the press appeal yesterday and came in with information. I took her statement.' He lifted up a sheet of paper. 'I'll read it to you.

"*I was looking out of my window on the evening of the fire and saw a motorbike pull up. I clearly remember a pizza sign on the back. I thought nothing of it, except it was still raining a little, and I became curious as they had parked at the bottom of the road, where there are no houses. The few houses are at the top of my road, and there was loads of room to park there. I watched him walk up the road in the rain, and through the gate leading to the back of the flats. I wondered why he hadn't parked nearer, or even at the front of their building.*" She couldn't give a description,' Luke told them, 'as the biker was head to toe in black leather and wearing a crash helmet, which he had kept on. I asked about height, she said average, but wasn't sure. I asked about the bike reg. She wasn't sure about that either, but thinks it was something similar to LW. I have just been looking up the bikes stolen from the pizza cafe. LH were the first letters of the bike that was stolen four weeks before the fire. Not too unlike, considering it was pouring rain.'

'Not unlike Del Harris's bike reg either,' Stephanie reminded them. 'His starts with LM.'

'OK,' Banham said. 'You interview him, Steph. Lean on him hard, threaten him, and find out every detail of how he knew Madara.'

'She'd frighten anyone into telling her anything if she leaned on them,' Crowther joked.

That sent a titter of amusement around the team. Even Hannah squeezed her lips to suppress a giggle.

'Shut up, Crowther,' Alison snapped. 'I've told you before: you treat your fellow female detectives with respect.'

228

'Just a joke, ma'am,' he said defensively.

'Yes. Well, not at the expense of the female detectives in my team,' Alison told him sharply. Her eyes flicked briefly to Hannah, then back to Crowther.

Hannah stared straight ahead, at the whiteboard at the top of the room.

'Let's get on,' Banham said, putting his hand up to hush the jibes that were now starting.

'Burton's still our guest here, in a cell,' Alison reminded them. 'His solicitor is going insane, apparently. We can only charge him with assaulting a police officer, and bail him. We've got nothing else, as yet. We are urgently waiting on Forensics.'

'Your witness said she thinks she saw the motorbike reg, something like LW,' Stephanie said to Luke. She was sipping a very large cappuccino, the froth from it had settled in the form of a moustache around her upper lip. 'Someone else said that, too, the woman at the pub. We have to remember that evening was rainy, therefore it was harder to read a registration. The reg on Harris's bike is LM.' She put her cup down and rubbed her hands. 'I've taken a dislike to Harris from the word go, and I am a woman of strong instincts.'

'Ring me after the interview,' Alison told her. 'We now have the search warrants, so we are off to Oxford to pay a visit to Mrs Burton. If she isn't there, we'll go in anyway. Les and Baz, you are with us, and round up some uniformed backup. Hannah and Crowther, you are doing the agency. I presume it's locked, so go in anyway with the warrant. I want that place turned upside down. Marconi and Camilla Agnelli both say they haven't got keys to the inner safe, so break it open. We want anything and everything that is in there.'

She turned to Luke. 'Keep on at Forensics. We need tests back as soon as – if they say they are working on it, ask them to work faster.'

'As we will all be out, apart from the few who are helping Luke, would you keep an eye on Babe after the interview?' Banham asked Stephanie. 'She'll need a loo break.'

Steph nodded and looked at Babe. 'You'll be OK with me,' she told the dog. 'I've got biscuits.'

'Right, that's about it then,' Banham said. 'Let's all get going.'

Alison's tone then became sharp and militant. 'Crowther, my office. Now,' she said, turning her back and walking speedily towards the door.

Hannah turned to Crowther, who didn't acknowledge her. He turned and followed Alison.

Alison glared at him as he walked into her office, after knocking, but not waiting. His jumper was on inside out, and, although he appeared to have matching socks on, his shoelaces were different colours, one black and one brown, and both undone.

'You look a mess. Did your alarm not go off?'

'Spit it out, Alison. What do you want to say?'

'Hannah came in wearing the clothes she went home in yesterday. Did she stay at yours last night?'

He pressed his tongue into the inside of his cheek, half-laughed and threw his eyes to heaven. 'Ask *her*, Alison. Although, let's be honest: friends as we are, it really is none of your business.'

'That's where you are wrong. I took her into my team, so I'm responsible for her. I put her with you because I knew your knowledge would help her. But I warned you not to seduce her. That's the last thing she needs at the moment.'

He stared at Alison. 'What are you, her mother? We've got a killer on the loose, ma'am. Five victims, Alison, and you are wasting your energy on my sex life.'

Before she had the chance to answer, he spoke again. 'And in answer to your question, no, I didn't seduce her.' He then turned and walked out the door, closing it with a bang as he left.

Chapter Thirty-five

Del Harris's hair was greasier than the last time Stephanie had spoken to him. He had been picking at one of the pimples by the side of his nose, and it was bleeding. His fingernails were filthy. She felt an urge to throw him in the shower.

Beside him sat the duty solicitor, Angela O'Dowd, a pleasant, no-nonsense woman in her mid- thirties. Stephanie and she got on well, out of the interview room.

'Interview is being videoed and recorded,' Stephanie said in a matter-of-fact tone, 'with me is DC Luke Hughes.'

'Why am I here?' Del Harris asked her. 'I should be at work. We're short-staffed—'

'The trains will hardly start running on time because you are flagging them in and out of Clapham,' Stephanie told him, pushing the photo of Madara in front of him. 'You told us you didn't know this woman. I asked you last night, and, again, you said you didn't know her. So, I am asking you for the third time,' she said in a cold tone. 'Do you know this woman?'

'No.'

She pushed another evidence bag in front of him, containing the dog-end of the spliff. 'I am showing Mr Harris exhibit 107fb. Forensics result on stub of marijuana cigarette.' She then leaned back, folding her arms across her oversized bosom. 'Could you, then, explain to me how your DNA found its way on to this spliff, which was retrieved from this same woman's flat?'

He coloured immediately, making his already ruddy pimples

231

look as if they had been lit up by a halogen light. His hand went to his forehead, and he used the back of it to flick back the pile of greasy hair that fell across his fingers.

'I lied,' he said quietly. 'I did know her.'

'Go on.'

'My mother must never know.'

Stephanie rolled her eyes. 'Tell us about knowing Madara,' she said.

'I met her through Danielle,' he said quietly. 'Danielle was her friend. She got her drugs from her. I didn't say before, because my mother has a heart condition and I didn't want her to know I smoked marijuana. If I was arrested, she could have a heart attack.'

'How did your DNA get on to the dog-end?' Stephanie repeated.

'Danielle introduced me to the odd smoke. And I enjoyed it. It calmed me down. She introduced me to Madara, too. Took me to her flat. We had the odd smoke together. I knew it was wrong, Danielle shouldn't have introduced me to a drug, but I forgave her, as I enjoyed the odd smoke, too.'

'You're a grown man. You can make your own decisions. Anyway, go on.'

'When I found out Danielle was a whore, I stopped seeing her, of course I did. I wasn't risking catching something. When our flats were burned, I was in a terrible state, and understandably very stressed. I had lost everything.' He looked up pleadingly. 'You must understand that. I lost everything, and I knew I would have to go back to living with my mother. I phoned Madara and asked for some stuff to calm me down. Check my phone, there'll be a text on there, proving it. She invited me round. She was very upset over Danielle. They were good friends. We smoked a joint between us. That's it.'

'Did you know Annabelle Perry?'

'I never met her. I knew of her.'

'How?'

'Through Danielle.'

'But you never met her?'

'No.'

'How do you know she knew Madara?'

'I don't want to get Madara into trouble.'

'You won't. She's been murdered.'

He seemed stunned. Stephanie and Luke both watched his reaction very carefully.

After a few seconds, he spoke. 'OK. Madara was a dealer. Annabelle, I believe, got drugs off her for her brother, who is an addict.' He leaned forward. 'I'm not gonna be charged with drug offences, am I?'

'Just answer the questions,' Stephanie said. 'Do you know Christopher Burton?'

'Who? No.'

'The politician? He was a close friend of Annabelle.'

Harris's voice became loud and angry. 'No. I've said no. I don't know these foul people. I had the odd spliff. I got in with the wrong crowd.' He banged his hands on the table and stood up. 'I have to think of my mother. If I am not under arrest—'

'Sit down, Mr Harris, or you will be,' Stephanie said firmly. 'You have already obstructed a murder inquiry by lying. I am going to check your phone, as you offered, then I will be back.' She got up and left the room.

Chapter Thirty-six

'Let's hope something turns up in here,' Hannah said as she and Crowther watched the uniformed team force the door of the Fabulous agency to open. 'I'd like to get back in the DI's good books. She glared at me all through this morning's meeting. She knows I didn't go home last night. She knows we slept together.'

Crowther shook his head. 'No, she doesn't,' he assured her. 'She asked me if I seduced you, and I said no.'

They both walked into the agency and to the files behind the reception desk. 'Why didn't you just admit it?' Hannah asked him. 'Why lie about it? It's not a crime. They'll find out, and then they'll call you a liar.'

He pulled the grin that reminded her of a naughty schoolboy. 'I wasn't lying. I didn't seduce you. You seduced me, if you care to remember.' He winked gently. 'I was prepared to be a perfect gentleman.'

'You didn't resist.'

'Who could resist you?' he said, obviously sensing she wasn't amused. 'If it worries you, I'm happy to even the balance. I'll seduce you later.'

She put her head down, pulled a drawer out, and rustled through its contents. 'Let's find something to help nail this killer,' she said. 'Alison's been good to me. I don't want to upset her.'

He frowned, and tilted his head to study her. 'I agree, let's get our minds on the job,' he said.

*

It was eleven in the morning when Alison and Banham arrived at the Oxford home of Christopher Burton. Alison flashed her warrant when his wife opened the front door.

'Police,' Alison said. 'We have a warrant to search this property. Can you let us in, please?'

Susan Burton immediately stepped aside to allow the team access. She was a tallish woman, and wore jeans and a sequinned jumper. Her feet bore red patent mid-heeled shoes. Her dyed-black hair was tied back in a neat ponytail, and her nails were painted in scarlet.

'Can I ask what this is about?' she said as the uniformed team made their way inside her house.

'We are investigating the murder of five people, and have authority to search your property,' Alison told her.

'This is about Christopher, I presume,' the woman said, sighing. 'If you think there is something in my house, go ahead. I can't stop you anyway.'

'Do you mind answering a few questions?' Alison asked. 'While my team have a look around.' She nodded to the four detectives, who were already pulling forensic blue-plastic gloves over their hands and waiting for the signal to start the search.

The woman shrugged. 'As long as I can have coffee while I do it. I had a lot to drink last night and I sort of need it.'

Banham and Alison made eye contact.

'Please sit,' Susan said. 'Make yourselves at home. I suspect this search will take a while.'

A pretty young Asian woman, who Susan introduced as her housekeeper, brought coffee on a tray a few minutes later.

'This is a sensitive question—' Alison started to say, but was interrupted by Susan.

'Has he been locked up for kerb-crawling again?' she asked, pouring cream into her own coffee. 'Only, he didn't come home last night, and he said he was looking for action.'

'No.' Alison said. 'Does he still visit prostitutes, then?'

'Yes. I believe so,' she said nonchalantly. She obviously noticed

235

Alison's expression change as she spoke, because she quickly added, 'Marriages are what they are, and ours works the way it works. I don't like sex, and he does, so I let him go and get it where he likes. The man is a fool.'

Banham pulled the photos of the three murdered prostitutes from his briefcase. He showed them to her. 'Did you know these women?' he asked.

Susan pointed to the photo of Annabelle. 'That's the Perry girl. Her father was a minister with Chris. Ghastly woman. She's a slag and a junkie. Her brother is worse.'

'Do you know if your husband had an affair with her?'

'Oh, for sure. Are these all hookers? He probably had affairs with all of them. I'd rather not know. As long as my son isn't hurt, and my lifestyle not affected, I couldn't give a hoot.'

'These *hookers*,' Banham said sarcastically, 'are all dead. Murdered. Two burned in their homes, and one battered to death in an alleyway. You might have read about it in the papers?'

'No,' she said quickly. 'I don't buy or read papers. Load of rubbish. Chris brings papers home, but he has been away on holiday.'

'Didn't you go with him?'

'No. We tend to holiday separately nowadays.'

'Where do you go, when you go?' Banham asked.

'To our villa on Ischia. The Italian island?'

'The one with the pure water in their spas?' Alison asked.

'Spot on.' She looked at the empty cups still on the tray. 'Are you not having coffee? Help yourselves.'

'No, thank you,' Banham said. 'Have you been to your villa recently?'

'Yes, as a matter of fact, I went just before Christopher. Do have a coffee. It came from Italy. Quite delicious.'

'Not for me,' Banham said.

'Nor me,' Alison agreed. 'Did you bring any spa water back?'

'Oh, er, yes. Gosh, I'm not going to be arrested for that, am I? I'm not sure I'm supposed to.'

236

'No. But I'd appreciate it if you would let me have a bottle,' Alison said.

'My pleasure.' The woman smiled. As she sipped her coffee, her over-lipsticked mouth bled its dark-red colour around the edge of both her cup and her lips.

Alison thought she resembled a clown. 'Does your husband always wear Italian socks?'

'I buy his clothes. All our clothes. I'm a fashion snob. So, yes, all Chris's socks are Italian silk. Ischia is straight across from Naples airport, but I usually fly to Milan first. I go to the fashion stores when I visit the villa.'

'Any special colour, his socks?' Alison pushed.

'I buy him a lot of navy, but he also has brown and black for winter months. Why do you ask? God, he hasn't been found dead, has he?'

'No, he hasn't,' Banham assured her.

'Are they all the same make?' Alison asked.

'Yes. I like the Aristo ones. I shop a lot for his clothes.' She looked at Alison. 'Well, I don't sleep with him or fondle his penis, but I do cook and shop for him. I am his wife, after all, even if he does behave like a filthy pig.'

'I will need a pair of his navy socks as well as the spa water,' Alison said.

The penny seemed to drop. 'Are you thinking he murdered these women?' Susan asked. 'You would be wrong there. A, he's been out of the country.' She searched Alison's face for confidence. Alison gave her nothing back. 'And B, I know him better than anyone. He doesn't have it in him.'

'Does he take drugs?' Banham asked her.

'Are you trying to ruin his career? No. He does not.' She shook her head. 'But if someone has given you that idea, then let me clear that one up. David Perry had a son. *Annabelle*'s brother. Jonathan is an addict. We tried to help him. Because of Chris's loyalty to David.' She waved her hand dismissively, before carrying on. 'Chris may have been fucking his daughter, Lord only knows – I

237

heard she had fucked most of England. She'd make Christine Keeler look like a nun, that's what I heard. Anyway, I know he introduced Annabelle to someone who got the drugs for her brother. Christopher merely made the introduction. That much I can tell you.'

'Who to? What was the name of this person? Male or female?' Banham pushed.

'I have no idea. I've told you what I know. Chris told me he helped the junkie son because of his loyalty to David Perry. David and his wife were killed in a car crash. Terrible tragedy, those children made orphans. He was Chris's friend. Chris said it was for David, but as I said, Chris can't resist a whore. I expect she sucked his dick for it.'

'Does he, or has he, ever owned a motorbike?'

Susan paused. 'No, my son had one. He lives in France now, and barely visits us, but God knows, who can blame him?'

'Why do you say that?'

She shook her head. 'He's just happy where he is.'

As Alison was about to bring the interview to a close, and ask for the socks and spa water, DS Les Mitchell came down the stairs. He was carrying a flyer.

'Thought this interesting, ma'am,' he said. 'It's from the pizza place in the road near where Danielle was burned to death. And there's a mobile number written on the back.'

'Put a trace in on the number,' Banham said immediately. 'We'll need that bottle of your spa water, and a pair of Christopher's socks,' he told Susan Burton.

'Oh my God. You *are* saying you think Chris is involved in a murder case. Gosh, that kind of publicity could lose him his job, and I could lose my house . . .'

238

Chapter Thirty-seven

Luke Hughes dragged his hands down his face. He was knackered; he had been up working all night. Last night he'd hardly slept, just the odd few minutes nodding off in his wheelchair behind his desk, as all the cells were full to overflowing.

He replaced his phone receiver and gulped another cup of black coffee. The number on the back of the pizza flyer was for an untraceable mobile. He had then rung Johnny Walsh, who had confirmed Christopher Burton had been in a couple of times, and also phoned orders through. Mr Burton, Walsh had said, would go out of his way to get an authentic Italian pizza, which was what Walsh supplied.

Luke then started to do some digging on the pizza-delivery boys, and was interested to find Joseph Perrino was born of an Italian mother from Naples, although his father was Jamaican. And then, even more interesting, the other delivery lad, Anthony Rossiti, had been brought up in Naples, and only arrived in England eighteen months ago. His family were still living in Naples, and he had been back four times in the last year. Christopher Burton's villa was in Ischia which, Luke knew, was a short boat ride from Naples. So, was this a coincidence, then, or a connection?

He turned to Stephanie. 'Guv, we may have something here,' he told her, handing over the notes he had made. 'I thought there might be some connection between Burton's villa and Oluwa Marconi's family links to Italy, but I can't find anything. Both the pizza-delivery boys have links to Naples, though. Burton's villa is just across the water there.'

Stephanie was eating a bag of crisps. She put the corner of the bag to her mouth and poured the remains in, then screwed the empty packet up, aimed, and threw it at the waste-paper bin. It missed.

She looked at the notes. 'That is interesting,' she agreed. 'I'll make a call to the guv'nor. Someone should interview those boys again, see if they recognise the phone number on that flyer.'

'That's the third packet of crisps you've eaten in the last twenty minutes, sarge,' Luke asked. 'Is something bothering you?'

She shook her head and shrugged. 'Harris bothers me. His story works, and the call he said he made to Madara was, as he said, on his mobile phone. I have to release and bail him. But I'm not happy. I just don't trust him.'

The Fabulous agency was proving fruitless. Hannah and Crowther had been through every drawer and cupboard. They had forced the second safe open and found it to be empty.

'We'll just have to hope that the technical guys get something from the old computer we took last night,' Crowther said. 'There's nothing in here now apart from a telephone, a few chairs, and . . .'

'A back room with a couch,' Hannah added with a grin. 'Is the front door locked?'

'Hannah, there's two uniforms standing outside. What will they think if we disappear into the back room?'

She lifted the bottom of her beige woollen jumper and peeled the garment over her head.

'What, no! Not here,' Crowther quickly protested, moving to block the view to the outside glass door. 'The uniform boys can see in.'

'Then we'd better get out of sight,' she said, unzipping her trousers and walking into the back room.

★

Alison took the call from Stephanie as they were leaving Christopher Burton's Oxford home. Steph told her about Harris. 'I checked his phone and his alibi stood up, so I've bailed him and let him go.' She then repeated what Luke had found out about the Italian connection with the delivery boys and the fact Burton had just visited an Italian Island, and the pizza cafe.

'I'll get Hannah and Crowther to go to the pizza place and bring both the delivery boys in for further questioning,' Alison told her. 'Must be a connection; their flyer was in the bedroom drawer of the Burtons' house, and that's in Oxford.'

'Shame the number on the back is untraceable, ma'am.'

Banham was mouthing to Alison, telling her to tell them to let Babe out.

'Can you take the dog out for a wee?' Alison added with a hint of irritation. 'We are on our way to Forensics. We've got Ischian spa water and another sample of Burton's socks. The wife confirmed Burton wears the same Italian brand most of the time, and mainly navy blue. Interesting.'

'Very,' Stephanie agreed. 'And I'm taking the dog out for a wee now. I don't want it staining my chair.'

Luke looked up and laughed. 'Like your chair is so scrupulously clean,' he teased.

Alison disconnected, then pressed Crowther's number. It went to voicemail. She left a message to tell him to go straight to the pizza shop next. She told him about the connection, and said she wanted him to bring in the delivery boys for further questioning. She then rang Hannah. That went to voicemail, too.

'Jesus, doesn't anyone answer their phone?' she said, shaking her head.

'OK, let's get these to Forensics and let's hope their testing isn't as slow as this traffic,' Banham said, reaching for the unit siren from the floor of the passenger seat. He turned it to *on*, unwound the window, and placed it on the roof of the car. He then pulled out into the fast lane, chasing cars out of his way as he sped back up the A40.

*

To the delight of both Hannah and Crowther, the sofa had turned out to be a sofa bed. Hannah was now getting dressed, and Crowther was pulling his trousers back on. 'Exciting, when you know there are two uniforms guarding the door outside,' she said. 'I bet they think we're being very thorough.'

Crowther dug into his pocket and checked his phone. 'Boss called,' he told Hannah. He checked his watch. 'About fifteen minutes ago.'

Hannah looked concerned. 'Call her back.' She was reassembling the sofa as she spoke. It was then that she felt something like a large button inside one of the cushions. She unzipped the cushion, pushed her hand inside the fabric and pulled out a tiny memory stick. In faint pink nail polish, someone had written the words *private contacts* on it. It was a slow realisation, then she quickly held it up as Crowther was returning his call to Alison.

'Sorry, our phones were in the outer room,' Crowther was saying. 'Hannah was in the back room and I was doing the toilet. Sadly, nothing . . .'

Hannah was now standing in front of him, wiggling the memory stick and pointing to the wording on it.

Crowther stopped talking, realising what Hannah had found, as she mouthed the words, 'Hidden inside the cushion.'

'Unless you count a memory stick, found hidden –' he watched carefully as Hannah mouthed the words again – 'inside one of the sofa cushions, boss,' he said to Alison, his tone now sounding less guilty. 'It's got the words "private contacts" written across it,' he added, reading from the casing. 'Yes. On the way, boss. We'll meet you there.'

He turned to Hannah. 'Let's go. Meeting the guv at the pizza joint.'

Hannah was driving. Crowther was quiet. She opened the conversation.

'So, both the pizza-delivery boys have very strong connections to Naples. Near where Christopher Burton has his villa.'

'Correct.'

'And the registration on the bike, seen by the witness at the first arson, could fit the registration of the bike stolen from the pizza cafe last month?' she questioned.

'Correct again.'

'What would the connection be between the delivery drivers and Christopher Burton?'

'We don't know yet.'

'And are you saying you think he used them to do his dirty work and kill the women?'

'It's a possibility.'

'Why them?'

'Guv'nor found a pizza flyer in Burton's Oxford home. There's a number on the back; it's untraceable, but it proves, without doubt, Burton has a connection with that pizza joint. The owner has now confirmed Burton has been in for pizza. And it's just down the road from the first arson.'

'And a long way from Burton's Oxford home.'

'Who knows?' Crowther's tone was sharp. 'We've got him connected to the victims, through the agency, and with Anna-belle Perry through her father, who was also a member of Parliament, and now the drugs for Jonathan Perry, according to his wife.'

'And the first victim lived near the pizza shop.'

'Correct.'

'Are you OK?'

'Yes, why?'

'You seem a bit off, or cool – yes, cool. That's a better description. Didn't you enjoy what we did?'

He turned away and looked out of the window. 'Hannah, we're supposed to be working. We missed our guv'nor's calls earlier. You seduced me on the job. That wasn't very professional.'

'You didn't resist.'

He turned back, but he wasn't grinning. 'You're hard to resist.'

243

'It's all me, is it?' Her face then became serious. 'You said you would seduce me later. I just gave you the opportunity.'

'I didn't seduce you, though. You seduced me, again.'

'Are you complaining?'

'I'm not complaining.'

'Sounds like you are to me.'

'I'm thinking.'

Her tone softened. 'Seduce me later, then. I'll let you.'

He didn't answer. Neither spoke another word until they got to the pizza shop.

Alison was there, waiting with Banham, as Hannah parked up and hurried out of the car. Alison gave them both a thorough look over, and then flicked her angry grey-green eyes in Crowther's direction. He got the message.

'We are en route to Forensics,' she told him, without taking her eyes off his guilty-looking face. 'I'll take the memory stick from you and drop it in to Luke on the way. Luke will check it out. We have spa water and a blue sock of Burton's that the wife gave us.' She pointed to the door of the cafe and handed Crowther the flyer with the phone number on the back. 'Cafe's closed for lunch. You two can wait, and when the staff come back, check their handwriting, get them to write this number on a separate piece of paper.' She wrote the number down in her notebook and tore the page and handed it to Crowther. 'Then bring the delivery boys into the station. The boss will have to shut shop again, so tell him we'll be as quick as possible with them.' She then cast her gaze down at Crowther's clothes, which were all crumpled. His hair, too, was uncombed and standing on end, but then he always looked as if he had got dressed in the dark, or a dustbin. Hannah, on the other hand, looked well groomed.

'Took you a long time to search the agency,' Alison sniped. Her angry eyes again bored into his.

'We're very thorough, ma'am. And we eventually found that memory stick.'

'Where did you find it?' she asked.

'In a cushion on the sofa, ma'am,' Hannah told her before Crowther could stop her.

'Well done. You obviously gave the sofa a thorough going over,' she said sarcastically. She then turned her back and walked way.

Chapter Thirty-eight

The sock and spa water from Susan Burton had been left with the forensic lab, and Alison was now back in the investigation room.

'Let's have an update,' she said to the detectives that were in the room, working behind their computers. 'We've still got Burton in custody, as well as Camilla Agnelli and Oluwa Marconi?'

'Yes, ma'am,' Luke told her. 'And all giving our custody sarge a hard time.'

'Well, Camilla and Marconi will go before a magistrate tomorrow now, so no bail for them. We are also waiting on forensic tests, so Burton's solicitor can shout as loudly as he likes. Crowther and Hannah are bringing the delivery boys in for questioning again.' She turned to Luke. 'What's on that memory stick?'

He shook his head. 'It's blank, ma'am.'

'Blank? You are kidding. Shit. *Shit.*'

He shook his head again. 'Completely empty, or maybe wiped.'

'Shit. Shit. Shit.'

'Burton's solicitor is going insane,' Banham said as he walked into the room. 'Are you going to bail him or charge him? He wants to know.'

'We are going to interview him again re the flyer,' Alison said.

'It's not an offence to have a pizza flyer in your house, but it is a coincidence, I agree,' Banham said.

'And another coincidence is that the bike used for the first arson nearly matches the registration of the bike stolen from the pizza place,' Alison reminded him. 'So, a lot of coincidences appearing around that pizza shop.'

'I checked with the DVLA,' Luke told her. 'Burton has a car licence only. But he had a bike licence twenty-five years ago.'

'So, he *can* ride a motorbike?' Alison said.

'All we know for sure is that he knew the victims,' Banham stated. 'We should talk to him again, however, it's not a crime to enjoy a genuine Italian pizza.'

'It could still have been Del Harris's registration,' Stephanie pointed out. 'That's very similar, too. I know coincidences are turning up now with Burton and the pizza shop, but I've still got a hunch about Harris.'

'Sadly, hunches don't count,' Alison snapped.

'You OK, guv?' Steph asked her.

Alison realised she was seething over Crowther and Hannah, but knew she shouldn't snap at Stephanie. 'Yes, thanks,' she said.

'Take the blank memory stick into Camilla and ask her what she knows about it,' Banham told Stephanie. He paused and then added, 'She is half Italian, too, as are Marconi and the delivery drivers. Is there something here that we are not seeing?'

'We need Forensics' reports back ASAP,' Alison stated. 'But testing isn't a few minutes' job and the clock is ticking. Right, I'm going to talk to Burton again, and then take it from there.'

Joseph and Anthony turned up at the pizza cafe together.

'Good afternoon,' Crowther said as they approached the cafe. 'Need to ask you both a few further questions about the theft of those motorbikes. Sorry, boys, going to have to drag you away from work for a while.'

Joseph scowled. 'Now what?' he said. 'Bad enough we're down to one bike. Delivering is tough, mate.'

'We think these bikes could be tied in with a murder we are investigating. We also have a flyer for your gaff with a mobile number on the back. Need your help on tracing that number.' He showed them the flyer.

'Not my handwriting,' Joseph told him as Anthony shook his head.

'Mine neither,' Anthony told them.

'Don't look like the boss's either, but you can ask him yourself,' Joseph suggested, indicating with his head as Johnny Walsh drew up in his car and quickly locked it, then walked up to them.

'Problem?' he said to Crowther and Hannah, then turned to look at the boys.

'Do you recognise this number?' Crowther asked him, showing him the flyer.

Walsh took the flyer and looked at the number, then shook his head. 'Don't immediately recognise it. It could be somewhere we've delivered. I can check our records,' he said. 'What's up?'

'The flyer was found in Oxford at the home of Christopher Burton, that MP.'

Walsh nodded. 'He has been in here. He likes our genuine Italian pizzas and he has a friend in the area, apparently. It could be we had to ring that number before delivering his pizza, then. Ask the boys, they would be more likely to know.'

Crowther nodded. 'Going to ask them to come down the station to give us full statements about the bike thefts, and such,' he said, not wishing to tell them he was suspicious of their strong links to Italy.

Walsh put his hands in the air. 'Can you get them back as soon as? I don't want to be losing my takeaway delivery trade, if there is any. I'll have to deliver in my car till they come back.'

Hannah had already stabbed numbers into her phone and requested a car to drive the boys to the station. It pulled up at that moment.

'We'll do our best,' Crowther told him as Hannah opened the door to the car, driven by Baz Butler. 'Here's service for you,' Crowther said, directing the two boys into the car. He then turned to Walsh. 'Mind if we come in and have a chat with you?' he asked.

'Course not. I'll need to start rolling a couple of pizzas, if that's OK?'

Chapter Thirty-nine

'I hope you know we are losing money,' Joseph snapped as Alison signed the delivery boys in and took them through towards separate interview rooms. 'You are stopping us from earning money. What is it you want from us?' he whined.

'This is an informal chat,' she told him politely, as she handed Anthony over to Banham and escorted Joseph into Interview Room B. 'But you are free to request a solicitor if you so wish.'

'Why would I want a solicitor? I'm losing money being here.' He was now looking nervous. 'I ain't done nothing.'

'Then you've nothing to worry about,' Alison told him. 'Just a few questions to help with our inquiries, and you can be on your way.'

'Go on then?'

'Do you want the duty solicitor present?'

'No. I want you to get on with it. I need to get back to work.'

'Tell me about your family. Your mum's Italian, I believe.'

'Yes. So?'

'So, did you grow up in Italy?'

'First few years of my life. My mum came to England ten years ago and she brought me with her.'

'What about your dad? Tell me about him.'

'Nothin' to tell ya,' He was looking unsettled. He kept looking around him and shifting about in his seat.' I ain't seen him for years. I never even hear from him.'

'But you've been back to Italy?'

'Just the once, with Tony, but I didn't see my so-called father. Why? What's this about my father?'

Alison ignored his question. 'Tell me about the theft of the bikes from the shop,' she asked.

'First one was around four weeks ago,' he said in a sing-song fashion. 'It was stolen from outside the shop. I wasn't there at the time. I had left for the night.' He shrugged and threw his eyes northwards in an irritable manner. 'I've told you all this before.'

'That was the bike with the registration starting LHA?' she questioned.

He gave a bored nod.

'And the second?'

'The second was stolen, as you know, when I did a drop earlier this week. I went to the Walden Estate, Bourne Street, and when I came out it was gone. I had to call Tony for a lift back. Bike thefts are up. You must know that.' He shrugged again dismissively. 'Not my fault.'

'Do you know a Christopher Burton? He is a member of Parliament.'

Joseph shook his head. 'No. Don't know no one posh,' he said.

'I believe he orders takeaways from you.'

Again the shrug. 'Don't know customers by name. I just deliver as quick as I can, and get back to get another drop. I'm paid for how many I do.'

'I believe Sergeant Crowther showed you a pizza flyer with a number on the back. You said you didn't write that number or recognise it?'

He nodded. 'We always take a number when delivering in case of not finding the joint. But that weren't my writing, so not my drop.'

'Would you mind writing that number down here, on this piece of paper. I have the number here. So, just write it as you would if you were taking it down.'

'The other police guy asked me to do that.'

She nodded, offering him a pen. 'Can you do it for me, please?'

250

He stared at her for a moment and then took the pen and scribbled the number at a rate of knots.

She watched him closely.

When Anthony was questioned, he said the same: not his handwriting.

'OK,' Banham said to him, after also getting him to write the number down again, and watching as he did so with a shaking hand. 'And how long have you known Christopher Burton?'

'Who?'

'Christopher Burton. I'll remind you. He's a member of Parliament.'

'I don't know any members of Parliament.'

'He owns a villa on an island in Italy. Ischia. Not too far from your family – they are in Naples. Am I right?'

Anthony looked surprised and a little nervous now. 'Yes. Why?'

'Tony, we know you have been home to Naples at least four times in the last year. That's a lot of visits.'

Anthony became immediately defensive. 'My mother is sick, so I go as often as I can afford. I can't be there all the time, there's no work for me, otherwise I would move back to be with her. I am worried for my mother, she's ill. I know Ischia, of course, but I haven't been there. It is a boat ride away. Why would I go there? I go to Naples to see my mother.'

'Not your handwriting, and you haven't even heard of Christopher Burton?'

Anthony hesitated, looked confused, and then said, 'No.'

Banham pushed a photo of Christopher Burton across the desk. 'Recognise him now?' he asked.

Again Anthony hesitated. He looked at the photo, and then up at Banham. He went to speak, then stopped, as if thinking. Then he said, 'I think he may have ordered from us. I can't be that sure.' He took a large intake of breath.

Banham watched him. 'Tell me about the motorbike thefts,' he said.

Now, Anthony looked even more frightened. 'The first one was a few weeks back. I'd left the shop and gone home for the night, so I wasn't there. When I came in, in the morning, the bike had been stolen. That's it.'

'And the second one?'

'That was last week, on Joseph's drop. It was nicked when he went in to deliver. Joseph phoned me and I went out to get him. That's it.'

Banham pulled his mouth into a tight smile. 'Thank you for your time,' he said. 'I'll just get this interview typed up, ask you to sign, and then I'll get you taken straight back to work.'

As Alison and Banham walked back into the murder room, Luke's head shot up from his computer. 'Got something very interesting,' he told them.

'Go on,' Banham said.

'I took a copy of the insurance claim that Johnny Walsh, the pizza-shop owner, put in for the first bike. I phoned the insurance company to check out the details they had. The claim is still outstanding, apparently. The company have a query on it, and referred me to the traffic incidents department. And I have just got an email back from a PC Gardener, in Traffic. Apparently, the insurance company got in touch with Traffic, asking them to look into the theft. Traffic checked the CCTV from the road the pizza cafe is in. The bike in question was there, in front of the shop, at five past five, the night it was reported stolen. And the CCTV went out of action at ten past five. I emailed Walsh, asking for details of the deliveries that night. He says he closed up at five past five, as there were no deliveries after that time.'

'So, Walsh leaves the shop at five past five. Five minutes later, the CCTV is put out of action. And this was three or four weeks before the first arson, you say?' Banham prompted.

'Yes, sir.'

'Who would leave a bike outside, in the main road, for the world to see, overnight?' Alison said. 'It's a known fact motorbike thefts are up. And that's the bike we think was used in the first arson?'

'Not sure, but it's possible.'

'Get on to Crowther,' Alison said. 'Tell him to bring Walsh in to talk to us.'

Banham then spoke. 'Tony Rossiti, the delivery driver, has visited his family home in Naples four times in the last year. Coincidentally, it's a short boat ride from Ischia, where Burton's villa is. Italy rears its head up again,' he added thoughtfully.

'We are waiting on Forensics on the water in the wellington, but I think we all now believe it will be pure spa water from Ischia, for which we have a comparison with the sample from Burton's wife,' Alison said.

'Burton has to be involved, somewhere,' Banham said, shaking his head. He then turned back to Luke. 'Get back on to Forensics. Tell them it's crisis time, we are hours away from having to release our main suspect. We need a result.'

'I'm going to interview Burton again,' Alison said, 'while we wait for Crowther to bring in Johnny Walsh.'

'It's also very possible that Rossiti is lying, and that he does know Burton,' Banham said. 'That he went to Ischia to get healing spa water for his sick mother. That he has met Burton, and maybe is the pawn in the game. I think we talk to the delivery boys again first; tell them we know about the suspected fraudulent insurance claim. See what they say,' Banham told her, overriding her decision as senior investigating officer to talk to Burton again first.

Stephanie caught Alison's furious face.

'You do that, then,' Alison said to him. 'As I said, I'm talking to Burton again. Steph, you are with me.'

'We'll take a break first,' Banham told the room. 'Alison, I'm going for a walk with the dog.' He indicated with his head for her to follow him to her office, where the dog was patiently waiting.

'Are you OK? he asked her as they walked round the block. 'You seem a bit distant.'

'I'm fine.' Her mind was on the case and she couldn't summon up the energy to ask him, yet again, to stop undermining her authority on it.

'So, what are you thinking?' he asked.

'I'm thinking you need a poo bag,' she told him. 'You'll have to get used to carrying all those things. Poo bags, and water, and a lead.'

'I've got one,' Banham told her, pulling a roll of green recyclable bags from his pocket. Babe must have noticed, because she immediately squatted down and did her business.

Alison felt a stab of pain in her heart as she watched him. He'd been so happy when she fell pregnant, he had spent a fortune on baby clothes. Since her miscarriage, so much had changed between them. Her maternal instincts were now non-existent, but he still yearned for a child. Were they growing apart? she wondered. She watched as he patted the dog's head, and made for the waste bin at the edge of the green.

Then her phone bleeped with a text.

'Burton wouldn't do his own dirty work,' Banham told her as he rejoined her after dumping the bag. 'Anthony Rossiti would be a perfect foil for him. The boy is malleable, and needs money. Say Burton pays his fare home to see his sick mother, but the deal is the boy brings back drugs, which Burton then gives the escort agency in return for the girls that he books for his masochistic sexual games. Maybe the girls were blackmailing him. We never found that video from Madara's flat. So, he has them killed.'

'Interesting that Burton's wife goes to the spa in Ischia and brings back the purest of waters,' Alison commented.

Banham looked at her. 'You think it's her?'

'She's his wife. She hated the women, or maybe she did it to protect him? She then lifted her phone towards Banham so he could read the text that had just pinged into her phone 'From the lab,' she said. 'The spa water from Mrs Burton's sample is a match to the water inside the wellington. That puts her in the frame, too. However, the fibres from the navy socks are not a match to the

254

ones Susan Burton gave us, belonging to her husband, nor are they a match to the ones Burton was wearing when arrested.'

'The spa water still could have come from Burton,' Banham reminded her. 'He could have given a bottle to Tony, to send to his sick mother. Then Tony panics and decides to use it to clean the residue off the wellington before he dumped the boot.'

'Maybe. You talk to Anthony Rossiti again; I'm going to interview Burton.'

'Shall we pick up Susan Burton, too?' Banham asked her.

'You're asking, not telling, me?' Alison answered sarcastically. She shook her head. 'Let's see what *he* says first.'

Chapter Forty

'Need you to come to the station with me,' Crowther told Johnny Walsh, as the man was bending down, cleaning out his oven. 'We need to ask you a few questions about the bike thefts.'

Walsh took a couple of seconds to take that in. 'The station?' he questioned. 'Can I do it later? My boys are already out of action. I've got a business to run.'

''Fraid not,' Crowther told him. His phone was to his ear, requesting a pick-up car to bring in a witness, as he spoke.

'What's going on?' Walsh asked. 'Is something wrong?'

'Problem with the claim, apparently,' Crowther told him. 'It's possible that the first stolen bike was used in the first arson attack. And there's an ongoing inquiry over the legitimacy of the insurance claim.'

Walsh stood up and turned to face Crowther. His face looked terrified. 'OK. I hold my hands up,' he said. 'It was stupid of me. I didn't think it through. Tony needed money to go back to his mother. She has cancer and time is running out. Business was slow. I was broke, so I came up with the idea of an insurance claim, and hiding the bike. We had another two bikes, so I knew we could cope. I am so ashamed, and very, very sorry.'

'That's fraud, mate,' Crowther reminded him.

Walsh nodded his head. 'I'm ashamed,' he said. 'But Tony was desperate.'

'Well, I'm not interested in fraud,' Crowther told him. 'But you'll still have to come and give us a statement about what happened, and then I'll be passing it on to the relevant department. What about the second bike?'

Walsh nodded. 'The same. I had that stolen, too. That boy is in bits. He's a good lad, and if I had the money, I would have lent it him. Truth is, the business isn't doing great. So, I falsified two theft claims.'

Hannah had been busying herself checking out the waiting room at the back of the pizza shop. She attempted to open the lockers and found them to be locked.

'What do you keep in those lockers?' she shouted through to Walsh. 'They're locked.'

'I had them put in for the delivery lads,' he shouted back. 'To leave their personals in, when they went out on a drop. They never use them, though. They just come in, grab a helmet, and go out again. They keep their phones on them in case of needing to call.'

'Do you have a master key?'

Walsh shook his head. 'No. The boys keep their keys. I'm surprised if they are locked. The boys never use them. But they'll have the keys.'

Hannah shook the two lockers, which stood, unsteadily, one on top of the other. 'Something's in there,' she said.

Johnny handed Crowther a flat pizza knife. 'Try that,' he said, 'Ease it in the side, it'll open the locker door. It's probably headphones and game stuff in there.'

Crowther handed Hannah the pizza slicer. She pushed into the side of the door of the top locker with it, wiggled it around, and then used force. After a few seconds, the door gave way.

'Crowther!' Hannah called out urgently. Crowther hurried through to her, followed by Walsh. The three of them stood staring at the contents of the top locker. A hammer with hair and dried blood over it, and a small revolver.

'Gloves,' Crowther said to Hannah, subtly telling her to bag the evidence. He pulled his phone from his pocket, and dialled Alison's number. It rang, unanswered, on her desk.

★

Burton was looking tired and angry. His fat red-faced solicitor was now more than a trifle argumentative.

'Are you charging my client?' the ruddy-faced man snapped as Stephanie and Alison walked into the interview room. He raised his voice. 'This is intolerable. If you have nothing to charge him with, you have to let him go.'

Alison ignored the man. She sat down with Stephanie noisily thumping herself into the chair beside her. She turned the tape and video to *on*, and told the machines who was present, then turned to Burton. 'You visited your Italian villa recently?'

'I did.'

'How often do you go?'

'Depends on what is happening in Parliament. You know all this.'

'Nice island,' Stephanie said sarcastically.

'Your point?' the ruddy-faced solicitor leaned in and interrupted.

Again, Alison ignored him. 'A spa island, isn't it?' she said. 'Is that why you look so tanned and clear-skinned?'

'Probably. What's this about?' replied Burton.

'The spa water your island home boasts, it's known to be the purest in the world. Am I right?'

'Yes.'

'Have you got some in your flat?'

'My wife will have some in our Oxford home, why? Is that a crime now?'

'For the third time –' the fat solicitor now raised his voice – 'what is this about?'

'Surely, you keep some in your London flat, too?' Stephanie pushed.

'I bring some back, occasionally, yes.' Burton's irritation was clear. 'My wife uses the villa, too, you know. She brings a good few bottles back. It keeps her calm or some load of rubbish.'

'Do you ever bring this water back and give it away as presents?' Alison asked.

'To the women you take out on the side, perhaps?' Stephanie added.

He shook his head, then smirked. 'The women I take out on the side prefer drugs and champagne.'

'How about the men that do your dirty work for you?' Alison almost spat.

'Are you insinuating my client dates men?' the fat solicitor immediately raised his voice again and sharpened his tone. 'Because if you are . . .'

'I'm insinuating nothing. I am asking Mr Burton about the men he *employs*.'

'I prefer to employ women when I can,' Burton answered smugly.

'And do you bring drugs back with you, for the women you entertain on the side?' Alison now asked.

Burton gave a heavy sigh and threw his eyes to the ceiling. 'I helped Jonathan Perry with his problem, once, but that was that. I do not have anything to do with drugs. It is more than my job's worth.'

'So, if I got a search warrant for your London flat, I would find no drugs or spa water, is that correct?' Alison asked him.

'Yes,' he said, shaking his head and speaking in a voice barely audible. 'No, you wouldn't.'

'Oh, and –' she pushed the pizza flyer across the table to him, then turned it over to show him the mobile number on the back – 'we found this in your Oxford home,' she said. 'Can you tell me who this mobile number belongs to?'

He glanced at the flyer, then turned away. 'I have no bloody idea,' he said.

'But you have bought pizzas from the Italian pizza shop down the road from where Danielle Low – she was a whore that you hired out from the escort agency, by the way, just in case it slipped your memory – was living when she died. You have bought pizza there, haven't you?'

The solicitor shook his head.

'No comment,' Burton said, turning to look away once again.

Alison leaned in and spoke to the recording device. 'Interview terminated. DI Grainger and DS Green leaving the room,' was all she said. She then stood up and left the room, followed by Stephanie, aware the solicitor was shouting after her.

'This is enough! It is outrageous. I will take this to the police complaints commission!'

Johnny Walsh stared first at the hammer and gun, and then at Crowther.

'Is this for real?' he said, as Hannah pulled a rubber glove, and then two forensic bags, from her pocket. The hammer went into one bag, and the revolver into another.

'Whose locker is it?' Crowther almost shouted at Walsh. 'Which one of them?'

'I don't know.' Johnny was very flustered. 'I've never seen either of them use the lockers. Jesus Christ,' he said again. 'Am I dreaming or what? I've never seen the boys use the lockers.'

'When Christopher Burton comes in for his pizza, does he ever wait in here while you cook?'

'Possibly. Yes, anyone who is waiting for their pizza is offered to wait in that room. Loads of customers have sat there. I can't remember' – he was shaking now and stuttering slightly – 'if he did or didn't. To be honest, I think he waits outside in his car while I cook.' Walsh was sounding nervous. 'But I honestly can't say for sure.'

'When was the last time he was in?'

'I really can't remember. Sorry, my brain, with all this—'

'Does he pay by cash or card?'

'Cash, always.'

'Do you have a receipt? Check your books.'

Walsh shook his head. 'Times are bad. Hard.' He squeezed his lips together and shook his head sheepishly. Then he said quietly. 'I don't put the cash ones through the books.'

*

260

Alison noticed the call from Crowther on her phone as she walked back into the investigation room. She ignored the call for the moment.

'We've just spoken to Burton again,' she told the team. 'As we know, the testing of his socks was negative, and he admits he helped Jonathan Perry with drugs, and has visited the agency, but we don't have enough to charge him with five murders. We need more. We all believe he is guilty as hell, but he hasn't done his own dirty work. He had someone do it for him, which is why he left the country.' She turned to Luke. 'Ask for an extension to hold him, on the grounds we now have further evidence. We have sent the local police round to pick up Susan Burton and bring her in for questioning. Meanwhile, we keep digging.'

'Just heard from Oxford police,' Steph said. 'She isn't there. They are outside her Oxford home, waiting for her to return.'

'Convenient,' Alison said.

'I'd like to talk to Del Harris again,' Stephanie said.

'You're like a dog with a bone about Harris,' Alison told her. 'What makes you so sure he's involved?'

Stephanie nodded. 'Gut feeling.'

Alison nodded. 'Go with it. But don't waste too much time on it.'

The internal phone rang at that moment. Luke took the call, and then looked up and said, 'Crowther has been trying to get hold of you, ma'am. He has found a bloodstained hammer and revolver in a locker at the pizza place. He's on his way in with the owner. Hannah is on her way to Forensics with the exhibits.'

The room went quiet.

Chapter Forty-one

Alison opened the door to the interview that Banham and Baz Butler were now conducting with Joseph Perrino. She indicated with her head for Banham to leave the interview for a moment. Once outside, she told him about the findings of the hammer and gun. She then re-entered Interview Room B with Banham, politely relieved Baz, and sat in his chair beside Banham. Joseph looked very uneasy.

'You knew the bike was being stolen for an insurance claim,' Banham said to him.

There were a few seconds before Joseph spoke, then he said, 'It was nothing to do with me, but I said nothing. I'm not a grass.'

'Tell us everything you know,' Banham told him sternly. 'We believe this bike was used in the first arson attack, and we also believe you knew about that.'

Joseph then started speaking very quickly, as if in a panic. 'Tony was crying. His mum is dying and he didn't have the fare to go to her. He asked Mr Walsh to lend him money.' Joseph shook his head. 'I knew Mr Walsh didn't have money to lend. The business isn't doing well, and Mr Walsh has high outgoings. He said he wanted to help Tony, and suggested we lose a bike for a while. He would hide it, he said, and claim on the insurance. When that came through, he would give it to Tony for his fare home.' Joseph shook his head. 'Now the insurance know they blocked the CCTV, and they won't pay out, so Tony can't get the money to go home.' He looked up. 'Nothing to do with me.'

'What about the night of the arson in Apple Tree Close?' Alison asked him. 'Who blocked the CCTV that night?'

Joseph held both his hands up, palms facing Alison. 'Not me. I swear. I was out on a drop. You have the proof I was. It took longer 'cause I had hassle and had to call Tony out to guard the bikes while I made the drop.'

'You said earlier that the gang that bothered you there weren't the gang that normally hang around that estate?'

'That's what was weird. It's one gang's territory, but I hadn't seen those boys before. I have seen them since, though.'

Alison then passed across the photo that Crowther had sent through to her phone of the bloodied hammer and the revolver. 'How about these? Have you seen these before?' she asked, watching his reaction very carefully.

He frowned as he stared at them. 'No,' he said. 'These are weapons.'

'They were found in your locker at your place of work.'

'I don't ever use a locker.'

'Which is your locker, the bottom one or the top one?' Alison asked him.

'Top locker, but I don't use it. I leave the key in the door, there ain't anything in it.'

'These were,' Alison told him, reading from Crowther's note on her phone saying they were found in the top locker.

'We are taking a break,' Alison told the tape, 'during which, I am advising Joseph Perrino to consider asking for a legal representative.'

Banham and Alison then walked into Interview Room C and sat opposite Anthony Rossiti.

'We know you lied to the insurance,' Alison said to him. 'There was no bike theft.'

Anthony sat back in his chair and looked terrified. 'It was Mr Walsh's idea.'

'But you agreed to do it.'

'I need money. My mother is dying, what would you do?'

'Well, I wouldn't break the law,' Alison said sarcastically. 'But we aren't here over a dodgy insurance claim. We believe that bike may be connected to five murders.'

Banham leaned into Anthony. 'Which means you start telling the truth or you may never see your mama again.'

Tears pricked Anthony's eyes.

'Do you know Christopher Burton?' Alison asked.

'I think I know who you mean,' Anthony said. 'I don't know him personally. He has been in a few times for pizza.'

'Does he have it delivered to an address?' Banham asked.

'No. He waits and takes it away.'

'Where does he wait?' Alison asked quickly.

'He talks to Mr Walsh, or sits in the back room, or in his car outside. I don't remember for sure. I hardly know him.' Anthony lifted a forearm to wipe away the perspiration that had broken out on his forehead. 'I have done wrong, I know. I shouldn't have agreed to the insurance claim—'

'How often does he come in?' Alison interrupted.

Anthony shrugged. 'I haven't seen him for a while. I think he knew someone who lived nearby, which is why—'

'Who? Who did he know that lives nearby?' Alison pushed.

'I don't know. I hardly spoke to him. He just ordered, then picked up a pizza and left. Will I be able to get home to my mamma? She is very ill.'

'Depends. We're interested in five murders. What can you tell us about those?' Alison said.

Anthony looked shocked. 'I only agreed to move a bike. I haven't killed anyone.'

'Where did you move the bike to?'

'I don't know. Mr Walsh did that.'

'How about these —' she showed him the photos from her phone, of the hammer and revolver across the table — 'what can you tell us about these?'

His eyes widened as he looked at them. He said nothing.

'They were found in your locker, at the shop,' Banham said, repeating the accusation he had previously used to Joseph.

'What? I don't use my locker.'

'Which is your locker, top or bottom one?' Banham asked him.

Tony hesitated and then said, 'Either one. We hardly use them, so we just choose whichever one is free. Keys are left in the locker if it's empty'

'Where are the keys now?'

'I don't know. In the lockers maybe. Or the back room somewhere, on the table. I never use it, so I don't know. Are you thinking that I murdered those women?'

'I'm thinking that you need to speak to a solicitor,' Alison said.

Chapter Forty-two

The afternoon duty solicitor had arrived. She was a large, grey-haired, middle-aged lady called Mrs Powley. Alison left her to speak to Anthony, while Joseph still insisted he didn't want a solicitor. Crowther had now arrived with Johnny Walsh, who was sitting in Interview Room D.

Alison and Banham walked into room D, and sat down, facing him. Alison turned the tape and video on and spoke the necessary into them.

'The hammer found on your property is with Forensics, as is the revolver. They were found in locked lockers on your property. You say the lockers belong to the delivery boys that you employ, and they have the only keys. Is this correct.'

'Yes.' Walsh took an intake of breath and nodded his head.

'You say customers wait in that room sometimes, while you cook,' Banham reminded him. 'And sometimes the lockers are unlocked ,and the keys left in the doors, with strangers in there. A bit careless, wouldn't you say?' Banham pushed.

Walsh shrugged. 'The lockers are usually empty. If there is anything in them, then the boys lock them and keep their keys.'

Alison then spoke. 'We feel confident that, when forensic results come through, they will confirm that they are the weapons used in the murder of two people. These two murders are also connected to three other murders. Five murders, Mr Walsh. How well do you know your delivery boys?'

Walsh shook his head. 'In a million years I would never believe either of those boys capable of killing. As I said, my customers sometimes wait in the back room while I cook their pizzas. I've known those boys for a while. In my opinion, they are both kind and honest.'

'Hardly honest, agreeing to be an accessory to making a fraudulent theft claim,' Alison argued.

'That was my idea,' Johnny told her, raising his voice. 'I hold my hands up to that one. Tony went along because he is desperate to get home to his mum. Who can blame him for that? But it was nothing whatsoever to do with Joseph. Please don't charge him.'

'I am passing all your details on to the fraud department,' Banham told him. 'They will deal with that. We are interested in those weapons, and how they got in the lockers in your shop.'

Walsh shook his head. 'All I know is that I didn't put them there, and I am finding it hard to accept either of those boys capable. As I said, sometimes my customers wait in there.'

'Including Christopher Burton?'

'It's possible, but no, my memory tells me he always goes back out to his car to wait.'

'We need a list of all your customers that have bought in the past few weeks.'

'I don't ask them for names and ID. I have statements for the ones that paid by card.'

'We'll have those,' Banham told him.

'What colour socks do you wear, Mr Walsh?' Alison asked him.

'What?'

'Answer the question, please.'

'Depends,' he said with a frown. 'If I'm cooking, I don't wear any. It gets very hot over that stove. If I go out in the cold then I wear whatever falls out of my drawer in the morning.'

'Do you have navy-blue socks?'

He frowned again. 'I think I do, but they may be black. It's a bugger to tell the difference in these dark early mornings.'

'What make are they?'

'What? I don't know. Primark, I think. I haven't bought socks for ages. As I say, I don't wear them often, cooking over a hot stove.'

'Do you know Christopher Burton's wife?'

Walsh frowned, then shook his head. 'No. I've never met her. I hardly know him. He just comes in occasionally, but I haven't seen him in a while.'

'But he has been in your back room where your lockers are?'

Walsh sighed, then lifted his hands in the air, palms up. 'In for a penny,' he said. 'If I'm being done for insurance fraud anyway, then I'll admit the truth. My boys need to earn. It's tough out there, business-wise. Burton has been in a few times and, yes, I got chatting with him on several occasions. We talked pizzas. He likes my authentic Italian cooking. I told him the business was struggling, and I was worried about keeping my delivery boys going.' He paused, then looked up. 'It went from there. Apparently Mr Burton needed stuff delivering. I don't ask questions. The boys deliver stuff for him, and he pays them. That's it, I keep out of that side, and the boys earn a bit more to help. It means I get to keep them, and they earn enough to get by. It's probably illegal what they deliver, it's in packages, no one asks questions, and my business survives.'

Banham looked at Alison. She leaned into the tape.

'Interview terminated,' she said.

Fifteen minutes later, she and Banham joined the overweight Mrs Powley, who now sat next to a trembling Anthony Rossiti, in Interview Room C.

Banham spoke first. 'You need to start telling the truth,' he told the shaking boy. 'You know Mr Burton quite well, don't you?'

When he didn't answer, Alison spoke. 'You deliver packages for him, don't you?'

Anthony nodded his head. 'I pick up stuff either from a bin on the corner or once from a woman who comes in. Then I delivered it to an address that she gave me. I don't know what's in the package and I don't ask.'

'What address?'

He was shaking now. 'I can't remember. It's in Earl's Court.'

Banham and Alison both took that in.

She then showed him the photos of the three women. 'Is she any of these women? Please look very closely.'

He studied the pictures, as his nose ran and he sniffed, wiping snot and tears away with the back of his hand. Then he shook his head. 'No,' he said. She wears dark glasses and hats and stuff. I don't know what she really looks like.' He started crying. 'I've been stupid.'

'How, how have you been stupid?' Banham pushed.

'I faked a stolen bike, and I delivered packages for that man.'

'What else?' Alison pushed.

'Nothing.' His voice was cracking and his nose was running still. 'Nothing, nothing.' His crying was becoming worse.

'Can we please take a break?' Mrs Powley spoke firmly, it wasn't a question but an order.

'Yes, I'd like one of your socks, please, Tony,' Alison told him. She then leaned in and told the tape they were taking a break.

Joseph was still sitting alone, with just a PC in the corner, as Alison entered the room. He was arrogant.

'I'm missing earning,' he said to her. 'I'm going to claim for this. Police harassment. I've done nothing wrong.'

'Nothing wrong?' Alison spoke sarcastically. 'Let's start with the drug delivering you do for Christopher Burton.'

Joseph stared back at her, then leaned into the desk. 'Mr Walsh said there was extra work for us, delivering a few packages for a friend. The parcels were wrapped and taped each time. No one said what they were. I just delivered them when and where I was told, and I got paid. End of.'

269

'Where did you deliver to?'

'Different places. Waste bins, all that. No addresses, to a dustbin, or somewhere like that.'

'And you are telling us you had no idea they were drugs, when you were making drops at waste bins and the like?' Banham said. 'You weren't born yesterday.'

'I didn't ask questions.'

'You knew Christopher Burton was involved,' Alison pushed.

'No one told me anything, and I asked no questions.'

'Where did you pick the stuff up from?'

'I just said: sometimes a waste bin, once a woman brought the stuff and gave us the address to go to, and cash for doing it. I jumped at the chance. Who wouldn't? I needed money. It was extra money.'

'Who was the woman?'

He shrugged. 'I don't know.'

Alison showed him pictures of the murdered women. 'Was she any of these women?'

'I don't know. She was always in a different wig with dark glasses on, and hats or a scarf. And I don't know her name.'

'So, she came in more than once?'

'Yeah, once for my job, and then once for Tony's drop. We only did it a couple of times.'

'Did she have an accent?' Banham asked.

'No.' Joseph pursed his bottom lip as if thinking. 'I don't think so.'

Alison pointed again to the photos of the three dead women. 'Take a good look,' she said. 'Do you recognise any of these women?'

He looked carefully, then shook his head. 'No,' he said. 'How many times? I've said no.'

'Trouble is, we don't believe you,' Banham said to him.

Alison pointed to Danielle. 'This woman lived at the top of the road your pizza shop is in. Did you never see her around, or deliver pizza to her?'

Joseph shook his head. 'Most people order over the phone and we don't even look as we give them the stuff. We're always in a hurry.'

'How well do you know Tony?' Alison asked him.

'I've been working with him for over a year. We get on well. Both our mums come from Italy. And we help each other out if we need backup on a drop. He's reliable.' He looked as if he was about to say something else, and then stopped.

'Go on,' Banham encouraged. 'You were saying.'

'Just something that I thought was strange. The gang that were at the flats, on the night of the burning of Apple Tree Close. The ones that hassled me, that were after my bike. They weren't the usual gang on there.'

'Why do you mention that?'

'Because I saw them again; they were hanging around the back of the shop a couple of days ago, and shortly after, a big car, it was a Range Rover, drew up and the driver leaned out and handed them money. I thought I recognised the driver as that Burton. I couldn't swear to it, but I think so.'

Banham and Alison took that in.

'Are those socks navy blue?' Alison asked Joseph after a few seconds of silence, pointing down at his jeans and trainers, where his socks peeped through.

Joseph frowned. 'Yes, why?'

'What make are they?'

'I don't know.'

'Where did you get them?'

He looked confused. 'A Christmas present from Tony.'

'I need you to remove one. We will replace it with another pair, until we can return your one to you.'

She then told the tape they were taking another break.

Alison then pushed the sock into a forensic bag and labelled it. She told the PC to take it to Baz, and to tell Baz to take it to Forensics.

★

She left Interview Room B and followed Banham into Interview Room C. After settling opposite the fat solicitor and Anthony Rossiti, she turned the tape back on and leaned into Anthony.

'Did Burton offer you money and health treatment for your mother?' she asked him. 'Is that why you killed those women for him? Talk to us, Tony. It will be easier for you in the long run.'

Chapter Forty-three

Anthony started crying. 'I haven't killed anyone. Please, please. I lied to the police. I said the bike was stolen, but we dumped it. I haven't killed anyone.'

'Where did you dump it?'

'I think near the wood. I didn't do it personally. Mr Walsh did.'

'And the other bike?' Banham pushed. 'Was that the same story?'

Anthony nodded and bowed his head. 'Yes. There was a hold-up with the other insurance money. This bike was insured somewhere else, so Mr Walsh said we could do the same with that one. Mr Walsh told me he would sort it. He was protecting me from getting into trouble.'

'He got you into delivering drugs, though,' Alison reminded him.

'Stupid –' Anthony nodded – 'I have been stupid. Mr Walsh suggested I could make some quick money delivering packages.'

'Who offered you quick money to burn those women?' Banham pushed again, niggling him.

'No.' Anthony looked up. 'I didn't do that.' He then turned and looked at fat Mrs Powley. She had sat there silently through the whole interview. 'Help me here,' he said. 'Am I going to go to prison?'

They were back in the investigation room. Alison perched on the side of Stephanie's desk and Banham stood at the front of the room.

'According to Johnny Walsh,' Alison said, 'the only people with keys to those lockers are the delivery boys.' She watched Stephanie dipping chocolate Hobnobs into her tea and sucking the melting chocolate off as bits of the biscuit dissolved into the liquid in the polystyrene cup. 'He said the lockers aren't always locked, and the boys don't use them.'

'And Walsh said he hasn't got a master key,' Crowther mentioned. 'What if he gave it to Burton. For storage of the packages of drugs. He's clearly in his pocket. And Burton used the locker for the hammer and gun.'

'He wasn't in the country to dump the hammer and gun,' Stephanie reminded him as she licked chocolate from her fat fingers. 'And he doesn't do his own dirty work.'

'I know,' Crowther snapped. 'Eat any more of those biscuits and you'll get so large you'll fall off your chair.'

'Oh, shut up, you two,' Banham said sharply to him.

'I'm suggesting Burton had access to the lockers and paid one of the boys to pick up the hammer and a revolver, and hide them,' Crowther said.

'Are you saying whichever one of those boys hid the evidence is most probably our killer?' Banham asked.

'Not necessarily, guv,' Crowther said. 'The boys deliver drugs for him. They could also have been told to pick up this evidence and hide it, not knowing it had been used on the murders. Doesn't mean they did it.'

'Did Forensics have any idea how long testing on those socks from the delivery boys might be?' Alison asked Luke. 'Surmising ain't gonna do it, right now. We need evidence to get people into court.'

'Or a confession,' Banham corrected her.

'It's marked "urgent". That's all I can say,' Luke told them.

'What did Camilla Agnelli say about the blank memory stick?' Alison asked Stephanie.

'She said she had no idea it existed. I advised her to help herself, by helping us. She spat at me. I told her she was being charged with

274

possession of a firearm, assaulting an officer, inciting women into prostitution, and possession of Class A drugs. She said nothing after that.'

'Good,' Alison nodded.

'Oluwa Marconi, the same,' Stephanie said. 'They'll go in front of a magistrate tomorrow and we know they'll both get custodials. So, that's the good news.'

'Have we any news back on the extension to holding Burton?' Alison asked Luke.

'Not yet.'

'If we tell Camilla that if she gives us a statement saying he is on their books as a pervert, and that he burned her with cigarette butts, then we'll tell the judge she helped us, and if she does, then we'll get our extension,' Crowther suggested.

'Even though Burton admitted getting his drugs, Jonathan Perry flatly refuses to testify against him on anything,' Alison reminded them.

'Burton, Jonathan Perry, the delivery boys, all have a connection to drugs and those women,' Banham said. 'Any could have wanted them killed.'

'And Burton's wife,' Alison added. 'Let's not forget her.'

'Del Harris didn't want his mother knowing he knew them, or that he smoked pot,' Stephanie reminded them. 'And his motorbike reg is very similar. Don't let's rule him out either.'

'You're like a dog with a bone over him,' Crowther told her. 'How would the murder weapons get into the lockers in that case?'

Luke's internal phone rang at that moment. He picked it up and nodded his head slowly, then thanked the caller. 'Forensics say they'll need three days to get the full results on the revolver and hammer,' he told them.

'Shit,' Alison said. 'OK. I'm thinking.'

Everyone was quiet for a few seconds, then Banham said, 'Col-the-know-all has an ex-lover in Forensics.' He turned to Crowther.

'Could you lean on her? Tell her this is a desperate situation for us and we need those results a lot sooner? Tell her you owe her a favour.'

'I'll give it a go, guv,' Crowther answered, as a few dirty jibes flew around the room.

The look on Hannah's face and her narrowed, jealous eyes, didn't go unnoticed by Alison.

'Even if we charge Burton with assaulting a police officer, he'll get bail,' Alison said. 'I don't want him let out of here.'

'I suggest we all go to the pub over the road and grab a quick lunch and a break,' Banham said. 'First, Col, ring your ex, and push hard for that favour.'

'Any questions?' Alison added as she watched Hannah mouth to Crowther, 'Meet me in the car park.'

Hannah then picked up her bag and left the room.

Crowther hadn't answered. He had noticed Alison glaring at him. He turned his back and picked up his phone, stabbing Penelope Starr's number into it.

A few minutes later, Crowther was in the car park and had zapped his key to open his car. Hannah followed shortly after, opened his door, and slid into the passenger seat. She leaned across and started kissing him. He pushed her off.

'What, are you on a death wish or something?' he said.

'It's lunchtime. They don't own us. We are adults. We can do what we like.'

'You make it very hard for a bloke.'

She slid her hand over his cock. 'I can feel just how hard I have made it,' she said as she slid down the seat, leaned into him, and was about to unzip his flies when she felt his firm grip grab her hands and moved them.

'No, Hannah. This is not on.'

'I thought you liked me seducing you,' she said.

'This is not the time or the place.'

'Don't you like me anymore?'

276

He sighed. 'Hannah, you need to wise up. This is a massive murder inquiry. We are all on tenterhooks waiting results and . . .'

'I'm offering to relieve some of that tension for you.'

He raised his voice. 'No. Listen. You were assigned to me, so I could help you as a detective. You are a trainee and you have a lot to learn. My job is to guide you professionally.'

She raised her voice back and spoke in an argumentative tone. 'You haven't objected before.'

'Then I was wrong,' he said gently. 'This has got to stop right now.'

'I'm sorry. I got the impression you liked me.'

'I do. Oh, Hannah, grow up!'

She glared at him for a second, then turned and opened the door and hurried out of the car, heading back into the station.

Crowther stayed in the car, noting his erection. After a few minutes, he noted it was safe to go and join the others. As he got out of the car, he came face to face with Alison and Banham. They had been taking the dog out for a walk.

'Everything OK?' Alison asked, sensing the discomfort Crowther felt at seeing her.

'Fine, boss.'

'Where's Hannah?' Banham asked him.

Crowther shrugged. 'Over in the pub, I expect. I was just catching up with Penny in Forensics.'

'Can she hurry the tests through?' Banham asked him.

'Says she'll do what she can,' Crowther told him. 'It's the testing, as you know, guv, you have to give it so much time. But she's on it.'

Alison popped back into the ladies' room at the station to go to the loo while Banham fed the dog. Hannah was at the mirror fixing her make-up. It was obvious she was upset.

'Are you OK?' Alison asked her.

'Yes, fine.' Hannah nodded, then shook her head. 'No, actually. I've just been dumped.'

'By Crowther?'

Hannah nodded again.

'I hadn't realised you and Crowther were an item. I thought I gave you the heads-up. He has a reputation for being romantically unreliable.'

Hannah shrugged. 'Well, now I know.'

Alison could barely hide her anger. 'Hopefully, we'll have this case put to bed soon. I won't put you two together again. I'll put you with Stephanie Green next time. You'll learn a lot from her.'

'I've learned a lot from Crowther.'

Alison bit her tongue. She was too angry to speak. Crowther had lied to her by saying he hadn't seduced the very vulnerable trainee. She'd wait until Forensics came through, then read him the riot act. Right now, forensic results were of top priority, and they were relying on him, and the fact he'd *also* had an affair with Dr Penny Starr, Head of Forensics.

During lunch, she watched Hannah and Crowther. They sat apart, and neither spoke to the other.

The team were now back in the investigation room.

'Even if we do get positive DNA from the hammer and the revolver,' Banham told them, 'it still wouldn't prove, conclusively, that either of the suspects murdered Danielle Low. She was burned alive, as were her neighbours, Mr and Mrs Dowd.'

'So, we are going to bluff our way through this,' Alison butted in. 'DCI Banham and I have discussed this, we have told both the boys that the weapons were found in their personal lockers. So, we are now going to tell both of them, separately, that we now have proof to charge them. That way we hope to get a full confession.'

'We're also going to bluff Burton, and tell him his prints are on the revolver,' Banham said. 'We need to trip him up.'

'First, we are going to grill Johnny Walsh,' Alison told them. 'We believe he is protecting someone. We are fairly sure it is Burton.'

'And then, Crowther, you can go with Alison to Burton's flat in London and turn it over,' Banham told him. 'We have the warrant through.'

Alison glared furiously at Crowther as she left the room and headed for the interview room. He smiled back at her.

Chapter Forty-four

Before they entered Interview Room D, Alison and Banham watched Walsh through the video. He was sitting with his head buried in his hands.

'Let's start at the beginning,' Banham said as they walked in and settled opposite Walsh. Alison switched the video and tape to *on*, and introduced herself and Banham as being there. 'We think you know who has the master key to your lockers, and we think you gave them permission to use it. Tell us who you are protecting.'

Walsh lifted his hands in a defensive manner. 'I am in debt,' he said, 'I've nothing to lose now. I'm going down for fraud.'

'So, who has the master key to the lockers?

Walsh shook his head. 'Me. I have been a gambler. Big time. Then I started taking drugs to forget my problems, and now I have a habit, an expensive one. Mr Burton helped me. I owed him.'

Got him, Alison thought to herself. Finally, they were getting something on Burton. 'How did he help you?' she asked.

'He lent me the money to pay my debts.'

'Why? Why would he go out of his way to lend you money? You said you hardly knew him.'

Walsh shook his head. 'I lied.' He then turned his head to the wall and clammed up.

'Go on,' Banham coaxed.

There was a few seconds before Walsh turned back and started talking again. 'I was working in Liverpool a few years ago. As a security guard at a pole-dancing club. They had girls for sale there.

They had game machines, too. That's where my gambling started. Mr Burton likes the girls. I got to know him there. He often drove up from London and bought a girl to take into the back room. Well away from home for him. He needed discretion. I looked out for him, helped him stay anonymous. He knew I liked a bit of coke, and he asked me who sold the gear at the club. I told him, and he got me a good supply of the stuff for having his back. I liked the stuff, but it wasn't a habit then. Burton then moved in on that club. Brought his boys in, like. The bloke who owned the club let him have the drug business there, cos he was who he was, and had so much clout, like. When I got my head kicked in for not paying my gambling debt, Mr Burton paid it for me to save me a second kicking. Said he would look after me, and I would work for him now. He moved me to London. He said he loved a pizza and sent me on a course for authentic Italian pizza-making. Said there was a big call for the classy bakes. He even found me the shop. Helped me start a new life. I was away from gambling and Mr Burton got me my drugs. All was good. I hired the delivery boys. Work was slow, we weren't bringing in enough to keep the boys, so Mr Burton got them to deliver his packages.'

'Of drugs?'

He nodded.

'For the tape, Mr Walsh is nodding,' Alison said. 'Go on,' she urged.

'I thought I was starting a new life, but my coke addiction was getting worse, and I started the gambling again on the side.'

'More debt?'

Again he nodded. 'More than I could manage. I was going to lose the shop.' Now his eyes filled with tears. 'I'd been stupid. Mr Burton said he would help me again. He said he'd pay my debts. But I owed him and if I wanted to keep the shop . . .' He clammed up then and put his head on his forearm which was across the desk.

'What?' Alison pushed 'What did Burton ask you to do in return for keeping your shop?'

Walsh lifted his head. There were tears in his eyes. 'I had to burn the girl. The one that came in with the packages. The one in Apple Tree Close. He got me the stuff, and said it would be a piece of cake. Even gave me his sacred water to clean any trace of petrol off with, after. Tony needed money to get home to his sick mother. I was in it up to my neck so I said I'd lose one of the bikes and report it stolen. I hid the bike and used it for the deed.'

'You said you couldn't ride a motorbike?'

'I lied. Again.'

'You killed two other people that night,' Alison said.

He was crying now. 'I know, and I'll never forgive myself.'

'And the other two women, you killed them, too?' Alison said in a tone that showed she just needed confirmation.

Again he nodded. 'I thought that was the end when I done the first one. But Mr Burton said I hadn't done enough for all he had done for me, and if I didn't do the other two then it would all lead back to me. If I did the other two, that would be the end of it, he would never mention my debt again. And would always look after me.' Walsh hiccupped now as he cried. 'Perry was easy. I kept trying to kill the Slovakian, but it was too hard. I hated doing it. He was on my back, made me get on with it. She had a kid; I didn't want her child to get burned. So, I done her in the alleyway.'

'Why did he want them murdered?' Banham asked him.

'They were blackmailing him,' he told me. 'They had videos of him, doing kinky sex. They wanted too much money for the videos. They also had proof he was a drug baron, and supplying the agency. He brought the Slovakian one, the last one I done, into the country. She had said she would say he kidnapped her and brought her over and put her into prostitution.' Walsh looked straight at them. 'He said they were nasty women, deserved what was coming to them. I was just—'

'The blood on the hammer we retrieved from your locker will turn out to be Madara Kowaska's?' Alison interrupted.

He nodded.

'Where did you get the revolver that was with it?'

'From Burton. He employs a gang that trades guns on the streets in South London. They were the gang that he sent to the estate where Joseph was delivering to, the evening I burned the first one. Joseph said they were a different gang, not the usual thugs that run that estate, and that's because they were. Burton has that gang on his payroll. He put them there to stall Joseph, knowing Joseph would call Tony out, leaving me free to close up earlier than I said and do the burning. There's a way out the back of the shop, no CCTV there. The gang blocked the CCTV in our street, then followed Joseph on his drop, and harassed him. He called out Tony and I was free to set fire to the . . . bitch.'

'Christopher Burton deals in drugs, and firearms, and prostitutes. Is that what you are saying?'

'Yes. I am.'

Alison shook her head and sighed.

'I know I deserve all I get. I can't sleep at night. I've made such a mess of my life. Can we leave the delivery boys out of all this? They truly are innocent.'

'Except for the handling and delivering of drugs,' Banham reminded him.

'And being accessories to fraud,' Alison added.

Walsh then raised his voice. 'Look. They have their lives ahead of them. I don't. I made my own bed. I got into gambling and drugs. Then I met *him*. He threatened me, said if I didn't agree to his terms, he would make sure I would never see my kid again. I've got a daughter in Liverpool. I wanted her to be safe.'

'It'll be a very long time until you see her again anyway,' Banham told him. 'You will go to prison for a very long time, Mr Walsh, and unless your daughter visits you, you will be a very, very old man when you next see her.'

Walsh's head dropped to his hands and his wailing could be heard the other end of the corridor.

Alison clicked the tape and video off, and both she and Banham left the room.

'Got him,' Alison said as they walked back along the corridor.

'Walsh, or Burton?' Banham asked.

'Burton,' Alison told him.

'Don't be so sure. His word against Walsh's. He'll deny everything and attempt to wriggle out of this. We still have no forensic proof to hold him as accessory to five murders. I wonder if his solicitor will still be shouting his rights now.'

'He's going nowhere, and Crowther and I will turn his London flat upside down.'

'You need a forensic result from there, or it'll be his word against Walsh,' Banham told her.

'I can't bear the thought of him walking away a free man,' Alison said.

'My God, we need a positive forensic result,' Banham told her.

Chapter Forty-five

'We have a full confession from Walsh,' Alison announced, acknowledging the cheer that followed from the full room of murder detectives. 'Burton paid him to kill all our victims.'

'Not there yet, though,' Banham told them. 'Burton is denying everything. We only have Walsh's words. Anything back from your lovely lady in Forensics?' Banham asked Crowther.

Alison looked at Hannah. She kept her head down.

'Not yet, guv,' Crowther told him. 'However, some good news. Camilla Agnelli has a copy of a video that shows Burton in bed with all three murdered women.'

'Still doesn't prove that he murdered them,' Banham said. 'Only that he knew them, which, of course, he has lied about. Still not a crime to bed three women at once.'

'Just as well, or Col-the-know-all would be in prison,' Stephanie tactlessly joked.

Banham ignored her. 'Burton has the best legal backup,' he reminded the team. 'If we're to nail him, we need solid proof.'

'Crowther and I are going to his London flat this afternoon. We'll turn it upside down,' Alison said. 'However, his wife also uses it, so I'm not holding my breath.'

'I never liked the sound of her,' Stephanie piped up.

'You didn't like Del Harris – you were convinced he was our murderer,' Crowther said. 'If I was you, I'd concentrate more on the job and less on your trips to McDonald's.'

'Shut up, Crowther,' Alison barked, letting him know he was

clearly not in her good books. She then said, 'And, I would like to say a special thanks to our new trainee detective for going under-cover into that agency, putting herself in danger, and getting so much information for us.'

Hannah looked up. 'Thank you, ma'am,' she said. 'And this is a good chance for me to thank the team for backing me and believing me. I have really enjoyed being on this case.'

Alison lowered her eyes, knowing what was now coming.

Hannah continued. 'However, I am not a hundred per cent ready to carry on with this career, so I have decided I will go back on compassionate leave until I feel stronger.'

Alison threw angry eyes in Crowther's direction, then looked back at Hannah. 'I'm sorry to hear that, Hannah,' she said. 'We all believe you have the makings of an excellent detective. I would welcome you back on my team. Feel free to take your time until you are ready.'

Alison didn't speak to Crowther on the drive over to Burton's London flat.

'I know why you asked me to come with you,' Crowther said as he indicated to turn the corner and then park alongside the May-fair block of flats.

'Why did you lie to me?'

'About?'

'Don't play games,' Alison snapped. 'You know what. About Hannah. You seduced her, after I blatantly told you not to, then you swore to me that you hadn't.'

'Oh, come on, Ali. I'm not one to kiss and tell. But let's be honest. I am irresistible.'

She looked at him exasperatedly.

He smiled. 'Maybe not to you, mate. I didn't lie to you, though. I didn't seduce her. She came on to me, and seduced me, seeing as you mention it. Told you I have that way with women.'

Alison unclipped her seat belt. 'Now I've heard it all,' she said, shaking her head and throwing her eyes heavenward yet again.

'And because of the fact you are so irresistible, the department has lost an excellent trainee detective.'

'And I'm sorry, too, but that isn't my fault. She threw her naked self at me. I am a man, and—'

'Too much information,' Alison interrupted, lifting her palm to face him. She gave a thumbs up to the police van standing by, waiting. They followed her and Crowther through the revolving doors and into the Mayfair block of flats where Burton lived. Alison flashed her identity card to the porter and told him to open Christopher Burton's second-floor flat, or else she would tell the team and take the door down.

The overweight, balding, middle-aged man fumbled in his desk for his large set of keys and did as he was told. He immediately picked up his phone and stabbed numbers into it as soon as the door to Burton's flat was unlocked.

The main bedroom was decorated with pictures of naked women, some with their legs astride chairs, one with her back to the camera, bending down, all X-rated. The bedroom was clearly used by Mrs Burton as well, as an array of perfume and cosmetics filled the top of the dressing table. There was also a small, framed wedding photo of the two of them.

Crowther picked it up. 'I wonder if she's as bent as he is,' he said.

Alison was already in the en suite. 'Take a look at this,' she called. She was holding up a box of bottles of Ischia spa water which had been left under the sink. The label described it as *one hundred per cent pure*. 'Walsh told us Burton gave him some of this to clear any remnants of the arson from him.' She pulled her phone from her bag and took some pictures, then turned to Crowther. 'Bag these,' she snapped at him.

The whole flat was turned over within the hour, but nothing else had manifested. 'We have the spa water, Walsh's statement, and Camilla's video,' Alison said. 'But not enough to stand up in court and win five murders.'

The noise of shouting and arguing from an obviously angry female immediately took Crowther and Alison's attention. As they both stopped what they were doing and walked towards the door to investigate, they came face to face with Susan Burton. The security porter had obviously tipped her off.

As she tried to step through the door, the guarding police constable stopped her. 'I'm allowed in my own flat, surely?' she said in an agitated voice.

'Your husband has been charged with five murders, the importing of Class A drugs and firearms, and people smuggling,' Alison told her. 'This is official police business. We have a search warrant, and I would ask that you stay out of the building.'

Mrs Burton sighed, then walked past the uniformed policeman, into the flat, and perched on the edge of the sofa. 'I knew it was him,' she said softly.

'How?' Alison asked quietly.

'I heard the police press conference, the appeal for knowledge of the owner of that ring, and the arson. The first woman lived near that pizza place, and I knew Chris had set up his pawn down there, that man Walsh. Those women sent Chris a copy of a video with them in a foursome. There was a revolver on the edge of the bed, and a hammer. He was dressed in rubber, and he was beating one of them. It was disgusting.'

'Why didn't you tell us this before?' Alison asked her.

'I was afraid of him. I told him I had seen it. He said if I went to the police, he would cut out my tongue.' She looked up. 'He would have done, too.' She paused and then said, 'If it is any help, the reason I stopped having sex with him was because he beat me, tried to strangle me, and has broken my nose in the past. He also burned one of my nipples off. My medical records will prove it. Does that help?'

'Yes,' Alison said gently. 'We have him locked in custody. He is going nowhere, now. Will you go to court and give evidence against him?'

'If you guarantee my safety. He deserves all he gets.'

'Yes. We will put you in witness protection if that is what you want.'

288

Susan nodded, then, after a few quiet seconds, she said, 'I have a copy of that video with him beating the three women. I hid it in case I could use it against him. And now I can. He would have killed me, no doubt, if he knew I had it hidden.'

Alison looked at Crowther; both knew if they got the video of Burton beating the women, and with a hammer and the revolver in shot, then they had him.

'And the ring,' Susan Burton then said. 'The one you put out the appeal for, asking if anyone knew the owner of it?'

'Is that your husband's?' Crowther asked, pulling the photo of the arm around the three women from the file he was holding.

She nodded immediately. 'Yes, it is. I bought it for him when we were courting.'

'Does he still have it?'

'It's in the rice container in the kitchen. I found it there the other day. There's a mobile in there, too. I found that in the toilet and I'm drying it out. I believe it has messages containing instructions of how to kill those women on it. They were sent to that man at the pizza shop. I thought of bringing it to the police, but I was too scared of what he would do to me. He's threatened and hurt me so many times.'

'We'll make sure he never does again,' Alison told her as they walked into the kitchen. Susan tipped the rice container up, and the ring and mobile fell onto the draining board. The inscription inside the ring read, *For my husband, Christopher Burton.*

At the same time, Crowther's phone rang.

Alison listened while Dr Penny Starr told him both the hammer and the revolver had DNA from both Christopher Burton and Johnny Walsh. Crowther handed the phone to Alison for her to hear.

'As I said, he won't hurt you ever again,' she told the shaking Susan Burton.

Two Weeks Later

'So, Hannah isn't coming back?' Banham asked Alison as they walked Babe, who was now sporting a pink-velvet lead and matching collar, accessorised with a bone-shaped chrome identity disc displaying Banham's name and mobile number.

'Maybe one day. Crowther told me she kept stripping naked at every, and any, given opportunity, and try as he might, he said he just couldn't resist.'

Banham burst out laughing. 'She'll be back. When the trial comes to the Old Bailey, and she sees how involved she was in bringing Burton to justice. She's just humiliated and feels embarrassed that she fell for him.'

'Well, if she does, Crowther won't be working closely with her, I'll make sure of that.'

'Good result, though,' Banham said. 'With luck, Burton will get five life sentences. Walsh the same. Camilla Agnelli and Oluwa Marconi will both get heavy custodials for illegal handling of firearms and selling Class As. They didn't get bail. Anthony Rossiti and Joseph Perrino may both get suspended sentences, if they get a lenient judge.'

She looked at Banham. 'Great teamwork, thank you for helping.'

'You headed the investigation,' Banham told her. 'You take that pat on the back. You're great at your job.'

'Thank you.' She bent down and patted Babe. 'She's a lovely dog,' she said. 'You adore her, don't you?'

'In a nutshell, yes,' Banham answered. 'I adore you, too, Ali, and I can wait.'

She knew he was talking about a baby. She wished she hadn't lost her maternal instincts, because she loved him and wanted to make him happy. But she was who she was and she now knew that wouldn't change.

'Thing is, I love my job,' she said. 'I know you really want a baby, but I'm just not ready yet. I love you but . . .'

His finger was against her lips. 'I know,' he said. 'All in good time. I can wait. Meanwhile, we have this needy little girl, who is gorgeous.' He stroked the dog's furry head. Babe wagged her tail. 'Her owner was murdered and she was left all alone in the world. I understand her, and will make sure she never feels abandoned or afraid ever again.' He turned back to Alison. 'It's OK, Alison. I know you're not ready.'

Before she could answer, he said, 'We should think about getting married, though, and see how it goes from there.'

She stood stock-still for a few seconds, in stunned silence. Then she said, 'Yes. Well, maybe.' Then, unable to think of anything better to say, she added, 'Meanwhile, I am going to cook you both dinner . . .'

Acknowledgements

Although writing is a lonely and often difficult profession, there are other people whose involvement in this book has not only been greatly welcomed, but has made it a better story.

I bow to the genius of my wonderful editor Greg, whose talented and creative eye keeps me on course.

I met my copy editor for the first time on this book and I am deeply grateful for her sharp eye and input.

Thank you too, to Toby Jones and Bea Grabowska at Headline who truly are delightful to work with, as well as a great support.

There are, of course, the wonderful detectives, police and professionals who have helped me get the procedural correct. I want to say an enormous thank you to DS Lisa Cutts who never tires of my endless questions. Also many thanks to Rob Gentry whose fine expertise was given so kindly.

Last, and far from least, my humble thankyous to you, the readers, for buying (or however you acquired this book). I truly appreciate you and look forward to saying 'Hi,' at any function you attend that I will be signing at.